W9-AOP-495

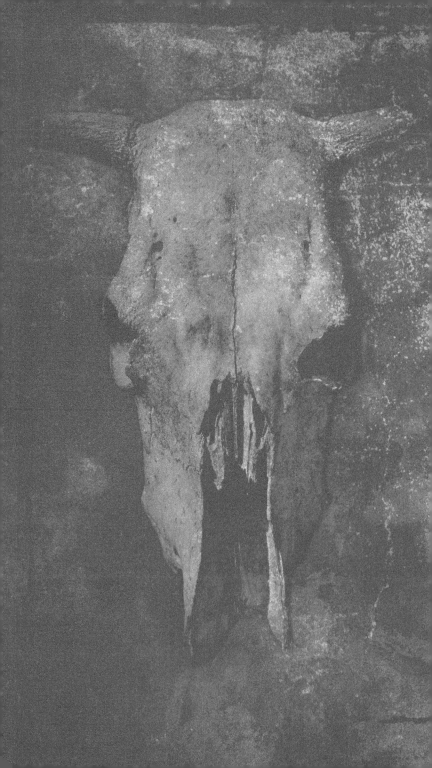

Flawless

Flawless

A Small Town Enemies to Lovers Romance

A Chestnut Springs Special Edition

Elsie Silver

Copyright © 2022 by Elsie Silver

All rights reserved.

No part of this book may be reproduced in any form or by any electronic or mechanical means, including information storage and retrieval systems, without written permission from the author, except for the use of brief quotations in a book review.

This is a work of fiction. Any names, characters, places or incidents are products of the author's imagination and used in a fictitious manner. Any resemblance to actual people, places, or events is purely coincidental or fictional.

Cover Design by Wildheart Graphics

Cover Photo by Madison Maltby

Editing by Lilypad Lit

Proofreading by My Notes in the Margin

Honestly, I wrote this book for myself.
For the girl who never quite knew what she wanted to do
with her life, and for the woman who figured it out.

Sometimes we seize the moment, and sometimes it seizes us.

— **Gregg Levoy**

Foreword

Dear Reader,

I'm so excited to bring Flawless to you with a special edition cover. Isn't it stunning?

My designer and I worked so hard on bringing this concept to life. When I first went to her I tossed out the idea of a skull "but make it pretty" and maybe something that gave "western vibes" and then I just left her to mull it all over. I try not to get too involved in the concept part but go in and do the tweaks.

Anyway, what she came back with blew my mind. The mirror, the water color effects, the burnt edges? We agree that it's Western meets fairytale meets old times fair poster (or something.)

I hope you love it just as much as we do. And I hope you love Rhett and Summer's story as well. Happy reading!

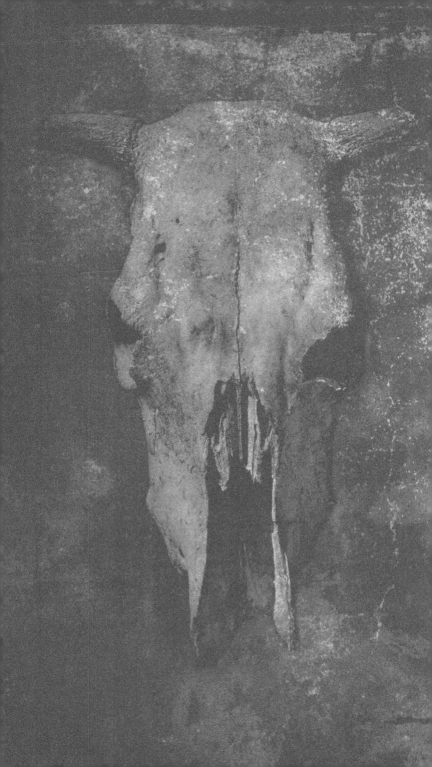

1

Summer

"*You got one angry motherfucker here, Eaton.*"

The handsome cowboy on the back of a huge bull scoffs and shifts his hand around the rope before him. His dark eyes twinkle on the screen, all the hard lines of his face peeking through the cage of his helmet. "*The harder they buck, the happier I am.*"

I can barely hear what they're saying over the din of the crowd in the vast arena with music blaring in the background, but the subtitles at the bottom of the screen clear up anything that might otherwise get missed.

The young man leaning over the pen chuckles and shakes his head. "*Must be all that milk you drink. No broken bones for the world-famous Rhett Eaton.*"

The easily recognizable cowboy grins behind the cage over his face, a flash of white teeth and the wink of an amber eye from beneath the black helmet. A charming grin I know from spending hours staring at a glossy, still version of it.

"Beat it, Theo. You know I fuckin' hate milk."

A teasing grin touches Theo's lips as he speaks. *"You look cute in those ads with it painted above your lip though. Cute for an old guy."*

The younger man winks and the two men share a friendly laugh as Rhett rubs a hand up the rope methodically.

"I'd rather get bucked off a bull every damn day than drink that shit."

Their laughter is all I hear as my father pauses the video on the large flatscreen, redness creeping up his neck and onto his face.

"Okay . . ." I venture cautiously, trying to piece together why that exchange requires this impromptu meeting with the two newest full-time hires at Hamilton Elite.

"No. Not okay. This guy is the face of professional bull riding, and he just skewered his biggest sponsors. But it gets worse. Keep watching."

He hits play again, aggressively, like the button did something wrong in this whole affair, and the screen flashes to a different scene. Rhett is walking outside of an arena, through the parking lot with a duffel bag slung over his shoulder. The helmet is now replaced by a cowboy hat and a slim man in dark baggy clothes is taking quick strides to keep up with his target while the cameraman follows and runs tape.

I don't think the paparazzi usually follow bull riders, but Rhett Eaton has become something of a household name over the years. Not a paragon of purity by any stretch, but a symbol of rough and tumble, rugged country men.

The reporter takes a little skip step to get far enough ahead that he can line his microphone up with Rhett's mouth.

"Rhett, can you comment on the video that's been circulating this weekend? Any apologies you'd like to make?"

The cowboy's lips thin, and he tries to hide his face behind the brim of his hat. A muscle in his jaw flexes, and his toned body goes taut. Tension lines every limb.

"No comment," he bites out through gritted teeth.

"Come on, man, give me something." The slender guy reaches out and presses the microphone against Rhett's cheek. Forcing it on him even though he declined to comment. *"Your fans deserve an explanation,"* the reporter demands.

"No, they don't," Rhett mutters, trying to create space between them.

Why do these people think they're *owed* a response when they ambush a person who is otherwise minding his own business?

"How about an apology?" the guy asks.

And then Rhett decks him in the face.

It happens so fast that I blink in an attempt to follow the now shaking and swiveling camera angles.

Well, shit.

Within seconds, the pushy paparazzi is on the ground clutching his face, and Rhett is shaking out his hand as he walks away without a word.

The screen switches back to news anchors sitting

behind a desk, and before they can give any input on what we just watched, my dad flicks the TV off and lets loose a rumbling sound of frustration.

"I hate these fucking cowboys. They're impossible to keep in line. I don't want to deal with him. So, lucky for you two, this job is up for grabs." He's practically vibrating with rage, but I just lean back in my chair. My father flies off the handle easily, but he gets over things quickly too. I'm pretty nonplussed by his mood swings at this point in my life. You don't last long at Hamilton Elite if you can't withstand Kip Hamilton.

Lucky for me, I have a lifetime of learning under my belt to brush off his moods, so I'm immune. I've come to think like it's part of his charm, so I don't take it personally. He's not mad at me. He's just . . . mad.

"I worked my ass off for years to get this country bumpkin sponsorships like he's never dreamed of, and then as his career is winding down, he goes and blows it all up like *this*." My father's hand flicks over at the wall-mounted screen. "Do you have any idea how much money these guys make for being nuts enough to climb up on an angry two-thousand-pound bull, Summer?"

"Nope." But I have a feeling he's about to tell me. I hold my father's dark eyes, the same shade as my own. Geoff, the other intern in the chair beside me, shrinks down in his seat.

"They make millions of dollars if they're as good as this asshole."

I never would have guessed this was such big business, but then they don't cover that in law school. I know all about Rhett Eaton, heartthrob bull riding sensation and mainstay teenaged crush, but almost nothing about the actual industry or sport. One corner of my lips tugs up as I think back on how a decade ago, I'd lie in my bed and gaze at that photo of him.

Rhett stepped up on a fence, glancing back over his shoulder at the camera. Open land behind him, a warm setting sun. A flirty smirk on his lips, eyes partially obscured by a worn cowboy hat, and the pièce de résistance . . . Wrangler jeans that hugged all the best parts.

So yeah, I know little about bull riding. But I know I spent an awful lot of time staring at that photo. The land. The light. It drew me in. It wasn't just the guy. It made me want to be there, watching that sunset for myself.

"George, do you know how much that milk sponsorship he just flushed down the toilet was worth? Not to mention all the other sponsors whose balls I'll be fondling to smooth this shit over?"

I swear to God I almost snort. *George.* I know my dad well enough to know that he's aware it's the wrong name, but it's also a test to see if Geoff has the cojones to say anything. From what I gather, it's not always a walk in the park working with entitled athletes and celebrities. I can already tell the guy beside me is going to struggle.

"Um . . ." He flips through the binder on the boardroom table in front of him, and I let my gaze linger out the floor-to-ceiling windows. The ones that offer sweeping views out over the Alberta prairies. From the 30th floor of this building, the view over Calgary is unparalleled. The snow-capped Rocky Mountains off in the distance are like a painting—it never gets old.

"The answer is tens of millions, Greg."

I bite the inside of my cheek to keep from chuckling. I like Geoff, and my dad is being a total dick, but after years of being on the spot in this same way, it's amusing to see someone else flounder the way I have in the past.

God knows my sister, Winter, was never on the receiving end of this kind of grilling. She and Kip have a different relationship than mine with our father. With me, he's playful and shoots from the hip; with her, he stays almost professional. I think she likes that better anyway.

Geoff looks over at me with a flat smile.

I've seen that expression on people's faces at work many times. It says, *Must be nice to be the boss's little girl.* It says, *How's that nepotism treating ya?* But I'm trained to take this kind of lashing. My skin is thicker. My give-a-fuck meter is less attuned. I know that in fifteen minutes, Kip Hamilton will crack jokes and be smiling. That perfect veneer he uses to suck up to clients will quickly slip back into place.

The man is a master, even if a bit of a weasel. But I think that comes with the territory of wheeling and dealing the contracts he does as a top-tier talent agent.

If I'm being honest, I'm still not so sure I'm cut out to be working here. Not sure I really want to. But it's always seemed like the right thing to do. I owe my dad that much.

"So, the question is, kids—how does one go about fixing this? I've got the Dairy King milk sponsorship hanging by a thread. I mean, a fucking professional bull rider just slammed his entire base. Farmers? Dairy producers? It seems like it shouldn't matter, but people are going to talk. They're going to put him under a microscope, and I don't think they'll love what they see. This will dent the idiot's bottom line more than you'd think. And his bottom line is *my* bottom line, because this nutjob makes us all a lot of money."

"How did the first recording even get out?" I ask, forcing my brain back onto the task at hand.

"A local station left their camera running." My dad scrubs a hand over his clean-shaven chin. "Caught the whole damn thing and then subtitled it and ran it on the evening news."

"Okay, so he needs to apologize," Geoff tosses out.

My dad rolls his eyes at the generic solution. "He's gonna need to do a hell of a lot more than apologize. I mean, he needs a bullet-proof plan for what's left of the season. He's got a couple of months until the World Championships in Vegas. We're gonna need to polish up that cowboy hat halo before then. Or other sponsors are going to drop like flies too."

I tap my pen against my lips, mind racing with what we could do to help salvage this situation. Of course, I have next to no experience, so I stick to leading questions. "So, he needs to be seen as the charming, wholesome country boy next door?"

My dad barks out a loud laugh, his hands coming to brace against the boardroom table across from us as he leans down. Geoff flinches, and I roll my eyes. *Pussy.*

"That right there is the issue. Rhett Eaton is not the

wholesome country boy next door. He's a cocky cowboy that parties too hard and has hordes of women throwing themselves at him every weekend. And he's not mad about it. It hasn't been an issue before, but they'll pick apart anything they can now. Like fucking vultures."

I quirk an eyebrow and lean back. Rhett is an adult, and surely, with an explanation of what's on the line, he can hold it together. After all, he pays for the company to manage this stuff for him. "So, he can't be on his best behavior for a couple of months?"

My dad drops his head with a deep chuckle. "Summer, this man's version of good behavior will not cut it."

"You're acting as if he's some sort of wild animal, Kip." I learned the hard way not to call him Dad at work. He's still my boss, even if we carpool together at the end of each day. "What does he need? A babysitter?"

The room is quiet for several beats while my dad stares at the tabletop between his hands. Eventually, his fingers tap the surface of it—something he does when he's deep in thought. A habit I've picked up from him over the years. His almost black eyes lift, and a wolfish grin takes over his entire face.

"Yeah, Summer. That's exactly what he needs. And I know the perfect person for the job."

And based on the way he's looking at me right now, I think Rhett Eaton's new babysitter just might be *me*.

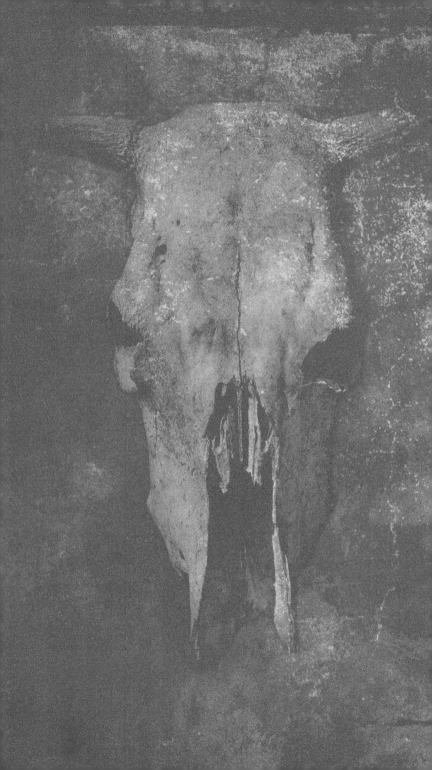

2

Rhett

Kip: Pick up your phone, you pretty motherfucker.

Rhett: You think I'm pretty?

Kip: I think you picking that one specific detail out of my text means you're an idiot.

Rhett: But a pretty one?

Kip: Answer. Your. Fucking. Phone.

Kip: Or be here at two p.m. so I can shake you in person.

The plane touches down at the Calgary airport, and I'm relieved to be home.

Especially after the clusterfuck that was the last couple of days.

The guy I punched isn't pressing charges, but I'm not sure how much money my agent, Kip, offered him to make that happen. It doesn't matter. If anyone can make this all go away, it's Kip.

He's been trying to call me, which is a clue he's losing his mind because we have more of a texting relationship. Which is why when I power my phone up before I'm supposed to, I'm not surprised to see his name lighting up my screen.

Again.

I haven't answered because I'm not in the mood for listening to him yell at me. I want to hide. I want silence. Birds. A hot shower. Some Tylenol. And a date with my hand to ease some tension.

Not necessarily in that order.

That's what I need to get my head back in the game. A quiet break at home while this blows over. The older I get, the longer the season seems, and somehow, at only thirty-two years old, I feel old as balls.

My body hurts, my mind is overfull, and I'm craving the quiet of my family ranch. Sure, my brothers are going to annoy the fuck out of me, and my dad is going to talk to me about when I'm planning on quitting, but that's family. That's home.

I suppose there's a reason us boys keep coming back.

We're co-dependent in a way our little sister isn't. She took one look at a bunch of grown-ass men living on a farm together and got the hell outta dodge.

I make a mental note to call Violet and check up on her all the same.

My head tips back against the cramped seat while the plane rolls to a stop on the runway. *"Welcome to beautiful Calgary, Alberta."* The cabin fills with the flight attendant's voice and the loud clicking of people undoing their seat-belts before they're supposed to.

I follow suit. Eager to get out of the small seat and stretch my limbs.

"If Calgary is home for you, welcome home . . ."

You'd think that after over a decade of playing this game, I'd be better at booking my flights and hotels. Instead, I'm constantly scrambling to grab a last-minute spot, which suits me just fine. Even though I'm feeling a little claustrophobic.

When the person beside me files out into the aisle, a sigh of relief whooshes from my lungs. I can't let myself sink into that intense tiredness yet. I still have to grab my truck and drive an hour outside the city to Chestnut Springs.

"Please remember that smoking is not permitted inside the terminal. . ."

And before that, I have to go meet with my pit bull of an agent. He's been barking at me since last night about not answering my phone.

Now, I'm going to have to face the music for my poor behavior.

I groan inwardly as I reach up to grab my duffel bag from the overhead compartment.

Kip Hamilton is the man I have to thank for my current financial situation. Truth be told, I like him a lot. He's been with me for ten years, and I almost consider him a friend. I also dream about punching his clean-shaven face pretty regularly. A double-edged sword, that one.

He reminds me of an older, more debonaire version of Ari Gold from *Entourage*, and I fucking love that show.

"Thank you for flying Air Acadia. We look forward to hosting you again."

The line of people finally starts to move toward the exit, and I shuffle toward the aisle of the plane, only to feel a firm poke in the middle of my chest.

When I peer down the bridge of my nose, I'm met with furious blue eyes and a pinched brow on a short frame. A woman well into her sixties glares up at me.

"You should be ashamed of yourself. Insulting your roots that way. Insulting us all who work so hard to put food on the tables of our fellow Canadians. And then assaulting a man. How dare you?"

This part of the country prides itself on farming and rural life. Calgary is home to one of the biggest rodeos in the world. Hell, some people call the city *Cowtown* for how tightly tied the ranching and farming community is to the city.

I grew up on a massive cattle ranch, I should know. I just never knew not liking milk was a crime.

But I give her a solemn nod anyhow. "No insult

intended, ma'am. We both know the farming community is the backbone of our fine province."

She holds my eyes as she rolls her shoulders back and sniffs a little. "You'd do well to remember that, Rhett Eaton."

All I offer back is a tight smile. "Of course," I say, and then I trudge through the airport with my head down. Hoping to avoid any more run-ins with offended fans.

The interaction sticks with me throughout baggage claim and out to my pickup truck. I don't feel bad about punching that guy—he deserved it—but a spark of guilt flicks in my chest for potentially hurting my hard-working fans. That's something I hadn't considered. Instead, I've spent the last several days rolling my eyes over my milk hatred making the news.

When my vintage truck comes into view in the covered parking garage, I breathe out a sigh of relief. Is it a practical vehicle? Maybe not. But my mom gave it to my dad as a gift, and I love it for that alone. Even though it's currently got rust spots and is painted with mismatched grays.

I have big plans for having it restored. A treat to myself. I want to paint it blue.

I don't remember my mom, but in pictures her eyes were a steely color, and that's what I want. A little nod to the woman I never really got to know.

Just need to find the time first.

Bag in hand, I hop into my truck. Cracked brown leather seats creaking slightly as I heave my tired body into place behind the wheel. It fires up to life, billowing a bit of dark exhaust as I pull out onto the freeway, heading straight to the city center. My eyes are on the road, but my head is somewhere else.

When my phone rings I take my eyes off the road only momentarily. I see my sister's name flashing on the screen and can't help but smile. Violet never fails to make me smile, even when everything around me is total shit. She's calling me before I even had the chance to dial her.

Stopped at a red light, I slide the button to answer and tap for speaker phone. This truck definitely isn't equipped with Bluetooth.

"Hey, Vi," I answer, almost shouting to project my voice at the phone on the seat next to me.

"Hi." Her voice overflows with concern. "How are you holding up?"

"Fine, I guess. Heading in to Kip's office right now to find out what sort of damage I've done."

"Yeah. Get ready. He's worked up," she mutters.

"How do you know?"

"I'm your emergency contact on file. He's been blowing up my phone about you ignoring him." Now she's laughing. "I don't even live there anymore. You need to update that."

I smirk as I merge onto the highway. "Yeah, but you're the only one who approves of my career and won't show up to lecture me about quitting if something goes wrong. Basically, you're stuck with the job."

"So, I'll have to leave my husband and kids to hop on a plane and sit at a hospital with you?"

Now that takes me back. Every time I got hurt as a teenager or young adult, it was Violet who took care of me.

"You're just so good at it. But fair point. I think Cole might kill me if I take you away from him."

I'm poking fun. I like her husband a lot, which is saying something because I never thought she'd meet someone good enough for her. But Cole is. He's also ex-military and kind of terrifying. I wouldn't want to piss him off.

My sister just giggles now. Still fucking giddy over the guy, and I couldn't be happier for her. "He would be fine. I could send him out your way if you need a bodyguard?"

"And leave his girls behind? He would never."

She doesn't laugh now. Instead, she makes a quiet grunting noise. "You know if you need me, I'm there, right? I know the others don't understand. But I do. I can be there for you if you need it."

And this is the thing with my little sister. She gets me. She's a bit of a daredevil herself. She doesn't condemn my career the way the rest of our family does. But she has her own life now. I don't need her coddling me. She's got her own kids to coddle.

"I'm good, Vi. Come for a visit with the whole family soon though, yeah? Or at the end of the season, I'll drag my sorry ass out to you. Race you on a fancy racehorse. Kick your ass." I try to joke, but I'm not sure my tone is all that convincing.

"Yeah," she replies. And I swear I can see her chewing on her lip the way she does, about to say something but stopping herself. "I'll probably just let you win because I feel so bad for you."

"Hey. A win is a win," I chuckle, trying to lighten the mood.

And all she responds with is, "I love you, Rhett. Be safe. But more than that, be yourself. You're very loveable when you stay true to who you are."

She's always reminding me of this. To be Rhett Eaton, boy from a small town. Not Rhett Eaton, cocky bull rider extraordinaire.

I usually roll my eyes, but deep down, I know it's good advice. One is the real me, the other is for show.

The problem is, not very many people know the real me anymore.

"Love you too, sis," I say before hanging up and getting lost in my head as I cruise down the highway toward the city.

When I pull up at Hamilton Elite and nab an unusual street parking spot, I realize I've been so lost in my thoughts that I barely remember the drive. I tip my head back against the seat. Again. And take a deep breath. It's hard to say for sure how much trouble I'm in, but based on how that woman scolded me publicly on the airplane, I'm going to go out on a limb and guess a fair bit of hot water.

But I know the people in this area. They're hard-working. They're proud. And they've got a chip on their shoulders from thinking that people from other walks of life don't understand their struggle.

And maybe they're right. Maybe the average Canadian doesn't *truly* understand the backbreaking work that goes into farming. Into stocking our grocery store shelves.

But me? I do.

I just fucking hate milk. The whole thing is so bizarre that it's almost funny.

I walk into the opulent building. Everything is shiny. The floor. The windows. The stainless-steel elevator doors. It makes me want to go smudge my hands all over them just to mess things up.

The security guard gives me a nod on the way past, and I step into the elevator with a bunch of well-dressed people. I roll my lips together to smother the smirk when one woman glares at me with barely restrained judgment.

Worn cowboy boots. Wouldn't surprise me if there was still cow shit on the sole. Perfectly broken-in jeans topped off with a brown shearling jacket. My hair is long, just how I like it.

Wild and unruly. Just like me.

But not how this woman likes it. In fact, the repulsion painted on her face is clear as day.

So, I wink at her and give her a way over the top, "Howdy, ma'am." Alberta boys don't have twangy accents, but when you spend your life at rodeos with guys who do, it's pretty easy to imitate. I only wish I had a cowboy hat with me to complete the picture.

The woman rolls her eyes and then jams a finger at the button that reads *CLOSE DOOR*. The next time the doors glide open, she storms through them without a backwards glance.

I'm still chuckling about it when I get to the floor that is home to Hamilton Elite, and based on the way the receptionist's eyes light when I walk in, she doesn't share the elevator woman's perception of me.

Truthfully, most women don't. Buckle bunnies, city

girls, country girls. I've always been equal-opportunity, and I do love women. Less so relationships.

A walk on the wild side is what one woman recently called me after we spent a full day locked up in a hotel room celebrating my win in a way that was fun in the moment but left me feeling a little hollow at the end.

"Rhett!" Kip's voice booms across the foyer before I even have a chance to chat up the girl at the front desk.

Total cock blocker.

"Thanks for coming straight here." He strides toward me and shoves a hand in my direction before shaking mine so hard that it's almost painful. This handshake is his way of taking out some aggression on me for whatever pickle I've gotten myself into. The fake, pinched smile on his face is proof of that. The owner of this agency doesn't make a habit of greeting his clients at reception, which means I've definitely stepped in it.

"Not a problem, Kip. I pay you the big bucks so that you can boss me around, right?"

We both laugh, but we also both know I just reminded him I'm the one paying him here. Not the other way around.

He claps me on the back, and my teeth shake. He's a big man. "Follow me. Let's chat in the conference room. Congratulations on your win this weekend. You're going on quite the streak this year."

I have no business winning as many events as I have been this season at my age. I should be on the downhill slide of my career, but the stars are aligning right now. And *Three-Time World Champion* sounds a lot better than *Two-*

Time World Champion. And three gold buckles on my shelf would look better than two.

"Sometimes the stars align." I grin at him as he ushers me into a room that holds a long table surrounded by generic-looking black office chairs with a generic-looking man sitting in one. Brownish, close-cut hair. Brownish eyes. Gray suit. Bored expression. Manicured nails. Soft hands. City boy.

Next to him is a woman who is anything but generic. Deep brown hair that shines an almost mahogany color when the sun hits where it's twisted into a tight bun on the crown of her head. Her black-rimmed glasses are a smidge too strong on her dainty, doll-like face, but her almost over-full lips painted a deep, warm pink somehow balance them out.

The ivory dress shirt she's wearing buttons all the way up, lace trim wrapped tight around her throat. There's a slightly bemused twist to her mouth, but her arms are crossed protectively across her chest and sparkling choco-late eyes give nothing away as she sizes me up from above the top rim of her glasses.

I know better than to judge a book by its cover. But the word *uptight* flits across my mind while I assess her all the same.

"Take a seat, Rhett." Kip pulls out a chair directly across from the woman and smoothly folds himself into the seat beside me before steepling his fingers beneath his chin.

I flop down and push away from the table, crossing a booted foot over my knee. "Alright. Give me my spanking so I can go home, Kip. I'm tired."

My agent quirks a brow and regards me carefully. "I don't need to give you a spanking. You've officially lost the Dairy King sponsorship, and I think that's probably bad enough."

I rear back, and my neck flushes. That same sensation of getting in trouble as a child. Missed curfew. Jumped off the bridge with the big kids when I wasn't supposed to. Trespassed on the Jansens' farm. There was always something. I was never *not* in trouble. But this is different. This isn't childhood fun and games. This is my livelihood. "You have to be kidding me."

"I wouldn't kid about this, Rhett." His lips flatten, and he shrugs. The look says *I'm not mad, I'm disappointed*. And I hate that distinction, because deep down, I hate failing people. When they're mad, it means they care about you. They want better for you. They know you're capable of better. When they're indifferent like this, it's almost like they expected you to blow it.

It's why I've always said I don't care what people think of me. Then they don't have the power to make me feel like this—clearly, it's not working.

I shift in my seat, eyes darting to the two other people in the room. The guy has the good sense to look down at the papers in front of himself.

But the woman holds my gaze. That same unflinching look on her face. And somehow, I just know she's judging me.

My hand swipes across my mouth as I clear my throat. "Well, how do we get them back?"

Kip leans back with a deep sigh, fingers tapping against

the armrests of the chair he's in. "I'm not sure we can. In fact, I think we might be doing damage control more than anything. Hoping other sponsors don't jump ship. Wrangler. Ariat. These are all companies who know their clientele. And their clientele are the people you've pissed off. Not to mention, punching a man with a camera rolling is a PR nightmare."

My eyes find the ceiling as I tip my head back and swallow audibly. "Who knew not liking milk was a crime? And that guy deserved to have his jaw adjusted."

The woman across from me huffs out a small scoff, and my eyes slide over to hers. Again, she doesn't look away. The fuck is she staring at?

She just smirks. Like me blowing a multimillion-dollar sponsorship is funny to her. I'm exhausted. I'm sore. My patience is beyond fried. But I'm a gentleman, so I rub my tongue along the front of my teeth and turn my focus back to Kip.

"If that camera hadn't been filming, it would have been fine. But don't let anyone hear you talking that way about assaulting someone. I worked my ass off to keep that fucker from pressing charges."

I roll my eyes. I'm pretty sure *worked my ass off* is code for *spent a bunch of my hard-earned money to shut the guy up*. "Why was the camera even rolling? Was it intentional?"

The older man sighs and shakes his head. "It doesn't really matter, does it? The damage is done."

"Fuck." I groan and let my eyes drift shut for a moment as I roll my shoulders, taking stock of how painful the right one is. The way I landed on that last ride was not ideal. Rookie dismount.

"So, I have a plan."

I peer back at Kip through the slits of my eyes. "I already hate it."

He laughs. And smiles. Because that fucker knows he has me over a barrel. We both know my days are numbered, and I've made the mistake of telling him my family needs more money to maintain the ranch long-term. I'll take what I need to live comfortably somewhere on our land and then work with my older brother, Cade, to keep Wishing Well Ranch up and running.

That's what you do for family. Whatever it takes.

"That's fine. We both know you'll do it anyway."

I glare at him. What a dick.

He gestures across the table. "This is Summer. She's new on the team. Has been an intern here for several years. She's also your new shadow."

My brows scrunch up along with my nose. Because this plan already smells like shit. "Elaborate."

"For the next two months, through the end of the World Championships in Las Vegas, she will work as your assistant. A media liaison. Someone who understands public perception and can help you polish your image. You two will discuss and come up with a plan. And then she'll consult with me so that I don't strangle you for being such a colossal cocksucker. I'm sure she'd be open to helping with any other administrative work you might need as well. Mostly, though, she'll be there to watch and keep you out of trouble."

I glance at the woman, and she nods, not seeming alarmed by this suggestion at all.

"Now I *know* you're kidding. Because there's no way you'd assign a man my age a glorified babysitter. That's just insulting, Kip."

I want him to burst out laughing and tell me this is his idea of pulling my leg.

But he doesn't. He just stares back at me, like the woman, giving my brain time to catch up to what he's already decided for me.

"The fuck outta here." I laugh in disbelief as I sit up straighter to glance around the room for some proof that this is a really excellent and hilarious joke. Something my brothers would pull on me for sure.

But the only thing I get is more silence.

This is not a drill, not a joke. This is a fucking nightmare.

"No, thanks. I'll take that guy." I point at the other dude. The one who can't even look me in the eye. He'll be perfect for me to pretend he doesn't exist. Not the uptight ball-buster who stares at me like I'm a dumb hick.

Kip steeples his hands again and crosses his legs. "No."

"No?" I sound incredulous. "I pay you, not the other way around."

"Then find someone else who will fix this shitstorm better than I can. It's only the future of your family farm on the line."

Heat slashes across my cheeks, barely hidden by the stubble there. And for once, I'm speechless. Utterly speechless. My jaw pops under the pressure of grinding my teeth against each other.

Milk. Taken down by fucking *milk*.

A piece of plain white paper slides in front of me from across the table. Nude polished fingernails tap on it twice. *Prissy.* "Write your address here, please."

"My address?" My gaze shoots up to meet hers.

"Yes. The place where you live." I swear her cheek twitches. It's fucking rude.

My head swivels to Kip. "Why am I giving this girl my address again?"

He smiles and reaches forward to clap me on the shoulder. "You're not Peter Pan, Rhett. You won't be losing your shadow. Not for the next two months."

My mind reels. He can't mean . . .

"Where you go, she goes."

Kip gives me a vicious smile, not the one he gave me when I walked in the room. No, this one is full of warning. "And Eaton, that *girl* is my daughter. *My* princess. So, mind your goddamn manners, keep your hands to yourself, and stay the hell out of trouble, yeah?"

The snarky *princess* is supposed to live at the ranch with me? Good God, this is so much worse than I imagined.

My weekend has been on a downhill spiral ever since that fucking video, and when I storm out of the shiny office, it doesn't get any better because I forgot to plug the meter on that *great* parking spot I got.

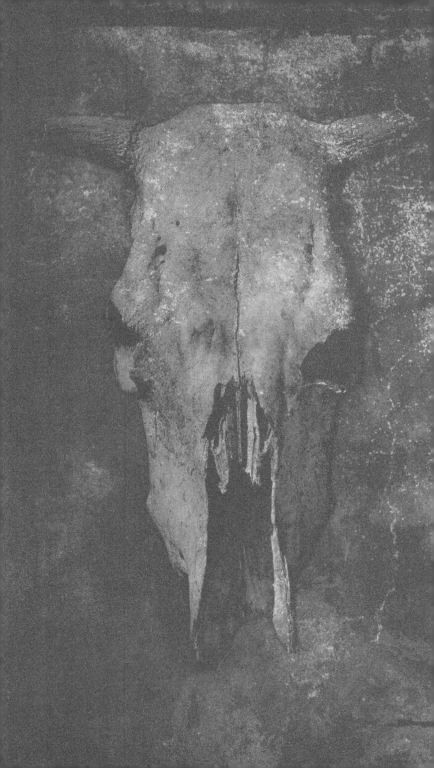

3

Summer

Summer: Heading out there
now.
Dad: Be safe. Don't let that
asshole in your pants.
Summer: I'm really more of
a skirt gal.
Dad: -_-

"Okay, wait. How long are you going to be
gone?"

"I mean, I'm not *gone*, Wils. I'm like an
hour outside of the city. The drive to your barn isn't that
much less from where you live."

"I need notice for things like this. Who am I supposed

to go for boozy brunches with? What if I find a whole new best friend while you're gone?"

I laugh at that. My best friend has a flair for the dramatic. It's part of her charm. "Then I guess you never really loved me," I reply wistfully.

"This is the worst news. For me anyway. You're probably all giddy and wet in the panties. Remember that photo you—"

"Willa, please. That was a long time ago. I'm an adult. I'm a professional. Hot athletes are my job every day. Don't make this weird for me."

She groans. "Why do you have to be so responsible? And mature? It makes me feel like a child."

"You're not a child. Possibly more like a teenager?" I peer around, trying to make sure I catch the right turn because the dusty back roads aren't the most well-marked. But I see the range road sign up ahead and turn just in time, tires wobbling on the gravel.

"I guess I can live with that. Growing up is the worst. It's just not for me, you know?"

I laugh at that. Willa is plenty grown up. She's just playful. She's *fun*. She's good for me. "You run a tight ship with all the guys at the bar. I think you're more grown up than you realize."

"Take that back!" She laughs before adding, "And bang the cowboy. Do it."

Willa has always been the one to loosen me up, the one to pick me up when I'm down, the one to rub my back when I cried over Rob.

But sometimes she's also wrong.

"You want me to ruin my budding career to sleep with my teenaged celebrity crush, who by all appearances hates my guts? Thanks. I'll take that under advisement."

"That's all I'm asking, ya know?" We chuckle together, like we have for the past fifteen years. I don't have a lot of friends. But I'd rather have one Willa than an entire pack of people who don't truly get me.

I catch sight of a driveway up ahead and slow to read the numbers on the fence. "I gotta go. I'll text later."

"You better. Love you."

"Love you back," I say absently before sighing with relief that the numbers are a match for what Rhett wrote on the piece of paper. I click off my Bluetooth and turn into the driveway, ready to face whatever mess I've been roped into by my father.

The raw-post fences that line the property usher me in through the main gate where those posts rise high above the driveway. The beam that crosses over the top is adorned with a wrought iron sign in the shape of a wishing well. And attached by two narrow chains, dangling beneath, is a slab of wood with the words *Wishing Well Ranch* branded into it.

The land around Chestnut Springs is truly something to behold. I feel like I've been transported onto the set of *Yellowstone*. And I'm downright giddy about it. Goodbye stuffy office, hello endless land.

Does Rhett Eaton look at me like I'm roadkill?

Yes.

But am I excited about getting out of the office and doing something different?

Also, yes.

I'm going to enjoy the hell out of this. I'm going to take the bull by the horns on this assignment. I chuckle at my joke as I reach forward and turn down the volume on The Sadies album I had blasting before Willa called me.

I peer around and slow my SUV to a crawl. My head is on a swivel as the gravel crunches and pops beneath my tires. I swear the view out every window is better than the last. March in Southern Alberta still has some bite. It can be cold and snowy, but then a chinook can roll in, and the air grows warm and soft against your skin. The grass isn't lush yet. It's just fields upon fields of this mossy brown color. Like you can see the green lurking beneath, ready to pop. But not quite yet.

For now, there's something monotone about the gently rolling fields that blend up into the gray peaks to the west. The Rocky Mountains provide a border to the foothills, jutting up all jagged and snow-capped with pristine white peaks.

I've spent years gazing out the windows of my dad's 30th floor windows, wishing I was out *there*. Imagining spending my summers exploring the mountains and the rustic small towns that lay between them, but being trapped inside his glossy office instead. Or, if I think even further back, stuck inside a pale green room without enough energy to get out of bed.

Is this work assignment ridiculous to the point where I had a hard time keeping a straight face through that meeting?

Absolutely.

But I'm going to make the most of it. If nothing else, I'll get to stare at the mountains with the wind in my face rather than the smell of burned coffee and those stale croissants that Martha sets out every morning. Or a room that reeks of antiseptic and antibacterial laundry soap. The kind that's supposed to be scent-free, but when you spend enough time wrapped up in it, you realize it's really not.

The long driveway stretches ahead of me until it disappears into a copse of closely planted, but leafless poplar trees. The outline of a large house peeks from between their branches.

I pull through, taking in the impressive home before me. Thick logs provide the frame for a house that is curved in a slight crescent shape, wrapping into trees and flowing with the lines of the hills behind it somehow. It's expansive with massive windows. The bottom retaining wall of the house is covered in a stone facade that swaps into some sort of vinyl siding in a soft sage color. It contrasts perfectly against the warm stained timber and cedar shake roof.

The houses where I grew up were almost at war with the landscape. Fighting it with their sharp corners and harsh tones. This house—big as it is—almost looks like it sprouted up from the ground. Like it's just part of the scenery, in perfect harmony.

It looks like it belongs here.

Unlike me.

I glance down at my outfit as I step out of my parked car. A black sweater-material skirt, silky tartan button-down, and a pair of brown heeled loafers with a pretty brogue toe are probably a ridiculous choice for the setting.

Even though this outfit slays.

I've grown so accustomed to getting dressed up every day, and I take so much pleasure in choosing pieces that make me feel more confident, that I didn't even consider how hilarious I might look pulling up wearing what I'm wearing.

But actually, I know *nothing* about what I'm supposed to be doing. When Rhett scribbled his address on the piece of paper, he pressed the pen so hard that it indented the pages beneath.

And then he stormed out without another word.

A smile teased my dad's lips as we all sat staring at Rhett Eaton's broad shoulders and long hair. But definitely *not* his ass.

I'm a professional, after all.

"Off to a good start," my dad joked once Rhett was out of earshot.

So, that was the extent of my instructions. An address. That and, "Fix this, Summer. I believe in you."

Oh, and, "Don't let that fucker charm his way into your bed."

I smiled and said, "What about his bed?"

"You'll be the death of me, girl," he groaned as he waltzed out of the boardroom, looking like the Cheshire Cat.

And that was that. Full trust that throwing me into the life of my childhood crush will be just fine. Though he probably doesn't even remember that.

I know that this is a test. Trial by fire. If I can knock this assignment out of the park, I'll impress my father, but I'll also prove I'm capable to everyone else at the company. Something he and I both know I need to do if I plan to move up the ranks at Hamilton Elite. If hiring me isn't going to seem like pure nepotism, then I need to be fantastic at what I do.

It's not an easy assignment, but nothing in my life has been easy, so maybe it doesn't seem as daunting as it should.

"You the babysitter?"

My head whips around to the front porch of the sprawling house, following the deep gravelly voice. An older man with silver hair leans against the big log pillar with his arms crossed over his chest and a smirk plastered on his face. A well-worn black cowboy hat sits atop his head, and it tips down in greeting as he swallows a chuckle.

"Been a while since I welcomed a babysitter up to the house for any of my boys."

I laugh out a breath and let my shoulders drop, immediately at ease around the man. Rhett may look at me like I'm a bug on his windshield, but this man is just plain charming.

I grin at him as I press my fists into my hips. "Been a while since I babysat someone."

"I reckon you'd have an easier time with even the most poorly behaved child," he says as he strides toward me.

I take a wild stab at who this man might be. "I suppose threatening to tell his dad isn't going to help me any, huh?"

The man smiles back, weathered skin crinkling around his eyes, and shoots his hand out in my direction. "That hellion has never given a shit what I have to say." He winks, and I take his palm in a firm handshake. "Harvey Eaton, Rhett's father. Pleasure to meet you. Welcome to Wishing Well Ranch."

"Summer Hamilton. Nice to meet you too. Wasn't sure what to expect when I pulled up. I'm not sure Rhett and I got off on the best foot yesterday," I confess.

Harvey waves me aside when I press the button to open my back hatch and reaches past me to retrieve my suitcase. "Well, I've got a room made up for you here in the main house. You can expect Rhett to sulk like a little boy who's gotten his favorite toy taken away. And when his brothers find out, I expect him to be downright foul because they are going to harass him something fierce."

I grimace. "Lucky me."

Harvey snorts and waves me along behind him toward the house. "Not to worry, Miss Hamilton. They're good boys. A little rough around the edges, but good boys none-theless." He peeks over his shoulder at me with an amused twist to his lips. "Plus, something tells me you'll be holding your own just fine with this crew."

I press my lips together. If I can make it to my age with Kip Hamilton as my father and boss, something tells me a couple of cowboys will be a cakewalk—but I don't say that. I'd rather not jinx things. Instead, I reply with, "Please, call me Summer."

He holds the front door open and gestures one arm wide. "Come on in, Summer. Let's get you settled and fed before you face the little monster."

I shake my head and chuckle as I move into the house. Clearly, my assessment of Rhett wasn't too far off. Or at least his dad isn't making me feel like I'm in for an easy time. A boulder of doubt drops into my stomach, anxiety seeping out through my body. *What if I'm not up to this? What if I fail? Will I always be the one who can't get things quite right?*

My internal monologue melts away as I take in the house before me. The warm wood theme from the exterior carries on inside. Wood beam ceilings and dark green walls give the space a cozy vibe despite the lofty open areas. The floors are dark hardwood, the wide planks slightly worn in heavy traffic areas. And as I watch Harvey march in with his boots on, I think I can guess why.

To my left, I can see the living room with overstuffed leather couches facing an enormous fireplace. Some sort of deer head with black marble eyes that sparkle enough to look real and antlers that reach high above it like thick, ornate branches, hangs above it.

My lips tug down into a small frown. I have no problem with hunting, not the type of hunting that's done responsibly anyway, but I'm such a city girl that the sight of this majestic animal hanging up in the house makes me a little sad about the deer and whatever end he might have faced.

Let's be honest. I'm thinking about *Bambi*.

I shake the thought away and tell myself to buck up. *Buck up?* God. What is wrong with me?

Before us is the gigantic kitchen with a large wood table smack dab in the middle of it, and I can already imagine all these cowboy-type guys rolling in here after a long day on the ranch to share a big family-style meal.

"Down here," Harvey's voice pulls me away, and we

turn right down a hallway lit by brass sconces on the walls. "I know this room is on the main floor. We'll try to keep it down in the mornings. Rhett and I have rooms upstairs, so I thought this might give you a little more space away from us men. It has an adjoining bathroom. The closet is the biggest in here, too."

He does one pull up with my suitcase. My very, very full suitcase. "Thinking I made the right choice with that."

My cheeks pink a bit. I must seem like a real city girl to a man like Harvey Eaton. "I wasn't sure what to expect with this assignment."

He chuckles good-naturedly. "Expect a rodeo, girl. I love my boy. But he's a handful. Has always been one. Come to think of it, I'm not sure anyone has ever truly handled Rhett at all. Youngest boy and all that. Even his baby sister ended up being the more mature of the two. The one who looked out for him—because Rhett needs looking out for. My advice? Don't push too hard. He'll just push back."

I nod, a little wide-eyed. He's making Rhett sound downright insane. "Sage advice, Mr. Eaton."

He drops my suitcase just inside the door of a room at the very end of the hall. "Girl, if I'm calling you Summer, you're calling me Harvey. We got it?"

I smile at him as I enter the room. "Got it."

"Good." He steps back out into the hall. "Take your time getting settled. I'll be in the kitchen when you're ready. We can eat, and I'll show you around."

"That's perfect." I give him the brightest smile I can muster before he ambles back down the hallway.

When I close the door behind him, I rest my head against the cool wood and suck in a deep breath to chase away the anxiety.

And then I pray for patience because something tells me I'm going to need it.

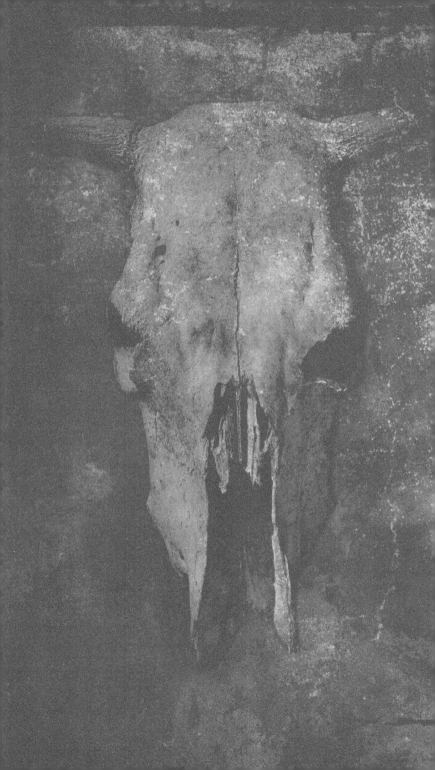

1

Rhett

Rhett: Want your daughter
back yet ? I promise I'll be
good.

Kip: She's not even there
yet.

Rhett: Think of all the time
you'll save her by calling
her back now.

Kip: No.

Rhett: Please?

Kip: Don't try to be polite.
It doesn't suit you.

Rhett: Suck a dick.

Kip: How do you think I'm
keeping all your sponsors?

Summer Hamilton pulled up in her fancy SUV and ridiculous prissy outfit like she's going out on the town rather than showing up on a cattle ranch.

So, I made myself scarce. I might be stuck with her, but I don't have to like it.

And I don't. I fucking hate being treated like a child, or like I'm stupid. Or worse, like I'm some sort of criminal. I had hoped that sleeping in my own bed and having some processing time to come to terms with my new arrangement might make it feel a little less stifling—less insulting.

But it still feels like trash.

Which is why I'm here pounding posts with my older brother. Setting new fence lines for some of his horses to be closer to his house, which is just over the crest of a big hill from where my dad and I live. Cade pulls a post out of the back of his pickup and hefts it over his shoulder with a grunt. He looks the most like our dad, wide shoulders and tightly cut hair. The only thing missing is a mustache. Something I love to harass him about, especially since he's one growly motherfucker. It's just too easy.

"When are you going to grow out the 'stache and go full Old Man Eaton?"

He glares at me before he drops the post and lines up the pointed end with the spot he wants. "Dunno. When you cutting your hair, Rapunzel?"

This feels good. This feels familiar. Pissing Cade off is

one of my favorite past-times. And he's so fucking grumbly that it never stops being satisfying. He's all bark and no bite, one of the nicest dudes I know.

If you can overlook what a prick he is.

I pull my cap off and flick my hair over my shoulder, trying not to wince at the shot of pain in my shoulder. Or the swelling in my knee. Or the ache in my back.

Never mind Rapunzel, I'm more like Humpty Dumpty.

"Never. How will I pull a princess through my window?"

He snorts and grabs the post pounder while I take over holding the post upright. "Just one princess, brother? Hardly seems like you."

I roll my eyes. Cade is the monk in this family. I don't think I've seen him with a single woman since his divorce.

"I'm just trying to have enough sex for the both of us," I lie. That part of me has changed. It doesn't hold the same appeal these last couple seasons. Not like it used to. It brings drama, and I've grown tired of having to spend time with people who only want something from me or who see me as some sort of trophy.

Cade reaches up and slaps the cap off my head. "Douche. You going to help do one or just stand there looking pretty?"

I step away and cross my arms. "I am pretty, aren't I? People keep telling me that," I deflect because I don't want to confess that my body is feeling utterly run down. All that will get me is a lecture about how I need to retire, how I've stuck with it too long.

The problem is, I'm addicted.

Riding bulls is a high I can't replace. A rush I can't stop chasing.

"Uncle Rhett!" The small, sugary voice makes me smile, and I'm grateful for the distraction.

Cade glances over his shoulder, brows drawn together in concern.

"Luke! What's up, little man? I thought you were with Mrs. Hill," I say.

My nephew smiles at me, exposing his little Chiclet teeth, a mischievous expression overtaking his face. "I told her I wanted to play hide and seek."

"Okay . . ."

Luke peeks at his dad from around my body, like he knows he's about to get in trouble. And then he leans in close to me and holds a hand up next to his mouth. "And then I ran over here instead."

His eyes go wide as he takes in my expression and then his dad's, who is probably scowling behind me. I try not to laugh.

But I fail. This cracks me up, and I bark out a loud laugh. This kid runs my brother into the ground. He keeps him light—and God knows Cade needs that.

That said, we're all a bunch of softies where Luke is concerned. Our little sister may have left the ranch, but we've got Luke to dote on now.

"Papa is looking for you," the boy continues.

"Luke." Cade walks up from behind me. "Are you telling me you ran away from your babysitter to help Papa find Rhett? Because that sounds an awful lot like not minding your business."

Luke rolls his little lips together, and I swear I can see the gears turning in his head. Almost five, smart as hell, a full-on troublemaker. But still too young to realize when he's blown it.

He side-steps that question, widening his eyes strategically. "Papa came looking for you at home. He's with a lady."

I groan because I know what this means. *Lady.* A more apt word has never been used to describe Summer Hamilton. My agent's *princess.*

My brother's eyes dart to my face. "Lady? Did you finally knock someone up?"

Cade is such a dick. "For fu—"

"What does knock someone up mean?" We both stare blankly down at the little boy, but before we can respond, my dad and Summer show up at the top of the hill.

"You making me a granddaddy again, Rhett?" My dad chuckles as he draws near. He has no business hearing this well for a man his age. It's annoying that nothing gets past him.

I brace my hands on my hips and turn my face up at the blue sky, blowing out a hot breath and watching it turn to steam that dances up into the air.

"Sorry to disappoint," I mutter as I turn back to them, trying to ignore the confused scowl on Cade's face. That's basically his range of looks: happy scowl, tired scowl . . . I imagine he even has some sort of horny scowl that he's hidden away for the past several years.

"Summer is here, Rhett," my dad starts, with a look that says I better behave myself. I've been seeing that look my entire life. "You didn't mention how delightful she is. Did you know she just finished law school?"

My brows pop up. I'm not above admitting that's a little bit impressive. But it's also worse somehow. She's prissy, smart, accomplished, and assigned to babysit me.

And also insanely beautiful. She's changed into jeans, and I'm trying like hell not to eye the way they hug her pint-sized frame.

With a few sure strides, my brother closes the space between himself and Summer, stretching one long, muscled arm out in her direction. "Cade Eaton." His voice is brusque, but I know he's not shaking her hand as hard as he usually does. She has a delicate air about her, and Cade may be a grumpy asshole, but he's also a gentleman.

"Summer Hamilton." She smiles, and it still borders on a smirk. Like she's amused by this whole thing. When she's alone, I bet she has a nice, long, rich-girl laugh at my expense.

"And sorry, how do you know Rhett?" Cade's scowl is now curious.

Here it is, the moment *everyone* has a big laugh at my expense. My dad already knows, but as much as he jokes around, I don't think he'd throw me under the bus. We both know my dickhead brothers are going to get a real kick out of Baby Brother being in trouble. Again.

He'll just sit back and enjoy watching it all unfold.

But Summer doesn't miss a beat. "I'm a new junior agent with his firm. Just trying to learn the ropes with someone established." Her smile is soft and demure —sincere.

And she's lying through her goddamn teeth.

The girl is good. I'll give her that.

My brother's brows tug together, and my dad's eyes twinkle as he watches the exchange. I hold my breath, hoping that's all there is to it. Maybe, just *maybe*, I'll get away with this without being completely embarrassed.

Cade's head quirks. "But why are you he—"

"I'm hungry," Luke announces.

"Bet you are," Summer replies. "What's your favorite snack?"

Instant redirection. My dad catches my eye and winks.

"Popcorn!" Why do kids always exclaim everything? Like they're going to win some sort of prize for shouting it out first.

Summer quirks a hip and crosses her arms, like she's weighing the child's response. "With M&M's mixed in?"

"Oooh!" Luke exclaims as the rest of us men wrinkle our noses. "I've never had that!"

"No?" Her eyes flare dramatically as she crouches down.

"What are emnems?" Luke asks, admitting he hasn't got a fucking clue what she's talking about. The exchange is cute, and my eyes snap to my brother, wondering if he's falling in love with Summer Hamilton on the spot. But he just seems perplexed.

"They're a candy. With chocolate. And peanuts. I saw stores on my way here that would have them for sure. I bet your dad would take you to get some."

And just like that, Cade looks colossally annoyed.

"Can we, Dad?" Luke's big blue eyes light up.

"After you ran away from poor old Mrs. Hill?" Cade's jaw pops, and he shoots Summer a disapproving glare. Some women would shrink under that scowl, but not this one.

She shrugs and mouths, "*Sorry*," looking a little chagrined as they turn toward their house to leave. But when she glances over her shoulder at me, that smug smirk touches her mouth.

And that's the moment I realize she wasn't chagrined at all. That entire exchange was a completely intentional way of cutting off my brother's line of questioning.

To help me save face.

"I'll go give Cade a hand with Luke," my dad says, dropping his head down to hide what I know has to be a grin under the brim of his cowboy hat.

Which means Summer and I are here on the top of the dry, scrubby knoll, all alone for the very first time. But she doesn't give me any attention. She just stands gazing out over the hills toward the peaks of the Rockies.

She's so still that for a few moments I can't help but watch her. The cool wind whistles through the bare branches of the sparse trees. There's a solid nip in the air, and when it gusts, her shoulders come up tight under her ears, the puffy down coat rubbing against her earrings as the breeze tosses her silky brown hair around behind her.

And then she sighs, deep and heavy, and I watch her shoulders slowly drop, entranced by her reaction. When my eyes track lower, I shake my head. I have to remember that even if she throws me a bone, she and I are not friends.

We're not even on the same team.

"Using a five-year-old boy to get your way. Is that a new low?"

She huffs out a laugh and shoves her hands into her back pockets before turning around to face me, all wide eyes. "I didn't use him. I enlightened him. Mixing candy with your popcorn is a life experience that every child deserves."

"Cade is going to hate you for that."

Her lips press together, and she shrugs, seeming truly unaffected by the prospect. "I guess I'll have to hope Brother Number Three likes me. Or maybe I'll go for the trifecta? Get you all to hate me? That might be nice for me."

The balls on this girl.

"You could have told the truth."

"I did."

My teeth grind. "Learning the ropes? We both know you're here to babysit me."

Her head tilts, and she stares at me in the most unnerving way. "I guess we all see things the way we want to. I *am* new at the firm. They only recently hired me as more than a summer intern. And you *are* established. And I'd be an idiot to think I'm not here to learn something. Or Kip would have sent someone with more experience, no?"

Then she walks back toward the main house.

"Why didn't you just throw me under the bus then? They're going to figure it out, eventually."

"Because that's not my job. Keep up, we need to go over some things."

I hang back for a few minutes, because when Summer Hamilton tells me to jump, I refuse to respond with, *How high?*

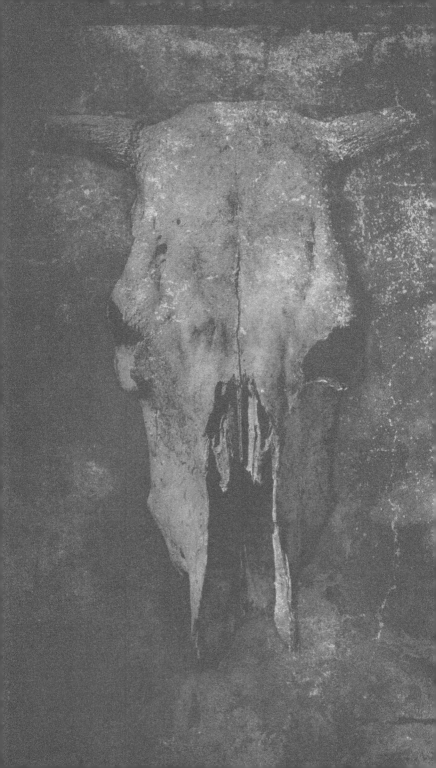

5

Summer

Dad: How's it going?

Summer: It's beautiful out here.

Dad: I meant the cowboy.

Summer: Oh, him? He hates me.

Dad: You'll win him over. Just make sure he keeps his dick in his pants.

Summer: I'll pass the message along. A sure way to win him over!

Men are so fragile.

I told Rhett to keep up, and I'm almost positive he stood in that field sulking just to prove a point. It's kind of amusing. My lips twitch as I set up my files and laptop on the living room table.

We need to hammer out a schedule for the coming months, and I'm going to need Rodeo King here to do that.

Eventually, I hear the back door slam and heavy footfalls traveling in my direction. Out of the corner of my eye, I catch sight of his frame. His broad shoulders, his unruly hair, and dark scruff. You'd have to be dead to not appreciate a man like Rhett Eaton.

He's not pretty and polished. He's rugged and a little rough around the edges.

He's all man.

One hundred percent different from any man I've met. Girls like me don't usually mix with men like him. We don't even mix in the same circles, but that doesn't stop me from appreciating him. The way a pair of Wranglers fit him hasn't changed since his early days on the circuit.

"I was worried a bear had attacked you," I announce as I seat myself on one of the tufted leather club chairs.

"Black bears rarely attack people," he husks as he strides into the living room, eyeing up my spread like it might be an explosive or something.

"Grizzlies?"

"Mostly stick to the mountains," he grumbles.

"Okay. Cougar?"

He towers above me and quirks a brow.

"Yeah," I sigh and lean back in the comfy chair, sensing the pressure of his honeyed stare on my body. "You definitely look like cougar bait."

He shakes his head while I bite back a grin. "This is going to be a long two months."

"You could always throw yourself down that well I saw on my way back to the house and put yourself right out of this misery."

That comment sobers him and instead of responding with something flippant, he flops down on the couch across from me and runs his hands through his hair. The silence stretches between us as I regard him carefully. "My mom used to make wishes down that well with my brothers and me. Don't remember it at all."

Fuuucckkk. Talk about stepping in it, Summer. The sinking feeling in my chest has me clearing my throat noisily. "I'm sorry," I say. Because I really am.

He just nods, and I opt to change the subject. Put the conversation back on the safe ground that is work. Our arrangement that he hates so much is preferable to where I just took things. "Tell me what the next two months looked like for you before I came onto the scene."

"You mean before I got saddled with you? It looked pretty great."

I just nod and say a quiet, "Yeehaw," as I twirl my finger around beside my head like I'm swinging a lasso. Because it's not like he's making this fun. He's acting like I'm some sort of enemy when I'm actually just here to make his life easier.

I reach for the day timer in front of me, grab my favorite

silver pen, and proceed to stare at him until he talks. I listen and note specific dates as he reads them off his phone while completely avoiding eye contact with me.

We exchange phone numbers and email addresses, and I make clear that he's to behave like a good little boy that no one can find fault in for the next eight weeks.

I don't get *too* specific, because I'm hoping he's picking up what I'm putting down as I speak in vague generalities about his behavior—that Little Rhett needs to stay in his pants. Because having to dictate a man's sexual activities is just way beyond my pay grade. Kip can call him and break those details down himself. Rhett and I are going to need to maintain some semblance of dignity if we're spending the next two months stuck together.

Rhett responds in grunts and stares up at the ceiling like he wishes it would open up and swallow him whole. And quite frankly, I can't blame him.

"Okay." I tap my fingers on the open page before me. "So, we have three qualifying events. Pine River is the first, then Blackwood Creek, then the one here in Calgary. That's kind of nice. Has there always been a stop here on your tour?"

"Yup."

"No rest for the wicked, huh? They bang these out back-to-back."

He sighs and finally holds my gaze for a moment. "The World Bull Riding Federation, or WBRF, is as competitive as it gets. If I wasn't sitting comfortably ahead and was chasing points instead, I'd probably be doing two more before Vegas. We usually go every weekend."

"Right. World Finals in Vegas." I stare down at the date on the calendar. That's the day I'll be free of this assignment and this grumpy cowboy.

"Championships, not finals. Do you even know anything about this sport?"

I draw a star on that calendar square and sigh wistfully before tipping my face back up to glare at Rhett, who is sitting across from me, taking up the maximum amount of space on the couch. Long arm draped over the back of it and jean-clad legs spread wide.

Man spreading.

"No. Just what I've searched on the internet. But I bet you'd love to tell me all about it."

He glares back like he's trying to figure out how his life turned into this, and then he asks, "Why do you need to go to law school to become an agent?"

"You don't. Well, not really. But it's a lot of contract work, so it definitely helps."

"Huh," is all he says while spinning the silver ring on his finger. "That's a lot of school. You must love it."

I give him a flat smile. I'm not sure I'd take it that far, but I'm not about to tell a client that. "Yeah. Can you explain the scoring? So I understand what I'm watching next weekend?"

He eyes me a suspiciously and then he starts. "So, you've got two judges. Each judge gives the rider a score out of twenty-five and the bull out of twenty-five. Add them up and you get an overall score out of one hundred."

"And what are they judging on?" My hope is that if I

can get him talking about something he likes, he'll warm up a bit.

"Several things. Their agility, speed, whether they turn. You pull a bull that runs down the arena in a straight line and you aren't going to get good style points. But you pull one that wants to kill you and will spin in a circle and toss his hooves to the roof? Then you're talking." Rhett is more animated than I've ever seen him as he explains the sport. His excitement is almost infectious.

"Now the rider is more about his form. His balance. His control." He shows me how that looks by moving his hands into the position. "The way he covers the bull. If you can spur 'em, they buck harder and there are extra points for that. And of course, you've gotta hang on for eight whole seconds."

"And if you don't?"

He clicks his tongue and tilts his head. "No score then."

I blow out a breath and tap my pen against the table. "Do or die, huh? I can't wait to see it live."

He eyes me up and down now, like he can't quite figure me out. "Yeah,"—his tongue pushes into his cheek—"that'll really be something."

I don't know what the hell a comment like that is supposed to mean, so I just forge ahead. "I'll book our flights and hotels for these dates. Fly in one day early and leave one day after?"

"Separate rooms."

I roll my eyes.

And there goes all that positive momentum. This guy

has some serious nerve. It makes all my professionalism fly out the window. "No shit."

"Just trying to keep the line clear, *Princess*." He's mocking me, but I don't bite. Even though I wish with every fiber of my being that Kip would stop calling me that—especially in front of other people. "Your dad made it seem like you were going to put me on a leash."

"Only if you're into that kind of thing." The words are out before I even comprehend what I'm saying. My head snaps up to gauge his reaction. I'm so accustomed to my father's biting commentary along with everyone else in the office that it's a comfortable role to fall into—even with someone as un-fun as Rhett Eaton.

He's glaring at me with his most unimpressed expression when the back door bangs open again, interrupting our exchange.

Luke flies into the house like a bat out of hell and launches himself into Rhett's lap, followed by more heavy feet and deep voices. Cade steps into the kitchen first, followed by his dad, and then a man who has to be the third brother.

He's a dead ringer for every other man in this family—except he smiles like his dad and his eyes are light.

"You must be Summer," he says, grinning at me appreciatively as he leans up against the door frame. His hair is trimmed tight and there's a polish about him that Rhett and Cade don't have.

"This is Beau," Harvey pipes up, pulling a seat out at the oversized table. "You caught him home between deployments." I can't help but smile back at the older man. His pride is spilling out of him all over the floor.

Harvey Eaton loves his boys with a fierceness I admire.

"Nice to meet you, Beau. I'm Summer Hamilton." I smile softly, already loving the family atmosphere here in the cozy house. Even if it is testosterone overload.

"You all finished with your meeting?" Harvey asks as Cade starts digging through the fridge and pulling out ingredients for dinner.

"Yes," Rhett announces before I can say anything.

I stand, feeling sufficiently dismissed by Rhett's cool tone. "I'll get out of your hair."

"Where you going, lady?" Luke asks. "It's dinner time. I thought you lived here now? I heard Grandpa say it."

I suck in a deep breath and glance down at Rhett, whose eyes have dropped shut, a small smile playing across his features.

It looks good on him.

"You live here now?" Cade's head snaps up, his face in what seems to be his favorite expression—bitchy.

"Um. Just for a while." My gaze settles on Harvey, who shakes his head and looks down like he knows what's coming.

"Hang on." Beau's head is swiveling between Rhett and me, amusement dancing on every feature. "Your *agent* is living with you? Why?"

"It's very temporary—" I start.

"Is this because you punched that guy?" Beau continues, intelligent eyes working through things so plainly.

"You punched someone?" Cade asks, brows knitting together.

"Bro. You need to turn a TV on now and then. You live in the dark ages." Beau laughs.

Cade turns to Rhett, who still hasn't opened his eyes. "Did he deserve it?"

Rhett smiles now, a real big smile. "So fucking much."

"Bad word, Uncle Rhett!" Luke's hands slap down over his ears with a shit-eating little grin.

My eyes bounce between everyone in the room, living for the level of comfort here. It's amusing. It's charming. It's so different from how my childhood home felt.

"He's in a tight spot with his sponsors, that's all," I clarify.

Cade grunts as he chops carrots. "When is he not in trouble?"

"Wait." Beau's face brightens. "Did you get assigned a babysitter?"

Rhett groans and drops his head back against the couch.

"I don't like my babysitter either, Uncle Rhett." Luke pats him like a dog and a laugh bubbles up out of me. Because Rhett called this. Harvey called this. They knew exactly how it was going to go down, and that level of familiarity is heartwarming to me. It's chaotic in here already, and I love it. I'm starry-eyed and giddy.

"Mind your manners, Lucas Eaton," Cade says while pulling a pan out from under the stove. "Answer the question, Rhett."

Rhett glances over at Beau and says, "You can contact my agent for a comment."

Beau barks out a laugh and looks over at me, hands held up in prayer position. "Please, Summer. Make my day. Tell me he's in time out. Tell me he's a thirty-two-year-old man with a full-time nanny."

I press my lips together, dedicated to not throwing Rhett under the bus—no matter how badly I'd like to. "I'm new at the firm. This job is so that I can get some experience under my belt outside of the office."

"Yeah. She told me that too," Cade interjects as he seasons a sizeable chunk of beef now. "I think Miss Hamilton might be full of shit though."

"Mind your manners, Daddy!" Luke shouts, right as Harvey scolds him, "Cade!"

I rub a hand over my mouth to cover my smile. You grow up around Kip Hamilton and a few bad words aren't going to phase you.

"I'll go grab dinner in town, leave you all to it. I don't want to be a nuisance."

Beau holds up a hand to stop me. "Not a chance, Summer. You're going to take a seat and tell us everything over Cade's famous pot roast. Then I'm going to take us all for drinks in town at The Railspur so you can get a warm Chestnut Springs welcome and meet my buddy, Jasper."

"Jasper is home?" Harvey's head snaps up from where he was watching his grandson with an amused expression on his face.

And just like that, I'm sucked into a dinner of hearty

home-cooked food, friendly taunting, and comfortable laughter.

Even Rhett lightens up now that it's not just us, but he still avoids looking at me throughout the meal.

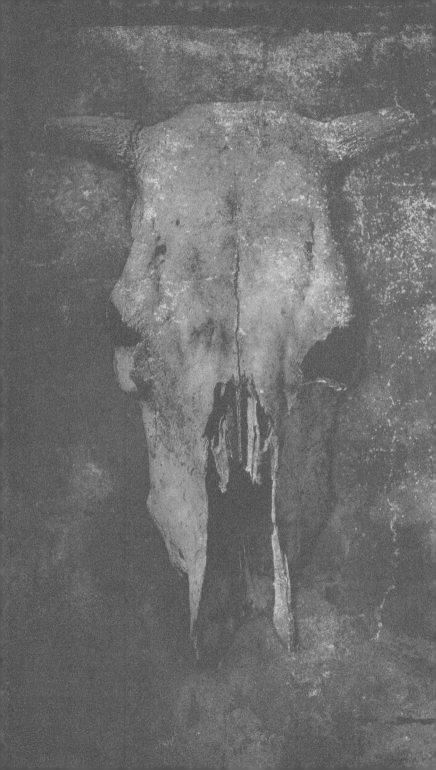

6

Summer

Willa: I miss your face already. Have fun playing Hell on Wheels?

Summer: What?

Willa: Your cowboy. I looked him up. He looks like the hot guy from Hell on Wheels. You know, the one with the long hair? Did you know they filmed that show out there?

Willa: You should bang him.

Summer: No.

Willa: Want me to print you a picture of him for your wall?

Summer: I don't miss you at all.

Rhett and I drive in utter silence, which is fine. It gives me the opportunity to get acquainted with everything out the window.

"Turn here." One small turn takes us to a dead-end side street, at the bottom of which sits The Railspur.

The pub is not what I was expecting from a small town. In fact, Chestnut Springs is not what I was expecting from a small town. I think my dad and I have watched a few too many old western movies, and I'm realizing that I am truly an oblivious city girl.

Because Chestnut Springs is beautiful. The main street has these adorable bricked-in sidewalks, ornate lamp posts with little town flags dangling from them, and the businesses down here have maintained the historic facades while modernizing or adding on to the rest. Old brick buildings with dramatic archways or charming colorful awnings line each side of Rosewood Street, the main thoroughfare in town.

And the pub is not some small-town dive either. It's like . . . cowboy chic.

"Is this an old train station?" I ask as I roll into the parking lot that Rhett just silently pointed to.

"Yup."

"I guess the name should have been clue enough," I say, mostly to myself since Rhett seems limited to grunts and one-word answers, before pulling to a stop in a space not too far from the door.

He grunts.

And I turn to him as he flings off his seatbelt, like he can't get away fast enough. "Are you always this monosyllabic? Or is this special just for me?"

"I don't need this," he mutters just before he slams the passenger door in my face and storms toward the bar.

I flop back against my seat and blow a raspberry out through my lips.

I ask myself what I always do.

If this were my last moment alive, how would I want it to be?

My eyes flutter shut, and I suck in a deep breath, like that might help me grow some extra patience to deal with the big asshole bull rider assigned to me. Because in my last moments, I'd want to feel happy. If I step out of this car and get run down, I want to go out feeling good, not pissed off at some long-haired, broad-shouldered, round-assed cowboy.

That is not how Summer Hamilton goes.

Not today, Satan.

Then my door is wrenched open. "Are you having a stroke?" Rhett peers down at me, lips curving toward the ground.

"What are you doing?" I ask, brows knitting in confusion. I thought he'd stormed into the bar.

"Opening your door for you. Now get out."

My lips tug up and a silent giggle fills me as I realize he's trying to be gentlemanlike while also being a grumpy dick. And with that, I step out of my SUV, patting the hood on the way past with a quiet, "Sorry." Because that dick slammed her door way too hard.

We don't look at each other as we walk, but he touches my shoulder gently and gestures me across his body. He moves me to the opposite side of him before taking up position by the road.

This man gives me whiplash.

He tugs the bar door open by grabbing one of the long brass pulls that stretches almost the full length of the wood frame. Once I pass through, Rhett is gone without a word, and I'm left admiring the interior of the pub.

Inside there's a long bar that runs the full length of the left side of the building and high-top tables dot the main area. Further back, I can see a slightly raised section with a pool table, burgundy leather couches, and a fireplace.

Rhett clearly made a beeline for the bar, and a few locals have cornered him. There are back pats and hand-shakes exchanged between the men, but there's also a tension to the greeting, and I can't help but wonder what they're saying to him.

Beau was stopping to pick up a friend and is a few minutes behind us, so I opt to do a walk-by behind Rhett and see if I can overhear anything before heading to the ladies' room to burn some time before people who actually acknowledge my existence arrive.

I'm still wearing my favorite skin-tight skinny jeans and white eyelet blouse. I even paired the outfit with a pair of super-cute booties that seem a tad country to me. Minus the heel, but whatever.

You can take the girl out of the city and all that.

But it must be obvious to the locals that I'm not from around here, because I'm definitely garnering some looks as I weave my way through the tables. Rhett's gaze darts to me as I ease myself in his direction, but aside from that one flick of the eyes, he doesn't acknowledge my existence.

It's an obvious hint that he'd rather not associate with me right now, so I trail past him, catching a whiff of whatever cologne he's wearing. There's a liquorice note to it I've never noticed before now, followed by leather. I don't know if it's his boots, or his belt, or just that a man that rugged is destined to smell like something equally masculine.

Either way, it's a heady combination. One that has me taking a deep breath on my way past, creepy as that makes me.

It is what it is.

One man squeezes Rhett's shoulder. "We know you, Rhett. We know your family. What the media tells us about you doesn't matter. You're a good boy."

I almost snort. *Boy.* Maybe that's the problem. Everyone still coddles him like he's a little boy rather than telling him to take some responsibility for his actions. Should he be in trouble for what he said? No. But he doesn't need a bunch of back pats over it either.

The bathrooms are straight off the end of the bar, and I push the door open to find far more women primping under the bright halogen lights than I was expecting on a Monday night.

I give them that weird closed-mouth smile I often give to strangers instead of just saying hi. I know it looks pained, forced—a little serial-killer-y—but I keep doing it anyway.

It's a problem, and I can't stop.

They eye me suspiciously as their conversation pauses, but as soon as I lock myself in the stall, they go on like I'm not even here.

"Did you see Rhett Eaton at the bar?" The girl's question is met with a chorus of moans and "oohs" like he's king crab and a bowl of butter or something.

Another one pipes up. "Nobody call Amber. She'll march down here and freak out when she sees him go home with someone else."

"She needs to get over him."

"Yeah." The first girl laughs. "Give the rest of us a turn."

"You? No. Me. I don't just want a turn though. I'd lock that shit down forever. Those Eaton boys take after their dad. And Harvey Eaton is a total DILF. GILF?"

"I guess we'll see who he chooses tonight, then." The girl who says it is trying to sound lighthearted, but I recognize the streak of venom in her voice.

They all dissolve into a fit of giggles that are dulled only by the sound of me peeing and rubbing my hands over my face.

Because it's only Day One, and I'm already going to be called upon to help keep Little Rhett in his pants.

Back out in the bar, the flock of women have descended on Rhett and are ushering him over to a table.

I'm standing at the end of the bar, steeling myself to walk over there and make Rhett Eaton hate me more than he already does. I've racked my brain for something I can do that doesn't involve me being an embarrassing wet blanket.

Kip would walk over there and dole out a firm but fair verbal spanking. But I'm not Kip. I'm a twenty-five-year-old woman who is brand new to the job and in way over her goddamn head.

What was my dad thinking?

"Summer!" I follow the sound of my name over the buzzing sea of tables toward the back couches. Beau is there, wearing a friendly smile and waving at me. The perfect out.

And I take it.

I opt to go sit there and plan rather than shoot from the hip. My heels clack against the wooden floor as I head in Beau's direction. When I reach the couches, I see the shape of his friend sitting with him on the couch, facing away from the main floor of the bar. It isn't until I get closer to the low-slung table between them that I get a good look at the other man. And even with a beard and cap pulled down over his face, I recognize him.

Everyone in this country probably does.

Jasper Gervais, professional hockey player. Goaltender extraordinaire. Canadian Olympic sensation. And another one of my dad's clients, whose name I know from spending the last several summers of my life doing paperwork at Hamilton Elite.

"Summer, this is my buddy, Jasper." Beau hikes a

thumb in his friend's direction and scootches down as I hit him with my stupid, awkward smile-greeting before I can reel it in. But I'm a little relieved when Jasper gives me a matching serial-killer smile back.

"Hi, Jasper," I say before flopping down onto the couch next to Beau.

"Hey," he huffs out. Clearly not chatty, which is fine by me.

"We ordered you a drink." Beau pushes a small wine glass, full to the top, in my direction with a bit of a grimace on his face. "Thought you seemed like a white wine gal."

Jasper chuckles and tips his beer back.

My eyes roll. These guys are having way too much fun with the city-girl jokes. The worst part is, they're not even wrong. "Wine and tequila. But this doesn't feel like a tequila night."

They both laugh, and I reach for the glass of wine, praying I don't spill it all over myself.

From here, I have a perfect view of Rhett, seated on a stool where two round tables have been pulled together. He's smiling, talking with his hands, and my eyes trail along them, the veined tops of them, catching on the glint of silver on his finger. The ring that matches the silver cuff bracelet around his wrist.

Only Rhett Eaton could make jewelry look so goddamn manly.

Outwardly, he seems like he's having a good time, but there's something off about it. Something is not quite right. His face looks serene and in his element, but his shoulders are tight. There's a set to his jaw and a pinch to the corners of his eyes. His smile doesn't quite stretch all the way.

"You trying to cast some sort of curse on my little brother?" Beau asks, head swiveling between my face and where I'm staring.

I snort and take a big gulp of wine. It tastes terrible, but I don't care. I need a little liquid courage. "No. I'm trying to figure out how to do my job without making him hate me more than he already does."

"Fair. He does seem to hate you."

"Rhett?" Jasper asks with a raised brow.

I nod absently just as Beau says, "Oh, hell yeah."

The hockey player snorts. "Nah. That kid doesn't have a mean bone in his body. He's nice to everyone."

But does he mean it? That's the question bouncing around in my head as I watch him sit there rigidly as a woman rubs his shoulder while staring at him with hearts in her eyes.

"You think he'll be nice to me when I walk over there and tell him he can't take all those girls home tonight? Or drink too much?" I probably should have put my foot down on going out at all tonight. All the ways tonight could go wrong flash through my head.

Jasper scoffs and shakes his head. But it's Beau who pipes up. "Rhett doesn't care about taking those girls home. He's just too nice to tell them to leave him alone."

"Facts," Jasper grumbles with a smirk before tipping the brown bottle back against his lips.

"If he was a prick like Jasper, he'd be fine."

Jasper doesn't even try to correct his friend's

assessment.

"I don't know . . ." My nose wrinkles as I weigh my options.

It's at that moment the server swings past. "Y'all doing okay? Can I grab you another round?"

And then Beau's eyes light up like a kid on Christmas.

"Yeah." He pulls a twenty-dollar bill out of his wallet and places it in the middle of the table. "I will give you another one of those for every ultra-girly milk-based beverage you take over to my brother."

The server's eyes widen. And so do mine.

Jasper holds a fist up over his lips and his shoulders shake. "Put an umbrella in it."

Beau's not done though. "And announce to the table that the drink is from his future wife and that she knows this is his favorite."

My jaw drops as I stare at Beau. "What are you doing?"

"Pissing him off enough to drag him away from that table for you."

I laugh. This is not the plan I had in mind. *Boys.*

The server nibbles at her lip, staring down at the cash as she hugs the brown plastic tray to her chest. "Is this a trick?"

"No, Bailey," Beau answers, his voice softening. "This has nothing to do with you. All in good fun."

She turns wide eyes on him, looking particularly young in this moment. Though I know to work in the bar, she has to be at least eighteen. "Okay. Fine."

And with that, she swipes the cash off the table and scurries away.

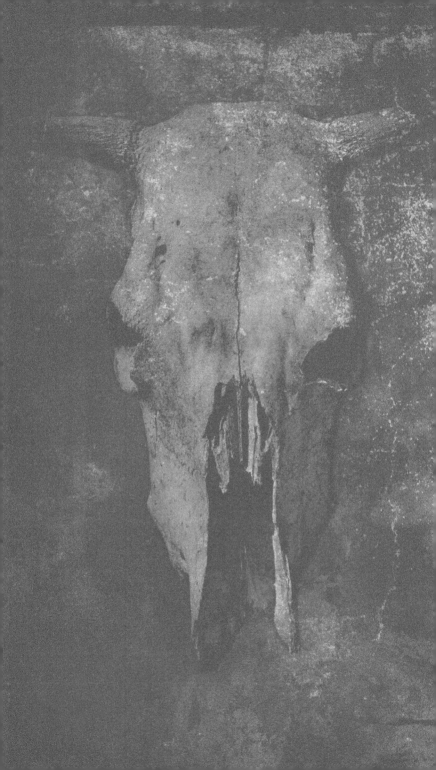

7

Rhett

Kip: Talked to the rest of your sponsors today. A couple were undecided on what they're going to do. But Wrangler and Ariat are still on . . . so long as you keep your shit together.

Kip: Hello? You going to thank me?

Rhett: Nope.

Kip: I know you love me.

Rhett: I don't. You sicced an attack dog on me. Your princess is a real ball-buster.

Kip: Good. Your balls could use some busting.

I'm in the middle of recounting one of my most recent rides, something I actually like talking about, when a glass slides in front of my spot at the table.

My eyes snap up to little Bailey Jansen, nibbling on her lip with rosy cheeks. "This is from your future wife." I rear back at that. "She says she knows it's your favorite." Bailey can barely get the words out.

I do some mental gymnastics as I glance around the table, but everyone here seems equally confused as I feel. The few men here are chuckling, but the girls range from looking confused to downright feral.

If one of them was smiling at me, I'd know it was her.

When I take a proper look at the drink, I'm even more confused.

"What is this?"

"It's . . . um . . . a White Russian?"

My brows knit together as I stare down at the milky drink, threads of dark liquor pulling up from the bottom. *What the fuck?*

"Enjoy!" Bailey squeaks before peeling away. If I didn't know she was the only good Jansen of the entire group, I'd suspect her. But the only thing I suspect is that someone else has put her up to this.

My first guess is Beau.

My eyes scan the bar for him as Laura, someone I've

known in passing since high school, tries to flag down a server like this milky umbrella drink is an affront to my masculinity. There's even a fucking maraschino cherry on top—plump and bright. And as I stare at it, I'm reminded of Summer's mouth.

I ditched her and didn't think twice about it when we got here. Not my finest moment. And definitely not a gentlemanly way to welcome her to town. I swivel on my stool, trying to see where she landed.

When I finally find her, she looks deep in conversation with my brother and his friend. They all seem relaxed, and oblivious to whatever this stunt is here. So, I rule them out. Though my eyes linger. She's talking, and those fuckers are hanging on every word like she's the most interesting person in the world.

And truth be told, if I wasn't so miffed about this whole thing, I might be interested in talking to her more. She does seem interesting. There's something intriguing about her. The way she looks, the way she talks, her confidence and spunk.

Summer Hamilton is an unusual combination.

"Excuse me, Rhett would *never* drink something like this." I almost scoff out loud. The way Laura is talking like she knows me grates on my nerves.

Someone promptly takes away the drink and replaces it with a bottle of local brew. Something I like.

But within minutes, Bailey is back, looking like she'd rather run out the front door than face our table again.

"Your future wife sent this over. She said she knows how much you love chocolate milkshakes." Then she darts away while I stare down at the creamy brown drink in a long-stem martini glass.

With an umbrella and cherry again.

These cherries are going to be the death of me. Somehow, my brain has connected them to the lipstick Summer wears, and the color isn't even that similar. But it's going there anyway.

It's going other places too. Like how that mouth would look wrapped around my dick.

When I peer up at her this time, her big brown eyes flit in my direction, but she purses her lips and turns away, like she finds something distasteful about me.

Some guys at the table are having a real good laugh now. "Thought you didn't like milk, Eaton?" one of the older men blurts out, and a smile tugs at my lips. At least these people don't hate me for saying what I said. And as usual, their attention feels good. I roll my shoulders back and choose to ignore whoever is pulling the hilarious prank.

"This is ridiculous," Laura hisses, rubbing my back like I'm upset. But I don't get mad, I get even. And when I figure out who is getting a kick out of sending me these milky fucking messes, it will be game on.

"Bailey, darlin', I don't want this."

She nods quickly and snatches it away before leaving us again.

Laura leans close, her lips brushing across my ear in a way that should be sexy, but makes me recoil as she whispers, "I'm so sorry someone is doing this to you. Mocking you like this. It's been a tough week for you already."

She's not wrong about that. But she won't be the factor

that turns this week around either. Things aren't going to turn around until I can ditch my babysitter once and for all —even if she isn't following me around like I thought she might.

I don't throw Laura any bones, but I don't push her away either. Even if I'm not remotely interested, I don't want to be rude. So, I tip my beer bottle in her direction before taking a swig.

"All good. I'm a big boy."

She smiles suggestively, reading an innuendo that isn't there, and I take another swallow. Because that was not how I intended for it to come out.

With a wink, she slides her hand up to play with the ends of my hair. "I've heard."

And *that* is why I don't hook up with women in this town anymore. I had one casual girlfriend before I learned my lesson. You get a blowjob from someone in Chestnut Springs and the next thing you know, it's in the newspaper, and the ladies at the salon are planning a fucking wedding. No, I keep that shit on the road where it belongs.

When I come home, I want privacy.

My eyes flit up to where my brother is sitting, and this time, I'm met with all three of them staring back at me. When they catch me looking, Summer and Beau quickly glance down and reach for their drinks.

Jasper grins at me from beneath the brim of his cap. The guy is quiet and doesn't smile that much. He gives thoughtful pauses and one-word answers until you get a few drinks into him. They say goaltenders are a different breed, and in Jasper's case, that's true. I should know, we grew up with the guy.

And more than anything, it gets me wondering why he's staring at me like the fucking Cheshire Cat. It's creeping me the hell out. The way it slowly widens further as his eyes drop to the table in front of me.

I glance over in time to see Bailey hustling away. This time, she didn't even say anything. Just dropped the drink and ran. Can't say that I blame her.

"Is that. . ." Laura looks offended, like someone just called her mother a whore.

The clear glass mug is one typically used for speciality coffee. But the liquid inside is solid white. It's topped with whipped cream.

And a fucking cherry.

When I touch the side, it's warm. Not hot. Warm, like I'd make hot chocolate for Luke.

"Is that warm milk?" Laura's voice is shrill, and I hear snickering from around the table, but I don't address them.

Instead, I tear my eyes away from the whipped cream melting down the sides of the mug, making a colossal mess, and peer up at the couches in the back.

Jasper is still staring at me, but this time, his hand is thrown over his mouth, shoulders shaking with barely restrained laughter. Beau, the cocksucker that he is, has flopped back on the couch, like this is the funniest joke in the world.

Spoiler alert: it's not.

I just lost a huge sponsorship over milk, and these dickheads are sitting around sending me *warm milk*. I almost shudder at the thought.

But it's Summer that really gets me. She's sitting there looking perfectly put together, perfectly smug. Legs crossed in the most lady-like way with the chocolate milk martini I sent back in her hand. She holds it up to me in a silent "cheers" and then plucks the cherry off the top and wraps her lips around it.

And then I'm moving across the bar. Storming up toward them. Half amused and half pissed off that these fucking traitors are playing tricks on me with the woman whose presence they know I don't like. It seems like they're taking her side when it's me they've known their entire lives. Am I having a minor internal temper tantrum over it?

Maybe.

I've always been the joke in this family. The one that gets poked fun at. The one nobody takes seriously.

"Rhett, you forgot your warm milk," Jasper says as I approach. Beau makes some honking noise as he tries, and fails, to keep himself from bursting out laughing. He always has been the giddy, lighthearted one of us. Which is fucking wild considering he's JTF2, Canada's top special forces unit.

"No, no, no." Beau gasps for air. "He's coming up here because he wants the White Russian instead."

I shake my head. The corners of my mouth tilt up, even though I'm working hard to keep them down. "You guys are such fucking losers." I prop my hands on my hips and stare up at the ceiling where an ornate brass chandelier hangs, completing the upscale country vibe this place has taken on under new ownership.

"Shouldn't talk to your future wife that way," Jasper bites before snorting and barking out another laugh.

Their laughter is infectious, and I'm trying to not let it overtake me. I don't want to find this funny. But if there was ever a person who could give me the giggles, it would be Beau. And right now, he is unhinged.

I peek down at Summer. Her wide, sparkling eyes looking up at me are downright disarming. She's trying not to laugh, and I'm trying not to get a boner from staring at her mouth. It's a fucking struggle for us both.

"Was this your idea?"

"No." She huffs outs a laugh, her composure finally cracking as a pink stain spreads out over her cheeks. "Not even a little bit. I am an innocent bystander."

I regard her with a raised brow, not entirely sure if I believe she wasn't playing a part in this. She already seems to be amused by my suffering, so I'm not sure why she'd draw the line here.

Plus, the fact that I can't stop staring at her gorgeous face makes me feel like she isn't innocent in my frustration at all.

"Hey now," Jasper interjects with his raspy tone before taking a big swig of his beer. "Don't pick on Summer. The warm milk was *my* idea. That was more fun than I've had in ages."

Beau slaps his knee and wheezes. "You should have seen your face!"

I shake my head and let out a chuckle that rumbles in my chest.

"I'm going to get you back for this," I say, but my eyes dart back to Summer's face. And then she nods, dropping my gaze for a moment as the shadows from her lashes fan across the apples of her cheeks. She looks almost shy, not smug at all.

Not what I expected.

With a deep sigh, I turn and kick Jasper's boot. "Shove over, asshole."

I flop down beside our childhood friend and feel immediately more at ease than I did at that other table—even with my lush-lipped babysitter princess here.

Then I reach forward and swipe the White Russian off the table in front of me and take a big swig of it as I throw an arm over the back of the couch.

"Fucking delicious," I announce with a cocky grin. Beau giggles like a schoolgirl all over again. *Idiot.* I roll my eyes at him and then turn my attention to Summer as I take another sip of the milky disaster in my hand. She's smiling at me now.

And as much as I hate to admit it, I like her eyes on me.

I thought a few drinks would provide me the pain relief I need to get a good sleep since that rough dismount last weekend, but I was wrong.

I've been lying here for the past two and a half hours

trying to get comfortable. Failing. And then berating myself for taking such a stupid fall. I've been at this for over a decade. The bull didn't pile drive me into the ground—no avoiding that—it was just a stupid landing.

And because I'm truthfully too old to still be doing what I'm doing, I don't bounce back like I used to. I'm trying so hard not to live on painkillers—only one set of kidneys and all that—but I've been popping them like candy for the better part of my life. I just didn't use to care.

Scrubbing my hands over my face, I let out a groan and roll myself out of bed, wincing as I do. The wooden floorboards are cold against my feet as I pad across my bedroom and turn the door handle. In the hallway, I tiptoe like a child.

I feel like one, too, trying not to wake my dad up. Can't say I ever imagined living with him at this age, but when I'm on the road for the better part of the year, maintaining my own house makes little sense.

Once I retire, I'll build, just like my brothers have.

Once I retire.

That's what I keep telling myself. That's what I keep putting off. Because without a bull to get on every weekend, I have no idea who I'll be. Or what I'll do.

It's a terrifying prospect. One I'm happy to continue ignoring.

Once I'm down the stairs, I take normal strides again, heading straight toward the kitchen where I keep my meds up high so Luke can't get his grubby, trouble-making hands on them.

Rounding the corner into the kitchen, I freeze when I find it's not empty.

Summer is sitting at the big family-sized table, scrolling through her phone with a glass of water in front of her. The light from her screen reflects on her bare face, capturing the look of surprise when she realizes I'm standing in the wide archway watching her.

"Hi," she says carefully, like she's not sure how I'll react to her presence.

Things seemed to settle between us at the bar after we all got a good laugh out of the way. I don't want to be a dick to Summer. None of this is her fault. But I'm pretty sure I've been one all the same. The woman can get a rise out of me without even trying.

"Hey. Everything okay?" I ask, sounding loud in the otherwise silent kitchen.

It's one thing I love about coming home. The silence. You just don't get that in hotels or in the city. Out here, it is truly quiet. Truly peaceful.

She places her phone down before lifting her glass in my direction. "A few too many sugary drinks mixed with the biggest glass of white wine ever. Thanks for driving back."

I click my tongue as I pull open the cupboard over the sink. "The Railspur has gotten a facelift in recent years. Still not the place for fancy-girl wine though."

She hums thoughtfully. "Good point. I'll go for the warm milk next time."

"You just gonna make fun of me for the next two months?" I pour a glass of water and then march back over to the table, not missing the way her eyes trail over my body. I'm only wearing boxers, not really accustomed to having to cover up for a woman in the house.

Her lips press into a thin line as I take a seat, deciding not to be a total dick and storm out of here. Her company isn't the worst. She could be Laura pawing at me like a bear on a beehive. That would be worse.

"Probably. It's my default when I'm uncomfortable." She doesn't whisper or drop my eyes; she just says something vulnerable like sharing that kind of shit is normal.

"You're uncomfortable?"

Summer blows a raspberry and flops against the worn ladder-back chair. And it's only now that I notice she's wearing some sort of silky tank top and matching shorts. They're light purple, and they shimmer in the dim light cast from the bulb over the stove.

"Of course, I am."

"Why? You're all smirks and quick comebacks. Winning everyone over."

She reaches up, combing her fingers through her long silky hair. Tresses that shimmer like her matching pajamas. And it's now I notice the scar on her chest, followed by the outline of her nipples through the top. They're not hard, but I can see the swell, the tease of the shape. It's almost more alluring to *imagine* what they might look like.

I flick my eyes up, but they land on her lips. Smirking lips. Which reminds me that Summer Hamilton pisses me off.

"You think this is ideal for me?" she asks. "Trial by fire? Having to follow around someone who clearly can't stand me as I try to do a brand-new job while also trying not to make him hate me more? Oh, yeah. Sign me up. Good times."

I raise a brow. "The embarrassing milk drinks were an excellent path to making me like you. Well played. Having you join in with my dickhead brother felt great."

That actually might be the worst part. I wanted her to pick my team, not Beau's. Everyone picks Beau because he's all sunny and handsome and shit.

She scoffs and squeezes her eyes shut. The first sign of frustration I've seen on her. "Would you have preferred I march over there and intervene? Embarrass you myself?"

My brow furrows as I swallow the pill. "Why would you?"

She levels a stare at me and very seriously says, "Because I was freaking out that we shouldn't have gone out at all. That I'm not going to be able to handle this—or you."

"I wasn't doing anything wrong." Jesus, is a few beers at my local watering hole off the table?

"I know that. But I'm supposed to keep Little Rhett in your pants. And that one girl was ready to pack him up and take him home."

"Pardon me?"

"Your dick." She points at my lap. "No coming out to play until this is all dealt with. Kip's orders. Your reputation can't take you getting caught up in any more drama. You're supposed to seem wholesome."

"I *am* wholesome. Does enjoying sex make a person less wholesome?"

She shivers, and then quickly rolls her eyes like she doesn't believe me. "It doesn't matter what you are or are not. You need to *look* wholesome, which means keep it in your pants. Keep your hands to yourself. Win the whole fucking thing so we can both put this behind us."

I stare at her. Is this fresh-out-of-law-school knockout seriously telling me what I can and cannot do with my dick? How must she see me?

"And for crying out loud, Rhett." She stands and swipes her phone off the table before pointing down at me. "Realize that I'm on your side. I don't *want* this to be miserable. I don't *want* to embarrass you. If you let me, we can be a team rather than fighting the entire time. Use your head."

I'm accustomed to getting dressed down. Getting in trouble isn't new, and I'm not about to roll over and take this from her. Which is why I reply with, "Which one?"

And with that, she storms out. Ass barely concealed by her silky shorts. Leaving me wondering if those are the new "team" uniform.

Because if so, I just might be in.

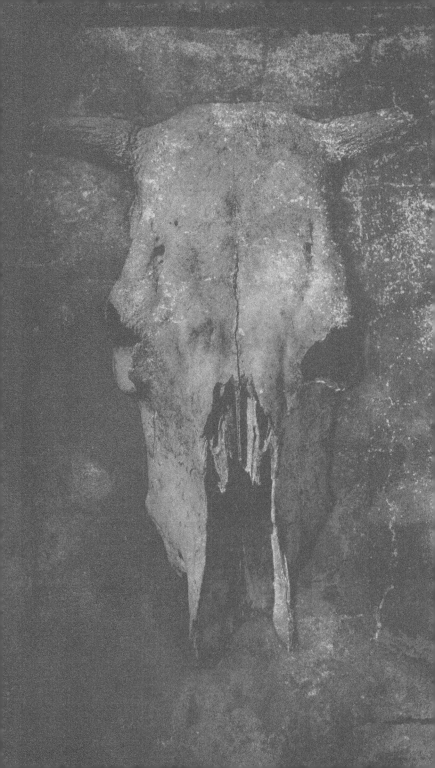

8

Summer

Dad: Is he being a dick?

Summer: No.

Dad: Would you tell me if he was?

Summer: Also no.

Dad: Summer, if you need backup, just tell me. I can send Gabriel.

Summer: That's not even his name. Plus, I grew up around you. I can handle dicks.

Summer: Fuck my life. Forget I said that.

Dad: Already deleted.

I sleep like shit. All the witty comebacks I wish I'd said to Rhett last night run through my head like the ticker on the bottom of a news channel.

He agitated me. I let him get under my skin, and I shouldn't have. I walked away like the bigger person, even though what I wanted to do was kick him in the shins. Which would have hurt like hell because everything about Rhett Eaton is hard, and toned, and cut.

He's not bulky, but he's *fit*. A swimmer's build. Strong enough to stay on, but not cumbersome.

And maybe that's why I'm agitated. Staring at a magazine ad of Rhett in Wranglers with hearts in my eyes as a teenager is funny, but seeing him stripped down as an adult is not.

It's frustrating. Something I need to work off, which is why I'm pulling on my favorite leggings, sports bra, and loose tee. A quick search on my phone brought up one option in town for a gym, and that's where I'm headed.

I march down the hallway, ponytail swinging behind me as I strut into the kitchen with my head held high, trying not to remember the way the light played off every ridge on Rhett's body last night—the shadows between every defined ab, the dip at the hollow of his throat, that perfect v heading toward the *other* head.

What a fucking dick.

And that dick's dad is already sitting at the table, sipping a coffee, and reading the newspaper.

"Good morning." Harvey smiles at me. "Early riser, huh?"

"Yeah." I reach for a mug and pour myself a coffee, making myself at home because, right now, I desperately need some caffeine. "Always have been."

"Me too," he tells me.

As I pass the fridge with my coffee in hand, I catch sight of a photo there, held up by a magnet in the shape of a horse's head. A petite blonde woman beams at the camera beside the shiniest black horse I've ever seen. She's wearing black and gold jockey silks and the horse has a blanket of roses draped over him.

"Who's this?" I ask Harvey curiously.

His responding smile is immediate. Deep and genuine. "That's my little girl. Violet. She's a championship race-horse jockey. Lives over near Vancouver with her husband and my other grandbabies."

I pull the chair out across from him, returning his grin. "You must be very proud of her."

A sad look flashes in his eyes, but he covers it quickly. "You have no idea."

I swallow thickly, sensing that's as far as I can go with this subject. So, I change the topic entirely. "I'm heading into town to try out the gym."

The older man nods. "Good for you. I bet you'll be back before Rhett even wakes up."

"Well, great. If he gets up, give him a tranquilizer until I return."

"He giving you trouble already?"

"No chance. He's a doll." I wink at Harvey, and we share a laugh before falling into an easy conversation.

I make Harvey and I each a piece of toast for breakfast,

and he seems thoroughly amused by me making him break-fast. When we hit a natural lull in the conversation, I clean up and head out the front door to hop in my car.

For the hour that follows, I work out until sweat pours down my body. I swear it smells like cheap wine. But I don't even care. My heart pumps blood out through my body, and I feel alive. I feel strong. The gym is quiet, and I monopolize a squat rack until my muscles burn and my legs shake.

And when I drive back through the front archway at Wishing Well Ranch, I feel substantially saner.

I breathe in the crisp morning air as I walk toward the sprawling house, admiring the way the frost on the dead grass has turned the landscape a sparkly white. Something that will melt away as soon as the bright prairie sun gets high enough in the bluebird sky.

When I head back into the kitchen to make another pot of coffee, Rhett is sitting at the table, looking as frosty as the grass.

"Good morning." I smirk at him because he reminds me of a pouty teenager scrolling through his phone with a forced frown on his face.

He grunts. Eyes don't even lift from his screen.

So, everything is going great.

"Who pissed in your Shreddies, Eaton?" I ask, unshaken by his sour attitude because there's already coffee made, ready and waiting for me. It's the little things in life.

"Everyone."

I snort. "Sounds delicious."

Rhett makes a growling noise and tosses his phone on

the table hard enough that it slides almost down the full length. "Am I just a big joke to you? I just lost another sponsor. You think everything I've worked for these past ten years circling the toilet is funny?"

I turn and regard him. Obviously, we're not doing the biting banter thing this morning. He's truly downtrodden.

"I don't find it remotely funny."

He props his elbows on the table and drops his head into his hands, his mane of hair falling around his face like a curtain that hides whatever expression might be there right now.

A sigh shudders through my body, and I approach to pull out the chair next to him, rather than across from him. When I sit beside him, he still doesn't look up. He's clearly trying out some sort of deep breathing technique, based on the whoosh of air from his nostrils.

My clay mug clunks on the table as I reach out with my opposite hand toward the broad expanse of his back. I hesitate, my hand fluttering above his plain white t-shirt, because I seriously wonder if touching him is a good idea.

It's a little like sticking your hand between the fence boards to pet a dog you don't know. They might be a very good boy who loves attention. Or they might bite you.

But I'm an empath. A caretaker. I can see the disappointment emanating from him. A hug never fails to make me feel better, but I won't hug him—mostly because I'd enjoy it far more than is professional. However, a gentle back pat never hurt anyone.

So, I drop my hand onto his shoulder. First, I give a

squeeze, but he flinches and sucks in a deep breath, like he's in pain.

I pull my hand away. But when his reaction ends there, and he doesn't make any other moves to get away from me, I put my hand back, a little lower this time. Running it along the ridge of his shoulder blade through the fabric of his shirt.

I move my hand in a soft circle, the way my dad used to do to me when I was having a rough day. He'd sit in that chair beside my hospital bed and rub my back for *hours*. And he never complained.

"I was unwell as a teenager. I had a surgery that went wrong," I say quietly, letting myself think back on that time. "I spent a lot of time in the hospital. I even spent some of that time thinking I'd never leave that hospital. So, I came up with a new way of looking at things. Are you interested in hearing the musings of an eternally optimistic teenager?"

"Sure." His voice is tight as he pushes his palms harder into his forehead.

"If these were your last few moments on earth, would you go happy?"

His responding sigh is ragged. He clears his throat. "No."

"But why? You have so much. You've achieved so much. No one's life is perfect."

He sits up straight now. Amber eyes regard me like I might not be the she-devil he took me for. "Have you googled my name? It's all just,"—he huffs out a sad laugh— "stupid."

"It is," I agree, solemnly nodding my head and letting my hand fall away.

"I got an email from your dad suggesting we spin this as I was joking about hating milk."

I lean back, turning slightly toward him as I sip my piping hot coffee, inhaling the caffeinated steam. If you could huff coffee, I would. I'm pretty sure I'm trying to right now. "You could."

"But I don't want to."

My head tilts. "Why?"

His hands fly up in frustration. "Because it's true! I fucking hate milk. And that shouldn't be a crime."

A breathy laugh escapes me, my cheeks twitching as I struggle to contain my smile.

"See? You're laughing at me." He scrubs a hand through the scruff on his chin before swinging his finger over my face in a U shape. "You have been since that first day in the office. That snarky little smirk."

I sit up straight now as his gaze drops again. "Rhett." His eyes roll, and he avoids making any eye contact with me, like a petulant child. I lean forward and nudge my knee against his. "Rhett."

When he turns his full attention on me, my heart skitters in my chest. No man has any business looking as good as he does. The dark lashes, the square jaw.

With one shake of my head, I regain my focus. "I was not laughing at you. I was laughing at this situation. Because you know what I think?"

"Yeah. That I'm a dumb cowboy."

I rear back, face scrunching. "No. I think they blew this

so far out of proportion that I can't help but laugh. Who the hell cares what you prefer as a beverage? I'm laughing, or smirking, or whatever you think, because this entire situation is so insulting and far-fetched that if I didn't laugh about it, I'd straight up quit my job and become a personal trainer."

He stares at me blankly, eyes darting over my face like he's searching for proof I'm joking.

"If I think about it too much, it makes me angry on your behalf. And I don't want to be angry."

He gazes down at his hands and spins the silver ring on his finger before whispering, "Okay."

God, he's really got this wounded, insecure little boy routine down. I nudge his knee again. "Okay," I repeat. "You gonna tell me why you hate milk so much?"

"Ever had raw farm milk?" he asks.

"No."

"Okay. Well, it's thick, and yellow, and fatty, and we had a cow growing up, and my dad would make us drink a glass of it every day, and I'm pretty sure it was borderline child abuse. Now, the thought of sitting down and just slugging back an entire glass . . ." He shudders. "I've never been happier than I was the day that cow died."

"That's dark!" I burst out laughing. "It sounds terrible though. I'll give you that."

"I'm properly traumatized." His cheek twitches, and he gives me a soft smile. A genuine one that makes butterflies swarm in my chest.

Did we just have some sort of breakthrough? It seems

like it. But so far, this guy gives me whiplash. So maybe I'm wrong.

What I know for sure is that I smell like sweat and look like a mess. So, I push to standing, not realizing how close I am to him when I do. Our knees brush, and his eyes lock on that spot.

I suck in a sharp breath and walk away. I'm very due for a shower, but I stop at the doorway, mulling over the conversation we just had. When I glance over my shoulder, I catch his eyes lower on my body than they should be, but they snap up to my face instantly. My cheeks heat all the same. After all, Rhett Eaton just checked out my ass in gym tights.

Which must be why my voice comes out more husky than usual. "Don't spin it if you don't want to. And don't let Kip bully you into it."

His lips press together, and he nods at me. Then I'm gone. Heading toward a shower.

A cold one.

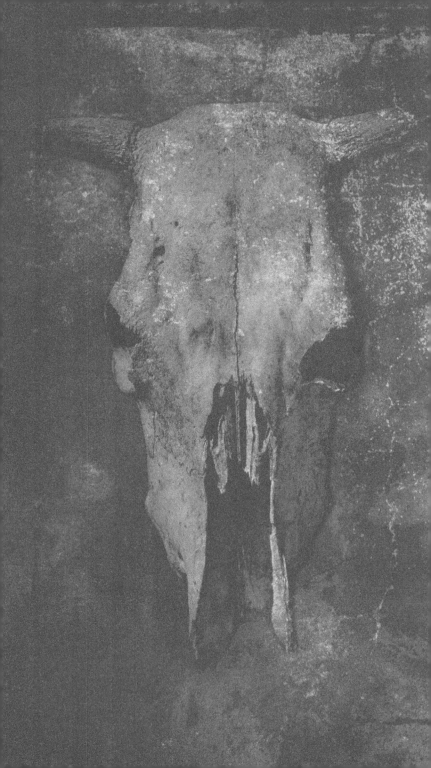

9

Rhett

Summer: Want to come to the gym with me? It will be good for you. You can't just lie around all week.

Rhett: Are you my new personal trainer now too?

Summer: Will that make you feel better about me being here?

Rhett: Maybe.

Summer: Well, then, I'm whatever you want me to be.

Rhett: That's a dangerous thing to say.

"I've been doing a bit of reading on good exercises for bull riders." Summer is waiting right outside the men's changing room, talking at me the second I clear the door.

"Uh huh," I say as I step ahead of her toward the cardio area, pulling my hair back with an elastic. Treadmills, bikes, and elliptical trainers face out the windows onto Rosewood Street.

"Do you usually work out much?" She peers up at me curiously as I opt for a bike, thinking it will help stretch out my hip, and shove my water bottle into the holder as I climb up.

"Usually. Lots of balance stuff. But not lately. It's harder on the road sometimes."

She hops up on the bike beside me. "I can also help you with exercises to accommodate whatever injuries you might have." And then she makes this adorable squeaking noise and falls forward onto the handles of her bike. "Shit."

I look down and stop one side of my mouth from hitching up. She was so busy talking to me that she failed to notice the seat on the bike she chose was way too high for someone as short as her and tipped forward when she reached for the pedal.

Her cheeks are all pink like she's embarrassed. I try to focus on the fact that she appears to be hilariously off balance rather than gawking at how insanely good she looks in gym clothes. The way they hug her curves could almost make a guy jealous.

"Should I ask if they have any child-sized bikes you can ride?"

"Very funny." She hops off and eyes the bike like it's personally offended her somehow. "I hate cardio."

"Is it because the machinery is too complicated for you?" I wink at her, and she scowls as I step off my bike and point at the too-high seat. "Stand next to it."

Her arms cross. "I'm perfectly capable of adjusting the seat on my own bike."

"Could have fooled me," I mumble as I rotate the knob to loosen the post and drop it down. I raise an eyebrow at her to see if she plans on stepping closer so I can measure the seat for her, but she just continues to mean-mug me. So, I eyeball the height, shrug when it looks good enough, and then hop back onto my bike and start the warmup program.

Eventually, she reaches out and readjusts the seat. Up. Down. And then settles on the exact same spot I had it in the first place.

Stubborn.

"Ah, yes. That looks so much better," I huff out while keeping my eyes trained on the road out front. I don't need to turn my gaze on her to know she's scowling at me.

"Like I said, I'm perfectly capable of doing it myself. Especially if you're going to be a snarky prick about helping me. What if I'd been injured?"

I shake my head and bite back a smile. "Are you injured, Princess?"

"No," she grumbles as she hops back on and pedals. "But you are."

"I'm not. I'm fine."

"You're a terrible liar." Now it's her turn to shake her head at me, but she doesn't push it any further. Instead, she pops her buds into her ears and blocks me out as she drops her head and gets to work.

And she works hard. Harder than me. Because I'm too busy stealing glances at her and trying not to get caught. There are enough locals in here already who'll be talking about the fact I was here with some girl. I don't need to give them more gossip fodder than that.

But the way sweat shimmers on her skin is fucking distracting. The way her chest heaves and the pulse point in her neck flutters.

It's almost annoying. That I can't stop stealing glances. That I'm so painfully aware of her right next to me.

But the most annoying thing of all is that she doesn't pay me any attention at all. And after twenty minutes, she hops off her bike, wipes it down, and walks away—giving me the most glorious view of her pert ass—without saying a goddamn word to me.

I'm fairly certain Shirley at the front desk sees me staring at Summer's ass while she walks across the gym toward a squat rack. She raises her eyebrows at me and smiles knowingly, erasing any questions about whether she saw me.

I drop my head back down and try to focus on my own workout, my own body. Taking physical inventory of every ache and pain. The more I move, the better my hip feels. I knew a few days of rest would help that. But my shoulder still isn't right, and it isn't getting better very quickly either.

Deep down, I suspect there's something more going on

than a simple strain that will take a few days off to heal. You beat your body up for this many years, and you know the difference.

But I don't want to admit it. Because if I let myself accept it, I'll just feel worse. I'll start second-guessing myself. And I can't afford to do that.

I peek over at Summer again. She's seated on the ground with her back pressed against a bench and a long barbell resting across her waist. When my gaze traces down to the end of it, my eyes bulge. The number of plates she has stacked there seems, well, almost impossible for a woman her size.

But then her hips thrust up, and she lifts the bar with the strength of her . . . I don't even know. Her ass? The way it's clenching, the way her lips part on a heavy breath.

It's all just confirmation that I'm a fucking pervert.

Just perverted enough to ditch my bike and wander over for a closer look. I don't have to *like* Summer to be impressed by her, right?

"What's this one called?" I ask as I approach.

"Hip thrust. Want to try?"

Do I ever.

The way she's staring up at me right now makes my dick twitch.

She points down at the bar, though, and my hip spasms just looking at it. "No, thanks."

"Is it because you're injured?" She gives me a flat, snarky little smile. I don't think I'm fooling her at all.

"I'm not injured," I reply, feeling her gaze coast over me, mimicking the sweat trailing down my spine.

She just sighs. "Okay. You're not injured. But . . ." She rolls the bar off herself and pushes to stand before me. I watch a bead of perspiration roll down her chest, through the valley between her breasts, and straight into her hot pink sports bra. "Pretend a bull rider was injured."

Summer flips a palm in my direction and widens her eyes slightly. "What would be a common injury for him to deal with?"

I regard her, seeing what she's doing here and trying to decide if I want to trust her enough to go with it.

"Hands and shoulders," I blurt. She nods as my eyes drop to the bar she was hip thrusting. "And sometimes hips."

Her finger taps against her lips, and she hums thoughtfully. "So, this pretend bull rider would probably benefit from a specialized workout that includes core exercises? And maybe some stretching?"

I feel some of my tension seep out. I feel relief that this hasn't turned into a scolding or a conversation about how reckless I am. And with my hands propped on my hips, I offer her a stiff nod.

One she returns before putting me to work until my abs burn.

Twenty minutes later, I wheeze, "I'm tapping out." I flop back on the mat, absolutely brutalized by the petite powerhouse who just tried to murder me with her "specialized workout."

Specialized to kill me.

"Okay, let's stretch," is how she responds as she tosses a mat down and kneels beside me. When I glance up at her, a faint smile touches her lips, and her eyes dart around my face.

"Why do you look so pleased with yourself? I can see that evil little smile," I pant out, still trying and failing to catch my breath.

She just laughs, reaching for some long piece of foam that she brought over earlier. "It's a satisfied smile. That was fun."

"You like to torture men for kicks. Got it."

She pats me on the shoulder. "Only the ones who deserve it."

I huff out a laugh. Because I probably do deserve it.

"Okay, sit up. I'm going to slide this under your back and let you lie on it for a bit. Open up the shoulders, stretch out the chest."

I'm pushed up to sitting before she even finishes her sentence and find myself face-to-face with her. Closer than I should be, eyes glued to the way her lips move and the flashes of white teeth behind them as she chatters away.

She has no idea how distracting she is.

When she reaches around me with the foam roller, I catch a whiff of cherries and the salty tang of sweat.

" . . . and then you'll let your shoulders drop to the floor."

I missed most of what she was saying, but she's oblivious. Her small palm lands carelessly in the middle of my chest and presses me back down to the floor.

I think about how bad a chicken farm smells to keep from getting hard. And once I'm lying flat, spine propped over the rounded foam piece, I force myself to focus on the banks of lights above me and the clanking of machinery around me rather than the way she looks hovering over me and the quiet way she murmurs, "Good job."

She counts under her breath, and I let my eyes close, trying to relax onto the roller, letting myself soften into the stretch across my back and chest. The pain slowly easing when her touch moves to the front of my shoulder, gently pressing down, deepening the stretch.

"How does that feel?" Summer's voice is curious.

I peer up at her, taking in the earnest expression on her face. The damp hairs at the base of her neck just below her ear. She really is fucking lovely.

And all her attention is on *me*.

"Really good," I reply, my voice all gravel. Then I risk looking her in the eye as I husk a deep, "Thank you."

She brightens, a soft, satisfied smile gracing her features. "You're welcome. Any time."

And just like that, I think I have my first gym crush.

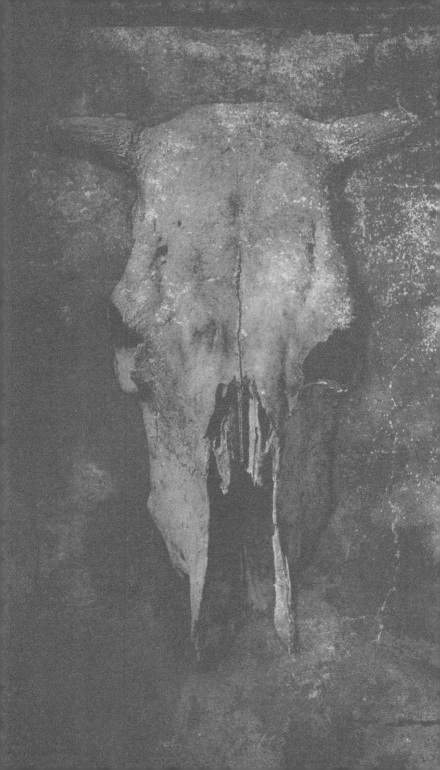

10

Summer

Dad: How many interviews have you set up for this weekend?

Summer: Two.

Dad: Good. You need to tell him what he'll need to say. He's refusing to play this off as a joke, so he needs to at least seem remorseful.

Summer: For punching a guy or for having a beverage preference?

Dad: Both. We could have him go out and order a glass of milk and call someone to snap photos.

Summer: No. We're not doing that. Don't even suggest it.

Dad: Why?

Summer: Because he doesn't

like it.

"How's the hot cowboy?" Willa asks, sounding somewhat distracted on the other end of the line.

"Good. Fine," I say, leaning on top of my leather duffel bag to close everything into it. I thought it would be perfect for our weekends away, but I don't pack light.

"Actually?" She sounds surprised, and I suppose after our last conversation, that makes sense.

"Yeah. I think we came to some sort of truce earlier this week. My days have involved working out every morning and then making travel arrangements and sending interview requests for the cities we're heading to. I'm thinking if I can curate some of these news stories for him, they might be more favorable."

I resolve not to mention that I almost climbed on top of him at the gym yesterday. That he looked good enough to eat and that he finally treated me like he might not totally hate me.

"Huh. And he's staying out of trouble?"

"Wils, he's not a dog who keeps getting out of the yard. He mostly sleeps, reads, and helps his dad and brothers around the ranch. He's not an idiot, and there's only so much to do out here. I'm not going to ride his ass unnecessarily."

She hums suggestively. "But would you let him ride yours?"

"Okay, it's been nice chatting! Bye!"

"Prude," she mutters.

"Love you too," I say before ending the call and putting my focus on the last section of zipper. When I finally realize that it's going to break the bag if I travel with the smaller duffel, I give up and pack everything into the hard-shell suitcase.

I drag my bag down the hallway and meet Rhett at the front door to leave for the airport. He holds a fist over his mouth for a moment to stifle a laugh. I suppose laughing *at* me is preferable to the scowling we started with.

"Is Kip hiding in that suitcase?"

My lips twitch. "Shut up."

He doesn't shut up. He says, "You know we're gone for four days, right?" But he smiles at me. And it stuns me. All masculine confidence and playful allure.

I think it might be the sexiest smile anyone has ever given me.

The plastic arena seat is cool beneath me. I scroll through my emails, which have all been read and responded to. Even the incessant texts from my dad about how things are going, what we're doing, and is he keeping his hands to himself.

Those parts have my eyes rolling, because even if Rhett

and I are on friendly-ish terms, he would never be interested in someone like me. He's made that abundantly clear. And that's fine because I can't take another heartbreak.

My ex, Rob, put my heart back together and then tore it to shreds. I wish I could say I hate him. I *should* hate him. But it's hard to extricate myself from him. There's something intensely personal about letting someone inside your body that way.

But right now, my heart feels just fine. Aside from the fact that it's pounding as I look out into the dirt ring.

I have to admit, this is quite the show. The stands are filling with happy chatter and laughter over the din of some twangy country songs in the big stadium. It's not some tiny rodeo, it's full-on entertainment. Big sponsors, high stakes.

The highest stakes. Because from the research I've done on the sport, the risk of serious injury is enough to keep the average person away. Statistically, it's a miracle that Rhett is still going at his age. That he hasn't been seriously injured. Though I'm suspecting he's more sore than he lets on. The painkillers. The way he flinches. The way he hobbles around like I do after doing too many split-squats at the gym.

It's obvious to me that he's in pain.

And I tell myself that's why I'm nervous right now. The knee I have crossed over my leg is still bouncing as I click off my phone, but it doesn't stop me from rapping my fingers anxiously against the screen.

When the lights go dark, I stop breathing. But then spotlights flash and the announcer talks about the points race for the upcoming finals. Rhett is firmly in first place, someone named Emmett Bush is sitting in second, and Theo Silva, the younger guy from the infamous milk clip, is in third.

Rhett told me earlier that he drew a good bull, and when I asked what that means, a slightly psychotic expression came over his face as his lips stretched into a toothy grin. "It means he's going to want to kill me, Princess."

Princess.

The fifteen-year-old in me fainted on the spot, because this time it didn't have the bite of an insult. But the twenty-five-year-old me lifted a finger at him and said, "Don't princess me, Eaton."

He chuckled and swaggered away to the locker rooms where all the riders get ready, not looking concerned at all. And I left him. Despite what Kip thinks I should do, I'm not barging into his dressing room to follow him around. We all have lines, and that's mine.

So, here I am, watching and nibbling on my lip. The energy in the arena is downright infectious. The smell of dust and popcorn waft through the stands as I look to the gated area at the closest end of the ring.

There's a brown bull in the chute. I can hear its snorts and see a few guys approaching the metal fences. Cowboy hats as far as the eye can see. Firm butts in tight Wranglers —the view isn't terrible.

Especially not when I catch sight of Rhett climbing onto the top of the fence. My heart stutter-steps. Yeah, I watched him on YouTube, but seeing it in real life is different.

There's something about a man who is damn good at

what he does that holds an appeal for me. Every step is sure. Practiced. Full of confidence. His warm-brown leather chaps, with darkened spots from wear, match his eyes. They're the color of the tiger's-eye stones I liked as a child. Bright and shiny, perfectly polished.

The collar of his dark blue shirt rubs against where his hair is pulled back in a short ponytail, and his broad shoulders peek out from the vest he wears. The one with padding to protect him from hard falls, or flying hooves, or well-placed horns.

It looks downright flimsy next to the snorting bull in the chute. Like a child with a foam sword about to battle a proper knight.

Theo hops down onto the bull and then glances up at Rhett's face with a shit-eating grin and a wink. They share a laugh and fist bump. There's this small sense of relief inside me that it's not Rhett who's getting on the bull just yet. I'm so busy watching the way his body balances on the top of the fence, that I jump when the gates fly open and the reddish bull surges out.

The bull's nose goes straight to the ground and his hooves fly up high behind Theo's head. A flimsy cowboy hat is the only protection he's wearing, and I feel like a mother hen wanting to rush down there and scold him for not wearing a helmet.

The bull turns in a tight circle and my eyes flash up to the timer, shocked to find that his eight seconds are almost up. When the buzzer sounds, the rodeo clowns rush over to help him dismount, but he leaps off and tosses a hand in the air before turning and pointing at Rhett, who is still sitting up in the fencing, clapping hard.

Looking so damn proud of the younger rider. Truthfully, it's adorable.

"You okay, sweetheart?" a woman beside me asks.

I smile back at her. "Yes. Just . . . nervous."

"I can tell." She nods her head down at my hands, which are currently fisted in the fabric of my skirt. "You here with one of the boys?"

"Oh." I laugh nervously, not wanting to throw Rhett under the bus to someone who is wearing a World Bull Riding Federation t-shirt with a longhorn skull on it. "I'm working on the business end. This is my first time."

"Now the skirt makes sense," she says kindly, eyeing my outfit. I don't particularly care if I appear out of place. I feel good in skirts. Look good, feel good. And after years of not feeling good, wearing pretty clothes makes me feel good. So, I do it. Even if I look overdressed.

I laugh politely all the same, but when she makes a grumbling noise, I follow her line of sight, and my eyes land right on Rhett, who is pulling a helmet with a cage over his head as a white and black bull trots into the chute. The gate slams closed behind the animal, trapping it between the panels, which it clearly does not like based on the way it's crashing against them. Rhett pulls himself back up, wincing as he does.

My throat tightens, but Rhett only pauses for a moment before descending onto the beast's back, like he's not terrified by the prospect.

I guess it's just me.

He runs his hands over the rope before him, and even from some distance away, I swear I can hear the rasp of his leather glove against the rope. The firm grip. The way his hand ripples over it.

It's downright hypnotic. Soothing.

"That boy thinks he's God's gift to this sport," the woman beside me says. Her statement has me sitting up a little taller, pinching my shoulder blades together, and tipping my chin up. Am I Rhett's number one fan? No. But after spending a week with the guy, after seeing how hard he's taking this whole thing—how vulnerable he was at the kitchen table that morning—my protective streak is fired up and ready to burn.

I bite my tongue and turn my body away. If these were my last moments alive, I'd rather spend them enjoying the thrill of watching Rhett ride than mouthing off to some snarky super fan.

I watch in rapt fascination as he secures his hand against the bull, the opposite one braced against the fence. For a beat, his eyes close and his body goes eerily still.

Then he nods.

And they fly.

The gate crashes open, and his bull goes nuts. I thought the other one bucked hard, but this one is truly terrifying. The way its body suspends in mid-air as it twists. The way saliva flies from its mouth and its eyes roll back as it unexpectedly changes direction.

It has me audibly gasping and pressing a hand against my chest to push away the ball of tension building there.

Rhett is poetry in motion. He doesn't fight the bull, it's

like he becomes an extension of it. One hand up high, body swaying naturally, never losing balance.

I check the clock, and somehow this ride feels much longer. It feels like he's going to get killed before the buzzer sounds.

The colors on the patches adorning his vest blur together as I watch him, the sound of the crowd and the announcer blending into white noise. I lean forward, swallowing on a dry throat, eyes darting between Rhett's toned body and the clock, sucked into the ride.

And when the buzzer finally sounds, all the noise and movement come rushing back in, everything in hyper focus as Rhett yanks at his hand.

It's not coming loose, he's struggling, and suddenly I'm up on my feet, watching with bated breath.

A cowboy on a horse gallops up beside him, and they reach for one another. With one solid tug, his hand comes free and the bull surges ahead as the cowboy sets Rhett back down on solid ground.

The announcer's voice crackles through the speakers. "A whopping 93 points for Rhett Eaton tonight, folks. That's going to be a tough score to beat and all but guarantees we'll see him back here tomorrow night."

The crowd cheers, but it's not nearly as loud it was for Theo. In fact, it's borderline quiet. Rhett stands in the middle of the ring, his shoulders drooping and his chin tipping down to his chest. His hand held protectively against his torso. He stares down at the toes of his boots, an almost-smile touching his lips, and I swear my heart breaks for him in that moment.

Over a decade of putting his life on the line to entertain these people, and this is what he gets?

So, I guess that's why I put two fingers in my mouth and pull out the most useless skill I've ever learned. One I've *mastered*.

I whistle so loud that you can hear it over everything. I whistle so loud that Rhett's head snaps up in my direction. And when he sees me in the crowd, grinning back at him, the sad look on his face washes away.

Replaced by one of surprise.

Our eyes lock, and for one moment, we trace each other's features. Then, almost like that moment never happened, he shakes his head, chuckles under his breath, and limps out of the ring, the fringes on his chaps swinging as he goes.

I gather my things to go meet him back in the staging area. I want to high-five him. Or give him a thumbs up. Or do some other equally professional celebration with him.

But not before I bend down to the woman beside me who just told me he thinks he's God's gift to this sport and say, "Maybe he is."

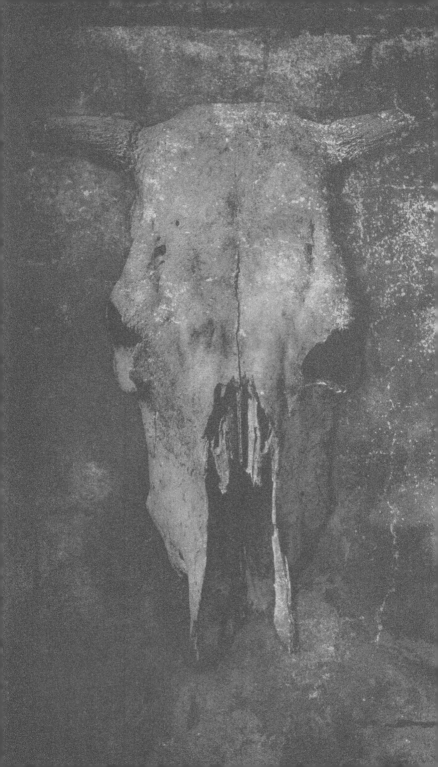

11

Rhett

Kip: Stop googling yourself.
That's my job. You just wear the
Wranglers and ride the bulls.

Rhett: This is the worst fatherly
advice you've ever given me.

Kip: Just do what Summer says,
you'll be fine. Don't stress. We got
this.

Rhett: Stop being nice to me. It's
fucking weird. And your daughter
is a pain in my ass.

Kip: Don't be such a pussy, Eaton.

Rhett: Better. Thank you,

"**R**hett!" Some girls are gathered right by the exit of the ring where I ditch my helmet and place the brown cowboy hat back on my head. I recognize a few. The rest . . . well, I recognize the type. "Hell of a ride," one says, biting her lip in a very intentional way.

"Thanks," I say and keep walking. Not in the mood to stop for them.

Lame as it sounds, part of what I love about this gig is the attention I get for being good at something. It makes me feel like I have something to offer, like people are invested in me. And not just riding my dick to say they did.

Because as close as I am to my dad and my brothers, none of them have ever taken my job seriously. It's more like they're all waiting for me to outgrow it. To grow up. And I hate that.

I grit my teeth as I walk through the staging area toward one of the locker rooms. The splash of heat burning on my cheeks. One of the best rides of my life, and the crowd gave me a fucking golf clap. I swear I could feel their disdain for me.

Except for Summer. That woman surprises me at every turn. I can't figure out what to make of her. I thought I had her pegged as a smug little princess, but I'm second-guessing that assessment more every day.

"Rhett!"

I start at the voice, and wince when pain shoots down from my shoulder. I said I wouldn't stop, but I'll stop for Summer.

I stop because there's no avoiding her. She's relentless, and she's really fucking nice. Which makes me feel like a total dick for being growly at her.

Turning stiffly, I see her petite form striding toward me like a splash of color in a sea of concrete, dirt, and brown fence panels. She's paired her dark yellow sweater with a flowing skirt covered in some sort of flower print and a pair of high-heeled boots. Her leather jacket and purse are slung over her arm, and her heels click against the concrete, drawing attention from all sides.

She carries herself like royalty, oblivious to the side-eye she's getting from the people back here. Especially the buckle bunnies hanging around by the gates.

"That was . . ." Her dark eyes go wide, sparkling like stars, and those cherry lips pop open wordlessly. "Just incredible. I think my heart is still racing."

Her excitement over my ride is real—not at all forced. The skin beneath the sprinkling of freckles across her nose and cheeks is a soft pink, and she sounds out of breath.

Her encouragement shouldn't feel this good. I shouldn't like that she's excited. So, I just say, "Welcome to the wild side, Princess."

I turn to walk away, wanting to get the vest off. Just the weight of it against my shoulder is agitating me. I wave her along but suck in a breath as I do. Pain lances up into my neck.

I hear the clicking of her heels behind me, and then her hand slips over my elbow, dainty fingers splayed over the joint as she leans close and whispers, "Did you make it worse?"

I grunt back because I don't want a bunch of people knowing I'm injured. It'll just give them one more thing to talk about, and I'm not feeling terribly trusting right about now.

"Let's just get back to the hotel." I want out of here before a tour doctor gets wind of this or before someone convinces me to come out and party tonight.

Her fingers rub gently, making the fabric of my shirt rasp against my skin. Heat blooms through the joint in an unfamiliar way before she pulls away with a stiff nod.

Our drive in the rental car from the arena is silent, something I don't entirely mind. And when we're back at the hotel, the silence continues all the way through the lobby.

In the elevator, we lean against opposite walls. Some shitty instrumental version of what I'm pretty sure is that song from *Titanic* filters through the speaker. My arms are crossed, and hers are pressed behind her.

And we stare. Actually, I glare. But this girl doesn't back down. My eyes on her don't make her nervous, and she just stares right back. Not saying a goddamn thing. Like she can read the thoughts running through my head.

"Staring is rude, Summer."

She doesn't smile. "Running yourself into the ground when you're already injured is stupid. You need to take care of yourself."

"Don't ride, don't get paid," I bite out. It sounds harsh—harsher than I intended—but this isn't a new conversation for me. Everyone in my family tries to get me to retire. They haven't succeeded, and neither will Summer.

"What are you doing to manage your injuries? Anything?"

I cross my arms tighter across my body and clamp my molars together. "You going to play nursemaid now too? Go all Mary Poppins on my ass?"

She sighs deeply, shoulders drooping as she does. "Do you remember the part where she daydreamed about holding one of those kids down and gagging them with a spoon full of sugar?"

I go back to glaring now.

"Yeah, me neither," she mutters.

When the doors slide open, I storm out, leaving her behind. And I feel like shit about not letting the lady go first the entire way to the door of my room and into the scalding hot shower. The guilt *almost* outweighs the pain of removing all my clothes with a mangled shoulder.

But not quite.

I've just gotten out of the shower, wrapped a towel around my waist, and am pouring a miniature sized bottle of cheap bourbon into a plastic cup when I hear a knock at the door.

"No!" I bark toward the door. These fucking buckle bunnies are relentless. It wouldn't be the first time one followed me back to my hotel. But I don't want that right now. And even if I did, I'm too sore to put out tonight. I'm not opening that fucking door for anyone.

"Yes!" Summer barks back, banging again. "Open up."

Except maybe Summer.

I sigh and take a huge swig, the liquor burning down my throat as I stride forward and pull the door open wide.

Summer shoots me a dirty look and barges past me—without being invited in—toward the desk near the window overlooking the parking lot. She plunks a plastic bag on top of it and starts pulling out small boxes and tubes of cream.

"What do you think you're doing?" I ask, taking another sip.

"Taking care of you," she mumbles, unboxing a bottle of pills with jerky movements.

"Why?"

"Because you're too dumb to take care of yourself. I went and bought some stuff at the pharmacy across the parking lot so we can try to patch you up."

"I don't need your help."

She makes this adorable little growling noise that sounds like an angry kitten as she props her palms on the desk and drops her head down, staring at the glossy expanse between her hands. "Has anyone ever told you what a massive prick you can be?"

I chuckle, kind of enjoying seeing her frustration bubble to the surface. I like our verbal sparring. Summer can keep up. She's witty, and I like that about her. "Nope. You're the first. Usually, it's more about what a massive prick I *have*."

She huffs out a quiet laugh but doesn't look up at me. "Nobody is going to care about your cock when you're too broken to bang them, Eaton. Now put some clothes on."

Jesus. The things that come out of those cherry lips.

I lift the cup back to my mouth and watch Summer. Her shiny hair tucked behind her ears, her back rising and falling under the weight of deep breaths.

I must really annoy her. And I kind of get off on that. I also get off on the way the word *cock* sounds on her lips.

When she turns her attention back to me, our eyes lock, and for the briefest moment hers trail down my bare chest, landing on the cheap white towel wrapped around my waist. "Was I unclear?"

All I do is snort, swipe a pair of sweats I laid out on the bed, and saunter into the bathroom to get changed. When I emerge back into the main part of the room, she's laid out an entire pharmacy.

"Shirt, too, please," she trills, tidying all the wrappers.

I ignore her request. The truth is, I don't think I can currently lift my arms high enough to put a shirt on. "Why are you doing this?"

"Because it's my job."

I go quiet because deep down that's not the answer I was hoping for.

"What did you hurt?"

My eyes drop to her lips, pursed in displeasure.

Need more bourbon.

"My shoulder."

She nods and holds up a bottle. "You can take one of these every twelve hours. And one of those"—she points at the desk—"every four. To start, though, let's double you up." She pours one of each into her palm and moves to stand right in front of me, head tipping up to gaze into my eyes as she holds her hand out flat. "Take them."

"Why?"

"Because you're going to get on a bull tomorrow either way. No point in suffering." She jiggles her hand at me. Pushy little thing that she is.

I take the pills from her palm and toss them into my mouth, holding her gaze the entire time, even as I chase them with my last sip of bourbon.

"Happy?"

"Happier." She turns away on a sigh and grabs two tubes of cream off the table. "This is arnica cream. It's homeopathic but I swear it works and it doesn't smell terrible. I also got you IcyHot that will burn and clear out your nostrils. Don't rub your eyes after using it. And when we get back home, you're seeing someone to help with this."

"We have a doctor on tour. I'm good, thanks. I'll do physio once the season is over."

"Then go see the doctor."

"No."

Her cheeks flush. "Why?"

I snort because she definitely doesn't get it. "He'll tell me not to ride. Everyone tells me not to ride."

Her eyes widen. "Then don't ride."

"I have to ride."

"Why?" Her voice is full of disbelief, like everyone else's. No one gets it. The high, the addiction, the thrill. That I'll have to face figuring out who I am without it.

With a few steps, I take a seat on the edge of the bed

and confess, "Because I'm more myself on the back of a bull than I am any other time. I've only ever been a bull rider."

The frustration leeches out of her at that confession, and she regards me with so many questions in her eyes. I look down at the plastic cup, small and flimsy between my hands, and after what seems like a long time, she finally talks again.

"Okay. When we get back to Chestnut Springs, will you at least agree to let me book you a massage or acupuncture appointment? Can we just manage the pain responsibly for the next couple of months until you win?"

My head flips up, the tips of my hair brushing against the top of my shoulders. "You think I'm going to win?"

All at once, I feel like the little boy who so badly wants attention, who wished his mom was there to see him do something impressive. The trouble-making shit disturber who didn't care about getting a scolding because it was still attention. It meant someone cared about me, and as one of four kids with a single dad breaking his back to run a ranch, I sometimes got lost in the shuffle.

She blows a raspberry as she moves toward the door. "You're pure magic up there. Of course, you will. Now put your cream on and go to bed."

My chest warms as she reaches for the knob, and suddenly I don't want her to leave at all.

I want to hear all about how I look to her.

It's fucking lame.

I clear my throat and blurt out what I've been trying to figure out since she mentioned the cream. "I don't think I can lift my arm to put the cream on my shoulder."

She freezes, skirt swishing against her knees. On a heavy sigh, she turns back to me with an expression I can't quite place on her face. Some cross between annoyance and sadness. And then she's kicking her boots off and padding across the room in socked feet, swiping both creams off the desk, and then crawling up on the bed until she's kneeling behind me.

"Which shoulder?" Her voice is tight as her breath dances across my bare back.

"The right one."

"Where?"

"Everywhere."

"Jesus, Rhett," she breathes.

"Getting hung up tonight didn't help." Nothing worse either because you can see the disaster coming in slow motion. This sense of panic settles into your gut that your hand is really fucking stuck in there.

"Okay, before tonight, where did it hurt?"

"Under the shoulder blade."

The tips of her fingers land gently right where the plate of my shoulder blade rests over my ribs, and I shiver. "Here?"

"Jesus, why are your hands so cold?"

"Because it's freezing outside, and I walked to get you all this, dumbass." Her fingers prod along the line of the blade, and I wince.

"Careful. Your dad told me to keep my hands off you."

"Yeah, well, he didn't tell me to keep *my* hands off *you*."

A quiet, strangled noise lodges in my throat as her hands flutter over my skin. Somehow, that one sentence from her lips has all my blood rushing in a singular direction. And suddenly, things feel awkward. Altogether too quiet. Too personal.

"Thank you," I mutter, it's so much easier to say without looking her in the eye.

She rests her hand flat against my back for a few beats and quietly replies with, "You're welcome."

I can hear her squeeze the cream out into her palm next, the sound of her hands rubbing together as she warms the ointment between them. And then she's slathering it over my shoulder, hands gliding against my skin with such tenderness that it doesn't even hurt. She massages gently, and I let my eyes fall shut, my shoulders drooping when I didn't even realize I had them tensed up.

Her fingers press and slide down every line of muscle, down into my mid-back, toward my spine and over the top of my shoulder.

"These muscles are hard as rocks," she mutters with a thread of annoyance in her voice.

Yeah, and so is something else.

When her fingertips push up the line from the top of my shoulder into my neck, I groan.

"Is your neck sore too?"

"I told you everything is sore."

She sighs and reaches for the other tube. I can smell the minty medicated scent the minute she squeezes it out. "Your neck is sore because all the muscles beneath it are so fucked."

"Is that the medical diagnosis? Fucked muscles?" I ask as she brushes my hair aside.

Her responding laugh is quiet, but then her hands are on my neck, digits digging in at the base of my skull and pulling down, thumbs working hard. And when I groan this time, it's in pleasure, not pain. I lean into her touch like a dog getting a scratch behind the ear.

I hate seeing the tour doctor on the best of days, but after The Summer Treatment, I will definitely dread his thick, rough hands when I could have her careful, soft ones instead.

My cock throbs between my legs, and I'm momentarily grateful for my loose sweatpants.

At least she'll never know.

She spreads the muscle balm over my shoulders, covering areas she's already soothed. And for a moment, I let myself imagine that she really likes this. Doting on me. Caring for me. Putting her hands on me. That it's not just a job. That she isn't just trying to prove herself in what I'm assuming is a brutally cutthroat industry.

When she pulls away, I bite my tongue to stop myself from asking her to keep going.

She swallows audibly before she crawls off the bed and straightens herself beside me. "Just make sure you cover that cream up with a shirt, so it gets nice and hot."

"Okay. Yeah." My eyes shift over to my luggage, wondering if I'll be able to lift my arms comfortably enough to pull a shirt on.

Summer must catch the look on my face because she sighs deeply and moves over to my open bag while shaking her head. "Is this t-shirt okay?" She turns, holding up a well-worn gray shirt.

"Yeah." I scrub at my beard, feeling a little embarrassed by her involvement here, but also relieved. Because I'm tired. Tired of hurting. Tired of knowing my body isn't keeping up but pretending it's fine. It's nice not having to pretend in front of someone.

She saunters back toward me, gathering the body of the shirt up and holding the right side arm hole out to me first as she comes to stand between my knees. I silently put my arm through, lifting it as little as possible, and inhale her scent. She even smells like cherries. Once both arms are through, she steps even closer, legs brushing against my inner thigh as she lifts the neck hole over my head and pulls it down.

All I can hear is the brush of fabric over my ears and the sound of us breathing the same air.

The t-shirt falls over my body, and she gives me a forced closed-lip smile. She brushes my shoulder, as though there's something there, and then quickly turns away. Almost like she can't get away from me fast enough.

And who could blame her? I'm sure dressing a grown-ass man wasn't what she imagined for herself when she went through law school.

"Thank you, Summer." My voice comes out gravelly in my dry throat.

"Of course. Just doing my job," she replies, pulling her boots up over toned calves. "You were incredible tonight. You should be very proud of yourself."

She says it as she walks out, not looking me in the eye. Which is fine, because she'd see how much it bothers me that she's just doing her job.

Because it does bother me, and I can't put my finger on why.

The worst part is, it doesn't bother me enough to stop me from limping over to the bathroom and fucking my hand while thinking about her cherry lips the minute she shuts the door.

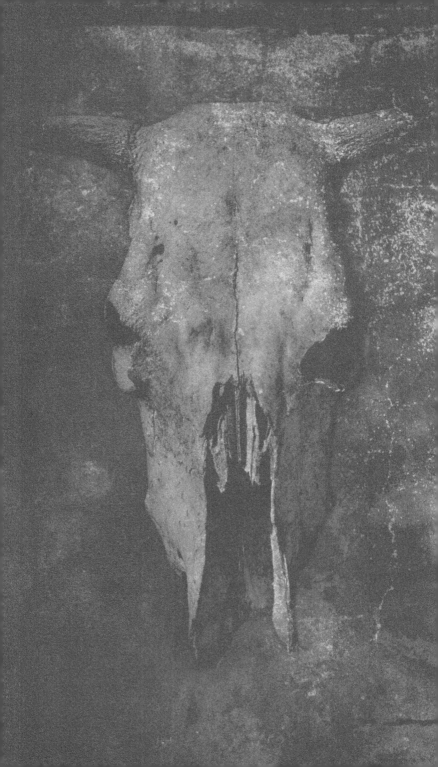

12

Rhett

Beau: How's Summer?

Rhett: Seriously?

Beau: Yeah. Are you being nice to her?

Rhett: Why is everyone so worried about Summer?

Beau: Because you're a dick and she's really nice.

Rhett: Oh, yeah. I'm sure it's her personality you're after.

Beau: It doesn't hurt that she seems really smart too.

Rhett: You done here?

Beau: I also really enjoy looking at her, so there's that. She's like the total package, ya know?

Rhett: Can you fuck off now?

Beau: Sadly, no. You're stuck with me forever. Don't die out there tonight!

Rhett: What if that was the last thing you ever said to me?

Beau: Then I'd think to myself: if only Rhett had listened to my good advice.

I'm sitting on the edge of my bed, scrubbing at my stubbled face with my hands, when I hear a soft knock at the door.

As I march toward the door, I realize that while I'm still tired, I'm not as sore as I was. Though the pain did wake me up at one point in the night, and I got up to take more pills—which Summer had laid out in a row for me.

Seeing them sitting out like that made my chest pinch in a completely new way.

In the same way it does when I swing the door open and see her petite frame standing in the hallway, bundled in a puffy down jacket holding a paper cup of what I'm assuming is coffee in her hand.

"Good morning," she says flatly, holding one cup out to me. She seems a little tired now that I get a closer look at her.

"You okay?" I ask, holding the door open wide for her to come in.

Summer sighs when she steps across the line and brushes past me toward the desk where her medicinal treatments are laid out. "I'm fine," she says, counting the pills that she left there. "How are you feeling this morning? You woke up to take a pill? Or have you just had one this morning? You need to take the twelve hour one."

"Yes, Boss." I swagger over, having an internal laugh at her fussing over me like this. I one hundred percent get off on it.

After grabbing the pills and the stale glass of water—the one that still tastes a smidge like bourbon—I toss back the medicine while noting the dark smudges beneath her eyes and the way her lashes flutter shut while she takes a deep swig of her coffee like she needs it to survive.

"You look tired."

She tilts her head and hits me with her most unimpressed look. All wide eyes and pursed lips. "Thank you. How charming. Now lose the shirt and get on your bed."

I blink slowly as I put together the real meaning behind what she's saying. "That's very forward, Summer."

"Don't test my patience this morning, Eaton. I need at least three cups of coffee before I can deal with this adorable version of you."

"It's alright. I like it when a woman knows what she wants and just asks for it." I chuckle as I head toward the bed, lowering myself to the edge in the exact spot I sat last night.

"Someone's in a good mood this morning," she grumbles as she exchanges her coffee for the two tubes of cream and tosses them onto the bed beside me.

She doesn't even ask; she just steps up between my legs and reaches for the bottom hem of my shirt before pulling it up. No fanfare, no *oohing* and *aahing* like some women have done in the past. Just straight to business.

But I also don't miss the way her eyes snag on my body as she lifts the shirt up and over my head. She seems generally indifferent toward me, but now and then, I swear something flickers between us.

"How can I not be? You just called me adorable."

She clambers up behind me. "Save it for the buckle bunnies, Rhett."

When her hands touch my skin, they're ice cold. I jump. "Jesus, Summer! You're freezing. Have you been outside already?"

"No," she says before wordlessly getting to work on my shoulder.

"How do you know about buckle bunnies?" I ask, trying to talk about something that will keep my cock from fixating on Summer's hands gliding across my skin.

"I didn't show up at your ranch without doing some Google research."

"Huh." I roll my lips together, wondering what she might have seen on there about me, about the sport.

She massages me like last night, but it doesn't feel quite the same in the morning light. Somehow less private, though no less kind. I try not to read into how she woke up, got coffees, and walked across the hallway to take care of me. Especially since she doesn't *need* to do this.

"Why are you so cold?"

She sighs, running a thumb into a deep knot. "The heat in my room isn't working."

"What?"

"That radiant heater thing." She points toward the metal grate beneath the window in my room. "It's not working."

"So, you slept in a freezing cold room?"

"Yeah. It was okay with my coat and blankets. I've survived worse."

I'm suddenly sitting up rigid, less focused on her hands than I am on the fact that after sleeping in a freezing room all night, she's here taking care of me. "They need to get you a different room. Did you call down and ask?"

"I did. The hotel is full, thanks to the WBRF event."

I turn to face her, gaze tracing the soft freckles across her button nose. "Then they need to get it fixed. Or we'll move hotels."

She sighs again, suddenly sounding just as weary as she appears. "I looked. Pine River isn't big. There are only so many hotels, and they're all sold out. They're going to send maintenance over today to take a look."

"Fucking right, they are." Suddenly I'm incensed that she spent an entire night freezing. That I've made her feel like she couldn't knock on my door and ask for help. "I'm going to talk to them."

"Okay, macho man." She laughs breathily. "Shut up and let me rub your back. It's warming my hands."

And I let her, because when she puts it like that, it sounds an awful lot like she's enjoying touching me.

I spent my day doing a few interviews and acting suitably humbled when people ask me about my comments and actions regarding the milk shitstorm.

Summer made me practice the right facial expression to make while feeding me little pills like some sort of Pez painkiller dispenser.

I told her I'm not really sorry, and she told me that sometimes we do or say things we don't mean to make other people comfortable. It's a sentiment I've been turning over in my head all day.

I'm not sure she's right.

We walked through the trade show attached to the rodeo, and when fans approached, she'd step away. Always there . . . but not really. As the day wore on, I felt like a bigger and bigger dick. But not the good kind.

Toward the end of our walk through the rows of vendors, she found a leatherworker that makes custom chaps and tried on a pre-made pair. They were charcoal leather with ivory highlights and ornate silver details. Her ass looked like an apple that I'd trade a limb to bite.

She checked the price tag, and I saw her consider it. I've only known Summer for a short time, but I already know she likes nice things. Nice boots, nice skirts—quality stuff. But she hesitated with these.

"You taking up riding, cowgirl?" I'd teased.

"I already know how." She smiled, a faraway look on

her face. "It's been a while though. I was pretty into it but quit when I got sick." And with that, she handed the chaps back to the man and carried on into the crowd, leaving me to catch up with her after I spent a few beats staring at her perfectly round ass. Again. And wishing she'd stuck around so I could ask her more about her past.

Now, I'm back in the locker room with the other guys, trying to get my head in the game. But it keeps wandering back to Summer.

Her fingers brushing my hair away.

Her breath on my neck.

Her lips when she purses them in disapproval.

Her ass in those goddamn jeans and chaps.

"Who's the hot new piece, Eaton?" Emmett asks from where he's lounging on a bench across the room. I don't hate Emmett, but I don't like him either. And that has nothing to do with him breathing down my neck in the standings this season.

He pretends he's so wholesome, all tightly cropped blond hair and big blue eyes that the girls seem to lose their minds over. But he's a sleaze bag. Something they find out quickly when he treats them like shit the morning after he gets what he wants.

I generally stick to a one-night stand. It's just less complicated that way. And I'm not above banging the odd buckle bunny. I'm just not a disrespectful dick about it. The difference between Emmett and me is I *like* women . . . with him, I'm not so sure. I wouldn't want my sister stuck in an elevator with him. That's for sure.

I also know he's reveling in my current scandal. He sees

it as an opportunity rather than something shitty that's happened to a friend or teammate.

Yeah, I trust this fucker about as far as I can throw him. Which, considering the current state of my shoulder, is not at all.

"She's not a new piece," I reply, my tone sharper than I intend as I tape my hands without bothering to glance up at him.

He chuckles, like he knows he's struck a chord I didn't even know was there. "So, fair game then?"

"She's my agent. So, no. Not fair game."

Emmett props a booted foot across his knee, knowing that he has the attention of the other guys in the room now too. "I thought Kip Hamilton was your agent?"

"Yeah. And she's his daughter."

"Hooo boy!" He slaps his knee and laughs, his hillbilly accent really shining through right now. "So not fair game for *you*. But fair game for me."

I hum in response. I'm pretty sure Summer could handle this fuckboy without my help, but I don't like the thought of it. Not at all.

"Just ignore him." Theo elbows me and mumbles, "You know he's trying to throw you off."

"You're smart for a baby, Theo."

He smiles and elbows me a little harder. His dad, a world-famous bull rider from Brazil, was my mentor, until a bull took him from us. So, I've taken Theo under my wing, and I make it my business to see him succeed. To give him all the support his old man gave to me once upon a time.

"Ready, old man?" He removes his ear buds and comes

to stand in front of me. He pulls me up and then we're off, walking through the staging area toward the din of the crowd and the flashing lights in the ring.

I drew another good bull for tonight. A real jumper. A vicious spinner. He'll toss me like a lawn dart or give me the ride of my life. Later Gator is just that kind of bull. I've ridden him before, and he hated it. But I loved my score. So, here's hoping he hates the feel of my spurs against his ribs again tonight because after that exchange, I sure as shit don't want Emmett Bush leaping me in the standings.

People say hello, but it's all in my periphery. This always happens to me before I step into the ring. The world melts away, and I hear nothing else. I see nothing else. My focus is singular, and I love this feeling.

Other riders take their turns. The cheering and color from the crowd becomes a backdrop for me and what I'm about to do.

Do I know a bull can kill me? Yeah. But I don't think about that. Half the battle in this sport is mental toughness. If I think that way, who knows what will happen. I've always told myself as soon as I look down at a bull and feel fear rather than anticipation, *that's* when I'll know my career is done.

So instead, I turn up the swagger. The confidence. The devil-may-care smile. It's a mask meant for the fans and competitors just as much as it's meant for me.

When my name is called, I shove my mouth guard in and swap my favorite brown hat for my favorite black helmet to climb up the fence while Later Gator makes his way down the chute.

My shoulder is sore, really fucking sore, but not like it was before Summer got her hands on it. She didn't even try to stop me from getting onto a bull tonight, something I appreciate more than she even realizes.

My chin turns momentarily to the stands where she sat last night. Exact same spot. A muscle in my chest twists when my eyes linger on her, leaned forward in her seat, elbows propped on her knees, one hand on each cheek. She looks *nervous*. And not because she thinks I'll get hurt. She looks like you do when your favorite hockey team is in a shootout for the win.

She looks *invested*.

And it makes me grin down at the vibrating two-thousand-pound bull beneath me.

Within moments, I jump down and rub at the bull rope, the rosin warms and softens as I do so that I can wrap it just the way I like.

It's going to be a good ride. Sometimes I have this gut feeling, and I roll with that feeling, letting it seep into every bone.

Theo says something to me, but I'm not sure what. He smacks my shoulder, and I sink down, finding my center of balance. I don't even register the pain.

Then I nod.

And the gate flies open.

The angry bull instantly drops his right shoulder into a spin. Dirt pelts my vest, and I find my balance, leaning away from the hole he creates in that turn. I definitely do not want to fall down in there.

Eight seconds feels like it lasts forever when all you

want to do is stay on and keep your arm in the perfect L shape. Because of my size, my form needs to be textbook for all the angles to work in my favor. And it is—that's sort of what I'm known for. I'm an anomaly.

I keep my chin dipped to my chest, because I know this fucker is going to veer left at some point.

And I know it's going to hurt.

A few breaths later, it comes to fruition. He leaps in the air, twisting like the athlete he is before dropping and turning. My shoulder screams, and I focus on keeping my fingers tight on the rope and my elbow tucked tight against my ribs. It's all I can do for now.

My body riots, but I force it into position, cursing under my breath as the bull continues his tour of destruction.

The buzzer sounds, and relief hits me.

I used to feel like I could go forever on the back of a bull bucking like this, but lately, the minute that buzzer goes, I want off. There's this little part of me that knows the statistics are less in my favor every time I hop on a bull. Something is bound to happen after how long I've been at it.

No one can be this lucky.

Tonight, my hand comes free, and I leap off, landing on my feet. The rodeo clowns take over, and Later Gator chases them toward the out gate while I race to the side fence.

Standing and celebrating in the middle of the ring always seems very cinematic—until you see a couple of unsuspecting guys get run over by a bull that comes back for seconds behind their back.

Safely on the sidelines, the first place my eyes go is to where Summer was sitting. For the second night in a row, she's on her feet, whistling like a grizzled, old sports fan. It makes me laugh. When she sees me laughing, she gives me a timid thumbs up, followed by a shy smile.

And fuck, it feels good.

Because that—right there—is not part of her job description.

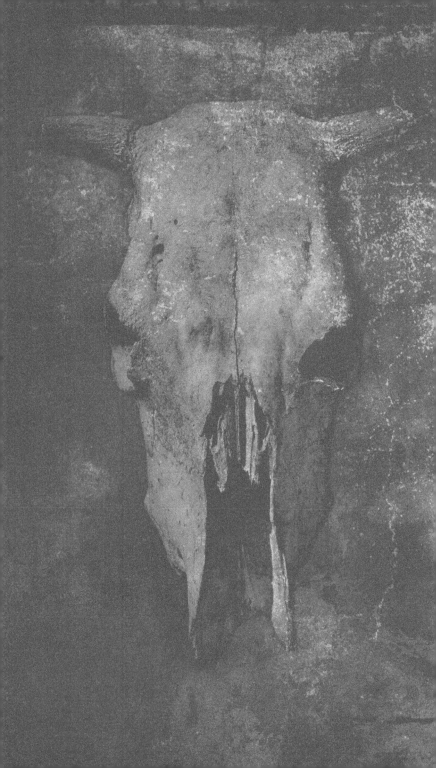

13

Summer

Dad: How'd the interviews go?

Summer: Good.

Dad: That's all I get? Did he behave himself?

Summer: He gave excellent interviews. The picture of professionalism. Unlike the way you talk about him, Kip. He's not a dog, you know.

Dad: Are you scolding your boss?

Summer: No. I'm scolding my dad. Unless you still haven't figured out your new employee's name. Then I might scold my boss.

Dad: Poor, poor Geronimo.

This is not a normal level of excitement for a person who is supposed to be doing a job. Watching Rhett ride a bull is a thrill I've never experienced. It's like the ultimate show of masculinity. Crazy enough to climb up on an animal that wants to kill you. Strong enough to stay on. And accomplished enough to look good doing it.

Pretty sure the throbbing between my legs means I'm a buckle bunny now.

I laugh inwardly at the thought as I dart down the stands toward the back staging area, flashing my lanyard pass at security as I go.

Excitement over his ride mixes in my gut with concern that he's making his injury worse by continuing to ride when what he needs is medical attention. But *that's* not my job.

My job is helping Rhett maintain his image. Taking care of him.

Or at least that's what I keep telling myself, even though I'm pretty sure Kip hasn't taken a road trip with any of the athletes he represents or spent an evening rubbing their muscular shoulders.

"Hey, Doll." Some Ken-Barbie looking cowboy is leaned up against the wall when I round the corner.

He reaches for my arm in a way that I don't appreciate,

but I slink past—avoiding his touch—and brush him off with a forced smile and, "The name is Summer."

The guy smiles back, but it doesn't touch his eyes. Which is right when a leather glove wraps around my elbow followed by a deep, raspy, "Hey."

Rhett doesn't have to pull me hard. My body moves toward him like butter melts onto hot toast.

I turn my back on the other guy and look up at Rhett's stubbled, rugged face. *Fuck*. He really is hot. I've been trying so hard not to admit that to myself. But every now and then, just a glimpse of him hits me in the gut.

His hair is loose around his shoulders and he's still wearing the vest covered in sponsor logos over a button-down shirt. A warm gray one this time, unbuttoned just enough for me to see the sprinkling of hair across what I already know is a perfectly toned chest.

I swallow, attempting to move my suddenly dry throat. "I don't even know what your score was," I blurt out stupidly. "But you were amazing."

His whiskey eyes go from pinched in the other guy's direction to warm and bright.

At me.

"Yeah?"

"Yeah." I take a step back, needing to put a little space between us and the tempting heat of his body. "You . . ." My hands flap around awkwardly as I search for what is the appropriate thing to say to him. "You rode the fuck outta that bull."

Rhett's head tips back as a deep, whole-hearted laugh

overtakes him. His Adam's apple bobs, and his fingers give my elbow a familiar squeeze.

"You should get them to put that in an ad about him." Theo Silva comes up from beside us, grinning. Handsome, but so damn baby-faced next to Rhett.

He holds his hands up and slides them out straight, like he's imagining a newspaper headline. "Old as balls but can still ride the fuck out of a bull."

"You little shit." Rhett's left hand shoots out and playfully punches at Theo's vest. They laugh.

Until the blond guy adds, "And every buckle bunny on tour," as he saunters away.

And that's when I step out of Rhett's hold. Because that guy may be a dick, but he's not wrong. Rhett has a reputation, and I have a bad habit of letting men I should stay away from break my heart.

Our drive back to the hotel is quiet. Strained almost.

Back at the arena, things felt natural. I was laughing, he was laughing, his hands were on me, and his friend was poking fun at him. He seemed himself.

And then that one snarky comment brought it all crashing down into reality. Because I'm here working, and he's the gig. It's something I have to remind myself.

This time in the elevator, we don't stare at each other. At least, I don't stare at him. Instead, I fixate on my boots as I wiggle my toes inside of them.

I can feel him staring at me, but I don't meet his gaze. Because when I gave him that thumbs up and he grinned back at me, my stomach flipped and then bottomed out. The same way it used to when Rob would wink at me, and I can't do that again.

"Did they fix the heater in your room?"

I think the only thing accomplished by him flashing his smile at the woman at the front desk while inquiring about the heater in my room this morning was her sliding her number to him across the countertop. Any comprehension of what he was talking to her about was gone the minute she caught sight of him.

I'd been waiting until we were out of earshot to crack a joke about it. But as soon as we walked away, he casually dropped the piece of paper with her number on it into a garbage can in the lobby.

"I'm not sure. I haven't been back to my room."

When I chance a look up at him, his eyes dart away, and he nods his head.

"How's your shoulder?" I ask, realizing I haven't checked yet.

"Not worse."

"Good." I lick my lips and rub them together. "That's good."

"Listen. About what Emmett said. . ." He trails off and I hold up a hand.

"You don't need to explain a thing."

"I feel like I do. I'm not really like that anymore." He sounds almost desperate.

"Truly, it's fine." Just talking about him with other

women makes a gnawing sensation take root at the base of my throat. I shimmy my shoulders then, standing up taller, refusing to curl in on myself.

"I've sown my wild oats, but a large part of what you see in the media is grossly exaggerated. I'm not a pig."

"Rhett." I don't know why he needs to keep talking about this. "I know. I know."

"How do you know?"

"Because I've glued myself to you for days on end now, and you haven't done a single thing to make me think you are. You've been a perfect gentleman."

We stare at each other now, and my lips twitch. "A grumpy, stubborn gentleman."

He huffs out a laugh and shakes his head. The elevator dings, and the moment evaporates. We wave and say our goodbyes before disappearing into our rooms.

Or, I should say, he disappears into his warm one, and I disappear into my cold one. Because they clearly didn't fix shit.

I opt to have a hot shower, layer up, and crawl under my covers to dream about the cozy room I've been assigned at Wishing Well Ranch. The hot coffee in the kitchen every morning. The charming family dinners where all the men on the ranch file into the main house to make fun of each other while cooking a meal.

But first, my phone rings.

Rob's name flashes across the screen. He calls now and then when the coast is clear. And I know I shouldn't answer, but our connections are so tangled that it's hard to tell right from wrong where he's concerned.

"Hey, what's up?" I shuck off my boots and flop into the armchair in the corner.

"Checking to see how you're feeling."

He always says that, and I don't believe him anymore.

"I'm fine. What's up?"

"I saw you on TV tonight."

My brows knit together. "For what?"

"At a rodeo. Giving thumbs up to some bull rider."

Ah. There it is. Anytime he sees me potentially moving on, he swoops in. I used to think it meant I had a chance to get him back. Now, I'm old enough to know it's his power play, it's how he keeps me in line. Under his thumb.

He sees my attention shift, and he dangles a carrot into my line of vision, thinking he'll make me lose focus. The problem is, I'm not all that into carrots these days. I'm favoring whiskey and leather.

"Yup. Listen, is there something wrong? I get worried when you call me that something is wrong."

"I just worry about you. You need to be careful. Specifically with guys like that."

I almost scoff, but there's still this pathetic part of me that purrs when he says things like that. Things that make me feel like he cares about me. Rob has groomed me almost beyond repair.

"I'm good, thanks. Don't need you looking out for me." My patience frays. I'm tired. I'm cold. And truth be told, I'm horny. This weekend has been jam-packed full of too much testosterone for one simple city girl to withstand.

I also have to confess I don't appreciate him talking about Rhett the way he is.

"Listen . . ."

"Yup," I cut him off. "It's bedtime for me here. We'll chat at my next appointment. Bye." I hang up on him.

Agitated, but also cast back in time, I stay in the chair, lost in memories of Rob and my times with him, for I don't know how long.

All I know is I can't feel my toes when a knock at the door pulls me out of my jog down memory lane. I woodenly move toward the door, trying to shake my chilled limbs out as I go. When I tug the door open, Rhett is freshly showered, smelling delicious, and looking even better.

His arms are across his chest and his eyes peruse the full length of my body—cream-colored sweater dress and camel peacoat. When I pulled the coat on, it reminded me of Rhett's chaps.

I wore it because it looked good, not because it's all that warm. And now, with his eyes tracing my body, I shiver.

"So, you're cold." His jaw pops as his teeth grind together, and he pushes past me into the room. "Summer. It's fucking freezing in here." The bite in his voice makes me flinch. "I thought they were fixing this today."

I lean against the wall, kind of enjoying watching him stalk around my room like a caveman. The only thing missing is a club in his hand. "I guess they didn't."

"You're not sleeping in here." His hands land on his hips when he turns and stares at me square in the eye.

"Oh, yes. I'll just take my pillow and blanket out into the hallway and sleep there." I smile at Rhett, but he doesn't smile back.

"Don't be ridiculous. You'll sleep in my room."

I blink slowly a few times, waiting for the punch line. And when it doesn't come, I burst out laughing. "That"—I point at him—"is *not* happening."

"I'll sleep in the chair. You can have the bed."

"That will be just great for your shoulder. No chance."

"Then I'll take my pillow and a blanket, and I'll sleep on the floor."

"Rhett," I scold, heat burning over my chest at how pushy he's being. "I'm not doing that. *We're* not doing that."

He smirks now, cocky prick he is. "Why? You worried you won't be able to resist me?"

My jaw drops. "Rude. And no. I'm more worried I might accidentally hold a pillow over your smug, pretty face until you stop breathing. I have a sweatsuit. I'll dress warm. I'll be fine."

He turns, and in a few strides he flips the top half of my suitcase closed, and I stand frowning at him as he zips my bag shut.

"What do you think you're doing?"

"All I heard was that you think I have a pretty face," he says as he marches past me, rolling my suitcase behind himself.

"Of course, you missed the part about me wanting to kill you."

When he gets to the door, he waves a hand over his shoulder and pushes out into the hallway. "Keep up, Princess. Kill me, don't kill me. At least you'll be warm. You're with me tonight."

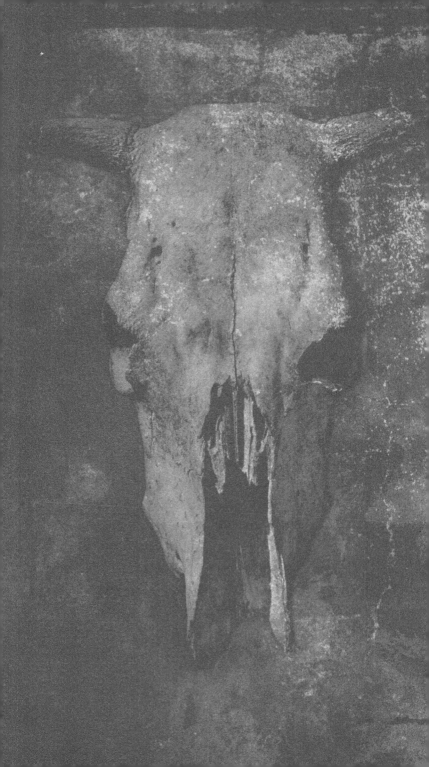

14

Summer

Willa: Did you bang him yet?

Summer: Goodnight, Willa.

Willa: You only live once, you know. This is a story you could tell your kids one day.

Summer: What the fuck kind of stories do you plan on telling your children, Wils?

I assess my matching bra and panties in the mirror of Rhett's bathroom. A set I splurged on. A silvery silk that I'm obsessed with. I contemplate taking them off and just slipping into the matching dusty pink sweatpants and sweatshirt that's folded on the counter beside me.

I'm overthinking this.

If I keep the lingerie on, what does it mean? Does it mean anything? If I go out there and pull out a different bra and panties, I'll just draw attention to myself. And if I'm being honest, none of my other sets are any better. I'm an absolute whore for fancy lingerie.

Long months spent in a hospital gown have made me appreciate all things that make me feel pretty. Sexy. Even the angry red scar down the center of my chest doesn't take away from that for me anymore. I've outgrown that insecurity.

But is going naked underneath the sweatsuit any better?

Yes. It's more casual. More comfortable for sure.

I pull my bra down and am about to flip it around to undo the clasps when I catch sight of my breasts in the mirror.

Full and pale. And peaked with rock-hard nipples.

"Fuck my life," I mutter, pulling the bra back up and replacing the straps.

Bra it is because I'm not facing Rhett Eaton with full headlights.

I slip on the sweatsuit and neatly fold my other clothes before making my way back into the basic hotel room.

The basic hotel room with one queen-size bed. And a queen-size bed has never looked quite so small as it does right at this moment. Deep down, I know I can't let Rhett sleep on the floor. Not with the current state of his body. It wouldn't be fair.

I'm still chilled from sitting in my ice-cold room, and I

shiver when I catch sight of him standing at the doorway talking to someone. His broad shoulders do nothing but pronounce the taper of his waist, which does nothing but pronounce his nice ass.

Letting my eyes trail over Rhett Eaton is like spending time at an amusement park. Each part is better than the last. When he turns to face me with takeout boxes in his large hands, my mind flashes to how they might feel on my bare skin. Big, warm, and calloused.

He looks nothing like the men I've grown accustomed to spending time with. They're all pale and smooth—well manicured. Some have been fans of literal manicures.

Rhett is weathered, his t-shirt tan line from last summer still faintly noticeable. And when he smiles, the skin beside his eyes crinkles in the most genuine way.

His work-hewn hands would feel like heaven sliding over my skin.

I shiver again, but this time I don't think it's because I'm cold.

"Food?" he asks, knocking me right out of my treacherous thoughts.

"Uh," I reply, scrambling to come up with something to say that doesn't involve me wondering out loud how it would feel to be man-handled by him. "I'm good."

He quirks a brow, like he doesn't believe me, and strides over to the bed. Food in hand, he perches on the end of the mattress before flicking on the TV. The channels flip until he lands on some type of gladiator show where people work their way through an extreme obstacle course and do their best not to die.

"You just gonna stand there, Princess?"

My mouth opens and closes silently. I am seriously not firing on all cylinders right now.

"Have you eaten?" He opens the white box.

"No." I worry my bottom lip between my teeth. I already feel like I'm imposing in his space, so I can't waltz in here and steal his food on top of that.

"Summer." He shakes his head and tosses a napkin toward the bed's opposite corner. "Sit. You need to eat."

I move toward the bed and fold myself onto the edge, sitting in a kneeling position across from him. "I'm good. You need . . ."

"What?" He squeezes a packet of ketchup into the box that's full of fries.

"Is this how you're eating?"

He chuckles but keeps setting his little spread up in front of himself.

"Rhett, you're an athlete. You can't treat your body this way." I glance at the French fries in one container and buffalo chicken wings in the other. "This food? The lack of physical therapy? Are you even working out?"

He grins at me now. "Why? Do you think I look good?"

"I think . . ." My eyes roam over him again as his leather scent blends with the tang of the wings. "I think you look like you're running yourself into the ground. If you're going to win, you need to be better to yourself."

"I like the way you put that. You might be the only person I know who isn't on my ass to retire."

My stomach picks this moment to growl like a grizzly bear.

"Listen, boss, if you eat something, I'll let you pamper me how you see fit for the next two weeks until the next rodeo. If I'd known you were coming, I'd have ordered more. We can order more. Just share this with me for now, so I won't drown in the guilt of holding a starving girl hostage in my room."

"If I eat, you'll do what I tell you to for the next two weeks?"

He stares back at me, all whiskey eyes and stubble and unruly hair. But his expression is sincere. "Yes."

I sigh in response. "Okay, fine. Deal."

He nods, but we're stuck in that weird limbo where we stare at each other. Like we want to say more but don't know where to start.

I opt to break the tension by reaching for a fry and shoving it in my mouth. Rhett smiles and does the same.

We watch the show, gasping when people fall and cheering when they seem like they're on a roll. I think the food tastes better just because we're sitting at the foot of a shitty hotel bed, legs crossed, takeout containers spread out beside us.

"I think I could do this," I finally announce.

"Yeah?" He looks at me curiously before pointing at the chicken wing box. "That's yours."

I peer down and see the last wing. "You should have it," I try to argue.

"No chance." Rhett licks his lips as he stares at the screen, and I can't look away. "You need your energy to put up with me. Have it."

I swear that one little drumstick is staring back at me.

Daring me to make this mean more than it does. But giving me the last piece is just so . . . sweet. I almost can't reconcile it. I almost want to ask myself what it means.

But even I don't want to be that pathetic. So, I lift the wing and start taking bites while getting back to my last statement. "Yeah, I think I could do this. I think I'm strong enough."

"Smart enough, too. I think half the battle with these is having a strategy. You can't just brute force your way through it. You know?"

I polish off the wing, nodding. Because he's right. And my heart is all aflutter over his compliment. "Thanks," I say with a smile.

He snorts. "You're welcome. But you've got sauce on your face. A big old smudge of it."

Immediately, I shoot a hand over my mouth. "Where?"

"Kinda hard to see with you covering half your face."

"But the minute I move my hand, you're going to laugh at me." I shift back up onto my knees, a somehow less vulnerable position.

His smile widens as he leans closer. "Oh, absolutely."

I let out an exasperated groan as I drop my hand and gaze up at the ceiling. "Fine. Tell me where it is. I'm too tired to go to the bathroom."

After a few beats, when my eyes go back to Rhett, he's not looking me in the eye anymore. He's looking at my mouth.

No. He's *staring* at my mouth.

His hand moves toward me, and my breath hitches in

my lungs. I'm like a deer caught in headlights, too shocked and mesmerized to run from danger.

"It's right . . ." His voice is low and rough. And I can't stop staring at his expression. The way he's watching my mouth is almost filthy, like I can read every thought flashing through his mind without even trying.

My lips pop open, ever so slightly at the thought of him closing the distance, gripping my head, and pressing his lips to mine. Giving me a taste of what I've fantasized about.

He's leaned close when his gentle fingers cup the bottom of my chin. His thumb hovers over the cleft there, like he's questioning touching me at all.

When the pad of his thumb brushes just beneath my lower lip, it's feather light. It makes the hair on my arms stand on end and my eyes flutter shut.

But he doesn't stop, doesn't hesitate.

His thumb caresses over my top lip, a strangled groan catching in the back of his throat. My breathing becomes more labored, and when I catch sight of the expression on his face, I'm panting.

The way he's looking at me . . . it's not polite. It's primal.

I lean forward—right into him—seeking his touch, seeking the promise in his eyes. And I make no move to distance myself from him.

When his thumb makes its next swipe, it's over my bottom lip and this time it's rougher, pressing my lip down to the side while his eyes go molten, his body held taut.

"There," he growls, still transfixed by my mouth.

"Rhett," I breathe, not sure what else to say. My nipples

rasp against the silk cups of the bra, and the trim of my panties graze my core in a way that has me sighing louder than is appropriate.

"Mm." His eyes flick up to mine, and there's a question in their depths. I swear if I closed the distance between us, he'd make me glad I did.

But his career is hanging by a thread, and I promised to help. To be a professional who can handle working with athletes. And knowing what I know of Rhett Eaton, my heart would be in shambles right along with his reputation if we were to close the distance between us.

"We should go to sleep." I clear my throat and sit back, pulling away.

I know I made the right decision. Even though my relief is laced with disappointment. The same disappointment I see flash across his face as he jolts back like I've slapped him.

But it disappears quickly, replaced by a blank face and eyes that won't meet mine as he silently starts tidying the room.

We almost kissed.

That's the thought playing on repeat in my head as I lie here. In his bed.

I'm new to a job that requires me to work with hot athletes every damn day, and after a short amount of time being out in the wild with one, I'm confused as fuck.

Excellent work, Summer.

The blanket feels like it's rubbing too heavily against my skin, and my heart is pounding erratically. Even under the covers, I can't seem to shake the chill. I almost got up to get myself a pair of socks, but I don't want to disturb Rhett.

I've been lying in the dark room for I don't know how long, listening to Rhett breathing, the hum of the heater every time it turns on, the ding of the elevator, and the dull thud of footfalls in the hallway followed by hushed voices as other people head to their rooms.

Sleep has evaded me so far, and based on the way my mind is spinning, it will continue to hover just beyond my grasp. Especially since all my thoughts and feelings are blending together with an intense sense of guilt that Rhett's injured and sleeping on the floor.

I was still too tongue-tied to put up a fight when he grabbed what he needed and set himself up on the carpet.

A sigh that borders on a groan filters from where he's sleeping.

"Are you awake?" I whisper.

"Yeah," he grumbles, shifting around.

"Are you sore?"

"No."

I roll my lips together and stare at the fire alarm above me, the tiny green dot a point to fix my gaze on. "Are you lying?"

He grunts in response, which I'm almost certain means he's lying.

"Rhett."

"Summer." He sounds exasperated with me.

"Stop being difficult and come sleep in the bed."

Silence fills the room, and I wonder if he heard me at all.

"I don't want to make you uncomfortable," he rasps.

I already am. Uncomfortably horny. But I don't say that. "You won't. What's making me uncomfortable is that you're sleeping on a dirty floor with an injured shoulder or back. Get your ass up here."

He blows out a deep breath in response, and I hear the rustling of blankets as his form takes shape across the room. When he comes to sit on the bed, the mattress dips beneath him and he scrubs at his face. The sound of his stubble rasping against his hands is more pronounced in the dark.

"You sure?"

His shoulder must be sore for him to have given in so easily.

"Eaton, stop being such a pussy and get in here. I thought you were good at hopping in and out of women's beds." I lift the blanket and scoot over to my side to make extra room for him.

He chuckles as he moves under the covers and drops his head onto the pillow he brought with him. "Most women aren't as terrifying as you."

"Yeah, right." I tuck the covers tight around myself, as though they'll protect me from the scent of liquorice and leather that envelops me. As if I won't feel the heat of his body sidled up close to mine and let my mind wander.

He lies flat on his back, hands clasped over his chiseled abs. Because, of fucking course, he's not wearing a shirt.

When his elbow bumps me, I try not to start. "I mean,

you told me you were going to kill me in my sleep. I have some sense of self-preservation, you know."

"You ride angry bulls for a living. I'm really not so sure about that."

He huffs out a small laugh, and we fall into an uncomfortable silence.

So, like the awkward mess I am, I blurt out, "Where's your mom? There's an awful lot of testosterone out at that ranch. Total sausage fest."

"She's gone." His voice gentles.

"Yeah. Mine too."

His head turns in my direction. "Really? I thought you had an older sister. I know I've heard Kip talk about his wife."

My face scrunches. "Yeah. Funny story that."

"I could use a laugh."

"The nanny is my mom."

Rhett's body goes rigid beside me, and I laugh. This story *always* horrifies people. "Come again?"

I clear my throat and reach up to push my hair off my forehead. "Kip was getting busy with the nanny. And ta-da! Along came me."

"Shit." I wish there were light so I could see his face right now.

"Yeah. Pretty much. My mother was travelling from abroad when she worked at our house. She basically had me, signed me over to my dad, and went back home. I don't even think I blame her. I'm not sure I'd want to be tied to the aftermath of that."

"That's . . . well, that's really fucked up."

I laugh and know he's looking at me like he can't quite decide how to tread into this. Most people don't.

"When did you find out?"

My eyebrows rise. This is usually when people promptly change the subject and run like hell toward another topic. "I think I've always known in some regard. My stepmom made sure that was the case."

"She stuck around?"

"She sure did."

"Huh."

"Yeah. I don't get it either. Particularly since she's always gone out of her way to make things strained between us. Between my sister and me. Between her and my dad. I almost feel bad for her. I know he shouldn't have cheated on her, obviously, but it's like she stuck around just to make everyone else miserable. I wish she could be happy."

"What does she do?" I know he's thinking she stuck with Kip for the money.

"She's a surgeon. Just like my sister. Or just like my sister will be."

"Wild." He sounds genuinely shocked. "And you and your sister?"

"Complicated." Really, really fucking complicated. "She's . . . well, she's pretty much the polar opposite from me. Looks. Personality. Shit, her name is even Winter. I think in my dad's misplaced desire to have us be one big happy family, he tried to stick with a trend of seasonal names, and instead we've just been pitted against each other. Even in moments that we weren't aware of it."

Silence stretches between us. "I'm sorry you grew up with that," he murmurs.

"Yeah, well, we adapt. I prefer the vibe at your ranch."

"Have you ever tried to find your mom?"

I suck in a sharp breath. "No. If she wanted to know me, she could easily find me. But she never has, and I don't want to be a burden to someone I don't even know."

He's silent at that, so after a few drawn-out moments, I ask, "What happened with your mom?"

"She died giving birth to my little sister."

I don't hesitate as I inch closer, pressing my arm against his, hoping to provide some sort of gentle comfort to him now that we've traveled down this path. Straight into heavy conversation, sharing secrets in the dark.

"I'm sorry, Rhett."

"I was not quite two, so I don't remember her. Actually, I think that's the worst part. I missed out on this whole facet of life. I'll never get to experience having a mom. And my dad never moved on."

Nodding, I say, "I can relate to that. But you know, at least your mom wanted you." I sound terribly tragic saying that, but I blurt it out before I can think better of it. "My dad has spent his entire life proving to me he loves me, and I think a lot of that is to make up for the clusterfuck that is everyone else around me."

"Kip pisses me off sometimes." I snort because Kip Hamilton *does* have a knack for pissing people off. "But I can see him being a good dad. A funny one. A protective one. *Obviously.* Can we not tell him about this bed-sharing thing?"

We both laugh. Thinking of his threats. The rules he set out for us.

"Yeah. It took me a while to reconcile, you know"—my hands flap in front of me—"the circumstances of my birth. That my dad can be a flawed but good man, all at once. When I was sick, he stayed with me every day. He literally worked from my hospital room and slept in the chair in the corner until some nurse took pity on him and snuck him a cot."

My voice breaks. This always gets me. That kind of love, well, it's scarce. Someone who doesn't leave your side, no matter what. Unlike my mother or stepmother.

This time, Rhett reaches down and tentatively threads his fingers through mine, giving my hand a gentle squeeze. His callouses rasp against my skin just like I knew they would, and against my better judgment, I don't pull away.

"I didn't know," is all he says, and somehow, that simple sentence and the feel of his warm hand brings me comfort.

"Yeah, lots of health issues growing up. Turned out to be an undiagnosed congenital heart defect. Fixable with surgery, except surgery went wrong, and there were complications. Big scary ones. Plus, a nice lingering infection. Kind of killed my teenaged years. Just really had to go all out on making myself an extra burden and all that."

He squeezes my hand. "I doubt he sees it that way."

I smile into the dark because I *know* my dad doesn't see me that way. Not at all. And it's nice to hear someone else notice that too. Notice that I have just as much right to that connection, that I don't need to feel guilty about loving my dad—no matter how complicated he might be.

So, I squeeze Rhett's hand back and turn toward him, feet crossing over to his side of the bed. Seeking warmth.

"Jesus, Summer." He startles but doesn't move away. "Your feet are freezing."

I pull them back instantly, grateful that he can't see me blushing in the dark. "Sorry!" I wince, sorrier that I took the freedom of touching him like that when things are already so tenuous between us tonight.

"The only thing you should be sorry for is not telling me you were an ice cube. I should have knocked on your door earlier," he grumps, right as his long legs stretch across the bed and he tangles them with mine, capturing my frozen feet between his calves.

"Okay," my voice comes out breathy as the warmth from his body seeps into mine. Heating me from the outside in.

And we fall quiet together. I hear the even rhythm of his breaths and feel his exhale across my chest. I fall asleep like that, lulled by the gentle steady sounds of him, by the solid comfort of him. My hand held tight in his, my feet cradled against his skin, and my heart warm wrapped up in his words.

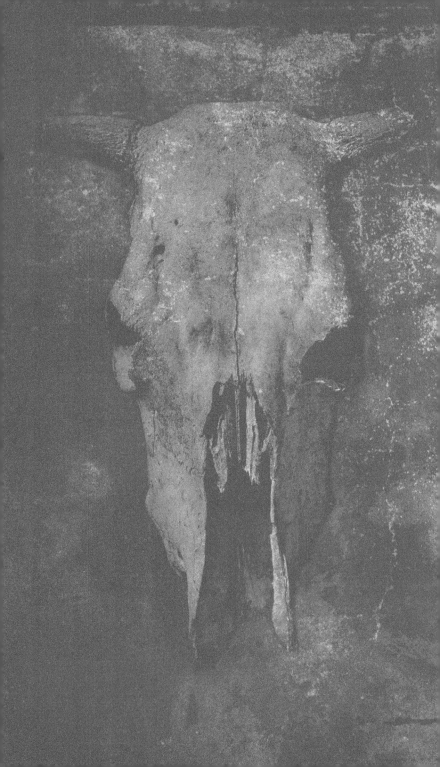

15

Rhett

Kip: Saw the interviews. You did well. You being good to my girl?

Rhett: Thanks. I laid awake all night, hoping I'd get your stamp of approval. And of course, I am.

Kip: But not too good, right?

Rhett: Is that what I'm aiming for? Good, but not too good? It's a wonder you raised an adult as functional as Summer.

Kip: Why aren't you complaining about her?

Rhett: Because she isn't so bad.

I 'm so fucked. I'm super fucked. I'm so super-mega fucked.

Summer was also right. I'm a massive prick. Because I've been awake for the better part of an hour, letting her cuddle me. Staring at her, trying to memorize every little freckle. Watching her sleep like a lovesick Ted Bundy or something.

I woke up when I felt her nuzzle against my bicep, and when I slowly opened my eyes, I was as close to her mouth as I had been the night before. When I'd done everything I could to not lick that hot sauce off her lips like a goddamn savage.

But now she's *on* me. Thigh slung over my legs, just below where my morning wood is saluting the world—Summer specifically.

Her small palm presses against the center of my chest, while her cheek rests against my arm. She's even still clutching my hand. Something that makes an ache throb in my chest.

I'm trying to be a gentleman. I really, *really* am. But I also haven't failed to notice how her sweatshirt has ridden up her mid-section. The way the waist band of her silky underwear is peeking out from her sweatpants.

Taunting me.

I want to do distinctly ungentlemanly things to Summer Hamilton. But I also want her to warm her cold feet up on me again. Anytime she wants. The thought of her being cold and uncomfortable infuriates me.

I want to take care of her, even though she doesn't need taking care of.

It's honestly really fucking confusing. It's also a terrible fucking idea. But then, good ideas haven't ever been my forte. Why start now?

She stirs, and I look at her shuttered eyes again. Soft lashes drawn down, a smattering of freckles over the bridge of her nose and the apples of her cheeks. I wonder if they show up on any other parts of her body.

My cock surges, and I don't think I can blame my current erection on morning time physiology anymore. It's just a straight boner because I want to bang my agent's daughter.

And then snuggle her. Trace her freckles.

Goddamn. I scrub my face with my spare hand and berate myself for not sucking it up and sleeping on the floor —no matter how badly it hurt. It couldn't have been worse than this realization.

I peel myself away from her, trying to extricate my tangled limbs and feelings.

But when I silently fuck my palm in the shower minutes later, I'm not all that sure I've succeeded. Especially since it's her name on my lips when I spill myself on the base of the porcelain tub.

"You'll be pleased to hear that while I was using the restroom on the flight back, Summer ordered me a glass of milk."

Summer snorts and takes another bite of the scone in her hand.

From the opposite side of the breakfast table, Beau cackles over the rim of his coffee mug. "Summer, will you marry me?"

My brother asks in jest. But my caveman brain misses the joke. Instead, it sounds like my big brother is hitting on her, and I want to scoop her up and hide her away. Because Beau is everything I'm not. Heroic, organized, dependable, clean-cut.

If I had to pick a type for Summer, I'd envision Beau.

To prevent myself from saying something I'll regret, I scald the back of my throat with hot coffee. To her credit, Summer just rolls her eyes. Which, pathetically, makes me feel better.

"You wound me!" Beau dramatically grabs at his chest. "Will you at least come out to The Railspur tonight?"

"Don't you need to deploy again soon?" I interrupt.

"Trying to get rid of me, baby brother?" Beau winks at me, and I momentarily wonder if he knows he's turning me into a jealous crybaby.

Summer ignores our antics. In fact, she's been the picture of professionalism ever since that night we shared a bed. Not weird, or cool, or awkward, just . . . professional.

Over the past week, I've often wished she'd be a little less professional. A little more reckless.

"Rhett has an MRI at the hospital," she says. "Then

acupuncture at four. Then he has a teleconference interview. So probably not tonight."

"You could come without him, you know?"

Summer smiles at my brother as she pushes out of her chair to stand. It's a kind enough smile, but not a full one. Not the one I saw on her face when she cheered for me in the stands.

It's the exact smirk that used to bug me. But now I see it in a different light—she thinks it's a polite smile. It's kind of the equivalent of a pat on the head.

"I could," she agrees as she turns and walks away.

My eyes drop to her ass in her skin-tight workout pants. She might be short, but fuck me, the girl has curves in all the right places. Firm muscles. She reminds me of a gymnast in spandex.

"Let's go, Rhett. It's gym time."

I groan and stand, still sore. Though I have to confess, this routine Summer has me on isn't terrible. I feel better every day. My biggest complaint is that I'm getting professional massages rather than ones from her.

I dump the dregs of my coffee and leave the cup in the sink. Beau can fucking wash it, put that military clean streak of his to use for flirting with my babysitter right in front of me.

"Have fun." He winks and hits me with a knowing smirk.

Dick.

I sneak my finger into my mouth and give him a big, slippery wet willy on the way past. And it's surprisingly satisfying.

"You don't have to stay here with me, you know." I nudge Summer's shoulder with mine and peer down at the glossy cooking magazine she's flipping through.

"I know." That's all she says. She doesn't elaborate or even look at me. In fact, she seems almost exasperated by me.

"You could leave and go hang out with Beau." Even saying it out loud is petty, but that jealous streak in me has fixated on the way my brother flirts with her. He's like that with everyone. But it bugs me when he does it with Summer.

Her lips press together, and she smirks down at the page. "I know."

"So why are you sitting here with me?"

Her head tips up and her eyes move over to meet mine. Sitting side by side in the radiology waiting room doesn't leave much space between us, especially if we're going to talk without everyone else hearing every word we say. Her lips open for a moment, like she's about to say something.

"That's the gig."

She says it, but it sounds like a lie to me, based on the way her lips were moving before she forced them into that line of bullshit.

She blinks rapidly and then stares back down at the magazine, that fake smirk firmly in place. "Plus, can't have you hitting on all the nurses here. Wouldn't be a good look."

"Ah, yes, because I'm an uncontrollable animal."

Her head tilts, and she shrugs. "There *is* a certain reputation."

"Have you seen any proof of that in the past few weeks?" Her lips roll together in the most alluring way, but she doesn't respond. "Imagine thinking someone doesn't change or grow up at all in the course of a decade."

Her eyes flit to the side.

"My dad, my brother, the entire WBRF fan base, it's like they still see me as the twenty-something World Champion with no boundaries. Or in my family's case, the unruly little boy who would do anything for attention."

I scoff, frustration bubbling to the surface as I continue. "Here I am, a man in his thirties and no matter what I do, people treat me like I'm a child. Like I'm irresponsible. And worse, they treat me like I'm stupid. And my job is to grin and ignore it because why? Money? That's how people want to see me? It's exhausting. All I wanted to do was ride bulls and chase that high that made me feel *something*. That high that gave me control of my destiny for a full eight seconds. Like I held the room's attention for a brief moment in time. And now I'm here bending over backwards to appease the masses because I've become some sort of household sex symbol or mascot for entire industries? I never asked for that kind of responsibility."

I'm almost out of breath when I finish my verbal rampage. Summer is staring at me, rich chocolate eyes wide and cheeks slightly pink. When I breathe out, she breathes in, the surrounding air a silent cocoon in a busy hospital.

She says it so quietly, I almost miss it. "I don't see you that way."

My heart thuds against my ribs, and my eyes drop to her lush cherry lips. Such a simple statement has never meant quite so much.

"Summer." A biting voice interrupts the moment, and we both fly away from each other like we've been caught doing something we shouldn't be.

Summer smooths her hands down the front of her corduroy jacket. "Winter. Hi. What a pleasant surprise." Her current smile isn't the smug one, it's one of forced brightness, and as I look between the two women, I put together why.

"Haven't seen you at family dinner lately." The other woman holds similar features to Summer, and yet, she couldn't be more different. Porcelain skin and pale blonde hair pulled back so tight her entire face looks equally taut. Cunning, icy eyes, just like her expression.

I almost chuckle over the names. Winter all frigid and biting. Summer all warm and soft.

"We've been on the road." Summer hikes a thumb at me. "Dad has me working with Rhett exclusively."

The woman wearing the long white coat over a boxy blue dress glances over at me with a dismissive smile, and I decide to jump in, feeling protective of Summer and not loving the way her sister is talking to her.

I stand, using my height to my advantage, staying close enough that Summer's knee brushes against my leg as I shove a hand in Winter's direction. "Rhett Eaton, pleasure to meet you."

She slips her hand into mine, and it's cold too. Her grip is firm, and her eyes flit down momentarily to her sister. A look passes between them before Winter seems almost gleeful. "Doctor Winter Valentine. I'm Summer's half-sister." Summer winces at that designation, but it's what her sister says next that has her all flustered. "And of course, I know who you are. Summer had your Wranglers ad plastered on her bedroom wall for *years*."

My mind stutters over what she's just spilled.

Summer clears her throat and glares at her sister, maintaining her composure beautifully despite the red splotches popping up on her cheeks, all the way down her neck and onto her chest.

Am I going to harass Summer about this later? Absolutely. I love to spar with her. It might as well be foreplay for how well she holds her own. But right now, I'm miffed. I see her older sister being intentionally cruel to her. *Trying* to embarrass her. It makes me plaster a vicious smile on my face while still gripping Winter's palm in a handshake that has now gone on for too long.

I wink at her. "Sounds like you remember it quite clearly yourself, darlin'."

Bitch.

Her lips flatten, and she yanks her hand from mine. "Maybe next family dinner you can join us. I know that would be a dream come true for Summer." She turns her scathing gaze down at Summer and then brightly adds, "Well, I have a patient's scans to tend to. It was a pleasure seeing you both."

And with that, she's gone. Same petite stature, but all

harsh, slim lines—almost sprite like—as she walks away, head held high, completely unrattled.

"Oof. Ice queen much?" I breathe out before flopping back down.

It's the small, strangled noise coming from Summer that has me turning in her direction. She's covered her face with both hands, and I'm not entirely sure what she's doing. But I think she might be laughing based on the way her body is vibrating.

Or crying. One of the two.

"You okay?"

"No," she wheezes.

"Are you hiding because your sister is a grade A bitch or because I now know that I'm your teenaged spank bank fodder?"

I'm pretty sure I hear her mumble a choked, "Oh, my God."

When she peeks out at me from between her fingers, I waggle my eyebrows. And when her only response is to groan and tip her head back against the vinyl chair back, I laugh.

"Can we please pretend that never happened?" Her palms muffle her voice.

I grin and shake my head, crossing my arms, irrationally pleased with the whole thing. "Not a fuckin' chance, Princess."

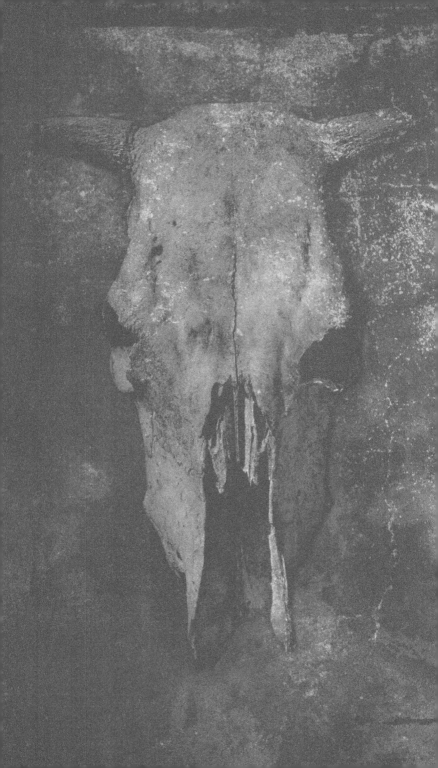

16

Summer

Dad: Can you come to the staff meeting this week?

Summer: Which day? What time?

Dad: Thursday at one.

Summer: Yeah, I might have to shuffle one of Rhett's appointments that will conflict with it.

Dad: I'm sure he can manage an appointment on his own. Seems like you've got him on a pretty tight leash.

Summer: Again. He's not a dog.

There's a chinook rolling through today. You'd think the breeze would cool my cheeks, but the air is downright balmy. All the hard work I did in the waiting room to compose myself while Rhett had his scan went right down the toilet the minute he came striding back out with a knowing grin on his face.

Cocky motherfucker.

On our walk out the main doors of the hospital, I avoid his eyes. It's awkward. Really fucking awkward. And it's such a Winter move. She's never outright mean to me. She's passive aggressive, she's calculated. Winter plays the long game. I can just see our dad mentioning what I've been up to and her filing that information away for the perfect moment to embarrass me with it.

I hate to call her conniving, because there's this little part of me that truly loves her. Admires her. I wish we'd been given the opportunity to forge our own type of relationship. But the evil stepmother got her fingers in there and played us both like puppets, easily making me out to be the source of all family strife. Winter never got a chance to like me, and no matter how hard I try, she doesn't seem interested. It's something that keeps me up at night. I long for a relationship with her. Yearn to have one more person I can consider family, rather than just Kip.

Seeing Rhett and his family together—even pestering each other the way they do—makes my chest ache. I want that one day.

"Did you doodle our names with a heart around them in your binders?"

That's how he breaks the silence.

I press my lips together into a firm line, willing myself not to smile. I don't want to give him the satisfaction of laughing at his joke. Even if it's funny.

"No."

"Did you. . ." He trails off, scrubbing at his beard. "Kiss the page you ripped out of a magazine?"

I scoff. "I didn't rip it out. I cut it out very carefully. And now I'm looking forward to throwing darts at it."

He barks out a laugh and grins down at me, looking altogether too handsome and pleased with himself. Which forces me to glance away and try to hide my smile. But when I do, my eyes land on the McLaren parked ahead of us, in a towaway zone with its hazards on. It's the license plate that makes me stop in my tracks.

DRHEART

As a teenager, I thought it was witty. Now I think it's lame beyond compare.

"You okay?" Rhett's hand lands on my lower back as he looks down at me, concern etched across his features. "I'm just joking around. You should probably fire me for sexual harassment."

"I . . ." I shake my head. "No. Just my ex." I nod my head toward the vehicle parked about ten car lengths ahead of us.

His eyes follow mine and then roll when they catch sight of the expensive sports car. "Of course, it is."

I just swallow in response.

"Do we like this ex?" His fingers pulse on my lower

back, and I lean into him, not forgetting the way he stepped up to protect me when Winter's claws came out.

"It's complicated," I breathe.

"Complicated how?" Rhett's voice takes on an edge that has me looking up at him and away from Rob's illegally parked car.

"Complicated like we're very, very over. He's moved on. But every time he catches wind of me doing the same, he crops back up in some capacity. Like, apparently, he saw a clip on TV of me giving you the thumbs up in Pine Lake and that was enough for him to start sniffing around."

Rhett's head drops down closer, erasing whatever little respectable space there was left between us. His eyes are trained on mine. Staring at me in that way he always does. With unmatched intensity. "That event wasn't televised. Which means he's going out of his way to figure out what you're doing and probably searching the events on YouTube for footage."

That night, when Rob told me he'd seen my gesture, I didn't even question it. But Rhett is right. I know which events are televised—Kip has been very exacting about that —so there's no way Rob just happened upon the footage. But Rhett is right, and I can't believe I didn't catch the lie.

"Shit. That's . . . creepy." I blink up at Rhett, who's opposite hand cups my elbow now, turning me in toward him.

"Maybe we should give him something to creep on. Do you think he's in that car?" The rugged man in front of me smirks in a way that has my entire body humming. "Rather than kissing your magazine pages, you can try out the real thing."

"You're an idiot," I mumble, but I also don't move away.

Would I do this? My heart races so hard that it drowns out the sounds around me. All I hear is that dull, rushing sound of my pulse in my ears.

"What if someone sees? What if this gets out?"

Rhett's thigh presses against mine while the hand on my lower back slides down to the waistline of my jeans, his fingers tightening in a way that has the spot just behind my hip bones aching.

He moves in close, his scent surrounding me as his wild hair fans down around us. The air between us hums and I stare at his mouth, wondering what the roughness of his beard might feel like on my lips, on my body.

I've never kissed a man like Rhett.

"You know, Princess," he rasps, and I should hate that goddamn nickname, borne of mocking me for being who I am, but suddenly it feels like a shot straight to my core. Like praise. Like worship. "I'm finding I don't really care what people think where you're concerned."

That comment strikes me speechless, and I momentarily let myself imagine a world in which I didn't care what people thought. Where I didn't constantly work to keep everyone around me appeased. Where there wasn't this ever-present need to make up for being born a burden. What might that kind of freedom feel like? To do something I want without worrying about every possible fallout.

And something about Rhett's impulsive ways and

rugged good looks makes me want to embrace it for one wild moment. I deserve a moment like that.

I swallow hard and nod once, getting lost in his glowing amber eyes. The hand on my elbow slides up, sending goosebumps out over my skin. The cool metal of his ring on my skin as that same hand glides over my shoulder, traces my collarbone, and slides up my throat.

And I'm on fire.

For all the times I imagined his hands on me, I never imagined my body reacting like *this*.

It's when his lips come down, only a hairsbreadth apart, and his knuckles graze my cheekbone that I notice the driver's side door of Rob's car shoot open from the corner of my eye. And it's then that I murmur, "Okay. But this means nothing."

In response, Rhett growls and dusts his lips across mine. Tingles shoot out like electricity, like every bristled point that touches me sends a spark dancing, twirling across my skin. Singeing every nerve ending.

His hands are possessive on my body. Pulling me tight against him almost aggressively, while cradling my skull so delicately, and kissing me so carefully. He lights me up. He burns me down. And I bask in his heat.

The buzz of the hospital around us fades away when his lips come back and press down more firmly this time. The people, the sirens, Rob's presence. It all blows away like dust on a dirt road as I kiss Rhett back.

I shouldn't. I really shouldn't be kissing this man. This *client*. I definitely should not be kissing him back. But sometimes being responsible is exhausting, especially in the face of someone as irresistible as Rhett Eaton.

It's me who pushes my tongue into his mouth. It's me who steps even closer, feeling his hand slide down to my ass as he crushes me against the steely bulge in his pants. It's me who moans when he presses it against me even harder.

The knowledge that *I* do *that* to *him* makes me wild. It seems unlikely. *We* seem unlikely.

And yet I'd have to be an idiot to deny there's a connection here. The bickering. The jokes. The goddamn teenaged crush.

His thumb trails down the column of my throat as his silky tongue tangles with mine. He wields it so well. He makes me weak in the knees. Suddenly, I want him closer—I want *more*.

And as I squeeze my thighs together and feel my core clench, I realize my body wants that too. Which is a problem. Because I still need to spend several weeks with this man. *Alone* with this man. Which means this needs to stop.

I pull back, panting. My hands are clenched, fisting the front of his shirt, and our hips still line up in a way that is entirely inappropriate for the main entrance of the hospital.

Rhett is breathless too, back to staring at me.

His eyes flit past me, and I follow them, not wanting him to look away yet. We glance over just in time to see Rob's coiffed head of golden hair slip into his fast car. The sound of his door slamming makes me jump. And then I'm staring back up at Rhett, whose jaw is clenched hard enough that it looks like the bone is trying to escape through his skin.

"Well . . . I think that worked." My voice sounds breathy and soft as I step away from Rhett's rock-hard body, the breeze whooshing in between us as though it's carrying away all the feelings that came fluttering up when we kissed.

I wish it could carry away my confusion.

We walk again, and I'm just trying to stay upright after the most mind-blowing kiss of my life. *Fake kiss.*

I wonder if we're going to talk about it, but Rhett just adjusts himself in his jeans and tries to steer the conversation back into safer territory. Mocking me.

"Did you plan our wedding while you were cooped up in the hospital? What about our wedding night? I'd love to hear about that."

I glance down at his crotch with a smirk. Secretly getting off on seeing the bulge there. "Bet you would."

His pinky finger wraps around mine tenderly before he moves his hand to the small of my back, guiding me safely across the road and making my chest flutter.

He's joking. But I did imagine a wedding night with him. A long time ago.

I haven't in years.

But I might be tonight.

"Tell me about him," Rhett says from the passenger seat while I focus too hard on an empty road.

"What?" I eye him suspiciously now, pretending I don't know what he's talking about.

"Doctor Douche."

I strangle a laugh in my throat as my tongue darts out over my lips and my knuckles turn white on the steering wheel. "He's not a douche."

"Get real. I saw his personalized license plate. His secret is officially out."

I smile now. "Okay, that *is* bad."

"Bad? It's worse than bad. I bet he loves milk-based drinks, too."

I huff out a laugh and shake my head.

"When did you break up?"

"I don't know if you could call it a breakup. We weren't together in the way you might be thinking." My top teeth graze my bottom lip as I turn things over in my mind. I've only ever told Willa about this, and it's scary to open up about it with Rhett.

"We . . . fuck. I don't know. I've told no one except my best friend about this."

"You mean Kip never met him?" The curiosity on his face is blatant.

"Well. No. He's met him."

"Summer, this isn't a Christopher Nolan film. I don't deserve to be this confused after giving you the best kiss of your—"

"He was my doctor," I blurt out.

Rhett goes still, all the jokes sliding away. Probably crushed by the wheels beneath us. "Like your family doctor?"

"No. He's a cardiothoracic surgeon. He performed the corrective heart procedures I had done as a teenager."

His head flops back on the rest behind him. "Jesus Christ. So . . . did you just say *teenager*?"

"Nothing happened until I was legal. Whatever we did mostly consisted of sneaking around," I add quickly, glancing over at him, because I can tell what he's thinking.

"Summer." He groans and throws a hand over his face. "That doesn't make it any better."

"I know," I reply, quietly.

"Someone should report him. Doctors can't go around dating their teenaged patients." His tone is biting.

My eyes go wide. I don't want to make this a thing. I want to leave it all in the past where it belongs. I don't hate Rob; I just want to move on from him. "Please, *please* don't say anything. I shouldn't have said anything to you. I was just . . . explaining myself, I guess."

Rhett sighs raggedly. "You don't owe me an explanation. It's him who should be explaining himself." He gazes out the window, shaking his head before muttering, "Saw you on TV, my ass."

I glance over again, almost nervously this time. My hands twist on the steering wheel. "I don't know. People pleaser, I guess. Things with Rob and I were complicated. I guess they still are. It's like, logically, I know that our relationship was fucked up. But he saved my life. Before him I was very sick, and he fixed me. And it's impossible to reconcile those two things."

Rhett grunts. I bet to him a lot of my family relationships seem awfully complicated.

"You deserve so much better, Summer. It's like you're so busy forcing yourself to smile and be happy all the time that you don't even realize when you're entitled to be pissed off."

His statement strikes me silent while I desperately search for something adequate to reply with. "Thank you for standing up for me today. To my sister. And with the . . ." I remove one hand from the wheel and wave it around eratically.

"Kiss?" he supplies.

"Yeah, that. I'm so glad we can go back to a professional working relationship after that."

Rhett quirks a brow in my direction, watching me lick my lips and swallow while avoiding his gaze.

"And thank you for keeping my secret about Rob."

Rhett's only reply is to grind his teeth.

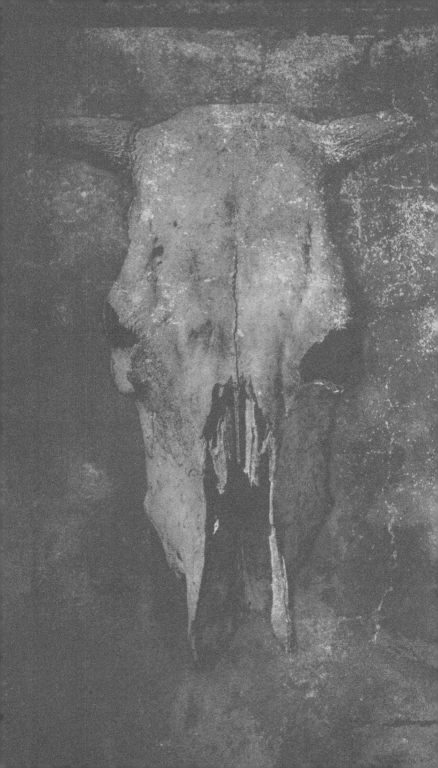

17

Rhett

Summer: Please don't do anything stupid while I'm at the staff meeting. I trust you to hold it together for one afternoon.

Rhett: Shit, Princess. I don't know. I might go crazy without you.

Summer: For ducks' sake.

Summer: Duck

Summer: *Duck

Summer: FUCK. Ugh. Why can't my phone learn that word? I'll be back around dinnertime.

Rhett: Quack.

"This is a bad fuckin' idea." Cade looks downright murderous on the back of his red mare as we ride through the pasture.

"No way." Beau, on the other hand, looks giddy. "This is fun. Like old times."

"Old times when we were, what? Teenagers?"

"Yeah. Exactly." Beau points back at him. "Our family is founded on fighting with the Jansens. We're like the Hatfields and McCoys."

Cade snorts. "We are not like the Hatfields and McCoys."

"It's more like Ebenezer Scrooge, Captain America, and I'm the cool guy from Tombstone who can twirl his guns really well," I reply.

"More like Fabio with all that fuckin' hair," Beau snorts. "And I'm Captain *Canada* thank you very much. Oh!" Beau slaps his thigh in the saddle. "No, no, no, I'm Maverick from *Top Gun*."

"Why the hell am I Ebenezer Scrooge?" Cade grumbles from under the brim of his hat.

Beau and I only need to glance at each other for a moment before we burst out laughing.

"Seriously?" Cade bites out, shaking his head. "If you spent your entire life being responsible for you two yahoos, and now a kid who takes after the likes of his fuckin' uncles, you'd be grumpy too."

That sobers me a bit. I know Cade has the weight of the world on his shoulders. In recent years, I've come to understand him better. I'm a split down the middle of my two brothers. At times, I can be quiet and grumbly like Cade, but I can also be playful and reckless like Beau.

The problem is Beau's lack of self-awareness. He's all about danger, and fun, and living life to the fullest. He's the happy-go-lucky middle child, who all the shit just seems to roll off. Like some sort of Teflon pan. Or at least that's the way it seems.

The unit he's a part of is ultra-secretive, which means we never really know where he is or what he's doing.

But we're all tight.

And I suppose that's why we're here, riding out to our property line together. When Cade mentioned the Jansens parked their tractor and tilling machine on our property —*again*—Beau hatched a plan that only someone with his level of maturity could.

I suppose I'm just agitated enough to go along with it. In the days since our kiss, Summer has gone on being completely professional, if a little wary. Like she's nervous about ticking me off now that I know a secret of hers.

When we go to the gym, she's not as hard on me. She'd enjoyed coming up with the hardest core exercises she could imagine. Like, tossing me a ball while I stand one-legged on a Bosu ball. When I would stumble, she'd laugh. But now, she offers me words of encouragement. And it's fucking weird. I hate it. I've grown to like her pestering. Her snarky little digs.

I crave those interactions with her.

So, here I am, falling into old habits. Doing something I know I shouldn't because, well, I guess it burns off steam.

What I refuse to acknowledge is that the risk of getting caught also brings the chance of attention.

Negative attention. From Summer, who is currently meeting with her dad in the city. And will freak out when she finds out I did this.

But even negative attention from Summer feels like a reward. If she wants to dress me down, I'll let her. I like the way her cheeks pink, the way her bottom lip pouts out, the way her eyes roll.

I'd like to make them roll in other ways too, tip back as her lashes flutter down. The view from between her legs would be spectacular, I just know it.

We crest the hill, and I will my boner away. If my brothers catch sight of that, there will be hell to pay.

"See?" Cade's jaw pops, and he shakes his head at where the blue tractor is parked. Does it matter? Probably not. But we're here anyway. "You'd think after years of this shit, they'd stop. I just know they did it on purpose. Trash, the lot of them."

The Jansens don't have a great reputation in town, they never have. If there's trouble, it's one of the Jansen boys. In the back of a police car, selling drugs, stealing shit, you name it. I don't think they're actually that scary, more just . . . well, like Cade said—trash.

We stay on our property, and they stay on theirs. The only spot of contention is near the creek where Beau built his house. He likes to fish out there and has had to chase those fuckers off our land twice for fishing where they don't belong.

Most of my pranks concerning the Jansens have been

limited to opening their chicken coop or sneaking around and cutting the twine on their bales of hay. Did I put sugar in their gas tank once? I'll never tell.

Basically, general shit-disturbing farm-boy behavior as a child.

"Bailey isn't so bad," Beau interjects.

"Yeah, I feel bad for Bailey," I agree. Bailey is quiet. She works her shifts at the pub at night and keeps her head down. I don't think being the baby sister of the criminal enterprise in a small town has been easy for her.

Cade grunts. I know he has a soft spot for Bailey. There's something about a baby sister that gets all three of us right in the chest.

"Alright, fellas." Beau grins and opens his saddle bag, pulling out a roll of toilet paper and holding it up. "Let's get to work."

Cade actually chuckles now, as he swings a leg up over his mount and jumps down onto the ground. "Let's do this."

I follow suit, pulling out my own rolls of toilet paper, trying to contain my grin and the childish glee bubbling up inside me. At my age, I should not be this giddy over toilet papering the neighbor's tractor.

But here we are.

We do the tires. The hitch. Beau gets underneath and does the axels. Cade does the pistons attached to the front bucket. Between the three of us, it doesn't take long to cover the whole goddamn thing.

We stand back to admire our handiwork, grinning from ear to ear. The three Eaton boys, united in their childish pranks. It feels good. It feels *normal*. There's no crush of expectations. There's no worry about sponsors, or fans, or scores.

Our horses' snort behind us, and I feel hilariously . . . at peace.

"I'm going to get the inside before we go," I announce.

"Yeah. Yeah. Get the pedals and shit," Beau prompts while Cade stands there, shaking his head.

"It's never enough for you, is it, Rhett? You're always looking for more." I dodge the truth of that statement by dropping my head and trudging back over the dry grass toward the tractor, toilet paper in hand, as the sun dips low in the sky.

I yank the door open and step up into the cage, immediately wrapping the wheel. It's when I bend down to get the pedals that I hear a commotion.

"Hey! What the fuck?"

"Oh, shit." That deep growl can only be Cade.

I don't shoot up right away. I keep myself folded down and peek over the dash into the field. There are two of the Jansen boys standing on the opposite side of a shallow ditch, looking red as beets, shouting and gesturing.

And then I glance over at my brothers. Fucking pussies that they are climbing up onto their horses, all while laughing.

The two others run toward them and spook my horse. Within moments, my brothers *and* my mount are taking off across the field, whooping and laughing as they go.

I can't help but snicker when I see Beau turn over his

shoulder and hold up three fingers in a sort of salute before he shouts, "May the odds be ever in your favor!"

Fucking dick.

The Jansens give chase, which is fucking stupid considering they're on foot.

I weigh my options. I can get out of the tractor and make a run for it, or I can stay down and hope they're too lazy to clean up the mess right now.

When I see the oldest one take a swig out of a tall boy can of beer, I opt to lie low. If I were a beer or two deep, I'd leave this mess until morning.

"I hate those Eaton motherfuckers." Lance Jansen kicks a rock.

"Should we move the tractor?" the younger one asks. I can't even remember his name. He's younger than me, where Lance was in my grade.

"Nah. Fuck that. I'm parking this here every goddamn day from now on. Just knowing it pisses them off is win enough."

I tilt my head. He has a point. Not that I'm about to say anything. I stay hidden until their chatter dies down, and once I'm sure they're gone, I finish doing the inside.

And I do it *real good*. I mean, I cover that shit from top to bottom. Then, I hop out and make my way over the hill, checking over my shoulder now and then to make sure those hillbilly motherfuckers don't come back for me. Someone smart would realize there were three horses and only two people.

But Lance and his brother are not that someone.

Spring is in the air, and I'm not even mad about the

walk. I get lost in my thoughts about my rides this weekend. We leave tomorrow, and I need to get my head in the game. My shoulder isn't too bad, but it's also not great—which makes sense considering the results of the scan say I need surgery on it.

Something I won't consider until I get this last World Championship under my belt. The doctor hated my refusal to do it right now. I don't think Summer liked it much either, based on the way she pressed her lips together all tight. But at least she didn't scold me about it.

She gets it.

For all she's been through, she understands my drive to succeed. To persevere. To not be a victim of my circumstances. And rather than talking me out of it, she snapped at the doctor to stop treating me like a child.

Her voice was all hard and snippy and—

"Rhett Eaton. What. The. Fuck. Do you think you're doing?"

Raspy. Just like that. I look up just in time to see her riding on my mount, in a flowy white dress and fucking snakeskin boots.

If her face was a little more *Please fuck me, sir* and a little less *I'm going to kill you*, I'd be hard at the mere sight of her.

"Walking home," I reply with a wink. Something I realize she hates. The wink. I mentally add it to my list of ways to rile her up.

She glares at me. "That." She points at the tractor.

"Oh. That. That's just my brothers and I blowing off some steam."

She halts the horse in front of me, body swaying gently with the horse beneath her. "That"—she points again—"is how three men in their thirties blow off some steam? Why can't you just be a normal male idiot and make me endure chasing you around while you try to fuck all the buckle bunnies?"

I stare back at her, a little taken aback by her outburst. "Is that really what you'd prefer?"

Her bottom lip pushes out as she raises her chin. I watch the column of her throat move as she glares at me, but she says nothing, even as the seconds stretch between us.

I eventually shrug and drop my gaze. "It was more about the nostalgia. I'm sure Beau will deploy any day now. With the two of us doing what we do, we never know when it will be our last time getting up to criminal mischief together."

She blinks at that. Like she hadn't considered that we both have jobs that risk our lives. And then, she pats the expanse of the horse's back behind the saddle while lifting one leg up to offer me the stirrup. "Get up, you big idiot."

"You making me ride bitch, Princess?" I wedge a boot in the stirrup and swing myself up a little awkwardly.

"If the shoe fits," she grumbles, urging the horse forward.

Instead of grabbing her waist, I slide my arms around her petite frame and cover her hands with my own. "I've got it."

For a minute, her fingers clench tight, like she doesn't

want to let go. Of the reins, or the control, or all the tension in her limbs.

But then she sighs, and I feel her body soften against mine as we both sway in time with the swinging gait of our mount. She seems out of breath, just like the poor horse we're riding.

"What did you do? Gallop into battle?"

"Not before reaming your brothers out. But yeah, I didn't know what kind of trouble you'd be in. If you'd need help."

She was rushing to help me. To be there for me.

Her fingers wrap around the horn of the saddle, and the blades of her shoulders brush against my chest. And I can't help myself. I take the reins in one hand and slide the other across her front. Splaying my fingers out over her ribs.

"How'd that go over?" I say quietly, feeling her body shake as a shiver rushes through her.

Summer clears her throat. "Well, Cade just crossed his arms and glared at me. Beau looked like a kicked puppy. Oh, and I think your dad and Luke might have peed their pants from laughing so hard."

A deep laugh rumbles in my chest, and I feel her push back into it, her back flush against my chest now as we crest another rolling foothill. It feels really fucking good holding her in the cage of my arms. She's relaxed with me, and I get off on that.

Without even thinking, my thumb starts to move in a gentle circle against her waist. Rubbing up against the bottom seam of her bra through the airy cotton. "I guess you weren't lying about being able to ride."

Her response is to reach forward and trail her fingers over my fingers that hold the reins. I suck in a breath, surprised by her sudden boldness. Her touch is pure heat as the delicate pads of her fingers trace the silver ring on my finger. But whatever hypnotic state she was just in evaporates before my eyes, and she snatches her hand back.

She sits up a little straighter, pulling away incrementally.

"Sorry. Yeah, no. I was pretty good before my heart problems worsened. It's how I met my best friend, Willa. It's also why I should have known riding in this dress would have pinched my thighs to shit." She shifts in the saddle.

I lean down and whisper into her ear, "Well, your chivalry is not lost on me," which earns me a firm elbow in the ribs.

"Your stupidity is not lost on me. If you'd been caught, *I'd* be the one in shit. I'd be letting people down."

"You ever get tired of living to please everyone else all the time? Doesn't it get boring?" I joke with a playful nip to the lobe of her ear, but based on the way Summer tenses, she doesn't see the humor.

"Let me off." She shoves one of my arms from where it's resting against hers.

"What?"

"Let. Me. Off."

"Summer, I didn't mean—"

"I know what you meant. And it's just further proof that you don't understand responsibility beyond what *you* want and what makes *you* feel good."

I move my arm away, and she swings her leg over the

horse's lowered neck and slides off easily. I even get a flash of her lacy nude underwear as she goes, but I look away quickly. She's clearly pissed, and it seems ungentlemanlike to ogle her while she tries to storm off.

"Summer, hold up."

She raises her hand to stop me. "Please. Just let me walk. I'm having a moment. I need to clear my head. I need space."

"I—"

Her head shakes, and she closes her eyes to suck in a breath. "Rhett. Please. I need *space*."

I don't miss the wobble in her voice, and as much as I want to stay and scoop her up and do everything in my power to make her feel better, I don't.

Because I *am* a gentleman. And I'll respect her wishes, even when I don't like them. I clearly struck a nerve. So, I urge my horse into a jog and offer her a casual tip of my hat on the way past.

I spend the next several minutes trying to figure out what that was. What chord did I strike with my comment? One that set her right the fuck off, that much is certain.

Back at the ranch, my brothers are nowhere to be found. They've skulked off to lick their wounds somewhere —something that brings a smile to my face. I wish I'd been here to see Summer go off on them. Her caretaker side is strong. But as much of a people pleaser as she might be, she has this vicious streak. This protective streak.

And I fucking live for that.

I untack my bay gelding, give him a quick brush, and turn him back out with a firm pat on the shoulder. Then I trudge back up to the gate that meets up with the main yard, lean myself against a fence post, and wait for Summer.

When she finally comes into sight, my breath freezes in my lungs. She's a vision in a billowing white dress, cinched tight around her waist, and tall boots. Toned thighs make the odd appearance through the slit in the skirt. Her small hands are curled into fists at her side, and she's staring at the ground, muttering to herself, dark strands floating across her face.

It sounds like she's having some sort of internal argument. She looks adorably pissed off, and one side of my mouth tips up in amusement.

"Rhett. I'm not in the mood for our bickering right now," she says when she glances up and catches me watching her.

"Yeah. Fair. It sounds like you're doing an excellent job of bickering with yourself."

Her lips part, but no noise comes out. It's fucking distracting. Distracting enough that I just stand here, propped up against the fence post while she meanders toward me.

With a heavy sigh, her shoulders droop. "Can you just stop? Please."

"Why?" I stretch my arms out to clasp the top board with my hands, because without something to grab, I might grab her. And that's not what she needs right now.

She runs her hands through her hair, pulling it back tight in her fists and tugging at it. She looks agitated, but also defeated.

"I just . . . I'm trying to do a good job. I'm trying hard not to let anyone down. My dad. His business. You. It's a lot of responsibility, and I kind of got tossed in the deep end with this gig."

The crack in her voice and the exhaustion in her frame really hits me now. She's only twenty-five, fresh out of school, and while I haven't been making her life a living hell or anything, I can see how I haven't been exactly helpful.

Summer gives so much of herself. Her dad. Her sister. Her stepmom. Everyone she meets.

Me.

But who the fuck is taking care of Summer?

She's sunny, and happy, and cracks a joke in the face of adversity. But right now, she seems tired. And after everything she's done for me, lending her strength seems like the most natural thing to do.

I let go of the fence post and hold my arms open wide, while crooking my fingers toward myself. "Come here."

"That's a bad idea." She rolls her eyes and nibbles at her bottom lip, but I get the sense that's mostly to chase away the glassiness shining in them. She makes me wait, but eventually, she steps into the cage of my arms, and I wrap them around her.

For the first moments she maintains a polite distance, but when I drop my head and let out a sigh against the crook of her neck, she melts closer. One arm slung over my shoulder while the other tentatively traces my ribs.

And I just hold her tighter.

She's healthy, and strong, and resilient, and yet so fragile. She feels small in my arms, and the way she clutches at me borders on desperate. I wish I could ease all her hurt, all her worry, all her anxiety.

It's almost like she doesn't see what a force she is.

But I do.

I wish I could make her see that too.

I'm not sure how long we stand here, holding one another as the golden sun sinks below the hills behind us.

When she finally pulls back a bit, her eyes hold mine. And what I see there is something akin to confusion.

"I'm sorry I made your job harder today." I say it, and I mean it. "I've spent so long fending for myself that it honestly just felt like a way to have some fun. I'm, well, I'm not accustomed to accounting for someone else." It's a sobering realization. I'm a man who's been living his day-to-day life for what feels good, with little regard for those around me.

She nods, eyes dipping down to my mouth. "Can you just wait until you win it all to have some fun? Then you can do whatever you want. It's not that long."

My fingers pulse on her waist and I take my turn staring at her mouth. I groan. *Whatever I want.* What a tempting way of putting that.

Her chest rises and falls with some strain now. "Rhett. You can't look at me like that," she says breathily. "You really, really can't." Her eyes press shut, like she might be able to erase me from her mind.

"Why not?" My voice is all gravel as I soak up the pained expression on her face.

"Because it's confusing."

Like hell. I reach down and hitch her leg up, wrapping it around my waist. Right where it belongs.

"I was so wrong about you. And now? Now I'm not confused at all." My fingers give her toned thigh a firm squeeze, and my mind runs wild with how it would feel to have her entirely wrapped around me.

This fucking body.

"Rhett?" She hasn't pulled away. In fact, her fingers are tangling in the hair at the base of my skull, pulling my face closer to hers, whether she realizes it or not.

And then her mouth tips up. Her body is saying yes, but her words are saying she's not so sure.

I let my hand trail up her torso, feeling her tremble slightly beneath my touch. I stroke the column of her throat with my thumb, her pulse beating beneath my fingers. The way it jumps wildly. "Tell me what you want, Summer." Our lips are so close, facing off in some sort of game without even touching. "If this were your last moment on earth, what would you want me to do?"

A desperate whimpering sound escapes her as her eyes squeeze shut again.

And then she pulls away. Her leg comes down, and the spring breeze pushes her out of my reach. Her expression is stricken, and her posture defeated.

Summer is proud and responsible. Two characteristics about her I absolutely admire.

So, there's the small part of me that isn't surprised. I stare at her trembling hand raised between us in a signal to not come any closer.

"Unfortunately, this is not my last moment on earth."

She swallows and glances over her shoulder, like she's embarrassed. "Mostly, I've been pushing papers at Hamilton Elite. I'm . . . I'm trying to keep this relationship professional. I *need* to keep this relationship professional if I'm going to work in this industry. I can't manage athletes if I'm hooking up with them. You need to find someone else to play this game with."

That last sentence is a slap to the face. Partly because she thinks all I want from her is some cheap hookup, partly because the thought of her with other men makes me insane, and partly because I know she's not wrong.

"I should go," she whispers sadly. "I need to pack. Our flight is early tomorrow."

And then she turns. I almost reach for her. But Luke comes running around the corner of the main barn waving a hand at me, shouting something about mutton bustin' as he races past Summer with an enthusiastic high five.

She turns to look back over her shoulder at me, her eyes pinched and confused. And I almost feel bad for touching her, because she wants it too, and I know she's going to go beat herself up about it.

That's what someone responsible would do.

But I'm not *that* responsible.

Which is why I only *almost* feel bad about touching Summer Hamilton. There isn't a single other woman I want to play this game with.

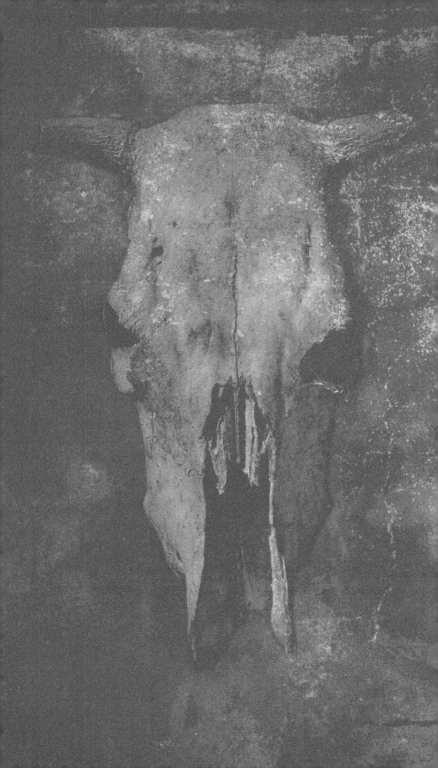

18

Summer

Summer: I almost kissed the
cowboy again.
Willa Calling

"Wait. So, you didn't kiss him?" Willa sounds
horrified by the prospect.

"No, Wils." I huff out a breath, still
jumbled this morning from my run in with Rhett yesterday.
Still slightly embarrassed by my outburst when I slid off his
horse and sulked the rest of the way back to the ranch. And
still a little obsessed with the way it felt to have him pressed
up against me while we doubled up on the way back.

Too good is what it felt like.

Oh, and I also have bruises on my inner thighs from

riding like a bat out of hell to rescue Rhett from what I was envisioning as some sort of hillbilly showdown in my head.

"That's disappointing. You're such a bore sometimes. A young, hot bore who should be living it up." She sighs and takes a bite of something crunchy on the other end of the line.

"Thank you for the vote of confidence, bestie. How's your dating life then if I'm so boring?"

"Meh. Every time I think I've met someone, they either end up boring me to death or just wanting to tell me what to do."

I laugh. "Godspeed to the man who tries to tell Willa Grant what to do."

"Amen," is my friend's solemn reply.

"It's okay to put yourself first. Don't settle, Wils."

She's quiet for a few moments. All I can hear is her chewing. Probably cookies. She loves baking. "You should take your own advice."

I grunt at that. I guess if I'm going to hit her with truth bombs, she can do the same to me. "I'll try if you do."

"Okay." I can hear the smile in her voice now. "Keep me posted on how riding the cowboy goes."

I shake my head and say, "Love you, psycho," before hanging up on her.

I head down to the cozy kitchen to have a cup of coffee before Rhett and I need to leave for the airport.

Butterflies dance in my stomach at the thought of coming face to face with him after practically climbing him last night. He was the perfect gentleman, never taking more than I was willing to give. But there's this part of me that wishes he had. Then I wouldn't be kicking myself for not telling him to kiss me again.

Because I just know that having Rhett Eaton kiss me for real, not because my ex is watching, would be different. *Good* different.

And I don't know if I'm ready to cross that line with him. We're already dangerously close, closer than is professional, but not career-ruining levels of unprofessional.

Friends.

I huff out a quiet laugh at how adept I am at lying to myself as I round the corner into the kitchen and plaster on my go-to smile, the one I wear like a suit of armor.

But I don't need it. The only people here are Harvey and Cade.

"Good morning," I sing-song as I breeze in and grab myself a mug from the wooden cabinet.

"Good morning, Summer," Harvey smiles kindly, as always.

Cade crosses his arms and leans back in his chair. I think he offers a low grunt and a tip of his chin in way of greeting.

"Not a morning person, Cade?" I ask, knowing that I'm poking the bear and not really caring. He could use some poking.

"I'm a rancher. Of course, I'm a morning person. I've been up for hours already."

I pour myself the last cup of coffee, lean back against the counter, and smile at him over the lip of the mug. "So, it's just good moods in general that you have something against?"

His cheek tugs up momentarily before he hides it with his own cup of coffee. "No, I'm just working myself up to apologizing."

"To who?" My head quirks as my eyes flip over to Harvey, who snorts.

"You," Cade grumbles, like it physically pains him to do this. "Rhett is my little brother. I shouldn't have left him there last night. I should have been the one to ride back and get him. I should have been there for him."

"Hm." I nod and sip at my coffee thoughtfully. "So, really you want to apologize to Rhett?"

His eyes roll. "Women," is all he says. And it makes me want to deck him in his manly, chiseled face.

"If he gets caught getting into more trouble, it'll tank his sponsorships. His career."

"Good. It's about time he outgrew riding bulls anyway."

"Oh, good. This conversation again," Rhett says, announcing his presence in the kitchen. He heads straight for the coffee maker.

"Shit, sorry, I'll make more." I reach for the container filled with beans just as Rhett does and our hands brush, sending sparks over my skin as I snatch my hand back and look up at him. At his scowl. At his warm golden eyes narrowed on where I'm clutching my hand against my chest now.

The Eaton boys are a whole *mood* this morning.

"It's fine. I've got it." He flicks a hand at me, signaling that I should move out of the way—away from him.

And it makes my stomach drop. He doesn't even want

to be near me. And who could blame him with the mixed signals I've been giving him?

"Did you know they developed rodeo events to showcase and develop usable ranching skills, Summer?" Cade asks as I gingerly pull out a seat at the table.

"I did not," I say warily, watching Rhett's back tense at the counter.

"And do you know what no one on a ranch or farm does?"

"No, but it sounds like you're itching to tell me," I mutter, knowing this is going to end poorly already. Years of watching Winter artfully set up an insult has my spidey senses tingling.

"Get on a bull," Cade carries on, not reading his brother's body language at all. "It serves no purpose, proves no point. It's just dangerous and frivolous. So, while Rhett is out fucking buckle bunnies and taking his life in his hands—"

"Cade," Harvey warns, eyes flicking between his two boys. I get the sense this isn't the first time he's been witness to this conversation.

"I'm here, day in and day out, working my ass off to keep this place afloat. Taking care of my son. Being responsible. Like I have been for years."

Rhett spins instantly. "If you're asking for my pity, brother, you have it. Your woe-is-me routine isn't even what gets me. It's that you have so *much* and you're still so *angry* about everything." He shakes his head and bites down on his cheek to keep from saying whatever he was about to, and then leaves the kitchen, tossing over his shoulder, "Let's go, Summer. We can get coffees in town."

I'm left in a deathly silent kitchen. All I can hear is the grandfather clock ticking from the living room, something that sounds ominous in the wake of that altercation.

Without saying a word, I dump my coffee into the sink and place my mug in the dishwasher. The air is thick with tension, and I want to escape it. Badly. I'm a people pleaser, and this is an unwinnable situation.

I head toward the hallway but stop when I hit the archway, grabbing it and tapping my fingers against it before I turn to face the two men in the kitchen.

"You know, it's not my place to say, but you should know that what Rhett is doing, he's doing for you. For this place."

Cade's jaw pops as he holds my eyes with his, and it's in those eyes that I see a flash of confusion.

"I wasn't joking. You owe him an apology. A big one." I knock on the wall and give him a flat smile. Then, I'm gone.

Because, while Rhett might not want to be near me right now, I'm finding I want nothing more than to be near him.

I've stuck close to Rhett since we arrived in Blackwood Creek. He's been distant, and to be frank, a growly dick.

But I don't let it get to me. I've come to know him well

enough over the last several weeks to know he sometimes just needs to lick his wounds. To process.

And I have no doubt that Cade embarrassed him this morning.

He's currently seated on a stool at a desk in front of a rolling camera, giving an interview. And doing an exceptional job of turning on the charm and leaning into his rural upbringing to un-offend his offended fans.

"You know, Sheila, having grown up on a cattle ranch, I know how hard our producers work to deliver a quality product to market. I've seen my dad work his fingers to the bone. He only stopped because of a workplace injury, and now my big brother spends his days running the place. It's my hope to do the same on the family farm at some point as well."

She smiles at him. A little *too* appreciatively for my taste and leans in toward him. "That's commendable, Rhett. Your family must be very proud of you."

His eyes dart to mine before he plasters a smile on his too-handsome face. "We're a tight-knit group."

My stomach sinks for him. He's so much harder on himself than anyone realizes. He does this showmanship thing so well and has everyone around him convinced he's much happier than he actually is.

Much healthier too.

Because I don't miss the way he winces as he unfolds himself from the stool. He's so sore, and all the therapy and exercise and stretching we've been doing can't hide that. His body is compensating for untreated injuries, and it's killing me to not tie him down and force him to get properly patched up.

But I also understand needing to do something to prove to yourself that you can, to do something that will be good for everyone around you. So, I bite the insides of my cheeks any time I have the desire to tell him what to do.

Just me being here is probably grating enough. I don't need to push my luck.

When he finally approaches me, he holds an arm out, gesturing toward the stairs out of the media room. As I move ahead of him, I glance over my shoulder. Only to bust him staring at my ass.

I bought myself a pair of light wash Wranglers this morning from one of the vendors on site and, clearly, Rhett approves. They aren't the beautiful custom chaps I was eyeing at the last event, but at least I stick out less like a sore thumb in these jeans and my new WBRF tee which is printed with a longhorn skull.

Plus, paired with the lacy bright red underwear I've got on under them, and my snakeskin boots, I feel like some sort of western-chic bombshell.

"You did good," I say, forcing his eyes to snap up to mine.

A blush creeps over my cheeks, and I drop his gaze when I add, "I'm proud of you."

Rhett's gloved hand rubs over the rope methodically, his jaw tight, his face focused. Last time, watching him get ready to ride excited me. Riveted me.

But today I'm antsy.

I'm not sure what's changed in the past few weeks. All I know is that watching him climb up onto a bull feels different tonight. It feels like my heart is pounding so hard that it's drilled its way right down into my stomach, my entire torso now thrums with the rush of adrenaline.

I know he knows what he's doing. I know he's one of the best. But when he nods his head, I think I might be sick.

The gates clank open and the black bull charges out, head down, hooves up, shaking Rhett all over the place. The crowd cheers this time, but I dig my elbows into my knees and clasp my hands over my mouth, feeling uncomfortably hot all over.

He's a sight to behold. The way he moves. The stillness in his body, his arm held up high. When the bull turns, his body softens and goes with him, everything in sync. Like the bull's rage is balanced by the look of peace on Rhett's face.

Yin and yang, somehow. Not every cowboy who steps in this ring has it. The serenity, the magic as the bull whips around violently. Rhett has something intangible that makes him just a cut above the rest. It's plain as day for me to see.

I wonder if everyone else here sees it too?

When the buzzer sounds, I flop back in my seat and rub at my sternum, hoping the ball of tension coiled there will unwind.

It's not until a rider has safely removed Rhett from the back of the bull that it does.

And when they call out his score of 91, I stand up and cheer. I do my loud whistle, except this time, it blends in with the crowd's cheering.

His eyes find me anyway, and I laugh, surrounded by the cheers of the people he thought he'd alienated. I hope he soaks this up. He deserves it.

Somehow, though, he doesn't look as happy as he should. He stands in the ring, helmet in hand, staring at me like he has before. With a gaze that feels like it goes right through me. Like he can see my patchwork heart right through my ribs.

With everyone around me screaming his name and cheering for him, someone who's been *theirs* for over a decade now, he feels like mine. Because he's staring at *me*.

He doesn't feel like theirs when he looks at me like that. I wonder for a moment if he feels like I'm his. This one person in the crowd that he continues to seek out.

Rhett's mouth twists in a wry grin and he shakes his head, pulling the elastic out of his wild hair, looking so fucking good that it hurts.

I watch him leave the ring, fringes of his chaps shaking, shoulders slumped—even though he has the buzz of the crowd firmly in hand. And I ask myself, if this were my last moment on earth, would I go happy?

The answer is, I'd go full of regrets. I'd go knowing I've done everything in my power to make everyone else around me happy, but failed to deliver that same treatment to myself.

I'm up and moving, saying "Excuse me" repeatedly as I push past people's knees in my row of seating, feeling the connection between Rhett and me more sharply than ever. Like a tug at the center of my chest, yanking me towards him. Like it's nature, and I'm helpless to deny the pull.

I jog down the steps before striding as quickly as my short legs will carry me toward the staging area, past the bull chute, and down the alleyway that leads to the locker rooms. I flash my pass at the security guard with a brief, flat smile.

He says something to me, but all I can hear is the healthy, even pounding of my heart in my chest. I catch sight of Rhett and almost smile before coming to a screeching halt.

He's got one arm propped up on a metal fence panel, his cowboy hat back on his head. I can see the tips of his hair brushing against his back as he leans forward toward the woman in front of him.

She's beautiful. And I recognize her from the last rodeo.

My stomach twists and my chest aches. This is exactly what I told him to do. He gave me a moment to tell him I wanted him too, and I told him I didn't. I told him to play this game with someone else. I should be happy he listened for once.

But I'm devastated. I've never been oblivious to Rhett's reputation, but he's never lived up to it in front of me. My tongue tastes sour at the sight.

I turn to walk away, not wanting to see any more than I already have, which is when I bump straight into a rock-hard chest and look up into the grinning face of Emmett Bush.

"Where you headed, darlin'?" he drawls.

I roll my lips together, weighing my options, taking stock of the warring emotions inside of me, and beating myself up for always being so goddamn responsible. So responsible, I drove a guy I might actually like to *that*.

"Not sure. My night is wide open. Got any ideas?" I ask, recklessness coursing through my veins.

Emmett smiles wider and slings an arm around my shoulder. "Well, have I got the bar for us."

I stiffen under his arm and pull away slightly. He doesn't give me the same sense of home that Rhett does when his arms wrap around me. But maybe I don't need feelings.

Maybe what I need is some fun.

"Hey, Eaton!" Emmett shouts, and I wince. "Grab your girl, and let's hit The Corral. Celebrate your old ass barely beating me tonight!" He laughs and tugs me along with him.

And I go, refusing to risk looking over my shoulder. I'm far too terrified of what I might see.

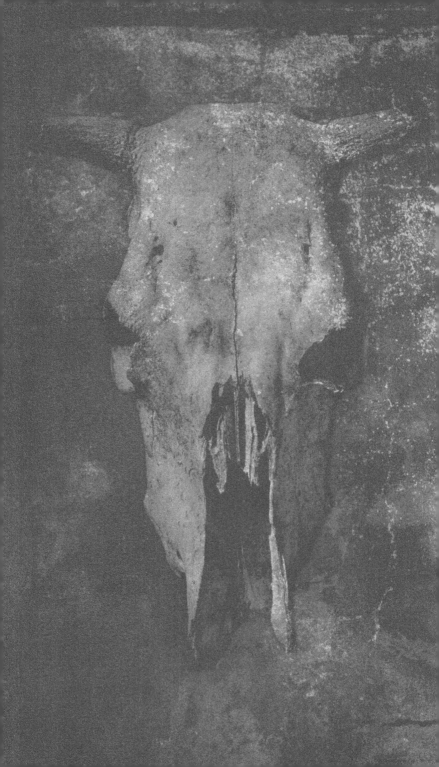

19

Rhett

Kip: Hell of a ride tonight, kid.

Rhett: Yup.

Kip: What's wrong?

Rhett: Your daughter is what's wrong.

Kip: I don't even believe you. That girl is one of the best people I know. And I'm not just saying that because I'm her dad.

Rhett: Yeah, she is. That's the problem.

I take an aggressive sip of the shitty beer in my hand before putting it back on the table with far more force than I intended.

"You're going to break that thing, Boss." Theo chuckles and takes a sip of his own, eyes alight with humor while he sits across from me at the high-top table.

Rather than replying to his goading, I roll the bottle between my hands, feeling more than hearing the clink of the glass against my silver rings over the country music blaring through this bar.

"Thought you'd be in a better mood after winning. Again. Would it kill you to give the rest of us a moment in the sun?"

"You're young, Theo. Work harder. Earn it. Spur your bull more and hold on for dear life rather than taking the path of least resistance. Mediocre isn't good enough to win on this tour."

I'm being harsh, but it's probably time for him to level up. If his old man were still around, he'd tell him the same thing. I remember him doing it with me.

He rubbed my back until one day he shoved me into the deep end. Tough love. It works when someone is as competitive as I am. Like a challenge to do better.

Theo snorts, his head rearing back a little. He's playing it cool, but I can tell by the spark in his eye that I've ticked him off a tad. Just the right amount to make him want to be better. Small increments all the time.

I get a real kick out of watching him develop, and I love

being there for him even if I wish it were his dad instead of me.

Try as I might to keep my eyes lasered on the brown bottle in my hands, they slip over to where I know Summer is sitting with that sleaze bag, Emmett. All I can see is her back, the taper of her waist where her brand new WBRF t-shirt is tucked into those tight-as-fuck jeans, cinched with some belt that has a colorful stitched pattern on it. The way they hug her hips where her body flares out is distracting beyond comparison.

His stool is too close to hers, and he leans close to say something to her while laughing and shit. All happy-go-lucky golden boy, while I'm sitting over here brooding like a Neanderthal.

"Do you think hooking up with Cindy is a bad idea?" Theo pulls my attention back to him with a complete subject change.

"I don't know. Why would it be a bad idea? She likes you. That's why she pulled me aside. To find out if I knew what you were up to tonight. Like I'm some fucking school-girl who wants to gossip about relationship status." I shake my head and take another swig of my beer.

During past seasons, if I felt like celebrating after a good ride, I'd roll out of the ring and snag myself a bunny. But the appeal has slowly but surely worn off, and the girls keep getting younger. Too young.

Or I keep getting older. I guess that's more likely.

"Because she's a buckle bunny, man. She's been with other guys on the tour too."

"When did you become a virgin again, Theo? Pretty

sure I saw you balls deep in one of her friends when I walked into the locker room once."

He laughs loudly now. "Forgot about that."

"But do you like her?"

He bobs his head back and forth with a shy smile. "Yeah. I guess I do."

"So, who cares? Maybe it works, maybe it doesn't. Just don't be a pig about it. Be up front. Buckle bunnies have feelings too." I wink at him.

"Ah, dating advice from the famous ladies' man, Rhett Eaton!" He holds his beer bottle up to me in cheers and I ignore it, opting to just take another swig. I'm not so sure my past behavior is to be celebrated.

I sneak a peek over at Summer again. I can't keep my eyes or mind from wandering to her. If she leaves with Emmett, I might combust.

He slings his arm over the back of her chair like he has a right to.

"Speaking of girls . . ." Theo waggles his eyebrows and points his chin over at Summer.

"What?" I bite out. "My babysitter?"

"I wouldn't judge. Fucking the babysitter is a thing for a reason."

"I thought I told you not to be a pig?" I have to remind myself he's only twenty-two—and walking around with a constant boner—before I bite his head off.

"Whatever, man. Just saying. You can't take your eyes off her. It's *almost* like you're jealous."

I resolve, right here and now, to not look over there again.

"Of Emmett Bush?" I snort. "That'll be the day. I'll start highlighting my hair and going for facials to get his Ken-doll glow just so I can be more like him."

"You definitely don't sound jealous *at all*," Theo mocks.

I take another aggravated swig. "Good. Cause I'm not."

"I can see why you would be though. She looks damn good on that bull."

"What?" I whip around so fast that I knock my bottle in the process, righting it just before it creates more than a small puddle of beer on the table.

But when I glance back up, sure enough, Summer has climbed onto the mechanical bull. It's surrounded by foam mats, and a crowd has gathered around the low barrier around the circle.

Her small hand is wrapped around the grip, and her pale jeans are so tight that I can see the fold where her thigh meets her hip.

She's grinning widely, and when she looks at Emmett, her top teeth dig into her bottom lip.

Those fucking lips.

She gives a small nod and giggles as she does it. Looking so carefree. So young. So much happier than she usually does in my company.

The guy operating the machine starts it up, and her hips rock with the motion.

I have to look away. My brain is fried, and my cock is thickening. I want to throw her over my shoulder and carry her out of here. Put my mark on her.

It's unlike anything I've ever felt.

But she doesn't want that. She doesn't need that, and I

keep reminding myself to be a gentleman. I told Theo not to be a pig, and I need to make sure I'm not being one either.

I swivel on my stool to face Theo and chug the rest of my beer before waving at the server to bring me another.

I need it.

"Hey, guys." Cindy walks up, looking at Theo like he's a cake and it's her birthday. "How's it going?"

"Great." Theo smiles and pats the stool beside himself.

I don't say anything. The pheromones between them do nothing but annoy me. I wish the only thing keeping Summer and me apart was that we were both too stupid to just talk to each other.

Instead, she has to be all smart, and responsible, and career driven. Making us a problem, when in any other setting we'd be a no-brainer.

"Your girl can ride, Rhett," Cindy says, nodding over at Summer.

Of course, she can. She's strong. That she can sit on a mechanical bull better than the average person doesn't surprise me one bit. I've watched her work out, watched that ass clench in her tights. I've watched sweat trickle down between her tits, her lips parted as she pants from a tough session.

I chance a glance over my shoulder because I'm a seriously weak son of a bitch where Summer Hamilton is concerned. Sure enough, she's looking damn fine up there. Arm up, chin down, shoulders back.

But it's not good for business when someone lasts too

long, and I turn away just as the operator jerks her in the other direction, forcing her to lose her seat.

"She's not my girl." I hear the cheers for her, knowing that she probably finally took her tumble.

I hope she's okay.

Theo rolls his eyes, but as he takes in the scene behind me, they go wide.

"You're right," Cindy agrees with a nod. "It looks like she might be Emmett's."

This time, I stand straight up, catching sight of Summer as she pulls Emmett's cowboy hat off and plunks it on her head as they head over to the bar across the room.

And that's it.

I'm striding across the bar, getting to her as fast as I can. It feels like it takes forever, but it has to have been under eight seconds.

Summer is tucking a shot into her cleavage when I get to her and knock that fucking hat right off her head.

"What the—" She stops talking when she catches sight of me. "What's wrong?" She looks genuinely confused. Like she truly has no goddamn idea how crazy she drives me.

How badly I want her.

"Hey, man." Emmett slithers up like the fucking snake he is. "You know the rules."

"Yeah, I do. But she doesn't. Keep your fucking hat to yourself."

"Whoa, whoa, whoa." Summer removes the shot glass from her cleavage and holds that hand up to stop us. "What rules?"

"Don't worry about it, doll. Let's do the body shot." Emmett tries to redirect the conversation, edging his body in front of mine to block me out.

But my limbs are longer, and I reach around him and steal the shot right out of Summer's hand. "Not a fucking chance."

Emmett turns to glare at me, all that polite, sunny, farm boy bullshit persona melting right off him. "Beat it, Eaton."

"Did you not hear me, Bush? I said not a fucking chance. I know your games. Play them somewhere else. Breathe on this girl the wrong way, and I'll end you right here rather than just kicking your ass in the ring."

His watery blue eyes narrow as he glares at me, jaw popping, shoulders drawn tight. It doesn't take a rocket scientist to know that he wants to hit me right now. I wish he would, so I could stomp on his stupid, shiny, predatory face.

It's Summer who steps up now, that sexy smirk plastered on her full lips as she raises a hand to point at me. I know she's trying to diffuse the situation, to keep me out of trouble, which is why I'm so surprised when she says, "Okay. Then you're doing the shot."

She doesn't drop my gaze as she steps in front of Emmett. He's behind her and the packed bar is beside us, but all I see is her.

Eyes twinkling, cheeks pink with exertion, dark hair loose and wild around her shoulders.

Summer puffs out her chest in my direction and my eyes drop to the swells of her breasts, the line of cleavage, and the vertical scar that traces up the center. "Put it in."

I groan. She nibbles on her lip, aware of what she's just said. So, I step closer, holding myself back from running my hands all over her, and lift the slender glass. Slowly, I press it between her soft breasts, trailing the pad of my ring finger over the rounded top of her flesh before tracing the line that goes up her entire chest. The scar that she doesn't bother covering up because she's so fucking strong. So brave.

I touch the raised skin, not caring how personal it feels to be doing this in public. Goosebumps erupt over her chest, and even over the blaring music, I can hear her quiet gasp. I feel the way her breath slides across my skin. It's fucking distracting. It has my cock swelling in my jeans.

Her hand darts out, and she holds up a can of whipping cream with a challenging glint in her eye. We've been dancing around each other awkwardly since that day at the fence. We've barely talked, but now she's looking at me like she wants to do an awful lot more than talk.

"In the mood for some dairy products, Rhett?" She shakes the can and before I can stop her, she sprays a line of it from the shot glass wedged between her tits right over the length of the scar.

It's fucking pornographic. Or maybe it's just been a while for me. Either way, I want to get her the hell out of here so I can bend her over and spank her perfect ass for putting Emmett's hat on. Put her on her knees and shove my cock between those lips that have been taunting me for weeks now. Watch her eyes widen when I hit the back of her throat.

She stares up at me, whipped cream trailing up the middle of her chest, ending where her pronounced collarbones dip down and meet the soft spot at the base of her throat. "Or is that going to be too milky for you?"

I drop my head in her direction, blocking some of the onlookers out with the brim of my own hat. "You want me to lick whipped cream off you, Princess?"

Her tongue darts out, wetting her bottom lip as her eyes peruse my body in the hungriest way.

"Yeah. I think I do."

I don't need her to ask twice. I crouch low, pressing my tongue to her bare skin as her hands mold to my shoulders. My mouth slides over her sternum, and I don't bother being polite about it either. I lick, I drag my teeth, and when I get to that soft dip, I suck at her skin before I press a gentle kiss against her.

Her fingers grasp my shirt, and her eyes are laser focused on me when I spare a glance up at her face.

I give her my best cocky, panty-melting smirk and dive back down between her breasts. One of her hands slides over the back of my neck, her fingers raking through my hair before taking hold. My lips wrap around the shot glass of something syrupy and sweet. Something I would never normally drink, but if Summer wants me to lick it off every square inch of her delectable body, I will happily spend hours obliging.

I stand tall and wrap an arm around her waist, tugging her against me as I tip my head back and down the shot.

I can feel her heart pounding against my ribs. She fits right under my arm, like that spot was meant for her.

"Okay, my turn." Emmett tries to step in, but I turn

Summer away under the shelter of my arm. The thought of letting her go now is almost unbearable. To him, to anyone.

Turn? This isn't bowling, asshole. "I already told you. Not a fuckin' chance."

I hear him try to say something to Summer, but I've got her by the wrist and have a clear shot to the door.

We're getting the fuck out of here.

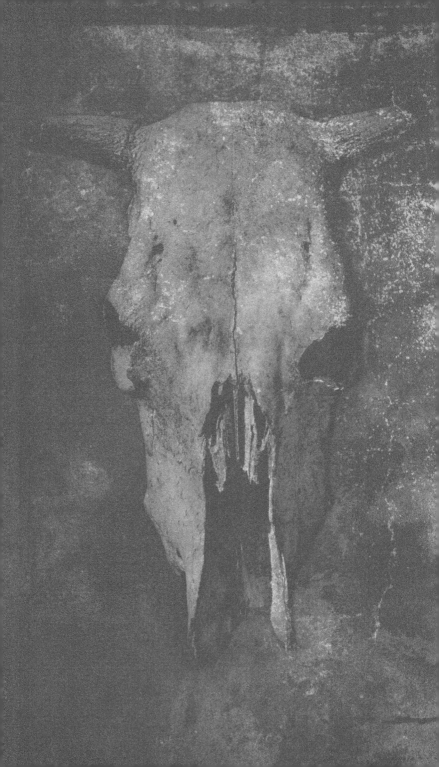

20

Summer

Dad: Summer, what did you do to that poor boy?

Summer: I don't know what you're talking about. But I do wish everyone would stop talking about a man in his thirties like he's a child. Or a dog.

Dad: Okay. You're defensive too. Got it.

Summer: I'm not being defensive. I'm just pointing something out.

Dad: Defensively.

"Where the hell do you think you're taking me?" I ask right as we clear the doors into the cool night air. Cool air that I desperately need after Rhett Eaton just set my entire body on fire.

I'm mad at him. I'm hot for him. And those two things blend until they're almost indecipherable.

Rhett's breath puffs out in front of him as we face off. "Away from Emmett. Before he tells you about the cowboy hat rule."

I scoff. "What the hell is the cowboy hat rule?"

"You wear the hat, you ride the cowboy."

My eyes bulge in their sockets. "What?"

"You heard me. You wanna take Emmett for a ride, Summer?" His voice is pure venom, and I lurch back, not recognizing this tone on him.

"What if I do?" I'm not backing down just because Rhett's going all caveman on me. "Seems an awful lot like none of your business, seeing as how the minute you had a chance you were all over some blonde buckle b—"

I go to hold up a hand between us, the one still holding the stupid whipped cream, and close my eyes. "You know what? It doesn't even matter. For a minute there I had a major lapse of judgment and just . . . forget about it."

Spinning on my heel, I turn and storm toward the crosswalk, relieved that our hotel is across the street. I jam my finger at the button, willing the light to change as quickly as possible so I can get the hell away from Rhett before I tumble right into the deep well of poor decision making that I'm staring down into.

I feel him come to stand beside me, but he says nothing. We walk in tense silence. The chirping sound of the walk signal is our only companion as the thumping music from the bar fades. My fingers wrap tightly around the whipped cream can, and I envision it being Rhett's neck for a moment, but truthfully, that just makes my palms sweat.

Why does he have to be the first guy since Rob who gives me butterflies in the chest? And not the same kind I got as a horned-up teenager staring at pictures of him. These butterflies almost hurt. They feel like they're writhing beneath my skin, taking over my stomach, impeding my vision.

Because all I can see is Rhett. On the back of my eyelids when I sleep, and with me all the fucking time when I'm not asleep.

It's like he's become an extension of me, a necessary part of my personal ecosystem. Infatuation by proximity. It's like I never even had a shot.

We walk into the hotel, him just a step or two behind me. We don't look at each other, we don't talk, but the most intense sense of anticipation grows in my chest. Expanding, pressing, aching.

I want it to stop and carry on forever all at once. I want to peek at him, but I think if I do, the reality of what we're about to do might scare me out of whatever trance I'm in. Whatever sense of resolve I've come to.

We wait at the bank of elevators with one other person, and when we step into the space, Rhett and I take opposite walls. I cross my arms under my breasts, the cool metal can pressing against my ribs and seeping through my shirt while I stare at him across from me.

The other man takes the space in the middle. He looks tired, ready for bed, not nearly as amped up as Rhett does. Rhett looks like a downed power line sparking in the dark.

And I think I'm about to pick that line up and let the electricity course through me.

When the man realizes he's standing in the middle of two people eyeing each other like they might set one another on fire with the power of their sight alone, he straightens up. I catch him peeking at us, head swiveling as he peers at each of us.

When we reach his floor, the elevator dings, and I swear he shakes his head as he gets out, like he knows there will be some sort of brawl between us.

When the doors slide shut behind him, my body tingles —the tips of my fingers, up my inner arm, into that dip behind my elbow, before shooting straight into an ache beneath my bra straps.

Rhett stares at me like no man has before in my life. And for all the times I couldn't decipher his look and thought he was glaring at me with irritation, or frustration, or distaste . . .

I realize I was wrong.

He's staring at me like he wants me. *Really* wants me. Like he aches for me. Like he might melt, just for me.

My breathing quickens, eyes scouring his features. Heavy brows, straight nose, deep, warm eyes, all that scruff. God knows I've stared enough at him over the years, and he just keeps getting better. Firm broad shoulders, narrow waist, and long, lean muscles.

When the elevator dings, I startle and swallow hard, watching his Adam's apple bob in a similar fashion as he holds a hand out to gesture that I go first.

My lips press together, but I exit, mind whirring with what to do next.

I should go to my room.

I should go to his room.

I should take a freezing fucking shower.

I should run straight down this hallway and jump through the window like James Bond getting away from a super villain because no matter what I do, this is going to end poorly. I just know it.

Rhett Eaton will ruin me if I give him the opportunity, and I don't even know what to do with that.

I think I might want him to ruin me.

As we walk toward our side-by-side rooms, I focus on breathing. I'm so hyperaware of his presence I might forget to breathe if I don't actively remind myself to do it.

When I finally reach my door, I place one palm flat against it to hold myself up as I wait for him to walk past me. This is hands down the most out of control, confounding feeling in the world. I want to stare at him all night long, and I want to squeeze my eyes shut and never look at him again.

"Rhett, I—"

"Go to bed, Summer."

I snap back, surprised by what he's saying. "Go to bed?"

"Yes. Before I do something distinctly ungentlemanlike to you."

My brows shoot up, taken aback by his directness.

"Like what?" My voice comes out quiet and uncertain. Our slightly hostile banter is my comfort zone, but alone with a man like Rhett Eaton, looking at me the way he is, well, it's way the hell and gone out of my wheelhouse.

Sex with Rob was rushed and unsatisfying.

The friends-with-benefits situation I had during law school ended with unrequited attachments.

And that one-night stand I had was . . . just bad.

I don't know where the hell that leaves me with Rhett. I don't know what I want from him. But I know I don't want to go to bed.

Not alone anyway.

A muscle in his neck jumps and he crosses his arms, shirt bunching around his biceps. "I'd start with those pretty fucking lips."

My lashes flutter and a whimper stalls out in my throat as I try to work out how I should respond to *that*.

I opt to take the bull by the horns. With one step forward, my hand darts out and I yank the saddle-brown cowboy hat off his head and place it on mine. His leather and licorice scent rushes in around me, and I sigh.

I'd like to bottle that if I could. Sweet and earthy and so damn masculine all at once.

He growls when I step away wearing his hat and push my back against the flat wall between our rooms, letting a small smirk play on my lips. Reveling in the way his eyes heat when I do.

With two steps, he's towering over me. My head tips back to take in all his agitated glory.

"You know what I'm sick of, Summer?" His hand comes to my throat, fluttering over the skin so gently that I arch toward him to increase the pressure.

"What's that?"

"Having you think I'm out fucking everything that moves when I've looked at nothing and no one since the first day I laid eyes on *you*. I stepped into that godforsaken boardroom, and you practically demanded I become obsessed with you."

I gasp for air, rendered speechless.

His finger pads stroke my neck with such tenderness that I blink up at him, more emotional than I banked on.

"Do you know what else I'm fucking sick of?"

"What?" My question is a breath, a whisper—a plea.

His hand moves up, and his thumb pushes down firmly on my chin, gently forcing my mouth open wide. There's something crude about it, but the way he's looking at me as he does it has me trembling with antici-pation, my pussy wet and slick when I squeeze my thighs together.

"Having to spend all day, every day, with you and this smart mouth . . ." His spare hand yanks the can of whipping cream from my sweaty grip. He holds it up, hitting me with the most sinful grin.

"And not being able to use it the way I want to. To fill it the way I want to." His voice is husky, but I barely have time to register it because the whoosh of the pressurized cream filling my mouth permeates the air between us.

When he stops, he presses my chin back up, closing my mouth. "How does that taste, Princess?"

"Mm," is all I can manage as my tastebuds dance with the creamy sweetness, while every nerve ending dances with scorching electricity.

"Good girl. You wish that was my cum, don't you?" A strangled whimper lodges in my throat as I nod back at him, trapped in his amber gaze. Then he leans in close, breath damp against my lips and growls, "Swallow, Summer."

Sharp anticipation races through my veins, and I make this desperate little moaning sound as I swallow for him. "Are we done playing games now?" His voice is heavy, full of promise, raising the hair on my arms.

I nod, nervously licking at my lips and unable to drop his gaze.

"Good." His thumb strokes the sensitive spot beneath my ear as he grips the back of my neck. "Now, tell me honestly, Summer. If this were your last moment on earth, what would you want me to do?"

I don't even need to think about it. I know what I want from him.

"Ruin me."

"Good. I'm about fucking done being a gentleman with you. And the only thing I'm ruining you for is anyone else."

He swipes his key card and shoves us through the door.

And it looks like I'm going to his room after all.

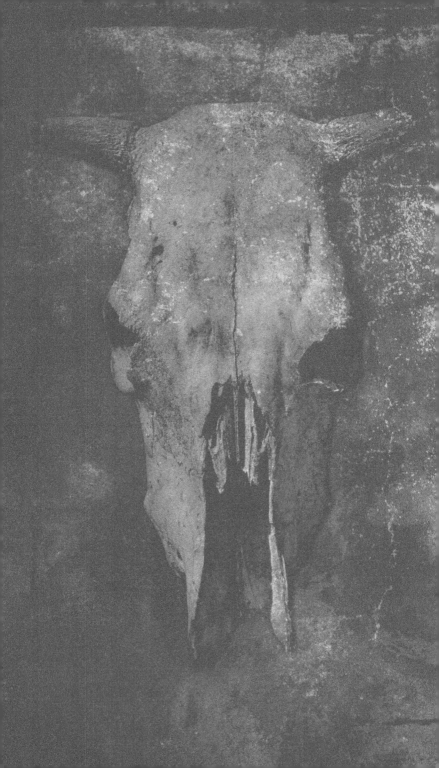

21

Rhett

I drop the can of cream on the carpet right as the heavy door clicks shut behind us, and all bets are off. My entire body hums with need. For *her*.

Ruin me.

She'd told me to ruin her. The only thing I'm going to ruin her for is any other man. I'm going to give her a night she'll never get over. A night that will keep her coming back for more.

I push her against the closed door, the brim of my hat on her head brushing against my face as I swoop in to taste her lips. But this time it's not for show. This time it's because she told me this is how she'd want to go out. Kissing *me*.

And fuck, a statement like that is a powerful drug.

I kiss her like my life depends on it, like hers does too. We latch onto each other, her arms curling around my neck while mine roam her body.

It's a desperate sort of kiss, full of angst and longing.

She seems rushed. Like she thinks this might end. Like there's a time limit on this thing we're doing.

I pull back just a little, cupping the base of her head, her hair silky beneath my hand, her breathing labored, her breath sweet like sugary cream, hands still feverishly tugging at me. "Stop rushing, Princess. We've got all night. Save your energy, you're going to need it."

"Fuck," she whispers as she sucks in a sharp breath.

"Let me show you. I'm going to take my time with you," I murmur before taking her lips slowly, swallowing the sweet little humming noise she makes, feeling her arms soften, hands tracing across my shoulders. Her nails drag and a shiver races down my spine.

I don't know what this is between Summer and me, but I want to worship at her throne. I want to give her the best of everything. The best of *me*.

She slides her tongue against mine, and I taste the whipped cream I just made her swallow. Even with my eyes closed, I can see the way her throat worked, the way she swallowed it the way I told her to. It's burned on the back of my eyelids.

Didn't think my cock could get any harder than it already is, but it pushes painfully at the zipper of my jeans at the memory.

I slide my hand down the curve of her body. My thumb flicks at her nipple through the thin cotton shirt as I clear her breast, and she whines into my mouth, trying to rush the leisurely pace I've set.

"Greedy girl," I growl as I pull back and press a kiss to the bottom line of her jaw.

I kiss just beside her mouth.

"Rhett." My name on her lips. *Fuck.* It's a prayer. It's a plea. It's my goddamn undoing.

I kiss her cheek.

"I thought I got off on hearing fans scream my name from the stands."

I kiss her temple.

"But hearing you moan it?"

She tilts her head, giving me more access. Asking for more.

"Hearing you moan it is so much more satisfying."

I kiss the spot just below her ear, and she squirms against me. She goes all breathy and moans my name again. "Rhett."

"You like that?" I nip at her ear.

"It's the beard. It feels so good. I . . . I've never had that before." The girl who is usually so put together and well-spoken is a puddle, all because of my beard.

And I get off on it. I get off on being the first man to give her beard burn. Her neck isn't safe tonight, neither are her inner thighs.

I chuckle and drag my teeth down the side of her throat, fueled by her moans. By her hips rocking toward me. By her fingers in the back of my hair.

My fingers land at the waistband of her tight fucking jeans and reach in to tug her shirt out. I instantly squeeze the taper of her waist, her smooth warm skin, noting the strap of whatever sexy fucking panties she's wearing coming up over her hip in the most alluring way.

And then, I'm pushing the white shirt up over her head,

wanting it off as quickly as possible. Wanting to see what she's hiding underneath this well put together exterior.

Her arms raise, and as the shirt clears her head, my hat topples to the ground at her feet. But I leave it there, just to take in Summer propped against the door, wild hair, chest heaving, full breasts pushed up high in the red lace bra. Straps of matching lace panties wedged up high over her jeans.

She looks a little unsteady and a lot desperate. Totally disheveled.

And I love this look on her.

I crouch quickly to swipe the hat and the can before replacing the hat on her head. *My hat.* I groan and shut my eyes at the fucking wet dream before me.

"You should see yourself right now." Her teeth dig into her puffy bottom lip, really completing the whole look. "So fucking pretty."

"Please, don't stop."

"Wasn't planning on it. Just admiring the view."

"Lose the shirt."

I chuckle. "There she is. My bossy girl." I step closer, crowding her against the door. "You want it off, do it yourself."

An expression of defiance flashes across her face, but within moments, she relents. Her small hands reach for the buttons of my shirt, and she nimbly works the first couple through the holes.

When she peeks up at me with that little smirk on her lips, I know she's about to pull something naughty. She grips my shirt and rips. Buttons fly all around us.

She seems amused until I yank her bra down, the sound of lace ripping loud in the quiet room.

"Hey!" she starts, but her bare tits are exposed right in front of me. All soft and full, nipples hard as rocks. The neon lights from the shitty bar across the street cast a blue glow in the room that adds to her ethereal beauty. Even the scar down the center of her chest suits her. A battle scar. A testament to how hard she's fought. How fucking strong she is.

I'm absolutely starstruck.

"That bra was La Perla. You owe m—"

I shut her up by spraying a circle of whipped cream over her right nipple. Instead of reaming me out, she swaps to moaning and running her hands through my hair when I drop my head and suck her breast into my mouth, taking a long pull.

Her chest arches into me as I lick the whipped cream from her body. A milk product has never tasted so good. I can feel the gooseflesh of her skin against my lips, and once I've cleaned her off, I graze her nipple with my teeth.

"Mm," I murmur, slightly leaning back to admire the way her breast glistens before reaching behind her and removing the torn bra entirely.

She watches, speechless.

I go for the other nipple, covering it in cream, pausing for a moment to appreciate how she looks all scandalized and painted with sugary cream.

It's giving me the filthiest ideas. Ideas I let play through my mind as I drop my head again and take my time cleaning her off while she moans and writhes.

When I straighten and drop the can on the floor, I cup her breasts and grin down at her.

"I thought you hated milk?" she huffs out, all glassy eyed and eager.

"I'm developing a taste for it." I growl as I lift her up, pressing her into the door and kissing her again. Her legs wrap around my waist, squeezing my hips as she sears me with a kiss, my hat toppling off her head to our feet.

All I can taste is whipped cream and cherries, and all I can smell is *her*.

All I want is *her*.

Which is how I find myself carrying her across the blue-lit hotel room with long sure strides, ignoring the twinge in my shoulder—because who needs a fucking shoulder with a girl like this?—and tossing her down on the bed, her dark hair shimmering out around her, like rays of sunshine off her sweet, freckled face.

We pause for a second, her splayed out across my bed while I stand entranced between her knees. This is the moment where we fully consider if we're about to do this.

"Do you want me, Princess?" I ask as I tug a boot off each of her feet.

Her lips part, and she stares back at me when I drop them on the floor with a heavy thud. "Yes."

I reach down and unbutton her jeans, stepping away only to drag them down her legs. "Why?"

"Because . . ."

I discard them and stare down at her, panties wedged high, showing the outline of her pussy. I groan. That paired with the knee-high socks she's wearing and her tits on display could make me blow on the spot. Paint her with something else entirely.

Stepping closer so my knees bump up against the mattress, I grip behind her knees and spread her legs wide. As I do, her panties slide over, exposing one of her bare lips.

"Fuck, Summer. Fucking look at you."

She whimpers, hands falling to her tits like she's trying to cover them. But I catch her rolling her nipples between her thumb and forefinger, clearly trying to avoid answering my question.

"Tell me. Tell me why you want me."

Her lips roll together, her panting audible.

"You want this?"

She nods.

"Talk to me, Summer. You want me to fill this tight little cunt?"

"Fuck," the word whooshes out of her as her eyes widen in surprise. Such a proper little princess.

"Have I got your attention now?"

"You've always had my attention, Rhett." Her confession comes out quiet and soft. Like a secret shared between lovers. And like a balm to my deepest wounds.

I groan and reach forward, running my thumb over the seam of her pussy, feeling her pulse and clench against me. Feeling how wet the lace there is already. Nudging the strip of fabric aside, I push a finger in and revel in her, smooth and slick. Drenched.

"You're soaked, Summer. Is that mess all for me?"

I swear I can see her cheeks flush pink, more of a purple in the blue glow.

"Yes," she says meekly, sounding almost embarrassed. And, well, that's just not going to do.

She needs to know how wild this makes me.

"I love it," I growl, dropping to one knee, slinging her leg over my shoulder and tugging her ass to the edge of the bed. When I pull the scrap of lace to the side, I feast my eyes on what I'd only felt before.

"All this for me." I rub her pussy again, feeling her leg clamp down on my shoulder as her head shyly flips to one side. "What a fucking treat."

She tries to press closed her free leg, and I slide one finger into her wet heat while tutting her. "Nah, nah, nah. Don't get all shy now. Legs wide open for me, Princess."

I slide one hand up the back of her thigh to open her as she breathes out a quiet, "Okay."

Pressing a kiss to the inside of her knee, making sure she feels the rasp of my beard, I ask, "Should I keep going?"

She takes a beat to respond. So, I wait, bestowing more kisses up her inner thigh, grinning when her hips buck. "I've never . . . well, this is new."

I freeze for a moment, looking over her outline from where I'm kneeling. "New? Like no one has tasted this?" I rub her again, and my cock jumps when I realize she's even wetter than before.

She shakes her head no.

Doctor Douche really is the fucking worst. But I don't say that. Instead, I reach for the lace underwear and drag them down her legs. If this is going to be her first time riding a man's face, it's going to be good. And there aren't going to be any fancy panties in the way.

When they clear her ankles, I resume my position. "That's a crime, Summer. A terrible shame." I slide a finger in and feel her contract around me as she gasps. "It seems I have some wrongs to right." I pump in and out, raptly watching her pussy take my finger, and then two. "And I'm not even sad about it. Do you know why?"

"Why?" she replies quickly, voice all raspy and thick.

"Because if this were my last moment on earth, that's how I'd want to go." I thrust in hard now, watching her body shake with the force, hearing her curse. "Head between these pretty little thighs, your pussy on my tongue."

I hold her wide open, drop my head, and get to work.

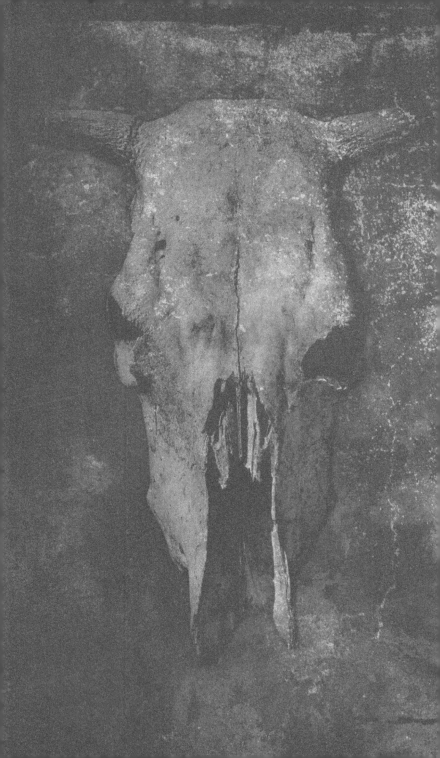

22

Summer

My eyes roll back in my head, and I see stars. Bright and shiny, almost blinding. I've heard good sex compares to an out-of-body experience, and I never quite understood that sentiment.

But with Rhett Eaton's face between my legs, I do.

Both his muscled arms loop around my legs, and one hand splays across my stomach, holding me down. The other is wrapped tight around my thigh, and his fingers dig in so hard that I feel like he might leave bruises right next to the ones from the saddle pinching me a few days earlier.

His tongue.

His. Tongue.

His goddamn tongue.

He's licking me, almost the way he did at the whipped cream on my breasts, reverently, but with just enough pressure. Just enough suction.

Just the right amount of teeth. He slides his tongue right into me, and when I try to squirm, his calloused hand pushes me harder into the too-soft mattress beneath my back. His beard is prickly and rough against my pussy. Grating on my inner thighs. Increasing my pleasure tenfold. Partly because of the actual sensation, and partly because, well, because it's Rhett.

Rhett Eaton. My teenaged crush. Rhett Eaton. Sex symbol. Rhett Eaton. Ladies' man.

Or is he? I'm thinking that's an outdated perception that he hasn't been able to shake.

He said he's been obsessed with me. That was almost as shocking as how good it feels to have his mouth between my legs.

I thought Rhett hated me but tolerated me.

But based on the things he's said, it seems I have been wrong. Very, *very*, wrong.

"Rhett!" I cry out, one hand still working at my nipple while my other shoots down to his head. I'm alternating between feeling self-conscious and not giving a fuck because it's just so damn good.

He pulls back, pausing, "Tell me what you want, Summer."

He's killing me with all this talking. Having to say things out loud is firmly outside my comfort zone. For a man who's never been huge on chatting, he sure has a lot to say once my clothes come off.

I push up onto my elbows and look down at him, his eyes still fixed on my pussy. "I want you to stop making me say things out loud." I half laugh.

His eyes flit up to mine and he grins, the most carnal

grin, before he licks his lips and winks at me. "What can I say? I like your pink cheeks and watching you squirm."

I blush harder.

He gently unhooks my legs and stands, towering over my exposed body. Making me feel remarkably vulnerable. He drops his ruined shirt on the floor and quirks a brow at me. "Did I tell you to stop?"

"Stop what?"

"Touching yourself. Keep going."

I swallow, wondering how I'm reacting to him this strongly. It's consuming, and I don't even consider saying no. Instead, I fall back onto the bed and slide one hand up my stomach before gripping my breast.

I do the same with the opposite, but when my knees tilt inward, his calloused palm gives one leg a little push open. "I'm not done with that," he growls as he shucks off his pants, turning briefly to pull something out of his bag, giving me a glorious view of his ass.

Round and muscled, and so goddamn grabbable.

When he comes back, he's holding a foil condom package. His cock is huge and hard and it's pointing straight at me. "You still want this, Summer?"

He sounds almost uncertain now, like he's concerned I might turn him away.

"Yes," I breathe, wanting to give him more. "I want you inside me."

The locks of his hair have flopped over his face. He looks messy and delicious, and I think even a little bit self-conscious. I wonder what he wants me to say? What he's trying to urge out of me?

I thought it was all dirty talk, but the way he's watching me now as he rolls a condom over his steely length has me wondering if it's something else.

"I want you on top of me," I blurt out awkwardly as I sit up. My dirty talk needs work. His eyes narrow as he fists his cock, but I keep my gaze on his face as he advances on me, my heart thundering against my ribs. Like it wants to jump out of my body and give itself to this man.

Like it knows something I don't.

With him finally hovering over me, I reach between us to grip his thick cock. And it is *thick*. "Jesus. I'm going to pay for this tomorrow, aren't I?"

Rhett smirks. "If you're not walking bow-legged tomorrow, I won't have done my job tonight."

Now he looks so playful, so delicious, so confident. His full attention is on me, and only me. He looks like the type of man I could easily get wrapped up in and be left standing with nothing but a broken heart at the end.

I swipe the head of his cock against my slick core, grinding on his tip, watching his eyes flutter shut.

He kisses me, a searing kiss that has my toes curling and my hips arching up to meet him. And then, he's pushing into me—slow, and steady, and delicious—filling me up and giving my body the time it needs to adjust. I lift a leg and wrap it around his back, pulling him nearer. Wanting him closer.

"Fuck, Summer," he growls against my lips. "Just fuck. How are you this fucking tight?"

My nails skate over his back as I let my hands roam in a way they never did while I massaged him. There is nothing remotely professional about the way I'm touching Rhett Eaton right now.

When he bottoms out, resting in the cradle of my hips, he groans. "Are you okay? Because I think this is about as long as I can handle being gentle."

I nip at his chin. "I thought I told you to ruin me?"

He rears up above me, deadly serious and painfully handsome. "Careful what you wish for, Princess."

He pulls all the way out before shoving himself back in. My body shakes and my head tips back. I feel every point of contact between us, every inch of skin, every hair. Even his gaze is heavy on me, like he's pulling my soul up to my skin with the look in his eye alone.

He sets a slow but powerful rhythm, fucking me hard, watching my every movement, absorbing every noise.

On one hand, it's borderline unnerving. On the other, I feel like a fucking goddess beneath Rhett Eaton. Like he can't tear his eyes away from me, like he has all the time in the world, like he'll never forget this.

Or get enough.

I know I never will.

My moans come at a higher pitch as he pushes my body taut, but he pulls out, drops to his knees, and feasts on me again.

The change in pressure, feel—the entire thing—it leaves my body reeling to catch up. A light sweat breaks out across my chest as he fucks me with his tongue like I'm the best thing he's ever tasted.

"Rhett," I gasp his name, completely lost to the sensation of him playing my body like an instrument he's mastered.

"Yes, Princess? You going to tell me why you want this now?" He stands tall, gripping my ankles as he goes, folding me how he wants, which at this current juncture, has my feet up near his shoulders while he looms over me like some sort of wild god.

Then he's lining himself up, sliding into me again. Going so deep. Filling me with every inch.

"I don't know," I pant, eyes lingering on the way his skin shimmers with perspiration.

"Try again." He thrusts into me, setting a more punishing pace. His head tips back, highlighting the bump of his Adam's apple. With every stroke, my moans grow louder, more frenzied—just like his movements. "I'll keep you screaming all night until you tell me."

Fuck, am I screaming?

Right when my nerve endings coil again, when I'm reaching for that spot that I so badly want to hit, he pulls out and ‘drops to the floor. Leaving me empty and breathless.

"I'll have you coming all night long, Summer. But not until you say it out loud. I want to hear it." His fingers slowly—so slowly—rub my swollen clit. He pumps two fingers in, the sound of how wet I am for him enough to make me blush. But he just chuckles softly, deeply. "You want to fuck a bull rider, baby?"

His head drops and he laps at me again, tongue flat, his movements measured, dragging me back away from the edge.

"No." My hands find my breasts of their own accord, body aching for release.

He sucks my clit into his mouth, grazing his teeth along my pussy.

"Take a walk on the wild side with a cowboy rather than your fancy city boys?" he murmurs, the sight of his head between my legs burning itself into my memory.

"No!" My response is more forceful this time.

He sucks harder, and my legs fall open wider. How I went from never having done this to devoured by the king of eating pussy, I'll never truly know. But I'm definitely not going to complain about it. Especially not when I'm finally barreling toward release, pushing myself down on him, fingers wantonly pinching my nipples.

But he pulls away.

I let out a frustrated growl and push up on my elbows. He gives me a devilish grin and quirk of a brow, like he knows exactly what he's doing.

"Tell me why you want it, Summer." His voice is gruff, with a bite that wasn't there before.

It.

It hits me that he talks about himself like a commodity. Maybe this isn't a game for him at all. Maybe he really is trying to figure out why a girl like me would want a man like him.

I pin him with my eyes as I sit up on the edge of the bed and reach for him. "I don't want *it*, Rhett. I want *you*."

My hands run over him, gently searching, but he stays quiet. Watching me like he always does. "I'm tired of doing what I *should* and ignoring what I want. And what I want is you. Inside me. All around me. I want you *with* me. And I want to be the only one."

Out loud, it sounds so insecure. But my heart can't take being broken again. It can't withstand a man like Rhett treating me like I'm nothing more than a roll in the hay. I don't know what it all means, but I know I want him to understand this isn't casual for me. I may not know what it is, but it's not that.

He stares at me, as though he's processing what I've just told him, before he leans back over me, cupping my skull in his big hands with so much tenderness that my chest aches.

"You've got me, Princess. Only you, I promise," he husks, before kissing me. A consuming kiss. I taste myself on his lips and feel his beard on my cheeks. His hair drops around us, closing us into an intimate bubble, and I smile against his mouth because he's all around me right now.

After a cool down moment, my body heats again for him so easily. Like I have a switch, and he's the only one who knows where it's located.

We exchange no more words as he gently lies me back down, keeping our bodies close as he does, kissing me as we go, dragging his mouth—his beard—until I'm a squirming, whimpering mess beneath him. His face hovers over mine, his elbows drop onto the bed beside my head, and he stares into my eyes.

Always staring. Like if he blinks, I might disappear.

The pad of his thumb swipes across my temple reverently, brushing a wispy lock of hair from my cheek. The blunt end of his cock nudges my thigh as we bask in this moment. This anticipation. Because suddenly, this night feels different.

"I've never wanted someone so badly in my life," I confess to him. His responding smile is soft, one I'm not sure I've ever seen on him.

His thumb still strokes at my temple with heart-aching gentleness as he slides himself into me. We sigh in unison, and then he says, "Me neither, Princess. Me neither."

We kiss, we touch, he rocks into me, he fucks me until I shake beneath him. On every surface we can find. He spends the entire night proving just how badly he wants me, pulling me apart at every seam, watching me crumble for him over and over again.

I think he crumbles a bit for me too though.

When we're both boneless and exhausted, he pulls me into the cradle of his body and holds me like he'll never let go.

And when he feels how cold my feet are, he tangles his warm legs against them.

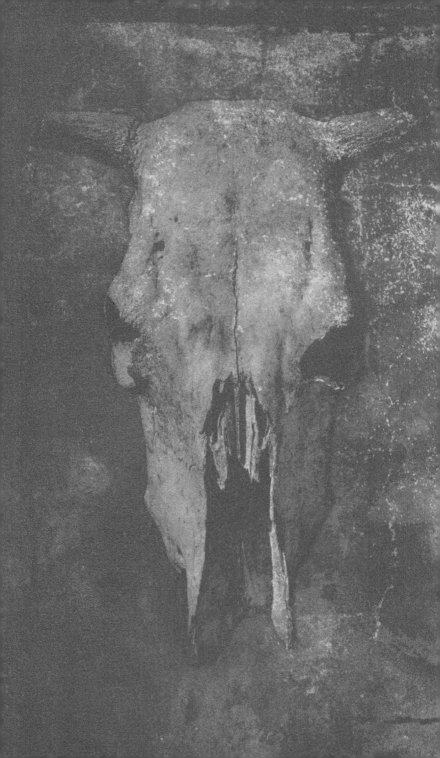

23

Rhett

Kip: Is everything okay? Neither of you have answered my texts about your meeting with the Ariat guys.

Rhett: Yes, Daddy. Everything is fine. Some of us sleep at night.

Kip: I was worried she might have killed you. Just looking out for you, son.

Rhett: She almost did.

I sleep more comfortably than I have in, well, ever. Summer fits against me like she was made for me. I don't even mind her cold-ass feet.

I wake up to pull her closer, or to thumb a piece of her silky hair, or to brush a featherlight kiss against those puffy lips. But it never really feels like waking up, just an extension of my blissful comfort. We smell like soap and minty toothpaste, because truthfully, we haven't been asleep for that long.

It's the sensation of being watched that finally draws my eyes open in the already light room. Summer is wedged under my arm, hair a tangled mess, lips all swollen and pink, bare face sprinkled with freckles like sugar on top of a cupcake.

When I meet her gaze, she doesn't look away.

"Is this when you kill me in my sleep? You mentioned that at one point." My morning voice is raspy, and so is her soft chuckle as I squeeze her tighter. "You've been playing the long game this entire time, haven't you? You didn't have a teenaged crush on me at all. You've been plotting my murder for over a decade."

She nuzzles her face into my chest. "Shut up."

Her eyelashes sweep against my skin as her fingers swirl in my chest hair.

"Are you hiding from me, Summer?" I fist her hair and give it a tug, forcing her chin up.

"I'm just working things out in my head."

Yeah, well, I can't say I didn't see this coming. I knew she'd take off in the morning. All the people who I want to stay never do. It's the ones I can't get away from fast enough that hang around. The ones who want something from me.

I grunt noncommittally, feeling irrationally attached to Summer after getting naked for one night. Which is brand spanking new for someone who only ever wants one night.

"Don't grunt at me, Rhett Eaton."

I sigh and scrub at my face, wanting to fall back into the quiet, happy lull before this conversation started. "What are you working out?"

She peeks up at me. "Well, for starters, how to convince you to go again."

My brows raise. "Yeah?"

She grins. "Yeah, but look at the time. You need to be at the arena for another interview and a meeting with a sponsor in one hour."

I roll her on top of me, not caring at all about the fucking time. Especially not when her legs straddle my waist, and she sighs like she knows she belongs there.

"Fuck the meetings." I grip her waist as she taps at her lip.

The sheet pools around her waist and the sun shines in brightly behind her, highlighting the beard burn across her chest, just above where her pert tits stare back at me.

"I'm also trying to figure out how I'm going to continue sleeping with a client who only has one-night stands."

"Fuck one-night stands." My hands glide up over her ribs, pushing her breasts together.

"It would be unprofessional for me to continue but . . ." She's smiling now, looking light and sweet and totally fuckable.

"Fuck professionalism," I growl, tweaking a nipple.

"Yes, well, Kip Hamilton might not share that sentiment. You're still a client." Her eyes sober.

"Fuck Kip Hamilton too. He's fired."

"Rhett—"

I silence her by sliding one hand up and pushing my thumb into her mouth, watching her lips part, and the flash of her pink tongue as I press down on it. "If you keep talking about things that don't matter, we're going to run out of time to do things that do."

She just nods and sucks my finger as I grind my rock-hard cock up into her bare ass. "Now shut up and ride me. I want to watch these pretty tits bounce while you come on my cock."

Her eyes widen, almost comically wide, but she pushes up onto her knees and drops herself down on me with a wanton little moan.

I told her I'd want to go with my head between her legs, but I think I'd settle for being anywhere close to her in my last moments.

"The interview went well." Summer paces in front of me while I methodically tape my hands.

"Yup." I can hear the music and the cheering from the arena all the way back here in the locker room.

"And I think the guy from Wrangler seemed happy

with what you were saying to them." From my periphery, I see her twisting her hands together.

"Mhm." I pay special attention to my thumb. It still twinges from getting hung up a few weeks back.

"Plus, you do wear them well."

I peek up at her now, all serious and anxious looking. "Was that a compliment?"

She furrows her brow. "Yeah."

"Huh." I go back to wrapping, lips tugging up as her fingers tap against the side of her thigh.

"I give you compliments," she tells me. Like that somehow makes it true.

"Okay."

"I do." Her snakeskin boot stomps. "Do you need me to gush over you like every other girl on tour? Or like every newscaster Barbie who interviews you?"

I grin down at my hands. If Summer's jealousy were water, I'd want to bathe in it. "No, Princess. Watching you get jealous over me is victory enough for a simple man like me. Never knew I'd like that so much. You are downright adorable, all pink cheeked and worked up like this."

"Ha!" she barks, loud with disbelief. "That's rich coming from you. You practically carried me out of that bar last night!"

"And I'd do it again. Emmett knows there are lots of great places to bury a body on my ranch. No one would ever find him again if he laid a hand on you."

I chuckle, but Summer goes quiet. Her fingers tap on her legs again, which pulls my gaze up to her pretty face from where I'm seated on the bench.

"What's wrong?"

"I kept you up too late last night. You should have been resting, getting ready for today. You're an athlete. You need to prepare."

She chews on her bottom lip. She seems worried.

"Summer, I'm fine. Come here." I open one arm, and she instantly steps across the ground separating us, hugging me to her chest. I press my cheek to her sternum. I feel her heartbeat as her fingers slide through the ends of my hair.

"Be careful, okay?" she whispers. "Don't give me a heart attack out there."

"That joke is in real poor taste for you, Summer."

She laughs, but it's thin. Tinny.

I hug her tighter, and she leans down to press a kiss to the top of my head. Understanding dawns on me what she's not saying. What we're both not saying. I can't, because if I went out there every weekend with even a small flickering of fear in me, I'd never get on that bull. Logic would take over. Survival instincts.

And I'd be done.

But I've got those instincts strapped down tight. One more championship and maybe I'll take my gold buckle and hang up my hat.

Preferably on Summer Hamilton's head.

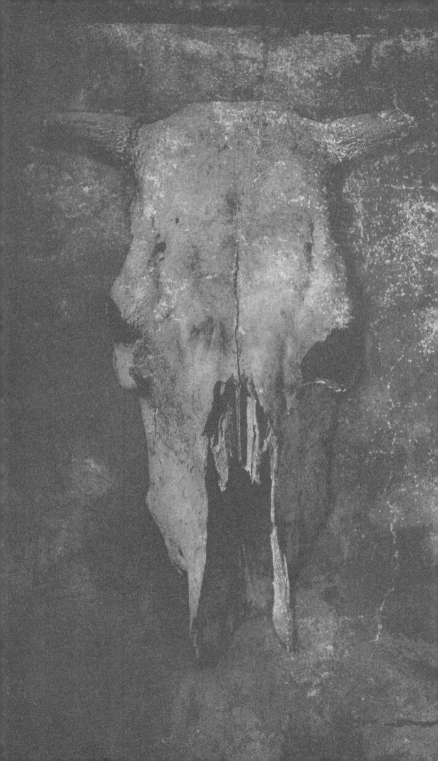

24

Summer

Kip: Why did Rhett send me a text saying that I'm fired?

Summer: He. Didn't.

Kip: He did. It said, "Fuck professionalism and fuck you. You're fired."

Summer: Well, he's not wrong. That certainly isn't very professional. I don't think you're actually fired though.

Kip: Of course I'm not fired. That asshole is stuck with me.

Summer: How is your shoulder? Are you taping it? Do you want me to come tape it?

Rhett: Fine. Don't come back here. It smells like sweaty balls.

Summer: Thank you for the vivid description. I was reading about pulsed electromagnetic field therapy for rotator cuff injuries. Maybe we should try it? There's a physiotherapist in the city who does it.

Rhett: I was kind of just hoping you'd give me more massages? But topless this time.

Summer: I'll do that if you go to the appointment I scheduled for next week.

Rhett: Daily massages. Where you ride my dick while rubbing my shoulder. Then I'll go.

Summer: Is your shoulder that bad?

Rhett: No, Princess. Your pussy is just that good.

Watching Rhett tonight has me wanting to hurl my fifteen-dollar arena beer all over the people in front of me. Emmett went first and had a great ride, something I know Rhett saw because he was sitting up on top of the gate with Theo watching.

I saw the flash of competition in his eye. He spent all night with his dick inside of me and still looks like he could kill the guy.

There's this tiny part of me that wishes he'd just hop off

that fence and retire on the spot. I want him safe. I want him to win too though. I want that for him.

But I also want him for myself.

It's fucking confusing. I've never worried about another person this way, and that's saying something, considering I've spent my entire life worrying about everyone around me.

Theo hops down onto his bull now, giving Rhett a bit of an unhinged grin as he does. I watch Rhett talk to him as Theo rubs at his bull rope, nodding—listening. There's an intensity about their conversation right now that I haven't noticed before.

Usually, things are lighthearted and friendly between them, but tonight there's a definite mentor feel to their interaction. It's heartwarming and nerve-wracking all at once.

The bull slams itself against the metal sides of the chute, and where I noticed Rhett back off in similar situations, Theo grins, drops his chin, and nods.

The gate flies, and so does the bull, like a bat out of hell. Theo looks like a younger, smaller Rhett, spurs riding up every time the bull bears down. He rides like his life depends on it. And based on how riled his bull is and how many times it switches directions, I would say his life actually does depend on it.

I barely know Theo, but I hold my breath all the same. On my nights spent sitting in the stands, I've seen other guys get head butted and stepped on. I've seen them leave strapped down on a stretcher.

In a lot of ways, it's hard to watch, in others . . . I can't tear my eyes away.

So, when Theo jumps off and tosses his hat in the air, I shoot up and cheer. The bull lopes out of the ring, chasing the clown, and Theo soaks up the cheers of the crowd. He scores himself a 90, which pushes him to the top of the standings for this weekend.

When I look back over at the fence, Rhett is sitting there, grinning ear to ear. So damn proud, chest puffed out, pride spilling off him.

He also looks fucking delicious. Dark and mysterious with his hat pulled down low on his face, charcoal shirt under his bull riding vest, and those simple warm brown chaps.

So. Good.

When he hops down to go stretch and warm up, my momentary calm dissolves and the nerves creep in.

I hate the feeling. I hate that I'm having it. I've come to terms with death in a lot of ways. Knowing that your time could come at any moment at such a young age does weird things to you. Somehow, the thought of me dying is easier to swallow than the thought of having to sit here in the stands while something might happen to Rhett.

I don't want to be this girl, telling him not to take risks because my heart can't take it. So, I push it down, like he told me he does.

I take a few big swigs of beer and let myself eavesdrop on the surrounding conversations. And when it's Rhett's turn, I take bigger gulps.

I watch him every moment, absently aware that it could

be the last. It's like time slows down. I see his cocky smile, the way his cheeks fold beside his mouth when he gives it. I can almost feel the raspiness of his beard on my neck just by watching him.

He pulls at the bull rope, looking hypnotized, and I try to slip into that too.

And then he does something he's never done. He peeks up at me from beneath the brim of his hat, like he knew exactly where I was sitting.

He winks at me.

And then he nods, and the gates fly open.

"You were so close."

The rippling of water sounds as Rhett swipes a face-cloth over my back. This shitty hotel bathtub is too small for the two of us, but we're packed into it anyway. He told me if I'm going to continue to force him to take Epsom salt baths that I have to come in with him.

So here I am, seated between his legs in the hottest, smallest bath known to man.

While Rhett Eaton washes me. And kisses me.

This is how I want to go.

"Ah, if I'm going to lose to someone, I'd have it be Theo. Give him a year or two, and he'll be winning left and right."

"So, like . . . a newer, shinier version of you?" I tease, but it ends in a gasp when he wraps my hair around his fist and gives it a tug.

"Watch that pretty little mouth, Summer," he murmurs against my ear.

His erection presses against my back, but we've mostly ignored that in favor of just soaking for a bit.

"Or what?" My lips tip up as I glance over my shoulder, hoping to egg him on.

He chuckles, making goosebumps race over my flushed skin. "Or nothing. I'm out of condoms."

"I don't know if they taught you this at cowboy school, but I can't get pregnant from giving blowjobs."

He reaches around and roughly squeezes one of my breasts as he pulls me back against him. "Jesus, woman. The things that come out of your mouth sometimes."

I giggle and soften against him. "Fine. *Fine.* You started it."

"Started what?"

"This."

I feel the rumble in his chest against my shoulders. "I did not."

"You did. You kissed me first," I joke.

"Huh. I thought you said that meant nothing." He trails the washcloth over my arms now.

I close my eyes and sigh. I did say that. And at the time I meant it, or at least I wanted to. "I needed it to mean nothing so I could maintain some sense of professionalism." It's a painfully honest statement, and there's a part of me that wishes I could take it back.

But for as much as Rhett and I rib each other, I don't think he takes me lightly. Men who take a woman lightly don't look at a woman the way Rhett looks at me.

That look could be all in my head.

Maybe I'm unraveling over a look that doesn't even exist.

"Is taking Epsom salt baths with your clients something they teach you at law school?" His chest shakes under the strain of trying not to laugh at his own joke. *Dork.*

I groan and cover my face with my hands. "Rhett."

He presses a kiss to the crown of my head. I'm pretty sure just to keep himself from laughing.

"It's not funny. I don't know what we're doing here. And I've spent years in school and tens of thousands of dollars on it to do this job. This is . . . I don't know what I'm doing."

"I think you do. I think you're doing what you want for the first time in your life and that's scary for you."

"Yeah. Maybe."

"I think you don't need to worry about if I'm a client or not. I think that has nothing to do with what's between you and me."

"It's the perception—" I try to say, but he interrupts me.

"What perception? Have you done this before? You planning to do it more in the future? Or does what's happened between us have nothing at all to do with what either of us do for work? Do you think if we'd met under different circumstances, it would be different?"

"You might have been less of a growly prick to me," I say, trying to steer the conversation away from what feels like something bigger than what I'm ready to face.

"I'm serious, Summer. I'm not sure why you keep talking about our jobs like it matters. We're not doing anything wrong. I think Doctor Douche has you scared that there's something shameful about being with another person. That you need to hide something you don't."

Well, shit. Is he right? I flip through the mental Rolodex of my past relationships.

I've never taken guys out with me. Never introduced them to my family. Once Willa straight out asked me if I was gay before assuring me she'd be cool with that.

Maybe the early input of thinking I needed to hide a relationship with genuine feelings made me believe that was true.

"I . . . well . . . fuck."

He squeezes me and nuzzles against the back of my head. "I've always done whatever I want. Never been big on what other people think I should be doing. I imagine a person somewhere in between the two of us would be ideal, because I've probably burned a few bridges along the way."

I snort at that. "You're probably not wrong. I—" I start to protest, but he cuts me off.

"What if you stopped worrying about everything that could go wrong and just let yourself enjoy how right this feels?"

He presses a wet kiss to my back and my body comes alive as his calloused palms slip over my soapy skin in the most sensual way. My head tips back and I sigh at the feel of him playing my body with such finesse.

It does feel right.

"I'll burn more bridges to take a kick at the can with you, Summer. Give me a shot."

My lashes open and close rapidly. My heart is flipping

over something that my brain can't quite process. My can feels thoroughly kicked by everything he's just said. My tongue is also thoroughly tied.

Rhett just leaves it, though, carrying on. "You said once that you'd become a personal trainer?"

I go still. Did I mention that? "I don't remember that."

"I do. I read between the lines. I've seen you work out. I've seen how hard you work and how reliable you are. If you could do anything as a job, would it be what you're doing right now? What Kip does?"

I roll my lips together, grateful that I don't have to face anyone right now. "Probably not." My voice cracks when I confess it.

"Then why do you do it? Why keep up the charade?"

I exhale. "It's not . . . it's not a charade. It's just, I enjoy seeing my dad happy. I know how proud he is of me. I know he likes having me at the office with him even though he acts like a psycho prick sometimes. He fractured his family to keep me. He gave up so much, and when I got sick, he dropped everything to be with me every day. I just feel like living up to some of those things for him is the least I can do, you know? I just feel like . . . God, this sounds terrible to say, but I feel like if it wasn't for me, his life would be so much easier. And if I can help him by being a part of the business he's spent his life building, if I can carry that on for him, well, that's the least I can do to repay him."

Rhett doesn't respond. He just keeps stroking my arm. "I can't speak for Kip, only the way he's talked about you and your sister over the years in passing. And he may be a psycho prick, but he doesn't strike me as the type of man who expects repayment for time spent with his daughter."

My eyes sting, and I nod. There's a little voice at the back of my people-pleasing head that's screaming *yes!* I think I know deep down that Rhett is right, but facing that also means facing that I've spent the last several years of my life relentlessly chasing a dream that isn't actually my own.

A breath whooshes out of me and I drop my chin to my chest, squeezing my eyes together tight, wanting to put that wall back up in my mind that Rhett just came crashing through.

This time, he kisses the back of my neck, lips moving against my wet skin as he whispers, "Let's go to bed."

He stands behind me, gathering our towels, while I sit in the draining tub, watching the water swirl in a cyclone. A perfect reflection of how I'm currently feeling inside.

Shaken up. Spinning. Thoroughly not myself and yet, more myself than I've ever felt.

"Summer?"

When I glance up at Rhett, in all his rugged glory, the tips of his long hair wet and dripping over his toned shoulders, a shiver runs down my spine. He's holding a towel open for me, and all I want to do is go to him.

So, I do. I stand, feeling the water slip off me like a skin I've shed. Like Rhett somehow scrubbed loose memories and hang-ups with that washcloth. When I step out of the tub, I expect him to drop his gaze over my body, but he takes a deep dive into my eyes.

I don't know why I didn't expect him to do that. He's

been nothing short of respectful. Is it the reputation? His look? The toe-curling things he says?

It seems unfair of me to think he'd be anything short of a gentleman. Small-town cowboy, rough around the edges, with a womanizing reputation, and he treats me better than any man ever has. Than any person has.

I sigh sleepily when he wraps the towel around my shoulders. But he doesn't leave it at that. He gently dries me. My hair, my neck, my back. He kneels beside me and dries my legs with so much care. I think he dries me better than I usually dry myself.

But he does place a gentle nip on the cheek of my ass before he stands back up, a boyish grin on his face and a devilish glint in his eye. "Go lie down." He points at the bed, and where I'd usually give him lip, I just go.

Because I want to. Because I don't *have* to fight him anymore. Because I don't want to fight him anymore.

When I get to the bed, I flop face down, feeling like I could fall asleep in place, on top of the bed, wrapped in a towel. I let my eyes shut, but after a few beats, they flutter open.

The towel is pulled off me. I hear the squeeze of lotion and the rasp of Rhett's palms rubbing together.

Those warm, calloused hands slide up over my bare back, and I moan because it feels good, but mostly because I can't get enough of Rhett touching me the way he does.

"I feel like I should be the one massaging you."

"I feel like you're wrong," he husks. And I melt into the bed, soaking up this side of him I didn't even know existed. Sweet, and tender, and swoony.

Somehow, the fact he looks so rough and tumble makes the swoon more intense. He doesn't look like a soft man, one to pull out pretty words or take you on lavish dates.

He is nothing like any man I've been with.

And that's a blessing.

"I love your freckles," he murmurs from behind me, the pad of his finger tracing lines across the expanse of my back. "They remind me of all the constellations. Like I could draw lines between them, and pictures would appear."

It's such an oddly worshipful thing to say. I wiggle my toes, hum softly, and tip my cheek against the bed to gaze back at him.

"Right here, there are two so close together they almost look like one."

"Like binary stars," I murmur.

"What are binary stars?" His finger tenderly swipes across the spot he's talking about.

"It's two stars that look like one to us when we see them in the sky. But really, they're two. Stuck together by a gravitational pull, always orbiting one another."

"Kind of like the two of us, stuck together," he muses.

It's that thought of us stuck together tumbling through my fading consciousness that leads into the sound of my phone buzzing on the bedside table.

Which leads to Rhett taking his hands off me.

Which leads to my stomach dropping, because what Rhett says next is, "It says Rob calling."

I push up on my elbows and look over my shoulder at Rhett.

"Why is he calling you?"

"I don't know," I say honestly. However, if I had to guess, it would be something to do with Rhett winking at me before *and* after his ride tonight. Tonight's event was broadcast, which means it's feasible that someone would have seen that. That someone being Rob, who used to give me tummy flutters when he called. But right now, regarding the lit screen of my phone in Rhett's hand, all I feel is dread.

"I don't want to talk to him," I say, flipping over and sitting up, pulling my towel back around myself. It opens up a jar of worms I'm not ready to show Rhett yet. I need to figure out where this is going before I go down that path and expose everything.

Rhett pushes the phone at me, his face hard and unreadable. "Answer it."

I quirk a brow at him, wondering if he can truly handle this. Based on the way he flew off the handle over Emmett, my guess is no. But I'm not in the mood to argue, so I push myself up to the top of the bed to lean against the headboard and take the phone from Rhett's hand. Without looking him in the eye, I swipe the screen to answer. "Hello?"

Rhett flops down on the bed beside me.

"Summer?" Rob asks, his voice polished and smooth. It doesn't make my hair stand on end at all. It doesn't sound rough and sexy, like tires crunching on gravel.

"Yeah." Obviously. Who the hell else would it be? "What's up? Is something wrong?"

"Why does something always have to be wrong for me to call you?"

My face pinches and my eyes roll. A year ago, that might have sounded sweet to me, now it just sounds stupid.

"You shouldn't be calling me at all."

Rhett's head turns in my direction, and I feel his gaze on me like a touch.

"I know," Rob says. Though I barely hear him over the rush of awareness Rhett's spurring on in me.

"Okay, so—" I stifle a squeal as Rhett suddenly reaches over and lifts me on top of him. My towel falls away, and I'm straddling Rhett Eaton, buck naked, his hands gripping my hips while he looks over my body like it might be his next snack.

"Sorry," I breathe, trying to not sound as shocked as I feel. "I, uh, dropped my phone." Rhett quirks a brow and then holds one finger up over his lips in the universal sign for *shh*.

I'm momentarily confused.

And then his hands push up on my hips, right as he pushes himself down the bed, lining his face up with my . . .

"Oh, God," I murmur, staring down into Rhett's honeyed irises. All trouble and promise. I widen my eyes at him, as if to say, *Are you fucking kidding me right now?*

But Rhett's mouth twists in a devilish smile.

"Everything okay?" Rob asks, which is right when Rhett's hands take hold of my hips, as though they're handles, and pulls my pussy down onto his stubbled face.

I suck in a breath and let my eyes go wide in their

sockets as Rhett spears me with his tongue. I can't look away. "Yeah, yeah. Sorry, just, uh, clumsy."

I think Rob laughs, but I'm not really listening. I'm too busy watching the bad boy between my legs do something very, *very* bad.

"Where are you right now?"

My brain stutters as Rhett sucks at my core. "In my hotel room." It's not my room, it's Rhett's. But I feel like I belong here, and based on the look in Rhett's eye, he likes the sound of it too.

"So, listen, I wanted to talk to you. Just check on you," Rob prattles on awkwardly, and it should be awkward for him, even if he doesn't know what's going on right now.

"Hm," I hum and let my eyes shutter when Rhett drags the pointed tip of his tongue over my clit.

"I saw you at the hospital the other day. With that bull rider."

"Rhett," I try to say his name, but it truly sounds like more of a moan. His strong hands grip my ass as he grinds me down onto his face.

"Yeah. Whatever." Rob sounds vaguely annoyed by the mention of his name, which kind of pisses me off. So, I swivel my hips onto Rhett's face, getting off on the way he groans happily when I do.

Fuck Rob for never doing this for me. He had no issue with me taking him in my mouth, and I'm not sure why I never saw the inequity in that. But I see it loud and fucking clear now.

"You need to be careful with men like that."

My body coils, that line up my inner thigh pulling tight

as Rhett's hands trace my torso with so much desire. I could just melt onto him and stay here forever.

"Men like what, Rob?" I bite out, my voice thick. I raise off Rhett's face, suddenly worried I might suffocate him, but when I stare down, all I see is victory in his eyes and my wetness shining on his beard as he licks at his lips.

It's lewd.

And I love it. So, I sit back down, tangling a hand in Rhett's hair and tugging at the roots.

"You know, Summer. Not like us." Has he always been such a pretentious prick? "Uneducated. Unruly. Just a different breed."

A protective streak lurches up in me. Rob thinks he can treat me the way he has and then insult Rhett? Continue to make it impossible for me to carry on with my life?

Fuck him.

"You know what he is, Rob?" I'm panting now, and I'm not entirely sure how he hasn't figured out that I'm not just sitting politely in my hotel room alone.

Guess you can be a doctor and still be stupid.

Rhett's tongue and lips work furiously between my legs, and he has me barreling toward release. And I'm not even resisting. I'm chasing it now.

"He's the breed that's man enough to eat pussy."

"Excuse me?" Rob sputters on the other end of the line, but it's Rhett's wide eyes I'm looking down into as I ride his face. And when his teeth graze my clit, I explode.

"Ahh! Rhett!" I click the side of the phone to hang up as I toss it and collapse forward on to the bed, bowled over by what feels like a tidal wave of scalding hot water covering me. My body trembles and shakes. I fall apart and love every second of my undoing.

All I can hear is the two of us panting for a few beats until Rhett breaks the silence.

"Well shit, Princess." He slaps my ass as I flop down beside him. "I hope that was as satisfying for you as it was for me."

I giggle. I can't help it. I think Rhett Eaton may have just melted a few of my brain cells. A few of my boundaries as well, because that was way, way, way out of left field for the polite, people-pleasing version of Summer.

"It really was." I throw an arm over my face to hide the blush building because of what I just did. What I just *said*. "But also, so goddamn rude, Rhett Eaton."

He completely ignores my scolding in favor of asking, "Do you think he heard you scream my name?" The glee in his voice isn't remotely concealed.

I giggle again and my other arm joins the first, covering my face from what was both an invigorating and somewhat embarrassing experience. "God. I don't know."

Rhett chuckles, his hands propped across his bare chest now. He's all smiles as he shakes his head and stares up at the ceiling. "I hope so. I think I get off on other people hearing you scream my name."

I grin and flop over onto my stomach, burying my face in the pillows because I think I might get off on it too. I want to dig a hole and crawl in there to hide, but I also want to burst out laughing because Rhett pushes all the boundaries I thought I had.

He's not ashamed, more like he's proud of me and

wants everyone to know I'm hooking up with him. Which is an altogether new experience.

I mull that over, feeling him get off the bed and hearing him shuffle around behind me. When he gets back on the bed beside me, he says, "I figured out what the freckles on your back spell."

"Oh, yeah?" I squeak out.

"Yeah."

I feel a fine point on my back. "Are you drawing on me?"

"No, I'm writing on you."

"What are you writing?" I laugh because it's ridiculous. I feel like I'm in junior high all over again.

His responding chuckle is low and deep. It makes my stomach flip and my core tingle. "You'll have to go look."

Rhett sounds so satisfied, so smug, and when I turn and glance back at him, his expression is a perfect match.

"Fine," I say, clambering off the bed. I pad into the bathroom, the one that still smells like lavender Epsom salts, and turn my back to the mirror. I give him a curious look as he watches me from the edge of the bed, and then I turn back to see what he's written.

He's connected the freckles to say *Mine*.

And God, in this moment, I feel like that might be true.

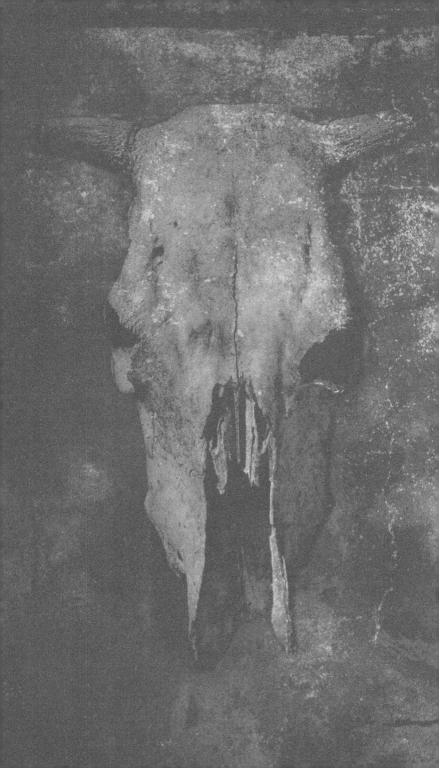

25

Rhett

Rhett: Come to my room.

Summer: No. I'm not tiptoeing around your dad's house and having sex with you on the same floor as him. That's tacky.

Rhett: There is no one I'd rather be tacky with.

Summer: My answer is still no.

Rhett: I'll come to your room. We won't be on the same floor that way. Everyone wins.

Summer: You're an animal.

Rhett: We can call it a team meeting.

Summer: You're going to call having sex a team meeting?

Rhett: Team building?

Summer: What are we building? LOL.

Rhett: Rapport.

Summer: Nice try.

Rhett: Will you at least send me a nude so I can jerk off all sad and alone?

Summer: You're pathetic. Wanna go for a midnight drive in the rust bucket? Look for the constellation that spells MINE? ;)

Rhett: Yeah. If I get you down on all fours, I'll find that one for sure.

"So, how's traveling together been going?" my dad asks over a mouthful of food from beside me. Table manners are a lost art in this house. It was enough for my dad to get a full meal down in front of three young boys. Well, four young boys, considering Jasper might as well be one of us for how much he hung around.

He's here tonight too. Made the trip out of the city for Sunday dinner before Beau deploys again.

"Anyone going to answer me?" Harvey prods.

I glance at Summer, who's at the opposite end of the table from me, wide-eyed, fork frozen in mid-air.

I almost laugh. She's a terrible liar.

"Great." I shrug and stare down at my spaghetti and meatballs. Cade may be a grumpy asshole. But he's a grumpy asshole who can cook.

"Yeah?" Beau asks, a curious smirk on his face. "The wild child treating you well, Summer?"

She promptly fills her mouth with a forkful of noodles, nodding with an awkward high-pitched laugh, before she points at her mouth apologetically, like that's the reason she's not answering.

Her eyes dart to mine. And I laugh. I can't help it.

"He's running you into the ground, isn't he?" Beau asks. Bless him. He's so sweet, he doesn't realize the button he's pressing. Cade does though. I can tell by the way he's glaring at me across the table.

It's hard to tell what type of scowl this is, but I think it might be one that says *You're not seriously fucking your agent's daughter, are you?*

I'm not so sure my dad is fooled either.

Me? I don't care. If I cared what they thought, I'd have stopped riding bulls years ago. I'd be happy to sit next to Summer and sling my arm across the back of her chair. But I know she's not there yet. Unlike me, Summer really, *really* cares what people think.

Summer lifts her napkin, primly dabbing at her lips as she takes a deep breath. I watch them flatten and fill back out under the pressure of her fingers and have to shift myself on the chair to accommodate the way my cock is expanding in my pants.

She smiles serenely at my brother. "No, everything has been absolutely fine. Very uneventful. When do you deploy? I'm assuming we'll see you all at the final rodeo weekend?" She looks around the table innocently. But I know her comment is anything but innocent. "It's just in the city. I'm sure you're all capable of driving to support Rhett."

That draws a lot of dropped eye contact and increased rates of chewing. I'm not surprised. My family doesn't support me in this venture. It's not a new conversation for me at this point.

"Sorry, Sum." My eyes narrow at Beau, shortening her name like he knows her well enough to do that. "I'm heading out early this week. Dad and I are making it a road trip across the country."

But Summer is a fixer. Summer supports the people she loves. I'm sure she can't quite wrap her head around this. So, she just continues to stare at everyone expectantly.

"I'll come!" Luke squeals. "I wanna be a bull rider, just like Uncle Rhett!"

Summer smiles. "Great, I can take y—"

"No." Cade's voice is downright arctic. This is not a conversation he likes to have. Not at all.

It's Jasper from beneath the brim of his team cap that takes over the conversation. "I'll join you, Summer. I live close to the arena, and we're off that night."

She perks up with a terse nod, rolling her shoulders back and glaring at my dad and brothers.

"Wouldn't matter if you had a game. You could take the night off. That's how far y'all are from clinching a playoff spot." Beau guffaws at his own joke.

Jasper rolls his eyes, shakes his head, and mutters,

"Fuckin' dick." His voice holds no venom though. Jasper and my middle brother are best friends, the kind most of us never get to have. Practically brothers. God knows Jasper needed someone.

Or a few someones. And those someones turned out to be the Eaton boys.

"Well," Beau exclaims, clapping his hands together, "who's up for a field trip to The Spur? I want to dance with Summer before I leave."

My teeth grind as I glare at my brother.

"You're gonna ruin your teeth doing that, son." Harvey slings a hand across the back of my chair and grins at me. It's a creepy grin. A knowing grin.

"Thanks, Dad."

"Any time. You know I'm a well-spring of good advice." He leans in closer while everyone else launches into talking about plans for later tonight. His voice goes lower. "That's why I'm going to give you this little tidbit of advice: cool your jets. If you ever have something that no one else wants, you gotta ask yourself where the value is."

I look over at my dad, face smushed together in confusion. "What?"

He smiles wistfully, observing everyone around the table. "It never mattered whose eyes were on your mom. Because her eyes were always on me." He pats my shoulder and then leans back into his chair, leaving me staring down at the old oak table beneath my elbows. The lines in the wood a testament to all the meals I've had in this exact spot over the course of my life.

While lively conversation rolls on around me, I think about my mom. I think about Summer.

And when I glance over at her, her eyes are on *me*.

I decide to take my dad's advice. To stop beating my chest like a fucking gorilla every time someone so much as looks Summer's way. I decide to sit back at The Spur and soak her up. Beau and Cade grabbed the couches on the raised part of the bar. It's the same spot they always take, and magically it's never in use.

I think we're just well-liked enough in town to warrant a special spot. Beau got here before Summer and I did, but I wouldn't be surprised if someone else moved from the table when they saw him walk in.

That, or Cade scowled at them and sent them scampering off.

Either way, from where I'm seated, I have a perfect view of the space they clear for a dance floor on Honky Tonk Sundays. I'm pretty sure it's just a way to get people out on Sunday nights—and it works.

Old school country music, line dancing, two-stepping. Chestnut Springs is a small enough town, but it's not all cowboys and ranchers. Which is why it always cracks me up to see people playing cowboy dress-up on Sunday nights.

Eric, the financial advisor from the bank, has a huge silver buckle on his belt and is wearing a fucking bolo tie.

This guy hasn't set foot outside a shiny clean bank in years, and I know he grew up attending a private school in the city.

Laura is here, so obviously trying to catch my eye that I almost feel bad for her. The second-hand embarrassment is thick. Unlike Cade, who mean-mugs every woman who approaches him and turns his back on them like that might make them disappear, I have a hard time turning women away.

Not in a physical sense, because I've spent many a night snuggled up to a woman at a bar just because I feel bad shutting them down. Even though nothing more than that happened, of course, all it takes is one photo of me with them for it to hit the internet and speculation to blow up.

That said, I've never felt like I needed to shut them down. I didn't owe anyone anything, and I wasn't hurting anyone.

But watching Summer two-stepping awkwardly with Beau right now, laughing and stumbling on each other's feet, my chest twists.

I'm not sure how I fell so hard, and so fast. I'm not sure of anything, really. My career. My health. But I'm pretty fucking sure Summer is a game-changer in more ways than one.

I'm also pretty sure I'm done being mature and watching my brother dance and enjoy my girl. I slam my beer bottle on the table and unfold myself from the couch. Cade gives me a speculative scowl, and I ignore him as I turn and stride to the dance floor.

I catch Summer's eye from over Beau's shoulder, and

she smiles at me. My stomach drops. The tips of my fingers itch to touch her—and fuck—those lips.

We've been back for half a day and not kissing her is driving me crazy.

After an entire season of wanting nothing more than to be at home, I suddenly want to be on the road, only because I get to be alone with Summer when I am.

My hand clamps down on Beau's shoulder. "I'm going to cut in now."

He looks over his shoulder with a grin. A knowing grin. *Fucking shit disturber.*

Beau acts like a goof, but the fact of the matter is, you don't get the level of clearance he has by being a doofus. Nah, he's a hell of a lot smarter than he lets on. And sometimes I wonder if he's a hell of a lot more fucked up than he lets on, too.

"Sure thing, baby bro." He claps me on the back and holds Summer's hand out to mine before turning away with a wink. Hopefully, to go keep a miserable looking Cade company and scare Laura away from talking to him too.

I step in front of Summer, sliding one hand around her waist and linking my fingers with hers before gazing down at her bright eyes and flushed cheeks. She looks happy. "Having fun?"

"Yes," she breathes. "I haven't been out dancing in forever." I lead her into an easy two-step, having had a lot more practice at country bars than Beau. I know how to lead without looking like a total buffoon. "It makes me miss Willa."

"Who is Willa?" I lean down closer, wishing I could

Thanos this place—snap my fingers and make everyone else disappear.

"My best friend. You'd like her." Summer snorts. "She's sort of the female version of you."

"Maybe that's why you handle me so well."

"Handle you? Rhett Eaton, I don't think anyone can truly handle you. I'm just along for the ride."

"Fuck yeah, you are."

She huffs out a laugh, and I feel her breath against my neck. The dress she's wearing is tight and scrunched up over her torso, and then soft and flowing around her legs. It's begging for me to flip it up and bend her over.

"I met Willa taking riding lessons. When I got sick again and had to quit, she kept coming to visit me in the hospital. Just never stopped. Sharing pictures, videos. I'm pretty sure we even watched you ride together."

Her head tips down shyly when she admits that.

"Does she know about us?" Us. That was a stupid thing to say. There's not an "us" yet. *Yet.* But I don't need to terrify Summer while I work on that *yet.*

But she doesn't seem scared. She just presses her lips together and looks up into my eyes. The song changes to something slower, and she automatically steps into me, lining our hips up and sliding her hand over my shoulder to wrap both arms around my neck.

"No. Well, not really. I believe a few weeks ago her suggestion was that I should—how did she put it—*ride you like a bucking bronco.*"

My dick twitches.

I lean down to whisper something in her ear but can't

resist pressing a kiss there first. "I approve of this friendship."

She giggles and runs her fingers up the base of my scalp, through my hair like she always seems to enjoy. "Careful. People here are going to think the infamous bachelor Rhett Eaton is taken."

I chuckle and spare a glance out to the bar.

"People are definitely looking," she murmurs.

I pull one hand up and shuck her chin back toward me. "Good. Let them look."

She just blinks at me. And I hate that anyone has ever made her feel like she isn't worth being seen with. Like she's some dirty secret to hide.

"They're going to talk."

"Then let them talk. You know I don't give a fuck what people think, Summer. And there is no one I'd rather ruin my reputation with."

With one hand still gripping her chin, I kiss her.

Fuck these people. Fuck *Rob*. Fuck her shitty sister. Fuck anyone who would make this woman feel like anything less than she is.

She stiffens at first—shocked—but when her fingers go back to moving in my hair and her lips slide against mine, I know I have her permission to keep going. To keep ruining my reputation, right here and now, with her.

If I were paying attention to anything other than the woman in my arms, I'd hear the hearts of girls breaking and the sound of my brothers whooping and laughing.

But all I hear is the pounding of my heart and the sweet

sighing noise Summer makes when my tongue dances with hers.

We stand here. In plain view. Kissing. In the middle of a makeshift dance floor. No doubt raising some eyebrows. Making a statement.

Doing what we want rather than what we should.

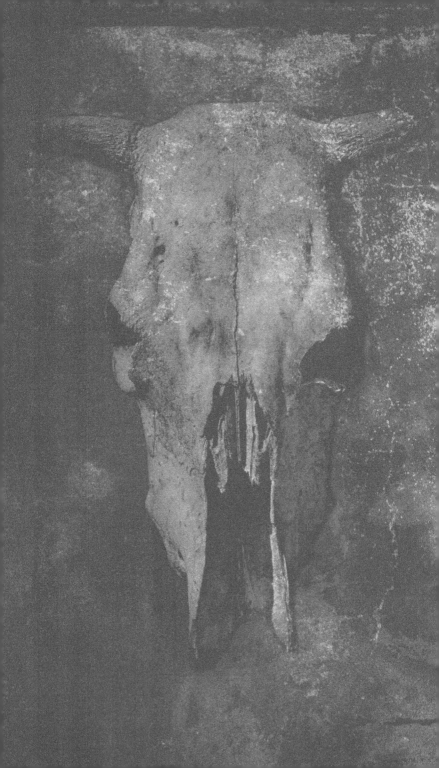

26

Rhett

Summer: Wanna go for a midnight drive?

Rhett: Now who's the animal?

Summer: Still you. I'm the princess.

Rhett: Fuckin' right you are. *My* princess.

Summer: Okay, Neanderthal. Meet outside? Bring a condom.

Summer: Actually, a few condoms.

Rhett: I just bought a whole box. You should have seen the look I got from the cashier.

Summer: Great. We'll probably be in the town newspaper tomorrow.

Rhett: What a headline that would be.

Summer: Gross. Are we going out or what?

Rhett: Wear one of those prissy skirts, but no panties. Meet at the rust bucket.

"What is this?" Summer places a gift bag in the middle of the table where I'm sitting, enjoying a coffee by myself. I'm feeling a little wrung out after saying goodbye to Beau this morning. He and my dad hit the road together to drive back to Ottawa, and while Summer's been at the gym, I've spent the last hour wondering if how I feel about saying goodbye to my brother is how they all feel every time I leave for an event.

"It's a bag, Summer."

I wonder how Summer feels when she watches me get onto the back of an angry bull. I don't know why, but I've never spent a lot of time considering how my job might make everyone else feel. I've been too busy not caring about what anyone thinks.

And trying not to terrify myself with the realities of this sport.

She juts out her hip and quirks her head, causing her

thick ponytail to flop down her slender neck. The flyaways over her forehead stick to her damp skin after her workout. "No shit, Eaton."

"Where'd it come from?"

I give her a lopsided smirk. "Me."

She rolls her lips together, appraising me. "What is it?"

We've spent the last few days stealing kisses in the hallway. Or driving my old truck out into the field to sink into each other under the open sky. It's romantic as fuck. It's also the best sex I've ever had.

While I've mostly convinced Summer to buck the rules, she's a real stickler for "not banging in your dad's house" and is still convinced she needs to hide what we're doing for some stupid reason—even though everyone knows what we're doing.

I've never been more motivated to get my own place so I can bend her over whenever I please.

"I don't know how you fancy types do gifts, but 'round here you find out what the gift is when you open it."

Her mouth turns down at the corners. "I don't have anything to give you."

I laugh. That's such a Summer thing to say, always worrying about everyone else.

"I don't want anything, Princess. It's a gift, just because. Now sit that fine ass down and open it."

Her head bobs from side to side as she pulls the chair out. "Well, I do love presents," she murmurs, eyes lighting as she pulls at the tissue paper I shoved in there kind of haphazardly.

When she reaches into the bag, she stills, eyes darting over to me. In a flash, she's tugging everything out.

With the chaps free of the bag, she makes this satisfied little sighing sound. "Rhett."

I sip at my coffee and enjoy watching her, every little drop of excitement that plays across her face. I've never gotten off on giving someone a gift quite like I'm enjoying this right now.

"Do you like them?"

"Do I *like* them? Are you kidding me? I *love* them. But these are from the first rodeo we went to?"

I shrug.

"Did you order them or something?"

"Nope."

"You bought them while we were there?"

"Yup."

Her mouth opens and closes as she holds them up again. They really are beautiful. The craftsmanship is top of the line. So was the price tag. When she surged ahead of me, I purchased them as fast as I could.

But it's not a completely unselfish gift. I'm dying to see her in them.

"Why?"

"Where else would you find a nice pair of child-sized chaps?"

She rolls her eyes.

"I got them because I saw you staring at them. I saw the look on your face. And then you told me you had to quit riding when you got sick. I thought you'd want to start again at some point. Maybe out here. With me. Then I saw you on my horse—a fucking natural—and I knew I'd made the right call."

She blinks at me, eyes shinier than they were seconds ago. Her smile is watery as she stares down and runs her dainty fingers over the polished silver studs. "I thought you hated me then."

I shake my head, a little sheepish over what a growly prick I'd been to her. "The only thing I hated was how badly I wanted you, Princess."

"Thank you." She says it so earnestly, it tugs on strings I didn't know exist. Those big brown soulful eyes—fuck—I'd do anything she wants me to. I'm an absolute goner for this girl, and I never even saw her coming.

"You're welcome." My voice is gruff, and I know I need to tell her what this is too. To tell her things I've been thinking about. Like that once the season is over, once I'm not a client to her, I'm going to commit my entire off-season to convincing her to give me a shot. A real shot.

A shot to be everything.

But I chicken out, not sure I can handle a rejection, or another person leaving me. Especially not one who's rapidly become as important to me as Summer is. So instead, I just say, "Put them on, then you can thank me on your knees."

Summer grumbles as I lead her up the stairs, her hand wrapped in mine so damn perfectly. Her grumbles are half-hearted and done with a small smile. Something about if the press found out I'm a sex addict, they'd have a field day.

When we get to my room, I shut the door and give her a little push into the sprawling space. Wood beam ceilings boast an antler chandelier hanging over a four-poster pine bed. Big sliding doors open onto a spacious second-floor patio, which holds a small wrought iron bistro set looking out over the range, pointed right at the Rocky Mountains.

"Wow," she breathes, struck by the view. She stops and stares. "Why the hell do you have your coffee downstairs with a view like that?"

I watch her as she admires the scenery—the slender column of her neck, the sharp angle of her jaw, dainty ear adorned with an understated gold stud. Summer is all class. All shiny and proper and well-educated.

It's fucking hot. It also makes me want to dirty her up a bit.

"The view downstairs has been better lately."

She shoots me a playful look, pursing her lips and shaking her head.

"Show me the chaps." I take a step back and point at the custom leather in her hand.

Summer turns to face me. "I'm wearing workout clothes. These need jeans." She holds them up in my direction.

"They need nothing. Lose the clothes. Let me see." I jut my chin in her direction.

Her dark eyes flare. "You want me to put them on with nothing under them?"

"Fuck yeah, I do."

Her cheeks turn pink right before my eyes. "I haven't had a shower. I'm all sweaty."

"Don't much care, Princess." I cross my arms over my chest. "Fully intend to get you all sweaty right now anyway."

Her cheeks twitch as she glances away momentarily. Shy but . . . eager.

She drops the chaps on the wooden floor with a heavy thud, rolling her lips together. The pink stain on the apples of her cheeks deepens to match the rose color of her lips.

She undresses, and I watch her like a total voyeur. She's literally just undressing and not even trying to be sexy. It's just that it's *her*, and everything she does is sexy to me.

Work out tank top and bra, gone. Perky golden tits pop out with a playful bounce. A sprinkling of freckles dust the tops of them, and I'd like to trace every one. Write *mine* on each of her tits.

She peels off the tight-as-fuck leggings, bending over to clear her ankles and toes, and tosses them toward the pile of gym clothes beside her before straightening and looking at me. All curves, soft lines, and toned muscle.

"Like this?" she breathes out, puffy lips parted, eyes a little hooded.

"No panties? Yeah. I agree with you about the view up here. Far superior."

She gives me a shy smile in return, and I stride forward, needing to be close to her. Needing contact. I slide my hands over her hips and the globes of her round ass as I drop to my knees in front of her. "You're too fucking much. Too pretty. Too good."

"No, you are." Her hand cups my cheek, fingernails rasping over my stubble. "I think I've wasted enough time with men who aren't good enough to know that you are better than good. More than enough."

I close my eyes and soak that up for a moment. Hearing that I'm enough for someone like Summer. I didn't know how badly I needed to hear that.

All I can do is shake my head, press a kiss to her stomach, and reach for the chaps beside her. I hitch them around her waist, feeding the soft leather strap through the buckle, watching the silver detailing glint beneath her hip bones.

Wrapping one loose piece of leather around her leg, I start the zipper at the top and pull it down, careful not to catch any bare skin as I go. When I move to the opposite side, I notice a light tremor in my hand and shake my head again.

Summer threads her fingers in my hair as I pull the zipper all the way down. I lean forward and give the slit of her pussy one long, firm lick. Because I can't be this close to it and not pay it some attention.

Her fingers tighten in my hair, and she pulls me closer. My chest rumbles as I give her clit a good hard pull with my mouth.

"For a girl who's never had her pussy eaten, you've sure developed a taste."

She tenses, pushing my head back. "Is it too much?" Her eyes are wide as she looks down at me and whispers, "Oh shit, I'm sorry."

Grabbing at my shoulders, she tries to pull me up, but I

shove two fingers inside her already slick, warm hole. So ready for me. "Summer, stop. It's *never* too much. I'm the one who's developed a taste."

I lean forward again, on my knees for this girl, and give her another long, firm lick. "There is never too much of this. I'll eat this pretty pussy all day, every day, if it means I get to watch you squirm around and beg for my cock. I love doing this for you."

My fingers pump into her languidly as I suck hard at her clit, knowing I can get her close and then pull away to watch her get all flustered and huffy. Desperate.

I love that too.

When she leans on me, I pull away and stand, gripping her skull to plant a firm kiss on her mouth. "You see how fucking good you taste?" I slide my tongue into her mouth, swallowing the dirty moaning sound she makes at the back of her throat.

That's where I plan to go next.

I step away to get a better view. Sexy, fancy leather chaps, tits heaving, eyes a little glassy.

Fuck.

Yeah, I love this.

"Spin." I twirl my finger and watch her swallow heavily. "Let me see you."

Her lips roll together, and her nipples pucker even tighter at my command. I can see the wetness glistening on her bare cunt. If I look too long, though, I'll just toss her down and go to town.

She slowly turns, and I'm struck by a tightness in my chest. And when I watch the creases beneath that perfect peach-shaped ass as she spins, a painful tightness in my jeans too. Bare ass surrounded by soft leather. Yeah, my perverted mind is *racing*.

Facing me again, she hits me with a quirk of her lips. "How do I look?"

"Perfect." My voice is gravel.

"Yeah?" Her head tilts.

I curl a finger at her, urging her to come closer. Her bare feet pad toward me, and I reach for her chin, tipping her fresh face up to mine, heart stuttering in my chest. "Such a pretty fucking princess," I muse, letting a grin touch my lips. "And do you know where pretty princesses belong, Summer?"

"Where?" Her voice is soft, but thick.

I point to the hardwood floor below me. "On their knees."

Her eyes widen, but her lips roll together to hide a hungry smile. My girl likes it when I talk to her like this.

"Lose the shirt, Rhett," is her only response.

I grab the back of my neckline with one hand and tug hard, ripping it off and tossing it away. Her palms trace over my chest, gentle on my shoulders—still so careful with me. She smiles when her fingers tighten on the bulge of my bicep.

It makes my dick twitch. And then her hands are sliding down my torso as she lowers herself to the ground at my feet. And suddenly, she's rushing, hands fumbling with my fly like she can't get to my cock fast enough. Like she's starving. The view from above is fantastic. Dark shiny hair and perky, pointed nipples.

My cock springs up between us when she tugs my boxers down, and she wastes no time wrapping her hands around my girth, licking a flat tongue over the head while tipping her wide eyes up at me.

"Keep looking at me like that, and I'm going to blow on your face, Summer."

She giggles and does it again. "Good. Do it."

I growl, a deep, feral sound.

But she doesn't give me a chance. She opens wide and takes me to the back of her throat, humming as she goes.

My head falls back and I close my eyes. "Fuck, Summer."

She sucks me slow, but firm, hands working the base, head bobbing eagerly.

When I finally get my act together and chance a look down at her, I find her staring up at me with an almost worshipful expression on her face.

I slide a hand over the line of her jaw. "You love this, don't you?"

She hums and nods, head tilting into my hand a little.

My opposite hand wraps in her thick ponytail. "Touch yourself."

She blinks but removes one hand, sliding it down between her legs, eyes hooding when she gets there.

"That's it." I thrust into her mouth slowly, letting her focus on herself, watching her slide one finger in and pull it back out to swirl at her clit, lids fluttering as she does.

When her eyes close and she moans, I almost explode on the spot. I squeeze her ponytail tighter, holding her head still, and increase the speed of my thrusts into her mouth.

"What a good fucking girl you are. Fucking your fingers while I fuck your throat."

Her eyes flip up to mine instantly, going wide right as her chest and neck go pink. She looks like a little rodeo doll down in front of me. She cries out around my cock, body shaking as she comes apart beneath me.

And I'm the lucky son of a bitch that gets to watch. It's too much. I can't wait any longer. My hands are under her arms, and I'm picking her up, kicking off my pants, bending her over, pushing her face first onto my bed.

She crawls up onto all fours, baring herself to me, whimpering desperately. "Rhett, please."

I squeeze my cock hard in my fist, eyes glued to her pussy clenching and releasing with the aftershocks of her orgasm.

"Fuck. Summer. Hang on. I need a condom."

"No," she whines. "I want it. I want you. Just you." She glances at me over her shoulder, eyes wild and sparkly. I don't think she means to, but her back arches, which pushes her ass out toward me.

"I've never not used a condom," I say, licking my lips.

"I have an IUD. I'm clean."

My hands are on her ass, rubbing. Spreading. Back to shaking just a bit. My cock throbs like it never has before, and my bed puts her at the perfect height to slide into.

"Are you sure, Summer?" I ask, slipping two fingers into her dripping pussy.

"Yes. Yes, yes, yes," she chants, rocking her hips back toward me.

I groan and notch the thick head of my cock against her.

"More." Her slender fingers grip the sheets. She doesn't move, but she's begging me to.

I wrap my hands around her hips and push into her slowly, carefully. She always feels so small, and looking down, watching the way her body stretches to take me, just drives that fact home.

"Fuck," she breathes out. "That feels . . ."

"Incredible," I finish, savoring the feel of being bare inside her as I seat myself to the hilt. Skin on skin. Memorizing every pulse, every twitch and flutter. It's other-fucking-worldly.

"Again."

"Princess, I need a second. You should see how you look from here."

"Tell me." She wiggles against me, peeking over her shoulder again. Flushed cheeks, wisps of hair on her temples. A hungry gleam in her eye. I feel her pussy clamp down on my cock when she says, "Tell me how I look."

I growl, sliding one hand up her back, pressing her down onto the bed while the other hand grabs the back strap of her chaps and hikes her ass up, positioning her how I want her.

I pull out and thrust back in. "You look perfect."

"More."

I pump in and out of her, letting one hand trail down her spine. "I love this indent down your back. And this ass." I squeeze hard, gripping it and letting go, watching the white fingerprints turn pink and smiling when she wiggles it at me again. I give her one firm slap and hear the breath whoosh out of her lungs.

I reach between us and rub a finger against her pussy where it hugs my cock. A shiver races down her spine as I do. "You look like you were born to take my cock."

She moans. "Jesus, I love it when you say shit like that."

I smile victoriously and slam into her, watching her body shake with the force of my thrust. "Princess, you look like you were made for me."

Her voice is hushed when she responds. But I catch it all the same.

"I feel like I was made for you."

That's all it takes for me to unleash. I grip the leather strap around her waist with one hand, her ass with my other, and fuck her like she was made for me.

She doesn't crumble. She meets every stroke, arching her back and pushing in for more. Letting me take her farther, deeper, than I ever have.

Perspiration trickles down my temple, and her moans turn into screams. "You're going to take it, Summer. Take every fucking inch. And you're going to scream my name when you come."

Like it was a command, I feel her body shake and buck beneath me.

And when she screams my name as I spill myself inside her, surge after surge, I'm hit with a realization that sends me reeling.

Summer wasn't just made for me.

She's it for me.

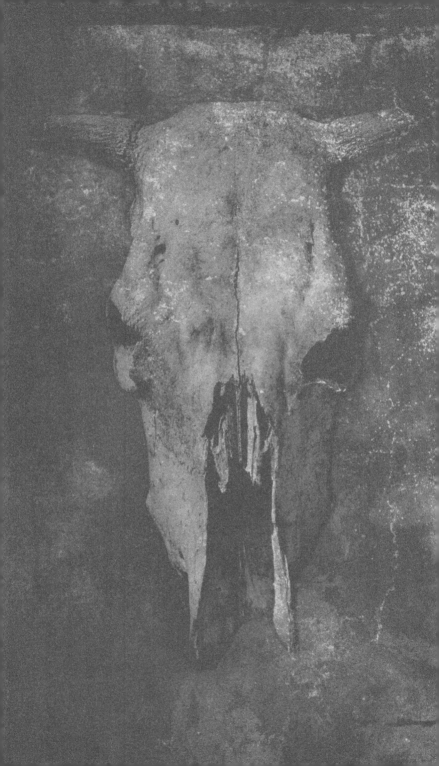

27

Summer

Summer: You going to come to the rodeo with me this weekend?

Dad: Wouldn't miss it. Beers are on me. Maybe some of those cinnamon mini donuts too.

Summer: Sounds healthy.

Dad: If this were my last moment on earth, I'd want to go with a beer in one hand and a mini donut in the other.

Summer: I hate you.

Dad: I love you too.

We step into the trendy downtown restaurant —all whites and silvers and modern lines— and Rhett looks out of place here. Frankly, I *feel* out of place here, like something inside of me has changed in the last couple months.

Before my time in Chestnut Springs, this was the type of place I would have loved to come for dinner. But spending long days in the prairies, seeing the mountains, being surrounded by people who value different things, well, I'm thinking they've rubbed off on me. That maybe my priorities have changed.

Rhett's hand bumps against mine as he peers around the restaurant. He's reached back for me without even looking, possibly without even thinking about it.

The girl who likes places like these pops up in my head, telling me I shouldn't hold his hand in public. That it's not appropriate. That I'll get one of us in trouble.

But the new girl—the windswept, sun-kissed girl with beautiful custom chaps who makes love in the back of a rusty old pickup in the middle of a field—doesn't give a fuck.

She tells me to slip my soft hand into Rhett's rough one and give it a squeeze.

When his cheek twitches, I know I listened to the right girl.

That smile is my kryptonite. And those hands. And that mouth, including the toe-curling things that come out of it. The dick, too. Big fan of Rhett Eaton's dick.

Actually, it would seem I'm just a big fan of Rhett

Eaton, and not the cocky cowboy everyone else gets to see. The man who kisses me sweetly, who makes me feel taken care of, like I'm not a burden—the one who's just a little bit vulnerable and insecure.

The man that no one else really sees. I'm not sure why he's opted to show me that side of himself, but I know I need to handle it with care. I know Rhett is far more sensitive than he lets on. His wounds run deep, and he's patched them with a public persona and a cocky grin that doesn't match the soulful man I've come to know.

"There he is." His opposite hand raises up in a salute, and he holds my hand tight as he strides across the room toward the table where Jasper is already seated.

Hilariously, Jasper doesn't look like he belongs here either. His scruffy beard covers most of his face, and his shaggy dark blond hair peeks out from under the team cap he's wearing.

"Hey, guys." Jasper's eyes drop to our intertwined hands and his lips press together. "Rhett, don't think I've ever seen you hold a girl's hand before," he continues as we pull out our chairs across from him.

I flush and pull my hand away, but the minute we're seated in the clear Lucite chairs, Rhett reaches across the space between us and grabs it again, thumb rubbing in reassuring strokes.

"Didn't know growing a playoff beard was a thing when you aren't even close to making the playoffs," Rhett deadpans.

Jasper smirks and dips his chin down to read the menu in front of him. "Vicious, little Eaton." He pops his head up just long enough to add, "Lovely to see you, Summer."

There's something different about Jasper. Something quiet and introspective. Something sweet, but also something very removed. I can't quite put my finger on him. The only thing I know is that I've heard my dad talk about goalies being a different type of athlete than your average hockey player.

"You too," I tell him honestly.

"Thanks for meeting us today," Rhett says. "I don't love dinners out before I ride."

Jasper grunts. "Yeah. I hear that. Playing on a full stomach makes me want to hurl."

My mouth twists. I'm in for an interesting evening of trying to make conversation with Jasper. At least it will distract me from the gnawing anxiety over Rhett riding again this weekend.

My phone rings loudly in my purse, much too loud in the quiet restaurant.

"Shit. Sorry guys." I rifle through my oversized purse, desperately hoping to find it and shut it up, silently chastising myself for dumping everything in here including receipts I'll never need.

My hand closes on the vibrating block and I pull it out right as the server comes to fill our tall, slender water glasses.

The name Doctor Douche flashes across my screen as I silence the ringer. My eyes shoot up to Rhett, who is staring at the phone in my hand looking equal parts amused and murderous.

"When did you do that?" I whisper.

"You left your phone unlocked one day," he mutters, peering just over my shoulder, looking like a scolded little boy who isn't sorry at all.

My mouth drops open, and I try to keep from laughing. "Really mature," I reply as I click the phone off and toss it back in my purse while shooting Jasper an apologetic glance. "Sorry about that. So, tell me, have you ever been to one of Rhett's events?"

"Not in a long time. Our seasons overlap and my schedule is usually packed with—"

My phone blares again, and I grimace, cringing internally as I yank my phone out again. I don't bother glancing at Rhett because I can tell by the set of his body next to mine that he's ready to break something.

We haven't talked much about what we are or where we're going. I want so badly to not be needy or clingy that I've been too afraid to ask. He hasn't told me anything, but his body says it all.

His body says I'm his.

When I pull out my phone this time, my sister's name flashes across the screen, which has my brow furrowing. She rarely calls me.

I shoot a concerned look at Rhett, whose expression tells me he's equally confused.

"Sorry, I'm just going to take this," I announce to the two men who respond with murmurs telling me to go ahead.

I slip my thumb across the screen and lift the phone to my ear. "Winter?"

"Summer, where are you right now?" Her voice is arctic, like usual, but there's also a thread of something else in there.

"I'm out for dinner."

"In the city or away?"

She's never taken an interest in where I am.

"I'm in the city. Winter, what's wrong?"

Rhett peers at me, concern etched on his face.

"Our dad had a heart attack."

My stomach plummets. "What?"

"It's very mild." She sniffs, and I can just imagine her inspecting her nails right now, like I'm some sort of simpleton because I didn't become a doctor. "He's going to be okay. But he's here at the hospital if you'd like to see him."

My heart thunders against my ribcage. "Of course, I want to see him!" The words come out more forcefully than I intend as panic seeps into my veins. "When did this happen?" I'm already standing, shoving my arms into my coat.

The guys are standing too, ready to follow, even though they don't know what's going on. A twinge pops up in my chest at knowing I have people who support me. It feels unusual, and despite the anxiety bubbling inside of me, their silent support soothes me.

"A few hours ago," Winter replies.

"Winter. Are you fucking kidding me? Dad had a heart attack a few hours ago, and you're just telling me now?"

"Don't be dramatic, Summer. It's not like there's

anything you could have done for him with a law degree," she scoffs, and tears sting my eyes.

"I could have been there with him! He's my dad too, Winter."

She sighs like I'm the most inconvenient person in the world to her. And I guess it's possible that I am. She didn't ask for this fucked up family tie. But neither did I, and I'm tired of being treated like I did.

"Well, he's here now. And he's fine. Staying a couple of days for observation. You're welcome to visit." She hangs up on me.

Rhett is talking to me, but all I see is white. White hot rage. Rage that I could have missed last moments with the only person who's ever really cared about me. Rage that Winter and my stepmother continue to treat me this way as an adult.

Rhett massages the back of my neck. "Let's go, Summer. I'll drive you."

"I'm sorry, Jasper," I say woodenly, trying to contain the anger bubbling beneath the surface.

He waves a hand at me. "Nothing to be sorry for. Go. Say hi to that nut for me."

I nod before Rhett ushers me out the door, straight to my vehicle, where he opens the passenger door and puts me in like I'm in some sort of coma. His motions are quick and efficient, full of worry—full of so much care.

He leans in and kisses my hair before slamming the door and bounding around to the driver's side. After he adjusts the seat and mirrors, he slings his hand over the back of my seat to reverse my car and says, "I'm against hitting women myself, but I fully support you decking your sister."

A dark laugh escapes me, and then, he hits the gas.

We fly into the cardiology wing. I recognize the mint-colored walls so well.

"Where is he?" My eyes narrow at my sister. She looks like a porcelain doll—pale blonde hair and perfect skin—next to me with all my freckles.

"He's speaking with the cardiologist. So, contain your tantrum." She flicks her hand up and inspects her nails. This is a way she insults me. Acting like her cuticles are more interesting than I am.

My voice shakes when I say, "I can't believe you didn't tell me." She sighs and glances over at the closed door to our dad's room. "Winter, what if it had been more serious? What if I'd missed my chance to be with him? All because...what?" My voice cracks and Rhett steps close behind me, his body firm and his hand steady at the small of my back.

Her eyes drop to where he's touching me, but she just blinks.

"Because you're carrying some vendetta against me for how I was conceived?" I continue. "You know I wasn't there for that, right? Didn't exactly have a choice in the matter. Did they cover that in medical school? Because that man in that room"—I point at the closed door—"he's all I've got. You and Marina have made sure of that. I'm not really certain what more you want from me."

Everything is spilling out of me, like this opened the dam, and I can't stop the water from gushing out. It's embarrassing.

It's cathartic.

Or it would be if Winter did anything other than stare at me blankly. She's so robotic, and I almost feel bad for her. *Almost.*

She brightens with a fake smile and moves her focus over my shoulder. "Oh, good. Rob, you're here."

Rhett stiffens behind me, and I freeze, refusing to turn around. In this moment, I realize that I've fucked up. Everything with Rhett moved too quickly, a blur of orgasms and lingering looks. I forgot about the world around us.

The world around me. And this is definitely something I should have told Rhett before walking into the hospital with him today.

When Rob Valentine strides into view, coiffed hair and collared shirt under some preppy sweater, I wonder what attracted me to him at all. Next to Rhett, he's just so . . . underwhelming.

"What the fuck is *he* doing here?" Rhett growls.

Winter's eyes widen and she rears back. "*He* is my husband. The question is, what are *you* doing here?"

"Hi, sweetheart." Rob pecks Winter on the cheek, obviously unaffected by her rude comment.

Now Rhett is stepping up, pushing an arm in front of me and guiding me behind him, using his body as a shield for me.

"Is this some sort of sick joke?" From behind Rhett's hulking frame, I see him turn his gaze on Rob, so slowly that it's almost eerie. A predator sizing up his prey.

I squeeze at his arm. "Can we please walk away now? I need to speak to you in private." My heart is pounding so hard that I can feel my chest vibrating. I'm always aware of my heart now. The change in rhythm, in intensity—I'll never not think about it.

And right now, it's pumping harder than I think it ever has. Because my deepest, darkest secret is dangerously close to seeing the light of day.

"No jokes here, fella." The way Rob says it is almost like he'd talk to a dog. And Rhett doesn't miss the insult. He strikes straight out.

"Preying on your teenaged patient wasn't bad enough? You had to turn around and marry her older sister?"

My stomach lurches into my throat. Fear immobilizes me, freezing me in place.

Everything feels like it's moving in slow motion. I'm grabbing at Rhett, feeling him moving forward. Kip's hospital room door is opening.

"Rhett, stop!" He doesn't hear me. I'm panicking now. This isn't how any of this was ever supposed to come out. "Rhett." I shake his arm. "Please stop."

"What?" Winter's skin is about the color of her hair. Her face is pale and drawn.

"Ignore the hillbilly, Winter. This is how people like him have fun. Let's go." He tries to pull his unmoving wife along with him.

Rob is so smug, so sure of himself, that he doesn't even

see it coming. Men like Rhett aren't a factor in his reality. Polite and restrained by social correctness when someone they care about has been hurt. It's all instinct and feeling.

Rhett's no hillbilly, he's more like a lion. And Rob is fucking with his pride.

It's why he doesn't hear me begging him to stop.

Rhett pushes his shoulders back. "Well, I'm sure glad that people like me don't get their kicks by breaking professional codes and spending years coercing young women into being a dirty little secret to save their own fucked up hide. People like me say what we mean." With a dark smile, he raises a finger and points right at Rob's face. "And you, *fella*, are the shit stuck to my boot."

My sister's mouth is slack. I can see thoughts rushing through her eyes. Everyone is watching. Their gazes itch on my skin, and I wish I could turn and run. Take Rhett with me and hide.

But I can't. Because Rob makes the stupidest decision he could make in this moment.

He rounds on me, eyes narrowed viciously, his voice pure venom. "You were supposed to keep your mouth shut."

It's a shitty thing to say to me, but I don't care much about Rob. It's my sister I can't peel my eyes from. She doesn't deserve this.

Rhett's arm shoots out in front of me again, and when his voice comes out, I hardly recognize it. It's so cold that a chill runs down my spine. "Talk to her like that again and I'll fucking bury you. And trust me, you won't be missed."

Rob waves a dismissive hand at him. "Down boy."

That's the wrong thing to say, because before I have a chance to beg Rhett to back down, he's pulled his arm back and is delivering a blow to Rob's shitty smug face.

"Rhett!" I shout right as blood spurts from Rob's nose, and the hospital around us buzzes to life. Nurses rush in, Rob bellows something about suing, and Winter stares at her husband like she's never seen him before. I feel the crack in my chest for her. She looks young. She looks lost.

I wish I could hug her.

As strained as our relationship is, she's still my big sister. And I'll never stop wishing for more with her.

My hands cover my mouth as I take in the scene before me, and when I turn to the right, I see my dad's open door, him sitting in his bed with pale skin and a grim expression on his face.

I press at my temples as I look up into Rhett's warm eyes.

"I'm sorry," he says as if he's just realizing the surrounding mayhem. "Fuck. I'm so sorry, Summer. I just . . . fuck. No one talks to you like that. No one. Not ever."

With a fat wad of gauze pressed to his nose, Rob butts in. "I'm going to take you for all you're worth."

I turn, holding a hand up, my patience fried. "Rob, *fuck off*. Go get your nose fixed and keep it where it belongs. Which is *not* in my business. You go after Rhett, and I'll start talking. So just shut up, okay?"

He shakes his head at me, like he can't believe the polite, pliant girl he's been stringing along for years just said that to him. And it's Winter who pulls him away. It's Winter who won't meet my eyes.

I turn my back on him, facing Rhett. "You need to leave."

"What?" He looks genuinely confused.

"Seriously, Rhett?" I whisper-shout. "This is a fucking mess. My dad is in the hospital, and you just dropped my biggest, most complicated secret in a very, very spectacular fashion. You need to leave. I'll talk to you later. I don't need you here doing the whole possessive thing right now."

Rhett blinks, a bit of color emerging under his stubble. After a deep sigh, he finally says, "Okay, fine." He steps in close, tipping my chin up, thumb taking one swipe just beneath my lower lip. "But I want to make one thing clear. I am not possessive. I am protective. And I'll never stop protecting you. I'd hit that fucker again in a heartbeat if it meant keeping him from talking to you that way."

I nod, a little overwhelmed by what he's just said, but too frazzled to do anything more. "Okay," is all I respond with.

I'm too flustered to work out my thoughts and feelings in this moment, and I fear what I'll find there. All I know is that I need to go be with my dad and clear my head.

Rhett leans in and presses a kiss to my forehead, the stubble rasping against my skin making my hair stand on end. He spins on his heel and strides out through the swinging doors. All the eyes in the room follow him.

Mine included.

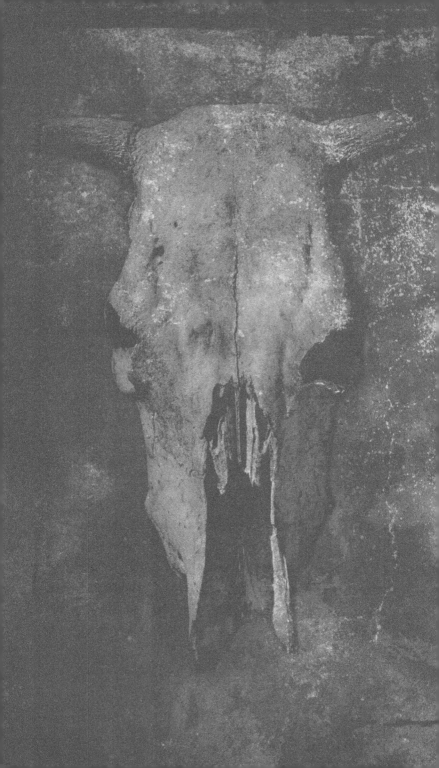

28

Summer

Rhett: I am so fucking sorry.

⟶⟵

"If I hadn't already had a heart attack today, that might have given me one."

I tip my head back against the back of the uncomfortable armchair angled in the corner of my dad's room and let my eyes flutter shut. "That isn't funny."

"Are heart problems contagious? Because I think you infected me."

I shake my head, lips quirking up at the corners. He's never let me live down asking that when I was young. I was worried about him getting too close or spending too much time around me, just in case my congenital heart defect was somehow contagious. "Still not funny."

"Do you think Rob's nose is broken?"

I sigh heavily. "I don't know. I'm not the doctor in this family."

"Does hoping it is make me a dick?"

I bark out a sad laugh now. Kip and I have this father-daughter relationship that borders on a friendship, and I wouldn't change it for the world. "You were already a dick."

"Yeah. That's true," he muses from the bed beside me. I peek an eye open at him. His dark hair is a little more mussed than usual, possibly even sporting a few more silver streaks than I remember. My dad looks . . . older. In a way I hadn't noticed until recently. I guess that happens when you creep up on your sixties.

But his mortality strikes me hard right now, laid up in a hospital bed, not looking like the suit wearing, tongue-wagging, shit disturber in a glossy office that he usually does.

My eyes sting as I study him. I roll my lips together to keep them from wobbling, to keep the shaky breaths inside.

When he looks over at me, I clamp my eyes shut. Squeezing them tight and willing away the tears building behind my lids.

"Summer, baby, come here. I'm okay." His voice is soft, so soothing. It tosses me right back into the long days spent in the children's ward with him at my side.

A sob lurches out of me, and he lifts an arm, gesturing me toward him. And as the tears spill out over the apples of my cheeks, I shuffle over and crawl into the narrow hospital bed and under my dad's arm. Even over the terrible plain scent of hospital sheets, I can smell him, that intrinsically comforting scent.

"I was so scared, Dad. I . . . As soon as I found out, I came. I should have been here earlier."

His broad palm rubs up and down my arm as he tips his cheek onto the top of my head. "No, you shouldn't have. It's not your job to take care of me. I asked Winter not to call you earlier. She wanted to. But I didn't want you worrying."

That just makes me cry harder. I nuzzle into his chest, rubbing my wet tears against the rough hospital gown he's still wearing. "Dad, I really fucked up."

"Yeah." He keeps rubbing my arm. "I saw."

"I didn't want it to come out that way. Winter. I didn't want her to . . ."

His voice goes deadly even as his fingers squeeze tight. "Did that fucker force you into anything?"

"No. He . . . I, well, you know, I always had a crush on him. Even when it turned into just check-ups." My dad grunts. It was a running joke, really. I wasn't subtle, and it's hard not to be starry-eyed over a handsome young doctor who saved your life like he saved mine. "It was around when I turned eighteen. I was legal and went out with friends to have some drinks. I ran into him at the bar and rather than partying, we ended up driving around all night talking. Things took off from there."

"For how long?"

I blow out a raspberry and turn my head to stare at the ceiling. "Two years."

"Jesus Christ," Kip mutters. "Then what?"

"Then . . .Winter." I swallow heavily, letting myself feel the excruciating pain I felt when he told me he was going out with her. I couldn't wrap my head around it back then. But I can now. I was young, and so fucking willing for a man with no professional boundaries. I don't know how I didn't see it that way. Winter started at the same hospital, and he was instantly taken.

And I was instantly forgotten.

He didn't love me, he used me and discarded me. And now it makes my skin crawl.

"I promised him I would never tell anyone. I didn't want to ruin his career. I mean, he's clearly good at what he does. But . . ."

"But what?" Kip sounds downright murderous.

"He just always kind of strung me along. The odd call, or text. A conversation at a family event. He was careful to never cross a physical line once Winter was in the picture, but he always kind of kept me thinking that maybe, *maybe*, things might change."

I bark out a sad laugh. Saying it out loud it seems so obvious.

"Because he wanted to keep you in line," my dad provides.

"Yeah. It seems so blatant now. So manipulative. To think of how my personal life has played out these past years, I just . . . I guess that's why they say hindsight is 20/20."

"Stupid fucking saying," Kip mutters as his hand slides up and down again. "Of course hindsight is 20/20."

I smile, but it's half-hearted. "I need to find Winter."

"You need to give her some time. And I'm going to have to deal with Marina. And you're going to have to spill the beans on why Rhett Eaton is acting like a fire-breathing dragon around you. But for now, just lie here with your old man for a minute. For old time's sake."

I don't argue with him, I just breathe in deeply through my nose, seeking comfort in a way that has me feeling like the little girl I once was. In this very hospital. In this very wing. With the one person who never stopped showing up for me.

And I doze off.

I'm woken by my stepmother, Marina, shoving at my shoulder in a dim room. Her hair is a pale blonde, and her features are severe. Just like her. She's wearing a gray pencil dress under her white coat. She's a well-respected doctor here, but she couldn't be bothered to come check on her husband in the last however many hours since he had a heart attack.

She's always been cruel, though.

"Get out." She points at the door.

She's never liked me. And on one hand, who can blame her? But on the other . . . grow the fuck up.

"No." I push up to sitting and comb my fingers through my hair, trying to get my bearings.

"Yes. You've done enough here for one day."

My heart plummets at the reminder of what happened earlier. With Winter. The muscles in my chest constrict and I drop her gaze.

One more reason for her to hate me. For my sister to hate me.

"Listen, I . . ."

Her hand shoots up, palm held flat to stop me talking, and her eyes blaze with icy fury. "Homewrecking is hereditary for you. You can't help it. I get it. But you're going to displace Kip's heart rate monitor and create more work for everyone. This isn't the time for a sleepover. Go home."

My jaw falls open as I stare back at this woman. This woman who only kind of raised me because Kip never let her get close enough. It didn't stop her from making comments like this to me through the years. I've developed a thick skin where Marina Hamilton is concerned. Her jabs used to hurt, but now . . .

I kiss my dad on his forehead and move off the narrow bed, limbs heavy like lead and eyes scratchy like there's sand in them. Most likely mascara crumbs from crying.

"I feel bad for you, Marina," I say evenly, brushing my clothes flat.

"I don't need your pity," she spits quietly, picking up my dad's chart and fixing her gaze on the papers before her.

"But you have it. And you have my forgiveness for how utterly awful you've been to me for my entire life."

She scoffs, and I pull myself up as tall as I can get as I aim for the door to leave. Battling with Marina isn't worth the effort. However, that doesn't stop me from sharing some parting words, even though my voice shakes as I do it.

"You've spent a lifetime hurting my dad, and I hate that. But whatever goes on between you and Kip is none of my business. You're both adults. But I will *never* forgive you for making it impossible for me to have a relationship with Winter. You think all your maneuvering throughout my life only hurt me, but it hurt Winter, too. It made it so that I felt like I couldn't tell her things that she deserved to know. It made it so that we were both isolated when we could have had each other. And that's"—I point at her, right in her face—"on *you* and *your* fucked up vendetta."

And then I spin on a heel and leave. Too angry to look at her for even another moment.

I stumble out of the room in search of a washroom to fix my face and relieve my bladder. And maybe to cry a little more by myself. I need to find Winter. Call Winter. Explain myself to my sister.

But when I wander around the corner and hit the waiting space, what I find is Rhett Eaton, corded arms crossed over his chest, hair loose around his shoulders, bearded chin tipped up, staring at the ceiling. His golden irises dance back and forth as though he's watching something.

"What are you doing here?" I ask.

He sits up straight, instantly looking at me as he clears his throat and grips at the armrests. "Waiting. I guess. Yeah, waiting. I wanted to make sure you were okay."

"What time is it?"

He nods at the wall behind me. "Almost two."

"Two a.m.?"

"Yeah."

I sigh and scrub at my face. "I asked you to leave."

The quiet hum of the hospital behind me is peaceful in its familiarity.

"Well, I didn't want to leave. I wanted to sit here and wait to make things right with you. I'll sit here all weekend if I have to."

"No, you won't. You ride tomorrow. You should be resting."

"Summer. Don't you get it?" He stands, holding out his hands in frustration. "I care about *you*."

I suck in a loud breath and nod as I drop my gaze to his worn boots. "Right. But not enough to stop talking when I begged you to. Not enough to think about the repercussions of you going off. The repercussions that land on *me*."

"He deserved it, Summer," Rhett growls.

"And what about me, Rhett?" My voice is borderline shrill. "What do I deserve? Do I not deserve the opportunity to tell my own story? Don't you get it? That was *my* secret to tell." My thumbs jab at my chest almost painfully before I point at him. "You promised to keep that secret. And you broke that promise. I *trusted* you."

He blinks, eyes softening as his shoulders sag. "Secrets like that will weigh you down, Princess. You never told me he was part of your family. I mean, fuck. How disgusting can one person be?"

"Don't princess me! We haven't known each other for that long! I'm *so sorry* I didn't spill all my dirtiest secrets to you right off the hop. How selfish of me." My voice goes up to another level, and I feel the sleepiness of earlier falling away, being replaced by panic. By heartache.

"You shouldn't keep secrets that eat you alive because you're worried about what people will think. And definitely not because someone is manipulating you into it."

"I know that! Don't you think I know that? But it was my story to tell, and you took that from me. In the most public, humiliating way possible. And as badly as Rob hurt me, I'm not out to tank his career." That one statement lands like an atomic bomb, silencing everything around us. Rhett's expression goes blank.

He glances away, like it hurts to keep his eyes on me, and gives his head a subtle shake. "Jesus. Do you still have a thing for him?"

I wave a hand in front of us while I comb the opposite one through my hair. "No! Of course not! No. It's just complicated. And it's not about him. Not really. I know you don't care what people think. But me? I do. And you keep steamrolling that. Maybe I shouldn't care so much about what people think, and maybe you should care more. Maybe your family is unsupportive of you, or maybe they're scared that every time you walk out that door, it might be the last time they ever see you."

I'm panting now, and Rhett looks stricken by what I've just said. "Other people's feelings are involved. It's not all about you and what you want, Rhett. Not when you love someone. I care what my sister thinks of me—even if I shouldn't, even if she's mean. And my dad?" I point behind me. "The man in that room, who could have died today, is the only person who really cares about me, the only person I've got. They both deserved better than hearing about this the way it just came out. Maybe Rob got what he deserves, but what about the rest of us?"

His teeth grind as he gazes down at me, unblinking. He wipes a hand across his mouth. "I get that. I do. And I'm so fucking sorry I blew up like I did. But Summer"—he reaches for me, but I step back—"you've got me too. I'm not sure how else to prove it. I keep telling you, and it's like you don't hear me."

My eyes sting. He's saying all the things I so badly want to hear. He's offering me all the support I so desperately want from him. But I'm also really fucking angry at him for betraying my trust and for being right about so much and wrong about so much all at once.

I'm angry that this isn't easier. That nothing in my life ever has been. At this moment, I'm not feeling very glass half full, and I take it out on the good man standing in front of me. Because as much as I want to, I can't rely on a man who's so busy not caring what anyone thinks that he'll hurt me to prove the point.

"Oh, I hear you, Rhett. I just don't believe you. What you did tonight doesn't feel like you caring about me. It feels like you losing control and flying off the handle." A surge of nausea hits me, and I hold a hand over my mouth as I pin him with watery eyes. "Go home. To your hotel. Just go. I can't deal with you right now."

"What does that mean? For you and me?"

My eyes close. Even that small movement hurts. Everything *hurts*. A laugh that blends into a sob leaps from my lips. "I don't know, Rhett. I'm not even sure there is a you and me. We've never been more than here and now."

And then I push past him to cry in the washroom, just like I planned.

Well, a little harder than I planned.

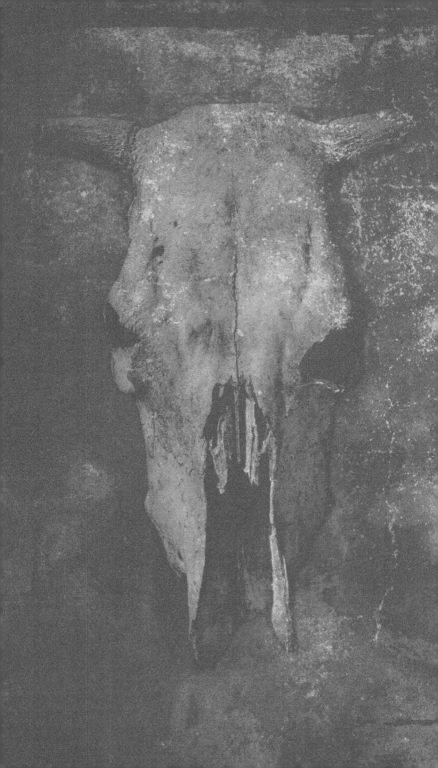

29

Summer

Summer: Winter, can we please talk? I'm coming back to the hospital today. I can meet you any place, any time. I don't expect you to forgive me. I would just like to tell you my side of the story.

Winter: There's nothing to forgive.

Summer: Okay. Can we please just still talk? I know things are strained between us, but I love you. I want to make sure you're okay.

Winter: I'm not okay. I'm pregnant. And the father of my child has been lying to me for years. I'm not ready to talk. Please stop asking. I'll contact you when I'm ready.

Rhett: How is Kip?

Summer: Apparently, fine.

Rhett: How are you?

Summer: Tired.

Rhett: What can I do to help? Just tell me.

Summer: Nothing.

Rhett: Have I mentioned how sorry I am?

Summer: Just be safe tonight, please.

"So, tell me about the cowboy."

I decide not to turn around. Instead, I busy myself rearranging some of my dad's flowers in their vase. "Hm?" I ask like I didn't hear him.

"You know. Long hair. Punches people who've wronged you. Featured on your wall as a teenager."

I groan, dropping my chin to my chest.

"Bet you thought I didn't remember that."

"Yup." I stare at the white sneakers on my feet. I finally snuck back to our house this morning. As though it might make me feel better, I took a shower, blow dried my hair, and put on a pretty matching bra and thong set. I threw on some jeans and a soft, gray jersey pullover and came back to keep Dad company.

Feeling right as rain. If this were my last moment, I'd want to be happy with my dad. So, I'm forcing myself to feel that. To do that. To control what I can.

And I'm failing because I'm sick about Winter. I was *literally* sick over that last message she sent me. I have to keep busy somehow. Rhett rides tonight, and Willa's bar is hosting some concert this weekend, so I'm here with Kip, who is now asking questions I don't want to answer.

With a sigh, I turn and face my dad, who appears awfully pleased with himself. "You should look worse. You just had a heart attack."

He waves me off. "A minor heart attack. And you know what would make me feel better?"

"What?" I perk up, eager for something to keep me busy and out of my head. Something other than arranging flowers that don't need arranging.

"Tell me about what went down with Rhett."

"Ugh." I stomp across the room, feeling notably childish as I flop down into the chair beside him. "I don't know what to tell you."

"Do you like him?"

Fuck me, this is awkward. I can't even look at Kip. He's found out more about my sex life in the past twenty-four hours than I'd have liked him to know in my entire lifetime.

"Yeah, Dad. I like him. He's not like he comes off. Nothing like everyone thinks."

"I know."

My head flips in his direction. "You do?"

"Of course, I know. Been helping that kid for over a decade now. He pisses me off because he's a loose fucking cannon, but I like him. I knew you two would get along eventually."

I blink, thinking back to the way Kip ranted and raved about him when this whole milk thing hit the fan. I saw it as frustration, but now, I'm thinking it might be affection. Frustration that things weren't going right for him rather than frustration directed *at* him.

"Well, cool," I say, slumping back in my chair. "Way to play weird matchmaker. It worked."

I can feel my dad staring at me. His gaze is burning a hole in my resolve to not say more.

"I let him get in my pants, okay?" I finally blurt.

My dad laughs.

I bring my hands up to my forehead as I stare at the ceiling. "You told me not to let him get into my pants, and I brushed you off like that was insane. And then I let him get in my pants. So, when we get back to work, you can just fire me and let me know what an unprofessional disappointment I am. Also, can we please never talk about my sex life again after this?"

Once Kip's laughter subsides, he looks over and gives my elbow a squeeze. "Right. Well, I don't think I told you not to fall in love with him."

"I don't love him."

He shrugs and gives me one of those sarcastic frowns that says, *Okay, sure, but we both know you're full of shit.*

I cross my arms, determined not to give him any further intel to harass me with. I don't want to talk about it. And I definitely don't want to consider the fact that I might be in love with Rhett Eaton.

The current state of things hurt bad enough without throwing the L word around.

"Wanna stream his event and talk about how terrible he is?"

I snort. The leg I have crossed jiggles as I try to avoid making eye contact with my dad. He's dangled a carrot I almost can't resist.

On one hand, I want to watch because I already miss Rhett so badly that there's a constant ache in my chest. On the other hand, I don't want to watch because there's a constant ache in my chest that will only worsen with the anxiety of watching him ride.

"Okay. Fine." I'm weak. I'm so fucking weak. A masochist, really.

Kip grins and reaches for his iPad, patting the bed as he scootches over. I fold myself onto the bed beside him and see that he already has the live stream queued and ready to go.

Traitor.

I cross my arms and lean back, settling in to watch. The start involves a lot of fireworks, girls in leather pants holding signs, and the announcers giving a rundown of the standings leading into the World Championships, which are two weeks from now. All they talk about is that goddamn gold buckle. They sound like Rhett.

I recognize the names of plenty of the guys as they take their turns. I tell my dad all that I've learned about the sport. The scoring, what makes a bull a good one, how they rub at their bull ropes to soften the rosin and mold it to their hands.

He listens raptly, even though there's a part of me that's certain he knows a lot of what I'm telling him. I think I just need to fill the space with something that isn't my sex life.

We hiss and groan in unison when guys fall or when the rodeo clown narrowly escapes. It's a terrifying sport.

"Oh, that's Theo." I point at the screen. "He's Rhett's protégé. Like a little brother."

"Oh, good. Another Rhett. Just what this world needs," my dad jokes. I laugh, but it's half-hearted, because the first thought that jumps into my head is, *Rhett is irreplaceable.*

The L word pops up again and I push it away, crossing my arms tighter across my ribs as though I can squeeze the thought right out of my body.

My lungs harden in my chest when I see Rhett climb up on the fence panels to help Theo. He's not a tour coach, so he doesn't need to be there. He just is. A flash of guilt hits me for saying what I said to him about not everything being about him.

It was a cruel thing to say.

I see the gate fly open and noise erupts from the tiny tablet screen. Theo's legs swing, arm held up in perfect position. The splattered-looking bull is bucking, straight and not overly high, so Theo digs in with his spurs.

And that's when it all goes to shit.

The bull turns hard and fast, and Theo isn't ready. He's chucked forward onto the bull's neck. His hat flies in one direction and his limp body in the other. I gasp, my hand coming up to cover my mouth as I shoot forward. When he hits the ground, dust floats up around him as he lies motionless.

"Shit." I hear Kip's voice, but I'm hardly processing because the bull has abandoned the clown he was chasing, and now all 2000 pounds of him barrels down on a lifeless-looking Theo.

I barely register what's happening outside the ring, which is why I hardly see it coming. Rhett runs out from the left of the screen and throws himself on Theo's body like a shield.

Selfless and heroic and stupid.

And just in time to bear the brunt of the bull's charge.

All I know is that I scream.

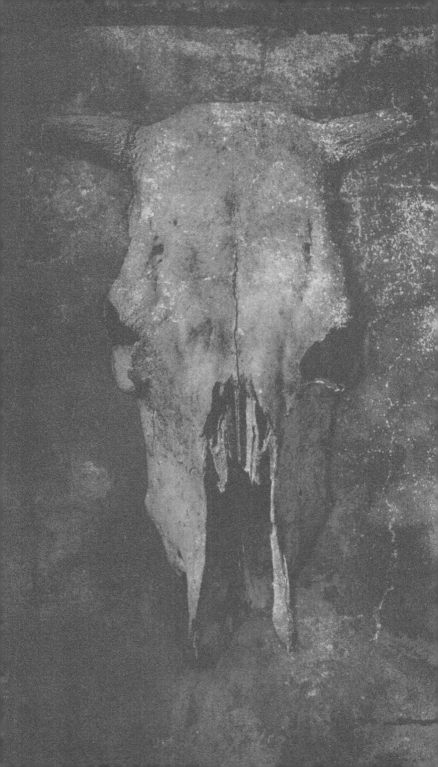

30

Rhett

Kip: I hope you're not dead, but only because my daughter is distraught over you right now, and if you're dead, I can't kick your ass for hurting her.

⋈

Red lights flash and project around the bay where the ambulance pulls up to the hospital. I've shooed the paramedics away at every turn. My ribs are fucked. I don't need a medical professional to tell me that.

Theo has been in and out of consciousness because he's too fucking stupid to wear a helmet, and I'm not leaving his side.

They pull the back doors open and lift Theo's stretcher. He's strapped down on a hard board. Something I'm hoping is just a precaution, considering he can easily move his feet. He was awake for long enough they were able to get him to do that much.

I follow, ignoring the lancing pain in my back and feeling every year of my age about a hundred times over. It doesn't help that I didn't sleep a wink last night.

When I closed my eyes, all I saw was Summer. Her perfect lips. Her deep brown eyes shrink-wrapped in tears.

Fucking haunting.

But right now, I just need to know that Theo is okay. I follow into the emergency room, ignoring the skeptical glances one paramedic gives me. She knows I'm lying to them about my injury. Plus, I made a huge scene about going with Theo, so I'm probably not in their good books.

I'll get a tour doctor to check me out later.

"You." She points at me. "Sit there." She points at the plastic chair just inside the door as they wheel Theo through, and this time, I listen.

I gasp when I bend to sit, dropping my head into my hands and breathing shallow, hoping the pain will subside if I don't move.

I'm not sure how long I sit here lost in the pain of my ribs and the worry about my friend when I hear, "Rhett. Long hair. Handsome. Probably a total asshole to you?"

It's Summer's distraught voice, brimming with pain and anxiety and panic. As if I didn't already feel sick enough about my dickhead behavior yesterday and making her cry

—fuck, that killed me—now I have to listen to her terrified voice.

It feels like rolling in glass, a thousand cuts all over my body, to hear her so upset.

And *I* did that to her. Yesterday. Today.

"Rhett!"

When I see her, I heave. Pain radiates everywhere. Mascara streams down her face as she jogs down the hallway toward me, fingers wrapped around the cuffs of her sleeves.

Beautiful and devastated.

I did that.

"Oh, my God. Are you okay?" She falls to her knees in front of me, hands fluttering above my legs before she lets herself touch me. "Are you okay?"

Her eyes scan me, as though she'll be able to see broken bones through my clothes and skin.

"I'm fine." I hurt too much to move. A part of me thinks I should touch her. The other part knows I should salvage her from the pain of this, of watching me do this. With my dad and brothers, their emotions are locked up. I don't know if they're actually afraid for me or just making fun of me.

But with Summer, I can see it plain as day.

Fear.

"I saw you." Her hands move lightly, so lightly, up my arms and over my shoulders. She sniffs as she takes me in. "I saw it happen."

My chest caves in. After the words we exchanged last

night, I don't know what to make of this. But I know that seeing her this upset is killing me. It's turning my stomach.

When she touches my ribs, I flinch. She lifts my shirt before I can stop her.

"Oh, God. Rhett." Her voice cracks, and I watch a fat tear fall from her eye. It rolls off her dark lashes and splatters on her cheek.

It breaks my fucking heart.

I haven't looked at my ribs yet, and I hadn't planned to. I feel her nail on the skin and jump, shoving her hand away as the shirt falls back down to cover what appears to be one hell of a bruise.

"I'll go get the doctor."

She turns to leave, and I grab her wrist. "No."

"No?" Her face twists in genuine confusion.

"No. I'll see a tour doctor later. A doctor here will want to admit me and keep me from riding."

She blinks. Once. Twice. Three times. The tip of her nose is red from crying. "You're going to ride?"

"Probably not tomorrow. But yes, I'm going to ride. I didn't make it this far to miss my shot at the buckle."

She shakes her head like she can't quite believe what she just heard. "Your ribs are probably broken. You could have internal damage."

"I'll be fine," I grumble, glancing away because I can't look at her anymore. It hurts worse than my ribs.

"Rhett, please. I know enough to know you won't ride your best like this. It's not safe."

I'm agitated because she's fucking killing me right now. And I want to relent. I do. For her, I do.

She's not wrong. But I also hate when people tell me to stop riding. I want the last win. It's all I have. She said things to me yesterday that stung. That resonated. That made me realize I don't *have* her, not really.

So maybe I'm mad. A little wounded.

I know it isn't fair to make her endure this when she's already been through so much. I want to protect her from any asshole who might hurt her. And that needs to include me.

Maybe that's why I say something I'll come to regret.

"We slept together for a couple of weeks, Summer. Don't tell me what to do." I spit the angry, petty words at her and watch her lips press together.

I hate myself instantly.

She pushes to standing, pulling in a deep breath and wiping at her nose as she straightens, so full of grace and class. So fucking far out of my league. Pulling away from me like I wanted her to, even though I could be sick over it.

Regret pulses through every limb. It courses through every vein. It singes every nerve.

She nods at me and walks away.

Taking my fucking heart with her as she goes.

"Where's Summer?" my dad asks as I enter the kitchen.

And there it is. The reason I went back to drinking coffee in my bedroom this morning. But even the view from my deck doesn't seem that impressive anymore.

While I mull over how to answer my dad's question, I limp over to the coffee maker for another cup, trying not to look as injured as I am but feeling like I've been hit by a fucking Mack truck.

Broken ribs, as confirmed by the tour docs. I stayed in the city for one more night. They discharged Theo with a severe concussion, but he rode the next night anyway. I wanted to tell him not to, and I bit my tongue so hard it bled.

I'd told Summer not to tell me what to do, so who the fuck am I to tell another guy just like me he shouldn't ride?

He rode well, and I watched from the sidelines. I might have a few screws loose, but I know my boundaries, and the amount of pain I'm in right now doesn't work for sitting on a bull. It puts me behind going into the World Championship, but only slides me into second. Emmett in first and Theo in third.

"In the city with her dad," I finally say. It's a safe answer, and it's true. I don't know where else we're at. I lasted all of a day before I was messaging her. Apologizing.

But fuck me, it's not even close to enough. I was so upset, so worried, in so much pain—but there's no excuse for what I said. Especially considering how far from the truth it is.

As the frustration burning in my gut cooled, it transformed into a heavy boulder. Making me feel sick. Nauseous. Dizzy.

I've never felt sick over a girl. I've never made a bigger mistake.

And she still hasn't responded.

Cade bursts through the back door, stalking straight into the kitchen, looking like some sort of avenging cowboy, angry and wearing black, the sun shining in from behind him. "Why are the boys in the bunkhouse talkin' about you getting rag-dolled by a fuckin' bull last night?"

I sense my dad go still as he looks up from his newspaper.

Of course, all those assholes are running their mouths.

"Rhett?" My dad quirks a brow while Cade breathes heavily and glares.

"One of the guys was knocked out. My guy. Gabriel's son. When the bull went gunning for him, I just . . ." I scrub at my beard, thinking back to that moment. What went through my mind? I'm not entirely sure. All I knew is I couldn't sit there and watch one of my best friends get gored by a bull. "Acted on instinct, I guess. Jumped on top of him."

"You what?" My dad exclaims at the same time Cade barks, "I always knew you were stupid, but that really takes the cake."

"Are you okay, son?"

I open my mouth to answer, but Cade cuts me off. "No, he's not okay. He rides fucking angry cows with testicles for a living. He's standing crooked like a broken cock. And he's clearly got more than a few screws rattling around in his thick head."

I stare back at my big brother, who is positively seething. "You always had a way with words."

My dad chuckles at that, but then is back on me. "You seem to be in one piece?"

"My ribs aren't," I reply, before tipping the steaming coffee back into my mouth.

"So, you're out for the season?" I don't miss the twinge of hope in my dad's voice.

Which means I feel like scum when I tell him the truth. "Nah. I'm still heading to Vegas. Last shot at that buckle."

"Did a horse kick you in the head as a child when I wasn't watching?" Cade asks. "Beau beat your ass too hard one time? If I shake you hard enough, will it get you thinking straight?"

Cade is mad, but my dad just looks sad. His blink lasts a few beats too long as he nods his head and folds his newspaper. "When is Summer coming back?" he asks as he pushes himself up from the table.

"I don't know." I stare at my feet when I say it.

Cade scoffs.

"Her dad had a heart attack, so she's with him right now."

"So, she'll be back soon? Is Kip okay?" My dad seems so hopeful. He likes Summer. I know the two of them enjoyed morning coffees and easy conversation. I think everyone enjoyed having her here on the ranch.

"Dad, I don't know. But I do know that Kip is going to be fine."

He gives me a flat smile and a wave before turning away. "Gotta run some errands in town. Be back later."

I say nothing. A house full of men hasn't been conducive to sitting around talking about our feelings. I've never had that kind of relationship with my dad. Or my brothers, for that matter. We care for each other, and we tease each other, and sometimes we fight with each other.

Which is what it looks like Cade is itching for as he takes a few menacing steps into the kitchen. "Smart girl," is what he says as he props a hip against the countertop and crosses his arms, the canvas of his black coat rasping as he does.

"Fuck you, Cade." I shake my head.

"No, Rhett. Fuck *you*. You fucking bolthead. You had something with that girl."

I huff out a laugh. "Cade, you don't even like her."

"I like her because she's good for you. I like her because she doesn't take our shit, and she doesn't roll over for you like some lovesick puppy dog. I don't like her because she's smarter than me, and that's fucking annoying."

My teeth clamp and grind as my big brother stares me down. "You were a different person with her. You were happy. You didn't have that sad, lost little boy look about you. The one constantly seeking attention and doing dumb shit to get it. Because you had *her* attention. You're just too stupid to see it."

"Is this your version of a pep talk?"

"No, you dolt. It's the closest thing to an ass kicking I can give you without beating on a man with broken ribs."

"I could still take you." I couldn't. Cade is bigger. Taller. And meaner.

"You're so busy running around being a showboat rodeo boy that you don't even realize what you've got. You think we all pick on you for riding bulls because we're just being dicks? It's because we love you. You don't remember when mom died. But I do. I was there. I watched our dad hold her while she bled out. Suddenly, at eight, I was wrangling you and Beau because dad was a shell of himself, focused on taking care of Violet. And now I'm a single dad. I watch Luke grow every day and dread the day I can't be the one to keep him safe."

I bite my inner cheek. I know Cade is serious right now because I don't think I can remember him ever telling me that he loves me.

"When you have a kid, everyone warns you about the sleepless nights. The explosive diaper changes. How they grow so fast that you hemorrhage money on clothing them. What they don't tell you is that you'll never spend another day of your life without worrying about another person. You'll never completely relax again because that person you created will always, *always* be on your mind. You'll wonder where they are, what they're doing, and if they're okay."

The bridge of my nose stings at his words, and I sniff to clear it. Pain lances through me as I do. *Fuck me, everything hurts.*

"Not knowing where Beau is or what he's doing is bad enough. But he's serving this country, he's got a good reason to be gone. But you? You fucking won it all. *Twice.* You make millions of dollars. If you had a brain, you would take that money and set yourself up real nice. When is it enough for you?"

I interrupt him there. "I fully intend to put my money toward this place. I plan to come back here and help you. I need something to do with myself."

Cade's gaze narrows. "When?"

"I don't know."

"After this season?"

I sigh. "I don't know. Some days, I don't even know if I like it anymore or if it's just what I know. Quitting is hard. My entire identity is wrapped up in riding bulls."

"With her, it wasn't. And I don't want an inheritance from you." He pushes off the counter, shaking his head. "I want to be poor and have you pissing me off for years to come."

From Cade, that sentiment is, well, like a shot to the heart. He leaves me, only stopping when he hits the door, fingers tapping against the frame. He glances at me over his shoulder.

"Rhett, working on the ranch isn't something to do with yourself. This is a job. A job I love. I wouldn't do it if I didn't. You need to figure out what you love and make that your life too."

The only word in my head when that screen door slams behind him is *Summer*.

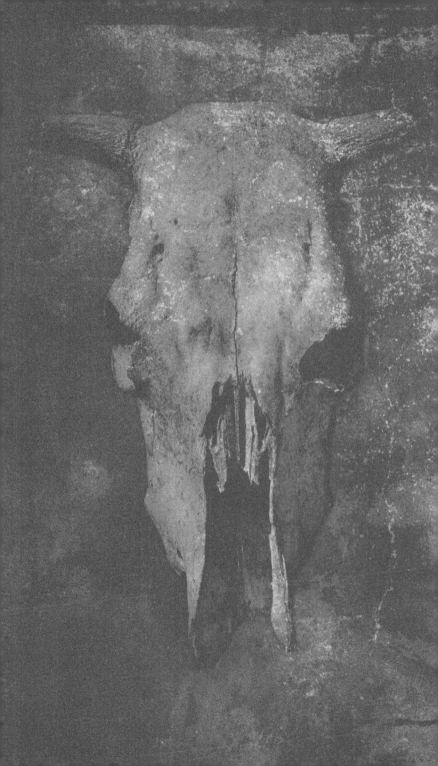

31

Summer

Rhett: Please answer your phone.

Rhett: I didn't mean what I said.

Rhett: Fuck, I hate myself so much for doing this to you.

Rhett: Are you okay? Can I just get some sign of life so I can stop walking around feeling sick all the time?

Rhett: Your dad told me you're still alive. He also says he's going to cut my hair off in my sleep.

Rhett: I want to explain myself. I want to apologize. I want to hear your voice. Even if it's you bitching me out. I deserve that. Please pick up.

Rhett: I'm going to blow your

phone up for the rest of your life.

Rhett: It wasn't just sleeping together. Not even close. It was everything. And it scared me.

Rhett: I can't lose you.

ᴡ

"I hear you're running a tight ship around here. Really cracking the whip."

My head snaps up from the contract I'm scouring as Kip saunters into my office like he didn't just have a heart attack last week.

"You're not supposed to be here."

He rolls his eyes before helping himself to the chair across from me. "You going to tattle on me, Princess?" I flinch, and my dad's head quirks in response. "Are you too old for that name now?"

My lips roll against each other, and I swallow the ache that crawls up the back of my throat. "Yeah," I croak. "I think so. Have you heard from Winter?"

I spin in my office chair and bend down to pull something—anything—out of my filing cabinet. I need a breather away from that goddamn nickname. A break from his incessant calls and texts. Leave it to Rhett Eaton to not only crush my heart but also ruin my favorite childhood dress-up game and nickname.

"No." Dad hesitates only slightly, but it's enough to

convince me I'm not getting the full story. "You enjoying your days here without me?" he jokes, perceptive enough to change the subject.

I sigh and lift the papers in front of me, tapping them against the desk to even all the edges before slipping a paperclip over the top corner. "Honestly, Dad, not really. I like it when you're here. You're a total nut." I smile and slip the sheets into the manilla folder beside me. "But you're my nut."

I expect him to laugh, but he steeples his fingers beneath his chin and regards me carefully, like he can't decide what to say next, which is truly something for a man like Kip Hamilton. "You're my nut too. But are you a happy nut?"

"Happy enough."

I straighten things on my desk like the nervous wreck that I am. My phone chimes and even that makes me start. Rhett has been relentless for an entire week now, but I'm still giving him the silent treatment. I'm not ready to talk to him. Or maybe I'm scared to talk to him.

"You gonna answer that?"

I finally meet my father's eyes. "No."

"You know that *happy enough* isn't actually happy enough, right?"

A sigh escapes me as I press my back into the chair, pushing my shoulders back.

"Especially since you don't seem all that happy to me."

I grunt. "I'm just having a day."

"Don't bullshit a bullshitter, Summer. I've watched you your entire life. I know what you look like happy, and it isn't how you are when you're here. Do you know why I work so hard here? Long hours? Weekends?"

I'm out of fucks to give, so I tell him the blunt truth. "Honestly, I always figured it was to avoid having to spend time around Marina." My stepmother isn't a pleasant human.

Now it's his turn to flinch. We don't talk much about his philandering. It's awkward, because I'm the by-product of it, and I don't want to hear him say he regrets it. "No. I do it because I love what I do. I built this company from the ground up and worked my ass off to get Hamilton Elite to where it is today."

"I know. And one day, you'll be able to pass it off to me and enjoy a lavish retirement."

"No, Summer. That was never my end game. I wanted to show you that anything was possible. That our transgressions don't define us. I did a shitty thing, but one of the very best things in my life came out of it. Things will always be strained between Marina and I because as much as I apologize to her, I can't bring myself to say that I regret it. Because I have you."

Tears spring up in my eyes. "Yeah, well, I bet you didn't know I'd be such a time suck when you signed up to keep me."

"Summer, stop." He leans forward, a broad hand spread out on the table between us. "If Marina or that piece of shit your sister married ever made you feel unworthy for even one moment, put it out of your mind. You are not a burden. You are not a waste of time. You are very wanted. And anyone who makes you feel you're anything less deserves Rhett Eaton's fist to their face. Or yours. You can hit back too, you know? I'll bail you out every fucking time."

A tear spills down my cheek, and I nod. "I know you will. And I want to be that for you, too. I want to be here helping you. Carrying on your legacy."

"Summer." His voice drops along with his shoulders. "This place isn't my legacy. This place is where I busy my mind and body. This place is my passion. My legacy is showing you that if you pursue something you love, you'll make it work. Blood. Sweat. Tears. And a whole lotta love. Do you feel that way about this place?"

I sniffle and blink rapidly, regarding the shiny, bright, immaculate and modern office. All I want is the smell of sweaty mats at a gym and the clanking of plates on the end of a barbell. I want open fields, crisp air, and the Rocky Mountains at the end of the horizon.

I want a man who smells like leather, looks like a glass of bourbon, and who calls me princess while drawing on my back.

I want Rhett to unsay what he said.

I want him to want me. More than he wants anything. I deserve that. He taught me that I do.

"No, I don't. I just don't want to let you down," I sob, my control cracking.

Kip reaches across the desk, holding his palm up and wiggling his fingers until I place my hand in his. "Listen to me carefully, Summer. The only way you could ever disappoint me is by not living your life to the fullest. Not going after what exhilarates you. You deserve that. And you deserve someone who wants that for you."

He wraps his fingers around my wrist as I attempt to pull away. "I'm not stupid. I know things are strained between you and Rhett after that explosion. But I also know that men don't look at a woman the way he looks at you unless they're out of their goddamn mind for that person. I know you're so accustomed to pleasing everyone that you give and give until you have nothing left to give. Rhett might be a little rough around the edges, but maybe you smooth him out and he scuffs you up. I don't know. Only you can make these decisions. But what I saw that night was a man who'd burn everything down to defend you. I saw a man who'd risk it all to take care of you."

"I don't need to be taken care of."

"Maybe not. But that man wears his love for you on his sleeve for the entire world to see. And he doesn't give a shit who sees it. He'd scream it from the mountain tops if you asked him to. It's written all over him. And you definitely need that."

I blow out a breath and stare up at the ceiling. Rhett loving me. It seems so unlikely. So far-fetched.

"Are you going to Vegas for the finals?"

Kip gets my attention with that comment. "Are you trying to play matchmaker again? It's fucking annoying."

"Well, are you?"

"Of course not. I'll be working to make up for your old ass being laid up," I try to joke. It's familiar footing for us, but it comes out all watery.

The thought of Rhett chasing his third title without a

soul in the stands who really knows him is a gut punch. I shouldn't care so much, but I do. It makes more tears fall thinking of the wild boy who lost his mom, who doesn't have the support of his family, riding injured for what could be the last time. A stadium full of strangers cheering him on, but not a single person who loves him there to witness it. No one to share it with.

"No, you won't. Because you're fired."

I still and meet my father's gaze, a sad smile playing at my lips. "Ha. Ha. Very funny."

"I'm not joking. You're fired. You have until the end of the day to clear out your desk, and I'll give you six weeks of severance."

"Are you kidding?" My heart rate accelerates. He can't be serious. "I went to law school so I could do this. So that I could be the best fit for you here."

He pushes to stand, dusting his hands off like he's done some great work here. "Yup. And now you're going to go find something to do that is the best fit for *you*. You're going to stop worrying about what everyone else thinks of you or wants from you. And you're going to waltz out in the world and be selfish for once. Take what you want and stop feeling guilty about it. Take it from me, guilt will eat you alive."

He knocks his fist on my desk and strides out of my office, tossing out, "Gotta get to my meeting," over his shoulder.

So casual, like he didn't just blow up my entire life to teach me some sort of tough-love lesson.

I stare at myself in the mirror, dabbing at my eyes and willing away the splotchy redness on my neck and chest. My heart is pounding so hard I can see the skin in my throat jumping every time it pumps.

It's comforting and distracting. I'm alive, but am I really living? Or have I just been scuttling along, putting everyone else first?

I press my palm to my chest, just above the scar there to feel the organ pumping.

Did I chase off the one man other than my father who put me first? Was he out of line? Or was I so tuned out from what I want that I missed the part where we fell in love? Did I dismiss him when that's what he was trying to tell me?

We spent weeks together. Traveling. Working out. Eating. He gave me his last chicken wing and let me warm my feet on him without complaint.

They weren't loud proclamations. But they were still there. And I missed them, while ignoring what I was feeling.

I shake my head and comb my fingers through my hair, smoothing my hands down the pretty maroon pencil skirt I'm wearing. All I have for clothes is what I retrieved from my hotel room and what I left at my dad's house in the city. All my favorite pieces are still out at Wishing Well Ranch, along with a good chunk of my favorite people.

With a deep centering breath, I turn and leave the washroom, striding down to my office on sky-high heels, refusing to walk around this place like I've just been fired. I hold my chin high and put my game face on, letting my hips sway.

I make this stupid hallway my runway.

Until I glance into the boardroom and see Rhett Eaton sitting in the same chair I met him in two months ago.

My steps falter and I stop to stare at him. He's leaned back in his chair, one booted foot casually slung across his knee.

He's devastating with his rugged lines, wild hair, and honeyed eyes. Far too masculine to be sitting in such a polished space. He overwhelms it.

He overwhelms me.

My throat aches just looking at him. And when his eyes slide over to meet mine through the glass, my chest feels like it's cracking right open.

I remember too keenly the sight of him moving above me, the appreciation in his gaze when I modeled my chaps for him, the way he kissed me so tenderly in a room full of people.

I also remember him calling what we did "sleeping together for a couple weeks." Rob said something similar to me when he broke things off with me to be with my sister, that we were *just sleeping together* so it shouldn't matter. It stung then, but it was excruciating this time around.

But I think what hurt the most was the way he brushed off my concern for him. That he made me feel like some overbearing crazy person for caring about him.

And that's enough to spur me into action. I turn my head and carry on down the hallway, resisting the urge to run and forcing myself to appear calm and collected.

I do not feel calm and collected. But I would rather fucking die than let Rhett see how deeply he wounded me.

"Summer!" He shoves the door open just as I pass. A whiff of his scent chases me like a haunting memory. "I want to talk to you."

"I'm good, thanks," I say without turning back to him.

"Please. Just five minutes." The pleading note in his voice almost makes me stop.

Almost.

"I think you've said enough, don't you?" I check my watch, wondering how soon I can get the hell out of here, and then I remember I don't work here anymore, so it doesn't matter.

"I haven't said nearly enough." I can feel him walking behind me, the warm solid presence of him looming over me but not overtaking me.

"You just walked out of a meeting. Go back."

"That meeting doesn't matter."

I scoff at that, turning into my office. My office? My old office?

"You're what matters." He reaches for my arm, and I yank it back.

Turning, I grit my teeth. Feeling . . . cornered. Like I could attack. "Rhett. Get. Out."

"Not a fucking chance, Princess." He shuts the door and leans against it, his hands captured behind his back. "I have some things I need to say to you, and you're going to listen."

I round my desk and try to look bored, lifting a file and opening it. "Well, seeing as how you've trapped me in here, I guess I don't really have a choice."

"No, I guess you don't. I've been trying to contact you for a week."

"Mhm." I stare down at the folder. I don't even know what I'm looking at though. My entire body is attuned to him. Truthfully, it's all I can focus on. "Been busy."

"Bullshit. You're ignoring me, and I deserve that."

I blink, not having seen that coming.

"Listen, Summer." He rakes a hand through his hair, and my fingers tingle with the memory of doing it myself. "I'm sorry. I'm so fucking sorry. I'm sorry I betrayed your trust. Believe me when I tell you it keeps me up at night."

My eyes flash up to check. He does look tired.

"I replay that interaction in my head when I lie in bed, thinking of all the ways I could have handled it better. Of all the ways I could have defended you without hurting you."

Tears spring up in my eyes, because apparently, that's my new thing.

For the past week, I cry at the drop of a hat. After years of seeing the glass as half full, I'm a mopey, whimpery, half-empty mess.

"Shit." He groans, and his body tenses as he pushes back against the door, like he's forcing himself away from me. "Please don't cry. I fucking hate it when you cry. It's like a bullet to my chest."

"Taken many bullets, have you?" My voice is weak, and I hate that.

"No," he husks, "but I would. For you, I would."

I whimper quietly at that, trying to cover it up with a, "Hmm."

"I said a lot of things I regret. Most of all, what I said about our time together. I can blame spilling your private business on coming to your defense in my own careless way. Because you may not know your worth yet, but I do. And I'll happily punch anyone in the face who makes you question it. But telling you what I did at the hospital that night, I said that to hurt you."

"Well, it worked."

He winces but carries on. "I'll never forgive myself for it."

And then we're back to like we were. Suspended in time. Staring at each other like we might find the answers to our problems written on the other person's face.

"Tell me what to do, Summer. Tell me, and I'll do it. Was I unclear before? Because I want to be crystal clear now. I love you. I loved you the moment you walked into that boardroom and smirked at me like you knew something I didn't. It bothered me, and I couldn't stop thinking about it. Wanting to know what you know. I fixated on it, but I think I was just fixated on you."

I process his words, soaking them in like a cat soaks up the sun. His cheeks flush, and his feet shift nervously. This is a lot of feeling talk for someone like Rhett Eaton.

"And I still am. I always will be. This thing between us? For me? It's everything. It's *it*. You're *it*. I've spent years thinking I didn't have someone who really supported me. But that was only because I hadn't met you yet. You were out there, wanting me. And all it took was one meeting with you for me to want you too. A few weeks for me to know that I'd do anything to support you too." He shakes his head and peers out the window. "You were out there this whole time, and now I know you exist, and I can never go back. Wouldn't want to if I could."

My tears are hot on my cheeks. His gaze back on me, tracking them as they spill.

"So, take your time. Do what you need to. Carry on with the cold shoulder, hate me, make a voodoo doll and needle the hell out of it. I don't fucking care. I'll take it all. Just think about what I'm telling you. Think about being everything with me. I'll keep coming back, no matter what. You're my priority. I'll keep trying because I'm not quitting on you. Ever."

I don't know when the tears spilled down over my cheeks, but two straight streams of them silently flow as I watch this man pour his heart out to me.

"Have I made myself clear?"

I nod. Struck dumb. Feeling incredibly fragile.

He nods back and turns to leave but stops when I speak. "How are your ribs?"

He looks over his shoulder. "Fine. They're fine, Summer."

I bite at my bottom lip, feeling a little awkward about my response to Rhett declaring his love for me. "Are you going to Vegas?"

He sighs and drops his eyes. "Yeah."

I nod again, unsure what to say to that. He says I'm his priority, but riding when he knows it's asking for trouble, when he knows it makes me frantic, when he knows I'll be left in a world without him if things go wrong . . .

That still feels like the bulls and the buckle are his priority.

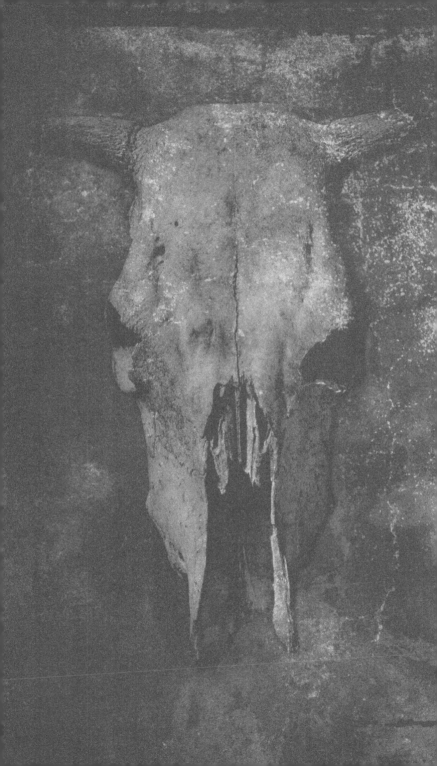

32

Summer

Summer: Wanna go for brunch?

Willa: It's Friday morning. Aren't we both working?

Summer: I got fired.

Willa: That's very unlike you! When did this happen?

Summer: A week ago.

Willa: Way to keep me in the loop. By the hot cowboy?

Summer: No. By my dad.

Willa: Well, shit. The Lark. 10:30. I'll get the mimosas started.

I walk into mine and Willa's favorite brunch location and spot her mane of red hair, poker straight around her shoulders, from the front door. Two mimosas sit in front of her . . . and two more parked across the table.

I guess it's going to be one of those mornings. The kind I need after moping around all week.

"Hey! You're here!" My best friend shoots out of her chair and wraps me in her arms. Willa gives the best hugs. She's much taller than me, which puts my head at about chest height.

So, I do what I've been doing since we were teenagers. It's a secret handshake at this point. I drop my head and jokingly motorboat her boobs. "I missed you," I say, mostly to her tits.

We both laugh. "That's what they all say." She ruffles my hair, and we step apart, smiling at each other. Sometimes, I'm so focused on feeling like I don't have any family that I forget about Willa. She might as well be my family.

"I was wondering why you've been radio silent," she tells me as she makes her way back to her seat and spreads a napkin across her lap. "Just figured you were working out the atomic bomb that got dropped at the hospital. Or possibly just saving horses left and right. Too busy riding cowboy pole to talk to me."

I roll my eyes, doing the same. "No. I've been moping."

"Because Daddy Hamilton fired you?"

"Can we not call him that?" I reach for a mimosa and take a gulp.

Willa waggles her eyebrows at me. She always jokes

about liking my dad. I don't actually know how much she's joking, though, because she's constantly checking out older men.

"So, he fired you. Why?"

I drink again. "Because he says I don't love working there like I should."

She snorts. "No shit. Glad he slapped some sense into you."

"Now, I have to figure out what I want to do with my life. Which is a hard question to answer. Basically, I've spent the past week in sweatpants mulling over the fact that all I've ever done is what I thought other people wanted me to do. I have no idea what I actually want."

"Well, as the twenty-five-year-old who works at her brother's bar full time with no other prospects to speak of, I'll drink to that."

"Well, you're a manager, doing office work during the day. It's not just bartending."

Her head quirks, green eyes appraising me with a smirk. "Am I? Or am I getting morning drunk with my bestie?"

We clink our glasses and polish off our first mimosa, immediately reaching for the second.

"So, do you have any ideas?" Willa asks.

"No," I say a little too quickly.

"Okay, if you don't want to talk about that, can we talk about the hottie in the Wranglers?"

"Ugh." I flop against the high back of the upholstered wing chair. This restaurant is eclectic to say the least. Mismatched chairs at each table. Antique chandeliers throughout. Floral wallpaper meets striped wallpaper, meets polka dot wallpaper. It makes me feel like I'm having a tea party at the Mad Hatter's place. Except with mimosas. "We're . . . I don't know what we are. He marched into my office the day I got fired."

Drink.

"Because you were ignoring all his calls and texts?"

"Yeah."

Drink.

"What did he say?"

Drink. I swipe my fingers across my lips and glance out the big windows at the sunny downtown street, thinking of how it felt to have Rhett touch my lips.

"That he loves me."

"Well, shit." Willa flops back in her chair too. "What did you say to that?"

I worry my bottom lip between my teeth. "I asked him how his ribs felt. I didn't know what to say. I had really dug in on being angry with him, so it took me by surprise. He said I was his priority. That he was always going to keep coming back."

Willa sighs wistfully. "So fucking romantic."

"Sure, and then he told me he was still going to ride in the finals, and I don't know what to make of that."

"What do you mean?"

Drink. Sigh. Look back at my best friend. "I mean, I don't want to be the girl who tells someone to stop doing something they love. Everyone tells him to stop. Do you know his family doesn't even come to watch him when the events are close? He's there alone. And I hate that for him."

I sigh again, thinking about how much that bothers me. All his close family, but still so alone.

"Between his shoulder and his rib injuries, he's injured enough that he won't be able to ride like he normally does. Not safely. I know it. He knows it. He knows it could end poorly—so damn poorly." Ire creeps into my voice. "And he's going to go out there and do it anyway. He'll leave me in the aftermath if something terrible happens. I've already picked up the pieces of so much heavy shit in my life. I'm not sure I want to sign up for caring about someone more than they care about themselves."

My friend sips elegantly while humming thoughtfully. I can see the wheels turning in her head as she mulls over my rant. "Maybe he doesn't know what making you a priority looks like because no one has ever made him a priority."

My mouth opens, but no sound comes out. I close it again, turning that thought around in my mind. Kip made sure I always knew I was his priority, no matter what else was going on in our lives. Winter, too.

But Rhett . . . he kind of got lost in the shuffle of life and tragedy and struggling to get by. Does he truly not know what it feels like to be someone's priority?

"I see I've struck you dumb. Thank you for coming to my TED Talk. Now tell me, do you love this man?"

My heart rate ratchets up, and I swear I can feel the blood pumping through my veins. I've only confessed this to myself. In my head. Saying it out loud makes it feel astonishingly real.

But maybe that's what Rhett needs from me.

I pull the mimosa up to my lips, throw a hand over my eyes, and mutter, "Yeah," before chasing back the rest of the drink. They really do serve them in small glasses.

And then I sit with my hand over my face, trying to figure out what that means. I hear Willa call out to a server that we'll have another round.

"Is she okay?" The guy sounds skeptical because I probably look hammered. I'm not, but two mimosas on an empty stomach isn't a great recipe for sobriety either.

"Her? Oh, nah. She's a mess. Get the lady a drink."

The guy chuckles, and I hear him depart as I continue to hide under the cover of my palm.

I smile, opening my eyes to tell Willa that I don't think I need another round, but she's got her head tipped down staring at her phone, thumbs swiping furiously across the screen.

"Who are you texting?"

"No one. I'm booking us flights."

I snort. She's always making shit like this up to throw me off. "Oh, yeah? Pray tell, bestie. Where are we going? Mexico? Ooh. A weekend in Paris? We can drink wine by the Eiffel Tower."

"You have expensive taste for an unemployed person."

"Please don't remind me of that."

"We're going to Vegas."

I lean forward and place my glass on the table in front of me. "Pardon me?"

"Don't play dumb. It's unbecoming. You heard me." She doesn't even glance up at me.

"When?"

A slow feline smile stretches across her lips. She looks far too satisfied with herself, something that immediately sets off alarm bells in my head.

"In a few hours. We'll get there in time to grab dinner and hit the rodeo. Maybe I'll ride a cowboy tonight too." She winks, and I stare slack-jawed at her.

"You're not even kidding, are you?"

"Why would I kid about this?" Her brows furrow.

"You're insane."

Willa laughs lightly, running a finger over the rim of her champagne glass. "Some people would say that's a redhead thing."

"I don't know if this is a good idea."

The server drops our drinks off and eyes me, probably checking to see if I'm swaying in my seat or something.

"It's a great idea. It will be fun. And you'll get your Prince Charming. You're welcome."

Silence stretches between us as I stare her down. The thing about Willa is that she can't be stared down. Not really. She's too ballsy. She just stares back, arching one shapely brow.

"If this we're your last moment on earth, would you—"

I hold up a hand to stop her, shaking my head. "I really wish people would stop using that saying against me." I let out a ragged sigh and drink. Because today I'm going to Vegas. Because in my last moments, I'd want to be with Rhett.

I'd want him to know I love him too. Every stupid, impulsive, broken bone in his body.

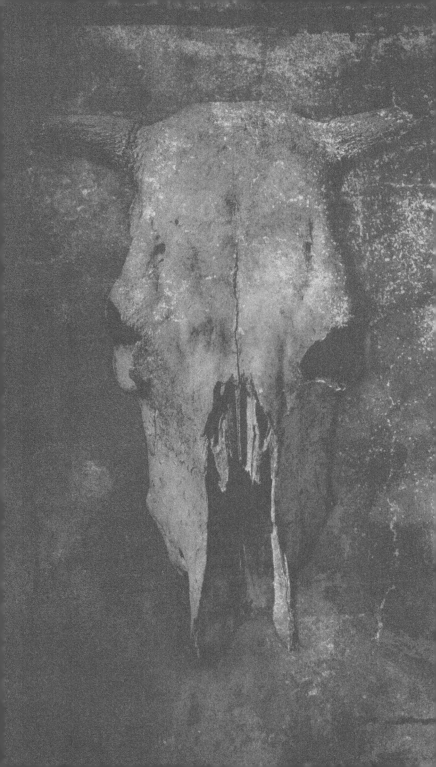

33

Rhett

Summer: Good luck tonight.
Rhett: I love you.

The guys chatter around me as I tape my hands. I try to tune them out so I can slip into that zone where everything falls away, and the job I came here to do tonight is the only thing I see.

Except the only thing I see is a beautiful girl with freckles over the bridge of her nose, wide doe eyes that look at me like I'm worth knowing, and a sharp tongue that makes me laugh.

The past two weeks I've spent playing everything between us out in my head. The care she put into healing me, the energy she put into planning favorable interviews for me, the way she whistles in the crowd for me. I find her there every time, and there's a twinge of regret in my chest knowing she won't be here tonight.

I got a taste of what it feels like to have someone show up for you, and now I'm greedy for it. It only took two months of spending every waking moment with one other person or thinking about that other person to slip into a place where it feels like she belongs with me.

And I belong with her.

It's the most insane, inexplicable thing that's ever happened to me. Which is saying something, considering all the shit I've done.

"Ready?" Theo claps down on my shoulder, and I wince. The ribs aren't as bad as they were. But they aren't great either—not by a long shot. There's really not any compensating for them, because my shoulder is still fucked, too. The tour doctors have pieced me together as best they can. And at least they didn't ride my ass about not getting on tonight. "You're not going to let Emmett win, right?"

A flicker of doubt flashes in my mind. I push it away. "Not a chance."

I pulled a good bull. A mean bull. A bull that makes or breaks the men who take him for a spin. I have the benefit of riding last, which means I'll know how hard I need to go to get that buckle.

The buckle I already have two of.

I haven't been able to shake my brother's words. *How much is enough?* That's the question I've tossed around for weeks. Turning it over in my mind from every perspective to see if I can answer it.

But I can't.

I don't know when it will be enough. All I know is that I still feel incomplete somehow. Like I'm not done just yet —like I'm still looking for something.

"I'm up first." Theo grins. "Balls to the wall. Right, Boss?"

I smile, but it feels forced. Before that night he got knocked out, I never felt nervous for him. I've convinced him he needs to be wearing a helmet. That the buckle bunnies will still want him if he wears a helmet because they prefer the walking, talking version of him to the vegetable version of him.

I nod. "You know it, kid. Hit 'em with the spurs."

We clap hands in a firm shake and give each other a smack on the shoulder. Which, for me, really fucking hurts. He turns and leaves the room, heading down the tunnel toward the ring.

Normally, I'd head out to watch him, but I'm not in the right headspace, and I know it. I don't need to watch other guys get chucked. I need to focus on myself right now. Mental walls up.

I watch them leave one by one, and mostly stay hunched over, elbows propped on my knees, hands dangling between them. My boots are worn, broken in, probably on their last legs. We're kindred spirits, my boots and me. I let my eyes wander over the sponsor patches on my vest, taking each one in. I've worn them with such pride, but today I can't help but wonder if risking my life to keep them is worth it. It's a thought that has genuinely never crossed my mind before.

I push it away.

The door opens and the sounds from the show outside filter into the room. The buzz of the crowd. The popping noises of the fireworks. The boom of the announcer's voice. All so familiar, like the soundtrack to my life.

"You're up, Eaton." Theo grins at me from the door.

"Why are you smiling like a serial killer?"

He smiles even bigger. He reminds me of his dad. This place reminds me of his dad. That year we all watched him fall. A shiver races down my spine.

"Emmett didn't beat my score."

One side of my cheek pulls up, and I take in his excitement and enthusiasm. I think I used to be that way too. Now, I'm going through the motions.

"Proud of you." I slap him on the back on my way past and walk down the darkened tunnel to the glitz and glam of the ring. There are even cheerleaders at this event. It's all a Vegas show.

I don't do my stretches because I don't think they matter tonight. Everything is tight and painful.

Three steps up and I'm at the staging area, pulling my helmet on, watching my bull, Filthy McNasty—a fitting fucking name—trot aggressively down the chute. He snorts and shakes his head, tail flicking against his side like a whip. Agitated.

And for the first time in my eleven-year pro career, I feel it.

Fear.

I push it aside as I climb up onto the fence and stare down at the bull's broad, muscled back. Two thousand pounds of pure muscle. He rattles the panels as he crashes around.

"Hop on when you're ready," one coach says, giving me a thumbs up.

A thumbs up.

This moment doesn't feel like a thumbs up situation. It feels like I'm about to spend eight seconds in excruciating pain.

I nod and climb down onto the bull, pushing it all away, trying to find that quiet—that calm. I run my hand over the bull rope, letting the bumps vibrate through my hand while watching the repetition of the motion, trying to get lost in it.

But the noise from the crowd picks up, and when I look up at the jumbotron, I see the footage of me leaping on top of an unconscious Theo playing. I haven't watched it yet, hadn't ever planned to.

I watch the bull hit me, tossing me into the air before turning back on a clown and leaving the ring. I land on my bad shoulder, and you see me roll over onto my knees, cupping my side.

It could have been so much worse.

That flicker of fear sparks at the back of my mind again. My stomach lurches.

I think about Summer. *Good luck.*

Shaking my head, I gaze back down and push my glove into the rope, tightening it until it's just right.

But it's not right.

A sharp whistle pulls my eye up to the stands. Before Summer, I was oblivious to the crowd, now I feel like I have a radar for her. And some asshole who whistles the same way is killing my concentration.

My eye catches on a flash of white, and the world around me goes fuzzy.

Summer's here.

She's wearing a white linen dress and sticks out like a sore fucking thumb.

My sore fucking thumb.

I blink. I blink again. Like she might not be real. Why would she come all the way here to watch me do something she clearly doesn't think I should do?

Kip told me he fired her, so I know it's not work.

I stare at her, and I think she stares back. Across the dirt ring. Across the crowd. We lock eyes and get lost in each other.

She offers me a small thumbs up, one that makes my chest ache at the memory of being on the road with her. All I can do is stare back. I'm always fucking staring at her.

I want to spend the rest of my life staring at her.

Then she mouths, *I love you.*

My jaw clamps down and something snaps inside me. That fear hits me like a tidal wave, and I yank my hand out, reaching for the fencing to pull myself up.

The fame. The buckle. None of it matters. Not one bit. All I want is to hear those words from her lips.

I don't want to spend my last moments on a bull. I want to spend them hearing her whisper that in my ear.

And then I'm off, swinging a leg over the fence.

"Eaton! What you doing?" one of the coaches calls out

to me as I drop onto the landing and toss my helmet, reaching for my favorite brown hat instead.

"I'm done."

"You're what?" The guy looks genuinely fucking confused.

"Consider this my retirement notice. I'm out. That bull gets a night off."

And I live to breathe another day. That part is pretty important too.

I stride through the staging area, heading straight for the door that leads out to the stands. It's all a guess because I only have a general idea of where Summer is seated.

But I told her I'd keep coming back for her. That I'd never stop. And that's what I'm going to do.

I turn up a flight of stairs and end up on the busy mezzanine, trying to decide between section 116 and 115. I choose 116, and shoot up those stairs, ignoring the stitch in my ribs as I do. I have tunnel vision, and I've overshot the section by one.

But I don't care. Rather than going back down, I turn down one of the aisles. I see Summer standing, palms pressed against her cheeks, face white as a sheet. Eyes brimming with wetness.

I did that. I want to never make her cry again.

"Pardon me. Excuse me." I smile and push my way down as people stand to let me pass.

"Can I grab an autograph?" someone asks.

"In a minute. Need to do something first."

Murmurs follow me across the entire section, and then I'm at Summer's aisle seat. Her back is turned to me, still facing down at the bull chute, standing on her tippy toes trying to see back to the staging area. Not a clue that I'm not back there anymore at all.

I'll definitely go down in this league for the most dramatic retirement, so maybe that's something.

And then I can't stop myself. I'm reaching for her. Sighing when my hands wrap around her upper arms. It's like all the anxiety that was coiling inside me just ebbs away.

Like I found what I was looking for—who I was looking for.

She spins on me, big brown doe eyes and perfect puffy lips. "What are you doing?" she breathes, hands falling instantly to my chest as though she's checking to see if I'm real.

"I could ask you the same thing, Princess."

"Fuck my life, he calls you princess, too? Ugh. Unfair." A lanky redhead standing behind her crosses her arms and rolls her eyes. But she's got a playful expression on her face. I like her instantly.

Summer ignores her, getting so lost in my eyes that she almost looks like she's somewhere else for a moment. "I just . . . I had to be here. I couldn't stand the thought of you being here alone. You're . . ." Her voice cracks and tears well in her eyes. "You're it for me too."

A stray tear streaks down one cheek and I swipe it away before gently combing her hair back behind her ear and cupping her head in my palm. "Please don't cry. It kills me when you cry." I pull her close, pressing her to my chest.

And it feels so fucking right. Her arms snake around

me gently, fingers trailing carefully over the sore side of my ribs. Always thinking about me.

Just like I'm always thinking about her. It took me a while to piece together why, what it means, and how I prove it to her.

Maybe I am just as dumb as Cade says.

"You need to go back down there and ride your bull. This is your championship to win." She sniffles against my chest.

I can hear surrounding chatter and the announcer's voice, but I don't make anything out. The woman in front of me is the center of my attention. The center of my universe.

A wry smile touches my lips and I tip her head up to look at me. She feels small and fragile in my arms, and I don't miss the way she trembles when I brush my thumb over her lips. "Say it. I want to hear it."

Her lashes flutter, clumped together with the wetness of her tears. And then she takes that deep dive into my eyes again. My chest twists and I pull her closer so our bodies wedge together.

I don't give a fuck who's watching.

"I love you," she says, her voice soft but sure.

I gaze down at her and wonder what the hell I did to get this fucking lucky. "I love you too. And I don't need to ride tonight. Or ever again. Hearing that from your lips is the biggest win of my life."

I take my hat, and I plunk it on her head. Just like I told myself I would.

And then I kiss her.

First soft and searching, before she grips at my shirt and turns things a little desperate. She moans and slips her tongue into my mouth. My eager girl is always the first to do that.

It's the best kiss of my life. It's the best moment of my life. Because I found the piece that was missing. I have no idea what I'm going to do with the rest of my life, but I know I'm going to do it with Summer. I'm going to keep coming back, keep proving to her we're better together.

So, we stand here kissing. With cameras rolling. In the middle of a huge crowd. No doubt raising some eyebrows. Making a statement and not giving a flying fuck who sees us.

Choosing each other. Finding each other. Showing up for each other.

And everything about the moment is flawless.

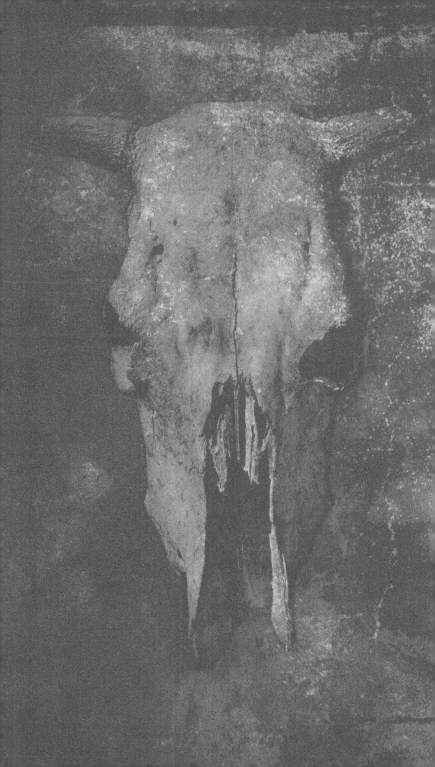

Epilogue
Rhett

One Year later . . .

I turn into the driveway at Wishing Well Ranch and take a deep breath.

Fuck it feels good to be home. It's been two weeks on the road. Which is about fourteen days longer than I want to be away from Summer.

But I'm happy. I'm fulfilled. I've got it all. My health. A job coaching on the WBRF circuit. And the girl of my fucking dreams waiting for me a couple minutes down this gravel road.

She better be naked. Naked and ready. I can feel myself swell in my jeans at the prospect. At the thought of our video chats while I've been away.

Usually, this gig only takes me away for a few days at a time. I fly in and I fly out, but I gave a clinic between weekend events this time to a bunch of young up-and-comers. It was fun.

But I miss my girl something fierce.

The road winds past the main house and then merges with a newer portion. *Our* portion. At the end of this driveway is *our house*. And I don't think I'll ever get tired of referring to it that way.

The only thing more satisfying would be being able to call Summer *my wife*.

"Mm," I hum and slap my hand against the steering wheel of my new truck. The one Summer made me buy because it's "safer." And because the old one kept breaking down because I never found the time to do any work on it.

But I think the new truck is worth it if only because it means that when I pull up to the newly constructed bungalow to see my girl sitting on the front steps next to . . .

My old truck.

But not my old truck. Because the one she's sitting next to is painted the prettiest blue. A steely blue.

The blue of my mom's eyes in my favorite picture of her.

The sight of it winds me. The girl I wish my mom could have met. Sitting next to a truck that now reminds me of her—that she bought for someone she loved.

In the strangest way, it seems like so much more than a pretty girl sitting next to a pretty truck.

Pulling up, I park beside it and step out on wobbly legs. Jaw hanging as I stare at the vehicle beside me. The bridge of my nose feels awfully tingly, and my vision is only slightly blurred when Summer walks around the front of it, small hand trailing across the hood. Simple white tank top and cut-off jeans making her look effortlessly sexy. The best thing she's wearing though is the soft look in her eyes and the tentative smile on her lips.

"Did I do okay?"

My lips press together as I try to suck in a centering breath. My gaze bounces between her and the truck. "Okay? Summer this is . . . how did you pull this off? Is this even the same truck? Does it run?"

She treads closer, bare feet on the freshly paved driveway. And before I know it, she's wedged herself underneath my arm, hand slung in the back pocket of my Wranglers as we stand there hip to hip staring at my new truck.

She laughs quietly and just stares for a moment. "Yes, it's the same truck. Every time you've been away this season, I've taken it into the shop to have them work on it." A choked laugh bubbles up in my chest and she tilts her head against me, painting herself flush against my side. "I hated you being gone for two weeks, but it was the perfect opportunity for the guys to finish it up."

"Wow." She's struck me nearly speechless. This was so far down my to-do list that I didn't even see it coming. I knew I wanted it. One day. After the house was finished, and there were a couple adorable little Summer clones running around the yard.

"Is the color right? I spent a lot of time looking at pictures of her. Trying to find just the right shade."

I wish I could say something to that, but I'm too choked up. So, I just fold her into a hug, take a deep inhale of the scent on her skin—cherries, always cherries—and whisper into the crook of her neck, "It's perfect, Princess. And so are you."

Life has never been better.

Work. Family. House. *Truck.*

The fact that Summer is on top of me. Riding me. Hips swiveling, head tilted back, dainty hands massaging her breasts, sporting a light sheen of sweat all over her golden skin. Her lips are slightly parted, and that's where my eyes snag. Puffy and pink and making the most delicious fucking whining noises.

She looks like a fucking goddess in the harsh afternoon light.

I've never loved her more.

"Did you miss me, Princess?" I ask, gripping her hips just above where those little creases form.

She stares down at me, eyes brimming with desire, cheeks rosy, hair in the messiest of buns. I remember the first day we met. Her bun was so tight that it looked border-line painful as she sat across from me in that boardroom.

But that was a year ago. And my girl has changed a lot since then. She's all undone right now—just the way I like her. Undone and riding my cock.

"Yes, so much. I'm coming next time."

I think I love her more with each passing moment.

A deep rumble in my chest sounds as I reach to rub at

her clit. "You're a business owner now. Can't go following your boyfriend around the country."

She stops now, glaring down at me. "Don't tell me what I can and can't do."

I especially love her when she gives me attitude.

I thrust up with a smirk. "Ride harder." I rub more firmly at her clit, knowing she won't be able to resist moving again if I do.

I smile when I'm right. She moves again with a playful little shake of her head. "Such a good girl, Summer. Ride it."

She moans, eyes fluttering shut. "I'm coming next time."

"Baby, you're coming a few seconds from now. Let's see those tits bounce. Go harder. Take it all."

"Fuck," she breathes as her head tips back, the sun catching her hair and making it shimmer. I let my hand trail up her body, her waist, the light line in her abdomen from spending her days working out.

I stop when my palm rests on the scar over her chest. And now, the look she gives me is soft, full of love and tenderness. I spent two weeks on the road and she's acting like I was gone for months on end.

"I hated being away from you," I confess, loving the way her lips tip up when I say shit like that. "But I love you. And I love watching you come on my cock. Let me watch. Let me see it. Let me hear it."

She bites down on her puffy bottom lip, and I almost explode on the spot. When she nods, I double my efforts, thrusting up to meet her, circling more tightly on her clit. Her wet heat clenches on me.

And then she's crying out, "Rhett!" with her head tipped back, lashes fluttering shut, looking like a goddamn angel. It's still the best sound in the world. And I follow, hand still on her heart, shooting up into her, while she falls forward on to me murmuring, "I love you."

"So fucking good," I murmur back, feeling like I should pinch myself. Like I have no idea how I stumbled into having a woman like Summer choose a man like me.

But that's just it. We're here, choosing each other every damn day. And I want to choose her for the rest of my life.

I'd have married her that day in the stands when I retired. Right there. On the fucking spot. But I'm greedy like that, and I know she needed time to sort her life out. Hell, I needed time to sort my life out.

Her sister still won't talk to her. And that's a wound I so desperately wish I could fix for her. But I can't. Not yet anyway. And her stepmom is lucky she doesn't come around because I'd have more than a few words for someone who's as cruel to my girl as Marina is to Summer. But she and her dad are closer than ever. And everyone in my family—hell, my entire town—loves her to pieces.

She's become the golden girl of Chestnut Springs since buying out the local gym and transforming it into Hamilton Athletics. The place geared toward training athletes. Or *torturing grown men* as I like to call it.

It's good for our small economy. And the ladies from town love it. They say they're going for a Pilates class, but really just sit around and stare at the hockey players and bull riders who train there during their off-seasons.

Summer flops forward and kisses me, warm and damp and smelling like cherries, fingers tangling in my hair. "I said I love you."

"I love you too, Princess. You know I do." I feel her smile against the skin of my chest before she rolls off me with a satisfied sigh.

I press a kiss to the scar on her chest and get up to get a warm cloth.

Over the sound of the running water, I hear her voice. "How much?"

Chuckling as I walk out of the bathroom, I catch sight of her, and the air in my lungs stills. She's heart-stopping, sprawled on our king-sized mattress. Right now, it's just a mattress on the floor. The unfinished floor. And she's surrounded by drywall that needs painting.

Our expansive rancher is definitely not complete yet, but we couldn't wait to move in. I was sick of her living in the studio loft above her gym. We built on our favorite hookup spot. The spot where we'd drive "the rust bucket"— as my truck has become lovingly known—toss a blanket in the back and make love under the stars. This spot has the best view of the mountains—and that's what Summer wanted.

And I want her with me all the time. It's fucking consuming. But she's my favorite human in the world. After a certain amount of time together, other people usually get on my nerves.

But not Summer. She's my person. And I'm hers. Two halves of the same whole.

"Tell me. Tell me how much you love me." Her lips tip up and her eyes dance.

"Woman, I'm wiping you with a hot washcloth after sex. That's how much I love you."

"Tell me more."

I crouch down beside her and get to wiping, mind racing as I do, dick filling again being this close to her pussy.

I feel her eyes on me. She's waiting for me to say more.

I slide her lacy thong back up her legs, because she looks fucking fantastic in expensive lingerie. "Turn over. I'll show you."

Her lips twist, questions dancing in her eyes, but she relents with a sigh, showing me her beautiful round ass.

I can't help but pop a nice loud smack on it before walking back across the room to chuck the cloth in the hamper, pull on a pair of sweats, and reach for the bag I dropped in the bedroom before losing all my clothes with her. Swiping a pen, I walk back over to her, catching the curious glance she gives me over her shoulder.

"Okay. Pay very close attention, Princess."

She giggles and nods her head. "Okay."

I straddle her, and it's a terrible idea, because all I can think about is sliding my dick between her legs. But I focus, uncapping the pen.

And then I start writing. Connecting the dots on her back the way I often do with the pad of my finger when we lay together. Her back is like the night sky, full of constellations. She and I really are binary stars, stuck in each other's orbit, drawn together by forces we can't see or understand—but that we can feel.

What I'm writing today is four words. And I swear I can almost hear her thinking, her body just a little bit tense, her head canted as she tries to decipher it.

"There," I say, right as I finish.

"Rhett?" She turns to glance over her shoulder now, but her eyes are less playful this time. More watery. "Did you just write what I think you did?"

I shrug and grin at her. "Guess you'll have to go look."

She shoots off the bed, and I watch her take quick steps across what is basically a construction zone, toward the bathroom. The creases under her ass, the lace framing it, and the words *Will you marry me?* written on her back.

It's so fucking satisfying.

I dart to my bag and grab the velvet box I hid. I go fast, not wanting to miss the expression on her face when she sees it.

My eyes trace her as she turns her back to the small temporary mirror in the ensuite bathroom. She casts a glance over her shoulder and then . . .

She smiles that little smirk that used to piss me off and now drives me wild. She doesn't even turn my way. She just stands there, staring at her reflection, smiling.

I drop to one knee and hold up the ring in my hand—a canary solitaire with smaller diamond points to make it look like a star—and I might as well be holding up my heart.

Because this girl owns every bit of me. And she has from the first day she smirked at me.

When Summer turns back to me, her smile grows larger. She doesn't even glance at the ring, she just stands there staring at me, her irises dancing with mine and speaking a language only the two of us know.

"Yes." She nods, tears springing up now.

"Princess, *please* don't cry." She pads closer to me, wrapping her arms around me and pressing my head to her chest. Her heart beats are loud, strong and steady, and so fucking sure. Just like I am of this—of her.

"They're happy tears."

I reach up, swiping a stray tear from her cheek. "I still hate them. But I'm glad you're happy. If these were your last moments, would you go happy?"

Taking her hand in mine, I slide the ring onto her finger, loving how perfectly it suits her.

We both spend a few seconds staring at it. Admiring it —but maybe more admiring what it means.

She grips my head, rubbing her thumbs across my beard. "Yeah, but this won't be my last moment. I've got too many things I want to do with you first."

A huge grin bursts across my face and I surge up, scooping her into my arms. I carry her back toward the mattress.

"Me too, Princess. Like take you to the main house and introduce the future Mrs. Eaton. Maybe make out with you at The Spur tonight so that everyone talks about it. But first," I toss her down onto the bed, thriving on the watery giggle that escapes her. "First, I'm going to spend the after- noon listening to you scream my name."

She laughs and holds her hand up to gaze at her ring. Looking so fucking happy.

And seeing her happy?

Seeing her happy is everything.

And I'm happy too, because I get to be stuck in her orbit for the rest of my life.

Visit www.elsiesilver.com and join Elsie's mailing list for a bonus scene of Rhett as a dad!

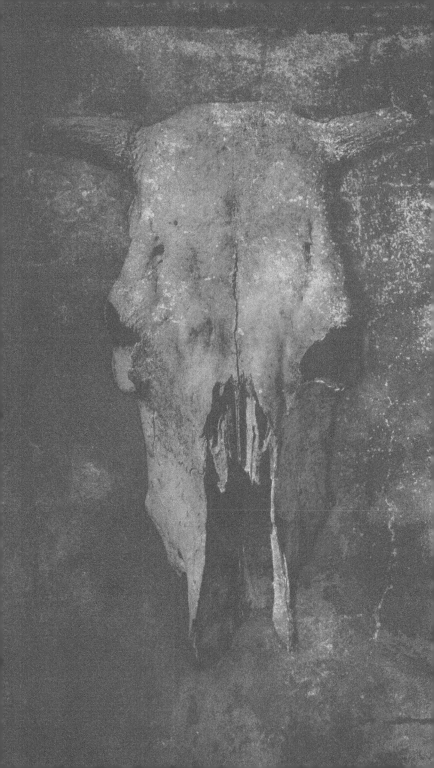

Bonus Epilogue
Seven Years Later

"We're gonna go fast, right Daddy?

"So fast, Baby." Rhett nods and looks up at our little girl like she hung the moon.

"We're gonna win, right?"

A knowing smile my touches my husband's lips as he looks down at the leather reins in his hands. "Hell yeah, baby girl. We're gonna win it all."

I can't help but shake my head as I cup the back of the small bald head pressed against my chest. Orion is fast asleep in his carrier, clearly not at all interested in his sister's very first rodeo.

Lead line barrel racing is about as riveting as it sounds. But we're all lined up at the gate, waiting for Stella's turn.

Rhett is going to run his fine ass around a huge arena, begging an old ranch horse to *maybe* jog around a few barrels.

And Stella is going to kick her tiny little four-year-old

legs and flap her arms around like she's some sort of rodeo queen.

The girl terrifies me. She *all* her dad. Dark hair, amber eyes, devil-may-care persona.

I'm already dreading the teenage years. Hopefully she'll keep looking at her dad like he walks on water because I already know she's going to scare the shit out of me.

"Y'alright, Princess?" Rhett calls at me with a sly wink from the opposite side of the exact same horse I rode across a field in a white dress to save his ass seven years ago.

The way things come full circle has me grinning at him. "Never better."

I sway without even thinking about it, the newborn tucked in tight against my chest.

"My girl and I are going to kick some ass today."

Rhett reaches up and gives Stella a high five. "Heck yeah we are, daddy."

Her smile is big, but her eyes are all focus. She's watching other kids get led around and it's all adorably clumsy. But judging from the way she's looking at "the competition" you'd swear she was at the Canadian Finals Rodeo.

"We're gonna come first place." She nods decisively, knuckles turning white as she grips the reins hard.

Rhett laughs into his fist and then pops around behind her back to mouth what looks an awful lot like, "Everyone gets the same ribbon."

I just laugh now, pressing a soft kiss onto Orion's bald head. Our sweet little boy. So wanted and so loved.

"He looks like you, you know?" Harvey comes to stand beside me. He was off helping somewhere as one of the founders of the new Chestnut Spring Rodeo.

"Only seems fair," I reply, and he chuckles. We can't even go out without people commenting on how much Stella looks like Rhett. "I grew them. I birthed them. I almost feel like I was owed a child who looks more like me."

Harvey's big hand comes down and he traces a thumb over the baby's brow. "The lot of you were written in the stars as far as I'm concerned. You and my son. These babies." He shakes his head. Baby-gazing at his newest grandchild. "Fate."

It's from my opposite side that I hear a scoff.

"Fate." Kip shakes his head. "Fate is not my name. Everyone can thank me for my genius idea of sending these two on the road together."

"Dad." I roll my eyes. "Shut up."

He shoves a sugary mini donut into his mouth and chases it with a cold beer from a plastic cup. "It's true. I knew you two would hit it off."

"You're full of shit, Hamilton!" Rhett calls from the other side of the horse. Stella nods seriously like she instantly agrees with her dad.

Adorable.

"It's true." Kip wobbles his head. "Well sort of."

Harvey snorts and I just arch an eyebrow at my dad. My dad who is exponentially happier since he finally kicked Marina to the curb.

It was the birth of Stella that did it. He told me he couldn't fathom subjecting his grand babies to her. There was also a very tearful apology for subjecting *me* to her for so long—something I didn't even realize how badly I needed to hear.

"What do you mean *sort of*?" I ask what everyone else is wondering, since all eyes are on Kip.

He shrugs. "I mean, I knew you'd bust his balls. And his balls needed busting. And . . ." He peeks over at me from behind his sunglasses a little sheepishly.

Rhett guffaws. "That's a promising look."

My dad just shrugs again, popping another mini donut into his mouth. "You know," he says around a mouthful of dough. "I just thought it would be kind of funny because you spent so much time staring at that magazine ad of him."

Rhett and Harvey are *howling* and I'm just standing here, agape, staring at my father. "You thought it would be *funny*?"

"Yeah, I mean, how many people get stuck on the road with their teenage crush? And let's be honest, that teenage crush was some next level shit. I was basically doing you a favor."

"Did you just say *next level shit*? You're too old to say that."

"Did she ever kiss it?" Rhett hollers over.

Kip points back at him and I feel heat creeping up my cheeks. "I caught her once!"

"Fuck my life," I mutter, burrowing my face against Orion's fuzzy head.

Rhett hoots like he's at a comedy show or something. *Asshole.*

"Did she write my name on her notepads? I asked you

that once, Princess. And you just ignored me. I think that was right before you begged me to kiss you."

"That kiss was your idea!" My hands fly out in a defensive gesture.

Harvey is laughing, and he reminds me of Beau when he gets the giggles.

But it's my dad's reply that really gets me. "No,"—he wipes at his mouth—"not her notebooks. Usually right on her arm like a tattoo."

"You're dead to me, Kip." I glare at my father dramatically before shaking my head on a laugh and looking over at my husband. His hair still wild, his shoulders still broad, his eyes still glowing.

So full of love and laughter, and whatever other cheesy shit people put up on their walls and call farmhouse chic.

"We getting tattoos, Princess?" He winks at me, his grin pure flirtation. Not giving a flying fuck that both our dads are standing right here to see it.

He's loved me out loud for seven years now and I don't ever want him to stop.

Princess started out as a nickname, but Rhett Eaton makes me feel like I really am one every goddamn day. I love him with every ounce of my being. I swear I feel it more acutely all the time. Like the most delicious ache.

"Sure. Let's do it."

"I'm doing it too, then," Stella announces with an upturned chin.

Rhett just laughs and runs a broad palm over her tiny back. Only four years old and up on a full-sized horse. Totally fearless.

"Stella Eaton!" The steward calls her name and we all crowd the fence to watch her round.

I smile so damn hard that my cheeks hurt. Stella is full on eye of the tiger. She's going to be a hell of rider one day if she keeps it up.

And Rhett? Well, he still wears the hell out of a pair of Wranglers.

When they cross the finish line to the cheers of our family he finds me along the fence line.

And he winks.

Then he mouths *I love you.*

And God. Don't I know it.

Acknowledgments

If a year ago someone told me I'd be here, doing this, I'd have laughed in their face. But the world works in mysterious ways, and like the quote at the front of this book says: sometimes the moment seizes you.

What a ride. What an adventure. What an absolute blessing to have stumbled into a career that brings me this much joy.

But this job is only this incredible because so many other people help make it that way.

To my readers, thank you. From the bottom of my heart. Thank you for spending your precious free time reading my stories. For loving them, for sharing them, for blowing up my inbox with your messages. I love it all.

To my husband, you're the ultimate book boyfriend. You inspire little pieces of my books every time. I love you beyond measure.

To my son, you make me laugh every day. You give the best hugs. I'm so lucky to be your mama. I love you to the moon and back.

To my parents, you always knew I'd figure out what to do with myself. Even when I wasn't so sure you were right. You're the two best cheerleaders a girl could ask for. I love you both with all my heart.

To my assistant Krista, I hate calling you my assistant. I feel like you're just my really cool fun friend who helps me with ALL OF THE THINGS. And I wouldn't have it any other way.

To Lena, you're my ride or die. My fellow delightful pervert. You make this gig more fun every day. Who else would I say all the inappropriate things to?

To Catherine, you are the most wonderful top secret mentor a girl could ask for. I feel so fortunate to have you in my corner.

To Kandi, you have to be one of my favorite people . . . ever. I will never forget your generosity and your kindness. I can't wait to pay it forward one day. I'm so lucky to call you my friend.

To Sarah from Social Butterfly, I love our working relationship. But I also can't wait to eat a waffle penis and do goat yoga with you.

To my beta readers, Amy, Krista, and Kelly, thank you for your hard work and keen eyes. You catch the things my brain is too jumbled to notice.

To my editor Paula, basically... I'm obsessed with you. Haha. Thank you for always being available to bounce ideas off of and joke around with. You are irreplaceable.

To my cover designer Casey/Echo, you worked so hard on this cover and goddamnit, it paid off. Your expertise and opinions are invaluable to me. You also crack me up, so there's that.

Finally, to my ARC readers and street team members . . . I don't even know where to start. You make a bigger difference than you'll ever realize. Every post makes me smile, every review has an impact. I don't care how many followers any of you have, you're all wonderful and deserving and I appreciate each and every one of you more than you know.

Books by Elsie Silver

The Chestnut Springs Series

Flawless

Heartless

Powerless

Reckless

The Gold Rush Ranch Series

Off to the Races

A Photo Finish

The Front Runner

A False Start

About the Author

Elsie Silver is a Canadian author of sassy, sexy, small town romance who loves a good book boyfriend and the strong heroines who bring them to their knees. She lives just outside of Vancouver, British Columbia with her husband, son, and three dogs and has been voraciously reading romance books since before she was probably supposed to.

She loves cooking and trying new foods, traveling, and spending time with her boys—especially outdoors. Elsie has also become a big fan of her quiet five o'clock mornings, which is when most of her writing happens. It's during this time that she can sip a cup of hot coffee and dream up a fictional world full of romantic stories to share with her readers.

www.elsiesilver.com

CPSIA information can be obtained
at www.ICGtesting.com
Printed in the USA
BVHW041507020723
666648BV00002B/21